STORM AND SEA

STORM AND SEA SAGA
BOOK ONE

TEREZA KANE

Cover and Back Art was done by "Quel" on Instagram

Cover Text and formatting was done by Amphi at AmphiStudios

Edited by Aly Hollis with Tawny Books

Published under Tawny Books

Photographs done by "Slava E. Photography"

 Formatted with Vellum

To the one who listened—thank you for giving me the chance to live my author dream and for believing in me, always. You nurtured my young imagination with stories whispered late into the night and, whether near or far, never turned down the ramblings of a little girl and her made-up worlds.

Love you dearly, always and forever.

WARNINGS

This story includes sensitive themes that may not be suitable for all readers. Please proceed with care if you are affected by any of the following:

1. **Homophobia and Social Stigma**
2. **Internalized Homophobia**
3. **Period-Accurate Prejudices**
4. **Parental/Family Rejection**
5. **Emotional Abuse**
6. **Subtle Religious Pressure**
7. **Mild Violence**
8. **Loss/Grief**
9. **Cultural Tensions**
10. **Ableism**
11. **Implied SA (not depicted on page)**
12. **Mentions of infant/child death**
13. **Suicidal ideation**

MUSIC

Immerse yourself in the world of *Storm and Sea* with my curated Spotify playlist—filled with songs that inspired the story and its characters. For the best reading experience, listen to my instrumental playlist, crafted as a personal "soundtrack" to accompany the book.

Curious about why I chose each song? Or which instrumental piece pairs with specific scenes? Check out my Google Doc, where I've detailed every track and its significance.

(*Warning: Some song descriptions may contain spoilers!*)

PRONOUCIATION GUIDE

<u>Baia Vita</u>

BY-uh VEE-tuh

- **"BY"** like "bye" in "goodbye."
- **"Uh"** like the relaxed "uh" in "umbrella."
- **"VEE"** like "vee" in "vehicle."
- **"Tuh"** like "tuh" in "tough."

<u>Nyel</u>

Nye-el

- **"Nye"** rhymes with "tie"
- **"el"** sounds like the letter "L"

<u>Atreus</u>

Uh-tray-us

- **"Uh"** sounds like "u" in "up"
- **"tray"** rhymes with "day"
- **"us"** sounds like "us" in "fuss"

Leofel

Leh-oh-fell

- **"Leh"** sounds like "le" in "let" or "e" in "elephant"
- **"oh"** sounds like "o" in "open"
- **"fell"** sounds like "fell" in "fell down"

(The shortened "Leo" is pronounced the same)

Mattias

Mah-tye-us

- **"Mah"** sounds like "ma" in "mama"
- **"tye"** rhymes with "tie"
- **"us"** sounds like "us" in "fuss"

Alvise

ahl-VEE-zay

- **"Ahl"** like "tall" but softer.
- **"VEE"** like "vee" in "vehicle."
- **"Zay"** rhymes with "bay."

Nephi

KNEE-fye

- **Ne** like "knee"
- **phi** like in "wifi"

GLOSSARY

Sireni – The plural form and name of the Mer native to the shallow, warm waters of the Mediterranean. Sireni are herbivores that live in close-knit family villages. Their green scales blend seamlessly with the kelp they cultivate, providing natural camouflage in their environment. Also known for their impeccable sense of smell and tracking abilities, Sireni can detect subtle changes in the water—whether it be the scent of distant predators, shifting currents, or sickness in their crops. Their keen noses allow them to recognize these traces even days after they've dispersed.

Sireno – A male Sireni.

Sirena – A female Sireni.

Rusalki – Another species of Mer. While little is known about them, they are believed to have blue scales and a carnivorous diet.

RaMaa – A species of Mer distinguished by their red scales and a presumed carnivorous diet. They function within a harem-based society, where dominant males, known as **Leviarchs**, control their clan of females and offspring, ensuring the safety of their lineage. A defining biological trait of the RaMaa is their ability to expand the fins along their back and tail, which can triple in size when agitated or threatened. This rapid expansion is caused by a surge of blood into hidden vessels within the fin membrane, making them appear luminous red.

Marvassa – The involuntary ability of a Mer to transform into a human body upon leaving the water and vice versa. This transformation is triggered solely by contact with air or water.

Thalaren – The Mer afterlife, where spirits are believed to go after death.

Tideway – A practice followed primarily by Sireni, where a bonded male and female pair journey with the winter tides in hopes of conceiving a child.

Opikun — A spirit guide responsible for escorting souls from mortality to *Thalaren*. It is said that, in dire circumstances, the Opikun may permit a soul to briefly return to the mortal realm to bring comfort to those left behind.

Halfling – A child born from the forbidden union of two different Mer species. Halflings are believed to be mentally unstable and irrationally violent. As a result, they are typically killed at birth.

Skraith – A demonic, evil spirit said to inhabit the minds of Halflings, driving them to madness and destruction.

The Seven Spirits

Dahest – *Spirit of Life and Death, overseeing the cycle of existence and the transition of souls to the afterlife.*

Spuragin – *Spirit of the Tide, the bridge between land and sea, carrying life-giving nutrients with each current.*

Pygon – *Spirit of the Sky, guardian of rain and wind, bringer of storms.*

Elowen – *Spirit of Bonds, embodying connection, unity, and the strength found in relationships.*

Lasidru – *Spirit of Fertility, bringing the promise of new life and abundance.*

Inju – *Spirit of War, bestower of Marvassa, and herald of change.*

Kaelmar – *Spirit of Beasts, protector, and overseer of all creatures within the waters and beyond.*

Because there's nothing more beautiful than the way the
ocean refuses to stop kissing the shoreline, no matter how
many times it's sent away.

—SARAH KAY

CHAPTER 1

ATREUS

Il Messaggero
Marzo, 1961

Despite its size and impact on the lives of every organism on Earth, the ocean remains a mystery. More than eighty percent of the ocean has never been mapped, explored, or even seen by humans. A greater percentage of the moon has been mapped when compared to the sea.

While there is still much to uncover, Italy's leading oceanographers have already made groundbreaking discoveries. Earlier this week, oceanographer Dr. Raphi mapped the first of what he suspects to be hundreds of deep ocean canyons he's dubbed 'trenches.' They range deep—

"M..mi...misteei?"

Atreus narrowed his eyes, demanding the letters on the page stay still.

"M— mistray—m..."

Atreus stumbled over the jumble of letters. The more he stared at the washed-up newspaper, the more the words taunted him. He'd found it dried out on the beach, and the black-and-white photos of men on boats sparked a flicker of hope that maybe some of the words would be familiar enough to decipher.

Guilt ate at him as the symbols refused to make sense. All Giovanni's efforts to teach him to read were wasted. He could handle three-lettered words like 'and' or 'sea.' He'd even patted himself on the back for quickly identifying the word 'earth.' He tried challenging himself with one of the longer ones like 'mystery,' but...

"My...Mi...eery?"

The sound coming off his tongue didn't sound like a word so much as a random jumble of sounds.

"Damn it!" he cursed. Crumpling the paper in frustration, he tossed the ball out the open window where it would fall over two hundred feet before sinking into the ocean.

Atreus ran a hand through his thick curls, irritated. He wanted to impress Giovanni, to prove that he'd been practicing his letters over the winter. Of course, his stupid brain wouldn't cooperate. He'd stared at the page less than five minutes before the letters began flipping and switching places like rowdy seal pups.

"Doesn't matter," he said to the random assortment of things he'd scavenged over the years, "I don't need to read to do my job."

He tugged at a long strand of curly hair, wondering if Leo's mom might be willing to cut it for him. It always turned out better when she cut it, instead of the uneven chunks he hacked off with a rusty knife in front of a shattered mirror propped against the wall.

Human hair was such a pain. It grew back way too fast.

He eyed the piles of his treasures, wishing they would talk back for once. Anything from fraying ropes, fishing gear, and the occasional tire washed ashore on his beach. He'd also found heavier objects like an entire wooden chair, panes of glass, and metal scrap on the ocean floor, likely remnants of old ship wreckage.

"As long as I work hard, he'll be...."

What? Proud? Happy? Satisfied with his employee's work? Atreus knew it was likely the last of those options, but a small part of him dared to hope it would be the first.

He took a steadying breath, trying to calm the anxiety that churned like a whirlpool in his chest.

Tomorrow. Tomorrow was the official start of the fishing season. He'd waited all winter for this day—all those miserable, freezing months when he was starved for both food and company. Forced to survive on his meager shellfish trappings and food stores, Atreus was disappointed with how much weight he'd lost. He'd done everything in his power to remain in shape, keeping his muscles strong and ready for the hours of lifting heavy fishing nets. But even more than the lack of nutrition, he was starved for the company of people. Atreus hadn't spoken a word to another soul in over two months. Other than his magpie's nest of random things, he was alone. He didn't mind the cold; in fact, Atreus rather enjoyed it. But he hated winter. Going so long without seeing another face made him feel like the last person alive.

The fishing season couldn't have come at a better time. He was down to his last half-dozen cans of sardines, and his traps hadn't caught anything in over a week. If he waited much longer, he would need to resort to stealing his food. The thought alone made Atreus sick, bringing unwanted flashes of his younger days to the surface.

Thirteen winters—that's how old he was when his father left. Every day, he'd waited on the sandy shore. Hour by hour, time stretched like a drought, leaving behind nothing but a husk of who he used to be. Yet his young heart dared hope for the day his father would come back.

He never did.

In those early days, Atreus learned the true meaning of the word hunger. It was an emptiness so painful he feared his stomach would cannibalize itself. But he survived. He fought. He adapted.

And if not for those starvation-fueled acts of desperation, he'd never be where he was now. He would never know the kindness in the hearts of humans—or one human in particular. Atreus's stomach tightened with guilt at the memory of his first meeting with Giovanni.

He'd been desperate in those early days of isolation. At thirteen winters, Atreus was skin and bone, barely strong enough to swim the quarter-mile channel that separated his lighthouse from the island of Baia Vita. His body trembled as he dragged himself onto the beach, the weight of his decision beating down on him as though he stood beneath a cascading waterfall. He was trespassing now, sneaking into the territory of the most terrifying creatures in the world—humans.

Bloodthirsty creatures without the ability to change. They were landlocked and had a penchant for ending the lives of anything that swam too close. For years, Atreus's father filled his mind with stories of humans and their greed and cruelty. He even showed Atreus scars on his body as evidence of their ruthlessness. As a child, the sound of a human boat puttering too close sent him shivering to his father with tears in his eyes.

But those were the days when he had someone to depend on. Now, there was no one.

Nobody to help him navigate the world. Nobody to teach him how to fish. How to maximize his resources. And when the easy-to-catch crustaceans on the seafloor migrated out of the bay... Atreus had nothing to eat.

And for weeks, he withered away. The beast of hunger grew so insistent that he tried to eat the kelp his father was so fond of, only for the vile sea plant to climb back up his throat as he wretched.

When starvation and a lonely death waited at his doorstep, Atreus faced his fear. Braving the human territory, he clambered onto their shore, the air thick with the scent of men. They smelled of oil and earth, instantly identifiable. A scent he'd learned meant danger. Instead of running away, he pushed further into the island until his feet no longer touched the sand but cobbled streets. His cadaverous body shivered as he crept behind a school of land dwellers. They milled about, busy with whatever it was humans did. Atreus ignored them, his focus narrowing to what his body so desperately needed—a stall brimming with fish. Fresh, cleaned, mouthwatering fish.

Atreus watched as humans exchanged what appeared to be shiny rocks for fish, and his heart sank—he didn't have any shiny rocks. Nerves billowed out of every pore, and Atreus *felt* the ghostly swish of his tail, even though it wasn't there.

He had no choice but to take what wasn't his.

Slinking behind a low wall made of red cube rock, Atreus waited for the school of humans to look away. When the moment finally came, he sprang forward, grabbing three fish at random, their slimy bodies slippery in his arms.

"Excuse me," a low voice boomed behind him.

Atreus jumped, dropping his loot, ready for a harpoon to pierce his chest. Beetle-black eyes bore into him, and Atreus gasped as the largest human he'd ever seen loomed like a mountain. The man-beast was built like a bull shark, with massive shoulders and tree trunk arms. His face was covered in curled black hair, sparsely tangled with strands of silver.

Atreus was so paralyzed with fear that it took him a moment to register the human's words. They shared the same language—something his father, despite all his cautionary tales, had never thought to mention.

Of course, this man had no idea what Atreus truly was. Without water on his skin, Atreus appeared perfectly human, which was likely the only reason he was still alive.

"Please... I didn't mean to..." Atreus pleaded before a coughing fit seized his lungs. His dry throat felt like it would crack from the strain, and he'd soon swallow blood.

The mountainous human picked up the scattered fish and wrapped them in black and white paper, which Atreus would later learn was 'newspaper,' before handing him the bundle.

"Come back tomorrow for more," he said and turned away.

Atreus ran from the square, down the beach, and behind an outcrop of stone before he dared look back. Nobody followed. Tears ran down his cheeks as he crouched, eating the fish raw, confused by the incredible act of mercy.

Memories of the deep white scars along his father's back and ribs resurfaced. The wounds were cruel. Deliberate. Given to him by humans in seas far to the north. So, how had Atreus managed to escape without so much as a scratch? He didn't ponder too long as his eyelids drooped, his belly full for the first time in months.

Three more days passed before the beast of hunger bared its fangs and gnawed at Atreus's stomach. He swam to the human town, chased by its insistent pangs. The monstrous man was there, working his stall, conversing with the other humans. Atreus cowered at his booming voice and wondered why the others didn't run in terror. Instead, they approached him like a friend.

Atreus only dared to leave his hiding place after observing the pleasant exchanges for the better part of the morning.

The hulking man's eyes found him quickly, and Atreus half expected him to shout, to tell him to get away like the scavenging mongrel he was. He hadn't expected the terrifying creature to soften. The human's features relaxed, and the lines at the edges of his mouth and eyes became more prominent as his face contorted into a bushy smile.

"I was worried about you, *ragazzo*. Glad you decided to return."

And it was that smile that changed Atreus's life forever. It was meant for him. There *because* of him. More than the pangs in his stomach, Atreus realized how starved he'd been for it—for someone to look at him and be glad he existed.

It was that smile that Atreus craved now. After a long winter of isolation, with only a few sparse glimpses of his human home, the hours couldn't pass quickly enough. He paced, circling his lighthouse over and over, looping around the dead beacon in the center like a vulture. He needed something to do. Something with his hands.

There wasn't much for resources on his small patch of land. He could walk around its perimeter in less than two hours. And he had. Probably over a thousand times in his seven winters of isolation. Or was it eight? He wasn't sure. Atreus wished he'd kept track of time when he was younger, but by the time it occurred to him, the years bled into one another. For that reason, Atreus wasn't sure how old he was. He figured somewhere between twenty and twenty-two winters.

Surrounded by a crescent-shaped sandbank on one side and a steep cliff on the other, Atreus's lighthouse stood isolated, cradled by a grove of trees that shielded his solitary refuge.

From his glass-paneled home, he had an unobstructed view stretching for miles in every direction. Yet the sight that captured his attention—the one he'd stared at with longing for months—was much closer: the island of Baia Vita.

"I'll be there tomorrow," he whispered, breath fogging the glass. "One more day."

One more day until he would see Giovanni. Until he would laugh with his best friend Leo and hear about all the trouble he'd gotten into over the winter. Just one more day, and he'd be waving to the familiar faces in Saul's café and *Signor* Rossi's gelato shop on the corner.

One more day.

And he'd be home.

Atreus sighed in frustration as he reorganized his dwindling food supplies for the third time. His ear twitched, and a moment later, the sky growled somewhere in the distance. A storm was coming, large and aggressive by the sound of it. He'd have to pull his traps from the water if he didn't want the violent waves to wash them away.

With bare feet, Atreus made his way down the tight spiral staircase leading to the base of the lighthouse. He tried not to let old memories wander as he walked through the house. Anything worth having was long gone from this place. Stripped bare after decades of abandonment, it was the perfect hiding place for Atreus and his father to live—far away from human dangers and the judgments of his own kind.

Memories of shared meals, nighttime stories, and stupid jokes clung to the walls like seaweed on rocks after high tide. It stank of happier times. After his father left, the stench became unbearable.

So, Atreus moved his few belongings to the top of the lighthouse, where only a broken beacon kept him company.

> *"He didn't leave. He abandoned you.*
> *Couldn't wait to leave behind*
> *his pathetic excuse of a son.*
> *You weren't worth staying for."*

A voice whispered in his mind. Not his voice, or at least, he didn't think it was. It didn't feel like his. But it was in his head, so what else could it be?

> *"Your father couldn't get away fast enough.*
> *You were nothing to him—*
> *just a dead weight he couldn't wait to drop.*
> *You're not worth anything.*
> *You never were."*

Atreus shook his head as though the words were an insect buzzing in his ear. He scolded himself for letting wayward memories crawl from the shallow grave where he'd buried them. This place was a ghost of his youth, and he would gladly leave it behind.

Yet, it still served a purpose. The house acted as an effective deterrent for thrill-seeking humans who occasionally invaded his island. Most of the time, they didn't brave the 'haunted' lighthouse, but on the rare occasions they did, they never made it past the first floor. Atreus wrecked the place into a state that promised only the most morbid hauntings.

He was quite proud of his handiwork, with broken shards of glass littering the floor (away from his walking path) and the deliberately placed smears of blood in the shape of handprints. He'd used fish's blood to set the scene and was happy with the result. Nobody would bother him here. Nobody would discover the creature that haunted the lighthouse.

"The freak not even a father could love."

Atreus silently exited his home, feet sinking into the soft carpet of grass that finally bloomed after a long winter of frozen ground. The scent of a storm wafted into his nose, promising one hell of a battle between the sea and sky.

"Why did you have to come now?" Atreus cursed at the mass of gray swirling above him.

If the rain didn't stop before tomorrow...

He shook his head, not allowing the thought to manifest. The storm would pass in time.

It had to.

Atreus filled his lungs to full capacity, tasting the spray of the sea. It was his favorite smell in the world—the salt, the untamable force of nature, the birthplace of life itself.

When Atreus was one with the sea, he was whole.

He allowed gravity to guide him over the cliff, eyes closed, relishing the whoosh of air as he dove. He fell, and the sea welcomed him home. The cool water stung his human flesh, but only for a moment. Because within the span of a heartbeat, *Marvassa* took his body.

The *change*.

The ability to transform from one state to another with the caress of water. Human skin evolved into a mosaic of scales and fins in less than a second. As he immersed himself in the frigid sea, Atreus's body relaxed, shifting from a warm-blooded land-dweller to a cold-blooded creature born of the ocean. An extra weight materialized in his lower back. Atreus flexed his powerful tail, fins rising in a display of sharp spines and hooked barbs. A shiver rippled through him as he reclaimed his true self.

Atreus was Mer.

He kicked at the water, marveling at how his webbed feet sliced through it with far more efficiency than his stubby human toes ever could. The sensation reminded him of the legless fountain in Baia Vita's town center. Humans knew of Mer only through myths and cautionary tales; creatures conjured from their imaginations rather than reality. The fountain depicted a *Donna del Mare*—a supposed sea goddess—with the upper body of a voluptuous woman and a single fishtail forming her lower half. Atreus had to suppress a laugh the first time he saw the sculpture. She was supposed to be regal and mysterious, but to him, she looked more like a manatee with hair.

Luckily, Atreus retained all four of his limbs upon transformation —but he did gain a powerful tail, so at least that part of the legend was accurate.

He ran his tongue over pointed teeth, enjoying the feel of elongated incisors behind his lips. Humans, with their flat teeth, relied on tools to hunt. They lacked the sharp claws and barbed fins that made Atreus deadly. Not only was their eyesight poor in the dark, but they were completely useless beneath the water.

He'd once seen Leo return from a swim with red, puffy eyes. That was when Atreus learned that humans kept their eyes closed underwater to avoid the stinging salt. The idea baffled him. Worst of all was how often Leo had to surface. Atreus's best friend remained below the surface for only two minutes before coming up for air.

"That's it?" Atreus asked the first time he watched his friend dive.

"What? Think you can do any better? Go on then," Leo challenged.

Of course, Atreus refused. He was careful to stay away from the water's edge whenever a human watched. Even his best friend.

But right now, he was alone and free to be himself.

Atreus pulled deeply, a sensation akin to inhaling, letting the seawater flow through the gills at his neck. The delicate layers fluttered as they extracted life-giving oxygen from the water. Even if he never surfaced again, Atreus wouldn't drown. And that is exactly what most Mer did. Live their lives hidden in the sea. Away from humans. They were content with life beneath the waves, never knowing the kiss of a summer wind. Atreus often wondered what it would be like to live as the others did.

*"But you aren't like the others.
Are you?"*

Atreus didn't need the reminder as he concentrated on untying the empty lobster traps.

The Mer in the local village, hidden within Baia Vita's bay, were covered in scales of varying shades of peridot and moss. Their bodies were small, fins rounded, and they blended into the kelp they so diligently farmed. Not for the first time, a pang of longing struck hard as Atreus imagined what his life might have been like if he'd been born to look like them.

From a distance, anyone who spotted him beneath the waves would say he was a unique shade of cerulean blue, that is, until they got close enough to see the truth. Sporadic scales in varying shades of indigo, séance, and cobalt mixed with flecks of midnight made him look like a mosaic of cool tones. These colors spread to his fins, where the purple became more dominant, and when the sun hit him just right, hidden streaks of magenta blended the outer edges of his dorsal and tail fins.

As a kid, he'd taken pride in having an identical tailfin color to his father—a vibrant purple fading to magenta along the spines. But therein lay the problem. While his father's body was entirely purple, Atreus's scales were predominantly blue. Something was wrong with Atreus, and it all started and ended with the color of his scales.

They never spoke of his birthplace—his home tribe across the sea. Even mentioning it soured his father's mood faster than fish skins left to rot in the sun. Over the years, though, using scraps of discarded comments, Atreus had managed to piece together this much:

His home tribe wanted him dead.

From the moment he was born, Atreus had been marked for death—all because of the color of his scales. But that hardly seemed like a good enough reason to murder an infant.

Atreus didn't fully understand it, and his father refused to explain. It was the threat to his life that forced his father to take him in the middle of the night and flee. Leaving behind a life Atreus would never know.

A mother he'd never remember.

Atreus sentenced his father to a life of exile for the crime of being born. He supposed that, after years of isolation, his father had enough. And left.

"Shouldn't be allowed to exist. They wanted you dead."

The voice hissed at him, each syllable a cruel reminder that his very presence was a crime in someone's eyes. Not for the first time, Atreus wondered if things would have been better if he'd been silenced as a babe. Never a burden.

His head shot up as the sound of a rumbling engine hummed above him. The underside of a boat glided across the surface as it returned to the harbor. Likely escaping the incoming storm. The sound of an engine alone would have sent most Mer diving beneath rocks.

Atreus smiled. He didn't need other Mer. He'd made a life for himself with their natural enemy. With humans. And since they were the only ones who would have him, the only ones who would accept him as one of their own — Atreus would gladly align himself with them.

"They only accept you because they don't know what you are."

The whisper in his head might as well have been a shout for how long it rang in his ears.

Doing his best to ignore it, Atreus untied the final lobster trap, glad to see the large pincers of a king male snacking on the bait inside. At least he'd eat well while the storm ravaged the sky.

But the voice wasn't done with him. It pressed against his mind, slithering inside like a sea snake ready to inject its venom. Atreus snapped and acknowledged the insistent whispers—anything to stop the internal assault.

They'll never know what I am. As far as they're concerned, I'm just like any other human. I'll be fine as long as I stay away from the water.

"And how long until that happens? How long until you slip, and they see you for what you are?"

Atreus blinked rapidly, his mind fuzzing as it always did when the voice grew so excited.

I've hidden my entire life. I know what I'm doing. They'll never find out. Now shut up.

And with that, he silenced the back-and-forth in his head, at least for now.

As he ascended the beach, rain dotted the sand, and the trees whipped with wind. Atreus tied his traps to a log and carefully removed the lobster, using the tips of his talons to avoid its clubbed pincers. The rain drenched every inch of his body, keeping him in Mer form. *Marvassa* didn't discriminate; any and all forms of water would transform him. Whether it be the sea or sky or the splash of a human fountain— the water would change him, returning him to his natural body, even against his will.

He climbed the winding staircase and was greeted by the sound of pelting rain on glass. The entire circular room was made of glass, intended for a beam of light to shine through. But that hadn't happened in decades. Still, even in disuse, the tower stood resolute, unyielding to the raging sea that beat upon its walls.

Placing the king lobster in a pail of seawater, Atreus began closing the black curtains hanging on one side of the room. He'd found the cloth years ago, dotted with holes, washed ashore on the beach. With a needle of bone and an endless supply of fishing line, he'd painstakingly mended every tear. Using a haphazard mix of metal pipes and sticks, he built a makeshift privacy wall, shielding the open glass that faced the town. Now, he could light a fire without fear of a human seeing the glow.

He set to work using his collection of dry tinder and a metal bowl he used as a firepit. He had to cut a hole in the lighthouse roof to let the smoke escape—a lesson learned the hard way after his first attempt at indoor cooking. An angled piece of glass shielded the room from the rain while letting the smoke ventilate. Each drop tapped against the thin pane with a soft, rhythmic 'pitter-patter,' like tiny fingers on a drum.

In minutes, a healthy fire roared, eating up the dry wood. Atreus let it burn, getting lost in the flames' glow while the wood transformed into hot white coals. The hypnotic flames danced in the bowl, jumping from coal to coal like seabirds along the rocky shore.

"It'll stop before tomorrow. It will," Atreus told himself as the rain attacked the glass with renewed ferocity.

His mind was so lost in thoughts of tomorrow that he didn't hear the distant cry from the floor below. The fire popped, regular and even, like footsteps.

No.

Those were footsteps. Steady and certain with a rhythmic 'clank' on the rusted metal stairs.

Someone was coming.

CHAPTER 2

NYEL

"You're stalling," Sonia said, absent-mindedly rubbing her swollen belly.

"Am not."

"Are too."

"I just want to make sure everything is locked up properly," Nyel argued, checking the knot for the third time. There was little chance of the goatfish escaping the woven wood cage, especially with Ripple standing guard.

"It's not going to go away, you know. And it'll be worse if you're

17

late. Might as well get it over with," his aunt said, her logic annoyingly sound.

Nyel sighed, a small stream of bubbles escaping his gills. "I'll be there in five minutes," he relented.

She gave him a pitying look before turning, her tail lazily propelling her through the water and into their domed clay home.

Nyel crossed his legs in the sand, his tail swishing and making a trench behind him. He wished he could blink and have the day be over. The so-called *casual* dinner his mother insisted on hosting would already be behind him, forgotten, so he could get back to his life and pretend it never happened. Yet every time he opened his eyes, only a second had passed, and the dinner loomed ever closer.

"What am I going to do?" he asked Ripple, who waddled beside him. The creature lumbered through the water with slow, loafing steps. Ripple's six legs moved in tandem as he plopped his flubby body on the sand with a grunt.

"Yeah, I feel the same way," Nyel said, scratching his most loyal friend behind the antenna where he liked it.

The sandwinder's broad head was flat and spade-shaped, with two fin-like appendages protruding on either side. Poking from beneath the fins and swaying with the ebb and flow of the water sprouted two long antennae. The organs at their tips emitted a faint, pulsating hum—invisible electromagnetic waves that effortlessly herded schools of fish without touching a single scale. Four tiny red eyes blinked lazily as Nyel rubbed him behind the flaps on his head. The sandwinder groaned, kicking one of his six legs in pleasure.

"Who's a good boy?" Nyel scratched his scaly body with both hands as the mossy two-ton beast rolled over, exposing his soft white belly.

"Who's a good boy? You are, yes you are, Ripple," Nyel cooed as Ripple's stubby tail waggled back and forth, his giant tongue lolling from the side of a gaping maw.

"Nyel!" His mother's shrill voice cut through the water.

"Coming!" he called before she could shout again, "Sorry boy, gotta go."

He gave Ripple one more scratch behind his antenna and slowly swam to their home. It was identical to all the others in Corallina. Made of hardened clay and mud, it was shaped into a dome and rested on a foundation of sea wood, keeping it lifted above the sand. A ramp wound its way from the base to the elevated entrance for the rare occasion Ripple was allowed to sleep inside. More often, the sandwinder slept beneath the hut or near the goatfish, always alert to the needs of the school.

It was the same scene, played on repeat every day of Nyel's life. Nyel was born in this home, lived here for eighteen springs, and would likely continue living here for many more. It was also the home where he would soon meet his Bond mate, or at least, that's what his mother hoped for.

"Hurry, the Ernestis will be here any second. Go change and be snappy," she said while simultaneously setting the perfectly laid-out dinner table. Despite dreading the meal to come, Nyel's stomach growled. The table was loaded with his favorites: Wakame kelp, hijiki, and sea prunes. They lay on clay plates, cut into flowery shapes with culinary scrutiny. Normally, delicacies like those were saved for holidays. He supposed tonight was more important than any holiday—at least in his mother's eyes.

Nyel swam to his private alcove of the home. The circular space was too small, but he only needed it to sleep. He sorted through his basket of various clothes made from anemone threads and driftweed fiber. He preferred to wear only the pants, as most men did, allowing his chest to remain bare. The village women most often wore loose-fitting sea-grass dresses or even a *fascia* and skirt.

But ordinary clothes wouldn't suffice tonight. With his mother dressed in her fine-fitted coral silk gown, Nyel knew that if he didn't wear his best outfit, she'd make him change. Groaning, he pulled on his pants, slipped his tail through the designated hole, and tied the itchy vest across his torso. He hated the way it tugged at the delicate scales across his chest and pinched the dorsal fin on his back.

Already uncomfortable, he forced himself back to the main room, where his mother and aunt were deep in conversation about where to set the clams.

"We simply can't have them at the table. They will make everyone lose their appetite," Bianca said, removing the plate of clams from the countertop with a disgusted look on her face.

Nyel didn't blame her. Even the smell of meat made him want to gag. His species of Mer, the *Sireni*, were vegetarians, only eating flesh in rare or dire cases. The swell in his aunt Sonia's middle was one of those rare times.

"You know I have to eat at least five a day," Sonia insisted. "I won't miss a single bite." She rubbed her belly in a protective gesture.

"Can you eat them now, then? Before the Ernestis arrive?" Bianca reasoned. "Please? I know you have to. I remember eating them when I was pregnant with Nyel," she said, eyeing the fleshy circles resting on their open shells. "But, they're gross."

"Fine," Sonia said, taking the stone plate and swimming to her room. She gave Nyel an exaggerated eye-roll before disappearing.

"Oh, there you are. I was about to fetch you. Okay, let me see," his mother said, wiping her hands on a cuttlefish-dyed apron and motioning for him to spin.

"Mom," Nyel groaned, but did as he was told and twirled in the water, feeling silly.

"When was the last time you polished?" she asked, rubbing at his scales as though her touch could make them shine.

"Last week," Nyel defended, "I'm not doing it before every single dinner, Mom. My scales will fall off."

"Well, at least the vest looks good. I can't believe how grown up you look," she said, getting that teary-eyed look only mothers could.

Nyel turned away, his tail curling behind him. "I'm only eighteen springs."

"That's old enough. A Lifebond can take place from the moment you become an adult. It could happen anytime; don't you realize how important that is? We can't waste a single day. And I have a good feeling about this one."

Nyel clenched his jaw, fingers curling at his sides. "I told you before, Chel and I are just friends."

"Exactly, childhood friends. Who's to say, now that you're both adults, something more won't set into place? The tides of fate have seen stranger things."

Nyel forced his mouth shut, unwilling to start another blowout minutes before guests arrived. Chel was not just any guest; she was his best friend. Ever since they were kids, they shared a comfortable companionship that Nyel never found with anyone else. The Ernesti family owned several acres of kombu, bladder, and ribbon kelp that fed not only their village but half a dozen other *Sireni* villages in the Mediterranean. Corallina was the largest *Sireni* settlement, with the highest crop yield. Hundreds of hungry mouths depended on their farms to eat. Nyel's family cared for a goatfish school as the local pest control. They went from farm to farm, releasing their four hundred head of goatfish to eat away any pests that might harm the crop. And with the vastness of the Ernesti's farm, Nyel frequently shepherded the school to their land and, thus, spent a lot of time with Chel.

A gentle "Hello?" sounded from the front of the house.

"That's them!" Bianca whispered in alarm. "Nyel, straighten up, chin high, show off those cheekbones."

"Chel's seen my cheekbones a hundred times," Nyel grumbled as his mother hastily removed the apron and swam to the front of the house.

Friendly chatter and pleasantries drifted from the front, and when his mother guided their guests inside, Nyel's heart sank. Chel was there with her parents, and she was dressed to perfection. Nyel didn't know if it was her parents' insistence or if she wanted to dress to impress. He hoped it was the first one.

Never once had Nyel viewed Chel as more than a friend. It didn't even cross his mind that she, a *sirena* (female), and he, a *sireno* (male), could be a potential mated pair. The thought made his stomach twist, and in an instant, the spread of delicious food lost all appeal.

"Hello, Nyel," Chel said with a shy wave.

"Hey, Chel," Nyel replied in kind.

It was awkward—so terribly awkward—as the five of them floated in the dining area, his mother and her parents watching them as though the Lifebond would spring into existence between them at any second.

"Let me get Don and Sonia, and we'll get started," Bianca said, excusing herself from the room.

Nyel was left alone with the three Ernesti members. Their appearance matched that of all *Sireni*: bodies covered in algae-green scales, rounded fins, and murky brown eyes. Scales matched the yellow-green hue of healthy kelp swaying in the sunlight while their fins draped in delicate layers over their heads, cascading down their backs and deepening into darker shades on their tails. The *Sireni* inherited their color from ancestors who camouflaged among the kelp back when the sea was ruled by monstrous predators ready to swallow them whole.

Now they had almost no natural predators, especially in the shallow, warm waters of the bay. Nyel supposed this was fortunate, as he, his mother, and his aunt Sonia were unique amongst the *Sireni*. Their scales shone the color of jade. Blue tones mixed and balanced the green before fading into dark azure at their fins and finally turning completely black at the tips. If they'd been born centuries earlier, they would have been easy targets and swiftly eliminated from the gene pool.

Nyel suspected that his unique scales were what constantly drew the attention of the village *sirena*. When he was little, the village girls would pretend they were *dating,* as children did, annoying Nyel with unwanted attention. But as he grew older and the first signs of maturity changed his body, their pursuits grew less playful and more serious.

Once the rounded fins along his tail flared high (the sign of a sexually mature Mer), the girls pursued him in earnest, asking him on dates, pestering him at every turn, and inevitably going home with tears and a broken heart when Nyel told them to stop. That was also the reason he had no *sireno* friends. The boys hated him for the attention he garnered, and that bitterness left Nyel isolated.

But that's what made Chel so perfect. She wasn't like that. She didn't push him for unwanted kisses or lock their webbed hands together. She didn't snuggle up too close or insist on discussing marriage, Lifebonds, and babies. She was just his friend. Plain and simple.

Now, this dinner jeopardized it all.

"The school looks good," Mr. Ernesti said, and Nyel gave him a grateful look when it was clear neither he nor Chel would start first.

"Yes, their spring colors are coming in. I like all the red and orange and... pinks," Nyel finished lamely.

"Ripple keeping them in check?" her father asked.

"Honestly, they're so well-behaved that Ripple is getting lazy. He sleeps most of the time."

"You have a good beast. Spirits know we're seeing fewer and fewer sandwinders. Is there any chance of finding a female and having a litter?"

Nyel shrugged. "We've been asking around for a while now, but it doesn't seem anyone has a female anywhere near here."

"Shame, they're magnificent beasts; I would hate to see them gone."

Nyel nodded, unsure of what else to add.

"Found them," Bianca said, hurrying into the room, Sonia and Don at her tail.

Nyel's father, Donato, had the characteristic yellow-green scales of all *Sireni*. In recent years, the darker fins atop his head had begun to recede, leaving him with a balding appearance.

As a kid, it confused Nyel why his parents were closer to the ages of his friend's grandparents. Bianca and Donato met late in life, and there was uncertainty about whether his mother could conceive at her age. Nyel was a miracle baby, which was also why he was an only child.

Well, the only child his mother ever had.

As though reading his mind, Mr. Ernesti broached the topic. "Will Nephi be joining us this evening?"

Everyone visibly tensed at the mention of the name, none more so than his mother.

"He had some errands to run, so we won't be seeing him. Now, shall we get started?" she said, quickly changing the topic.

The tension in the water eased as everyone put Nyel's estranged half-brother out of their minds. He hated how quickly the mood darkened at the mere mention of Nephi.

But...he understood why. There were too many stories, too many old fears about *his* kind.

The water shifted as everyone settled around the table, picking at the food in uncomfortable silence. Finally, Mrs. Ernesti broke the awkwardness and directed her next question at Sonia. "How are you fairing, dear? Everything is going okay?" she asked, referencing the bump in Sonia's middle.

"I'm doing well, thank you for asking," his aunt replied kindly.

"I am so glad you have Bianca and Don. I can't imagine caring for a little one alone. Especially after everything that happened. If you need anything and Bianca and Don are unavailable, you can come to us."

Sonia's jaw tensed, but her voice remained calm and polite. "Thank you; you're very kind. I'm lucky to have my sister and brother-in-law. I'm grateful they're letting me stay until the baby comes."

"And after that," Bianca chimed in, "I want plenty of time with my niece or nephew before you set off on your own."

Sonia forced a courteous smile but said nothing else. Nyel was proud of how far his aunt had come. She was much younger than his mom, and Nyel's relationship with her felt closer to brother and sister rather than aunt and nephew. Sonia found her mate fairly early in life and became pregnant shortly after.

That was when his aunt's idyllic world plunged into despair.

Nyel's uncle, Santé, was found deceased while working the feather kelp fields. There were no wounds on his body, and most assumed it was a failure of his heart, but there was no way of knowing for certain.

Nyel suspected—no, he was positive that if not for the babe inside her, his aunt Sonia would have followed him to *Thalaren*. The beyond. The next life. The loss of a Lifemate, the shattering of a Lifebond was… Nyel didn't understand it. Couldn't. His mother had once told him it would feel like his very soul was torn in two.

Before, even broaching the subject would have sent Sonia into a grief-stricken spiral. Now she was healing, and Nyel knew it was for her unborn child. He was proud of her.

Fortunately, his father chose that moment to ask about the neighbor's farm, diverting attention from Sonia and allowing the conversation to flow smoothly as everyone dined. They discussed crop yield, recent sightings of Great Whites (mostly rumors), and the predicted storms this spring. Mr. Ernesti became very animated, complaining that some of his fields were going gray. Other farmers were having the same problem, with entire sections of kelp turning gray before rotting off the stalk.

"A few of my farm hands are getting sick just touching the rotting stuff. I can't figure out what it could possibly be," Mr. Ernesti said, looking concerned. "And whatever it is, it's spreading."

Donato suggested an extra pass with the goatfish school in case of a parasite. Nyel listened to the ever-present talk of farming, kelp, annoying pests, and so forth. These were words and speculations he'd heard all his life, which was comforting. Normal dinner talk was more than he dared hope for. Nyel was actually beginning to enjoy himself when his name rang through the water.

"Nyel, tell Chel what you told me yesterday; it was such a good idea," his mother said in a less-than-smooth segway to force him to speak to the *sirena*.

Nyel sighed internally. He'd mentioned the idea two months ago and regretted opening his mouth ever since. When his mother's eyes widened dangerously, he forced the words out. "I had this idea of starting a starfish colony."

"Why is that, honey?" his mother pushed him when he didn't expand.

He sighed. "The goatfish are great about picking off barnacles and smaller pests, but they won't touch the sea urchins. Starfish prey on them naturally. It could be a good way to manage their numbers."

"Spirits know I can't stand those buggers." Mr. Ernesti nodded, agreeing right away. "No matter how many hands I hire to get rid of them, they come back in droves."

"Right?" Bianca said, "I can't believe nobody has thought of it before. It's such an inspired idea, right, Don?" She turned to his father.

"Yes. Of course. Brilliant," his father said shortly.

"It's not a big deal," Nyel grumbled, but nobody heard him.

"Chel, what do you think? Would you mind being a starfish farmer's wife?" Mrs. Ernesti asked, nudging her daughter conspiratorially.

Nyel choked on his sea prune. "W-wife?" he coughed.

He hated how the color in Chel's cheeks deepened as blood rushed to her face. He hated how his mother looked as if she might float to the ceiling with joy. But most of all, he hated the way his chest grew heavy. The idea of marrying Chel and taking her as a Lifemate was...

Across the table, Chel didn't seem to mind at all. Though her cheeks brightened, she was smiling, twisting her hands in a shy gesture. Some might call it cute. No, all the eligible *sireno* boys in the village would call her cute, adorable, beautiful even. Chel was a young and stunning *sirena*, deserving of a mate who would adore her in all seven seas.

Nyel wanted that for her. But he also knew—it couldn't be him.

Mrs. Ernesti looked at Bianca. "You haven't told him?"

"I thought it would be good for him to see Chel tonight before breaking the news."

"What news?" Nyel asked, his tone harsher than he intended, and Chel's face fell.

Bianca didn't miss this and glared at him as she spoke. "Mr. and Mrs. Ernesti have been talking with Don and me, and we all agree that a Tideway would be a great idea for you two."

Chel gave him a hopeful smile, but no matter how much he wanted to, he couldn't return the gesture.

"A Tideway—Isn't that only for mated pairs? *Bonded* pairs?" Nyel urged.

"Yes, well, our theory was that if a Tideway can help couples conceive, it might also help set the wheels of fate in motion."

Nyel knew what that meant. They were all hoping for the Lifebond to take root.

A Tideway was when an already Bonded pair, who were struggling to conceive, followed the winter tide for several weeks. *Sirena* were only fertile in the winter months. The idea was that by following cooler waters, the window of fertility would be extended, thus giving them a higher chance of conceiving that year. Not to mention, it was supposed to be extremely romantic. The tide followed a stretch of ocean lush with coral reefs, great planes of seagrass, and incredible blooms of pearl poppies and wave orchids.

A *Sireni* couple's dream vacation.

Nyel's worst nightmare.

Weeks on end with nobody else around—just him and Chel making small talk and maintaining each other's virtue while waiting for the Lifebond to take hold. Not that Nyel was even remotely tempted to sully their *virtue*.

Because mating, or even worse, conceiving while Unbonded, well... there was no greater shame. Unbonded couples were driven out of Corallina and left to navigate the wild seas alone. Being Bonded with your mate was not optional. Lifebonds were the center of everything they knew. Everything they were. Everything they sought to be.

And now, the weight of that connection, the expectation for him to forge such a Bond with a *sirena,* made the water around him thick as mud. Nyel could hardly breathe, his gills heavy. He was eighteen. Old enough to find a mate. Old enough to experience what it was to be Bonded.

He couldn't do it.

"No."

The word rolled from his lips before he registered that he'd spoken.

Nobody heard him as they chattered enthusiastically about all the sightseeing Chel and Nyel would experience during the Tideway. Nobody noticed how pale he'd grown. Nobody noticed the shake in his hands. Nobody... but Sonia. Her eyes met his across the table as incoherent words faded to a mumble in his ears.

It was like looking into a mirror. The same scales, same sad expression. Even their eyes were the same, brown with scattered flecks of gold. Nyel supposed his mother had eyes like that, too, but he'd never looked long enough to notice. She'd never held his gaze long enough to see him. Not the way Sonia did.

When it was clear nobody was going to stop for breath anytime soon, Sonia cleared her throat, forcing the chatter to cease. The water grew still again, and Nyel's shoulders shook as he found his voice.

"I... I have to decline."

"What are you talking about?" Bianca said, brows scrunched, "Of course, you're going. Where else would two young *Sireni* hope for a Lifebond to take hold? It's the perfect environment."

"I can't," Nyel stuttered again.

"Nyel," his mother said with an air of exasperation, "We've had dinner with every eligible *sirena* in the village. I saved the lovely Chel Ernesti for last at your insistence. Even you have to admit this is the best fit for you. You two are long-time friends, and your interests are aligned. It's a match blessed by *Elowen* herself. Don't you worry my little minnow; it'll be singing and Lifebond ceremonies in no time."

Nyel cringed at the mention of *Elowen*, the Spirit of Bonds.

"It's not that, I—"

"When do you think is the best time for them to depart?" His mother addressed the Ernesti couple. "The tide is already moving; I say the sooner, the better," Bianca continued as though Nyel weren't there.

"My nephew and his mate left last week," Mrs. Ernesti said. "They've been trying for a baby for two winters now, *Lasidru* bless them."

"How much did they pack to carry along? I already started a travel bag for Nyel, though I'm worried that—"

"I'm not going," Nyel said, his voice loud and slightly hysterical.

All fell silent.

Bianca rounded on him, her voice a heated whisper, though everyone could hear. "You will not start one of your scenes right now, Nyel."

"I'm not going. I don't agree with this," Nyel said again. Chel's eyes welled in front of him; all her previous joy evaporated. "I'm sorry, Chel. This... this wasn't my idea. I never wanted—"

"You hush right this instant!" Bianca hissed. "Not another word to this poor girl. What do you think you're doing? This is your best chance for a Bonding, for a Lifemate. I will not let you throw it all away because of foolish nerves."

Nyel's mouth went sour. His stomach threatened a rebellion as all eyes were glued to him. But he forced himself to speak, knowing he might never get another chance. "I can't do this, Mom. I'm sorry."

"Do you want to spend the rest of your life alone? Huh? Go about your life as a lone *sireno* with no family and no connections? You want to spend your entire life never knowing the joys of being Bonded?" She gave a mirthless laugh. "Or are you planning on running away and pairing yourself off Unbonded?"

"No, it's not that I—"

"Well, if you're going to be an Unbonded heathen, might as well take a lover that isn't *Sireni*. Fill the world with more half-breeds."

"Bianca." His father's voice was firm, stopping her rant before she could go any further. "That's enough. I think he gets the idea."

Bianca looked like she wanted to continue her verbal tirade, but stopped. She took a deep breath, composing herself. "Well. Now that the stakes are clear, we can move forward." She shook herself, plastering on a perfect smile like she hadn't just torn her son's heart in two. "Back to what I was saying. Next week would be the best time for Nyel and Chel to— Nyel!"

Bianca shrieked as he darted from the room. He was out of their house in one lunge, shoving Mrs. Ernesti in his haste. He didn't know if it was the rush of adrenaline or the repressed sobs that made pulling water through his gills impossible as he swam. Only when he escaped the boundaries of their property did a distant voice break through the pounding in his head.

"Nyel!" Sonia chased after him.

He flattened his fins, slowing his momentum. "You shouldn't be swimming so fast," Nyel called as she swam to meet him.

"I'm fine," she said, but her gills worked hard, the delicate layers of tissue pulsing in and out as she panted. "I needed to talk to you before—"

"I know I shouldn't have," Nyel interrupted, his tears mixing with the water around him as his voice broke. "I know, I know, I'm so sorry, I just—"

"Nyel, stop. You did the right thing. What Bianca did in there, what she's been doing since you turned eighteen, I should have stepped in sooner."

"It's not your problem."

"You're my nephew. You're blood. And your mother..." She let out a weary breath. "She is a difficult person."

They floated there, letting the words drift through the water. He knew she was about to tell him to come back and make things right.

And he'd do it.

"She isn't going to let this go anytime soon. I think it's best to let her cool down for a few days."

Nyel recoiled. "Really?"

"Yes. I'll talk to her and try to smooth things out with the Ernestis. She's probably making a scene as we speak."

Nyel imagined his mother's reaction and shivered at the thought of it being directed at him.

"Stay with a friend for a while. Come back when you feel ready."

"I... I don't have anywhere to stay," Nyel confessed. The only person he knew well enough to ask such a favor was Chel, and he assumed that was off the table. Remembering the hurt look in her eyes made Nyel's chest tighten. Chel didn't deserve this.

Sonia tilted her head, considering him. "Then go to the surface for a while. Bianca won't look for you there."

"S-surface?" Nyel's head shot up in surprise.

"The old human tower island—you know the one. The humans won't bother you there; they abandoned it long ago." Sonia didn't miss his hesitation. "What? You've... tell me you've experienced *Marvassa* before, right? You've *changed?*"

Nyel swished his tail uncomfortably. "Only once, and it was by accident. I got caught up in a rogue wave, and it washed me ashore and..." He remembered the sensation. The tickling. The nakedness of having no scales. The impact of the sun on his skin.

"Then it shouldn't be a problem. The first time is the hardest. I still think it was a mistake on your parents' part to shelter you. By your age, you should have more experience surfacing. But that's neither here nor there. The point is to stay in the tower house, and I'll come to get you when things have settled."

"No, Sonia, you can't surface. Not in your state."

She rubbed at the small bulge on her belly. "I'll send word then. Staying here won't help you or Bianca right now. Give it time."

Nyel's shoulders dropped in resignation. It was the best option. Undoubtedly, his mother would look for him when Sonia came to say he wasn't coming back. But she wouldn't dare surface. He never asked, but Nyel got the feeling that both his parents were scared of *Marvassa*.

"Hey." Sonia touched his cheek with a gentle hand. "Everything will be okay. You did the right thing."

Nyel nodded, though he wasn't so sure. She hugged him before turning and swimming slowly to their home. The adrenaline of his escape was finally fading away, and the shake in his shoulders trickled to the tip of his tail.

How could Mom do that to me?

He knew she wanted to see him Bonded. But didn't that also mean he had to be happy? That it was still his choice? The dinners with potential mates had been pleasant at best and awkward at worst. Yet tonight felt different. It was like his mother had placed all her cuttlefish eggs in one basket—and that basket was named Chel.

"No" wasn't an option.

Is it even my life anymore?

Nyel didn't know. The lingering feeling of being a passenger on his own Spirits blessed journey was unnerving. Frustration built in his chest until the burn in his eyes became too much. He clenched his fists, teeth grinding as the ocean snatched the tears from his cheeks.

This is my life. Not hers.

With nowhere else to go, he turned toward the island. It was time to take his life and shape it with his own claws.

CHAPTER 3

NYEL

HE SHOULD HAVE given himself time to calm down before dashing into the darkening waters, half-blind with residual tears. Maybe then he would have spotted the figure resting on the sandbank. Nyel wiped away another irritating layer of tears when a voice made him jump.

"What has your tail in a twist?"

"Ahh!" Nyel shouted, kicking with all four limbs to put distance between him and the silent figure that watched with a raised brow.

"And here I thought after three months of having me around, you'd stop screaming at the sight of me."

"Y-you should have said something," Nyel said, placing a palm over his chest to ease his flailing heart.

"I take it from the tears that dinner didn't go well."

"I'm not crying," Nyel said stubbornly.

"Uh-huh, and I'm the Kraken."

Nyel regarded his half-brother carefully. Nephi lay on the sand dune in a leisurely pose, his tail swishing back and forth in lazy strokes. He chewed on a sliver of wood between his sharp teeth.

"I thought Mom sent you on some errands," Nyel said, taking a spot on the sand beside him, close enough to be heard but not too close.

Nephi laughed. "I know what *'can you do some mundane task while we have guests'* stands for."

Nyel sighed. He knew too but pretended not to.

Nephi continued. "Bianca isn't very subtle. Doesn't take a genius to figure out she doesn't want her husband's bastard child hanging around."

"Don't.... say that," Nyel said, feeling uncomfortable.

Nephi shrugged, moving the sliver of wood from one side of his mouth to another. "I know what I am."

Nyel tried not to stare, but sitting on Nephi's right side, it was impossible to look away. His brother was a halfling, a child born of two opposing species of Mer. Their father had an Unbonded relationship in his youth. It was taboo in every sense of the word—a crime against the Spirits. And Nephi was the result.

Nephi was half *Sireni* and half *RaMaa*. Nyel didn't know much about them, only that the *RaMaa* lived in seas far to the south. Their scales were red as fresh blood, and their bodies were large and muscular. Nephi was by far the largest Mer in the village, towering over everyone else. The fins along his back and tail were twice as tall as a *sireni's,* with the potential to flare even wider when he flexed. Because of the mixing, Nephi's body was primarily green, like their father's, before merging into the red of a bleeding sun. His teeth were sharp, and, much to Nyel's disgust, Nephi consumed meat.

But that wasn't what made Nyel stare now.

Nephi's right side bore the twisted, scarred remains of savage burns, his skin a grotesque display of seared flesh. The scales melted into one another, cracking in unnatural ways. In a few places, the scales were gone entirely, revealing tortured skin beneath. The fins along the right side of his head were gone, giving him a half-bald look, and the fins protecting his ear canal were nothing but stubs. The worst part was the foggy film over his right eye, as though smoke were trapped inside. His iris and slit pupil were barely visible, and he seemed to struggle to open it fully, giving one side a perpetually squinted appearance. Nyel didn't know if Nephi was completely blind in that eye and didn't dare ask.

"Getting a good look?"

"Sorry." Nyel quickly turned his head.

He wanted to ask how it happened. He wanted to ask...everything. What had his brother been doing for the past three years? Why did he come back now?

Despite sharing half their blood, the Mer sitting beside him felt like a stranger. Nephi had been absent for most of Nyel's life and was older by nine springs—a gap that only deepened the chasm between them. They had painfully little to talk about. And it didn't help that after Nephi left all those years ago, their family pretended he never existed to begin with.

Their father included.

"You better go back," Nephi said dismissively, "before Bianca comes looking. I'm not in the mood for her glares at the moment."

"I'm not going back."

"And where will you go?" He snorted as though the idea of his helpless little brother leaving home was a joke.

"You don't think I can be alone for a few days?" Nyel bit back.

Nephi chewed on the stick in his mouth. "I think you're a sheltered kid with no business leaving your perfect pampered life."

Nyel stiffened, the fins along his back flaring. "I'm not a kid. And you don't know a thing about me."

"Well, Bianca made sure of that."

"Don't blame Mom. You could have stuck around."

"No. I couldn't," he said with finality. His words dissipated in the water like a drawn-out echo. After a brief pause, during which Nephi crunched loudly on the twig in his mouth, he asked, "So none of the *sirena* she dragged in appealed to your tastes?"

"No *sirena* has ever appealed to my tastes. I don't even know if I have tastes," Nyel replied bitterly. "And I'm tired of being shown around the village like a prize crab at the fair."

"Interesting," Nephi said, tilting his head and narrowing his eyes thoughtfully.

"What is?"

"Nothing. Where are you going?" he asked again.

"The tower island. Just until mom calms down."

At this, Nephi bolted upright, fins flared, his relaxed demeanor vanishing. "That's a human island," he said, his tone biting. "You're going to surface on human land? Do you have a death wish?" The growl in his voice sent vibrations rippling through the water.

Nyel flinched and floated away a few inches despite himself. He knew Nephi had no reason to hurt him.

Probably.

Yet, the scars along Nephi's body told a story of violence, and that visual warning kept Nyel at a tail's distance. Even when Nephi first arrived—his wounds fresh, the pain making him whimper through the night—Nyel couldn't bring himself to go to him. He couldn't leave the safety of his bed to comfort the Mer, who shared half his blood. As Nephi's labored breathing echoed through the floorboards, Nyel lay frozen, too afraid to move, too afraid to sleep. The warning to never approach a wounded animal, to never back it into a corner, rang in his mind.

There was a reason halflings were taboo. There was a reason Nyel's mother didn't allow Nephi into the house—a precaution Nyel was secretly grateful for. When two species of Mer interbred, it was seen as defiance against the Seven Spirits, a direct rebellion against the gift of life. As punishment, the resulting child was born severed from Them.

Disconnected and cursed.

These were the stories told to him as a child; cautionary tales pounded into his mind—the monsters he grew to fear. Halflings were cursed. From their first breath, *Skraith* lived within them: dark spirits that drove a Mer to madness. Violent. Dangerous. Nyel was privy to many stories of halfling children turning on their families. Even killing their own flesh and blood. That's why they were silenced at birth. It's why everyone in the village, including his family, treated Nephi like a dangerous animal.

Because he might be.

The scars on his body were only a testament to the violence he'd experienced—the horrors he'd taken part in. And even though there was no possible way they were interconnected, the fact that mere days after Nephi arrived, his uncle Santé was found dead only served as another bad omen—a curse brought to their village by the halfling carrying *Skraith* in his body.

Nyel couldn't stop himself from flinching as Nephi turned toward him—a motion his half-brother didn't miss. For a moment, Nephi's face softened, and a guilty knot tightened in Nyel's stomach. But that fleeting moment of vulnerability vanished as quickly as it appeared, replaced by the sharp gleam of fangs and slitted pupils.

"S-sorry, I didn't mean to—" Nyel tried to correct.

"Forget it," Nephi said, rising, "Go to the human's den. Anywhere is safer than with a halfling monster, right?" And before Nyel could speak, Nephi was gone, darting farther from the village and into the darkening sea.

THE UNDERSIDE OF the waves rolled as the water crested and crashed in a flurry of foam. Nyel squinted as beams of light distorted with each ocean pull. He could do this. He could go up there and let *Marvassa* change him.

"Just go. Now... now.... now."

He kept saying the word like it might magically transport him to the surface, and he wouldn't have to do it himself.

The waves continued to roll above him. Sonia assured him the humans left the island a long time ago, and he trusted her. Nephi was paranoid. He was obsessed and acted like the humans were hiding behind each crevice and hollow, ready to kill anything that moved. *Sireni* were cautious of the land dwellers, but Nephi's views were extreme.

Still, Nyel had never met a human, and he wanted to keep it that way.

"There is nobody there. No boats," Nyel said to himself. "Just.... Go!"

Swishing his tail, Nyel propelled himself through the water and, with a gasp, broke the surface. A wave carried him to the shore, where he tumbled on the soft sand, sputtering. He choked a moment, the pull in his gills no longer working. Nyel opened his mouth, sucking air as something inside him inflated. It was like a blowfish, continuing to puff up and deflate with every breath. He supposed this is how land creatures breathed, awkward as it was. It took him a moment to realize that nothing about his exterior had changed.

Rain pelted him, the sky alive with tears and rage as veins of light flashed in the clouds. And when the air above him cracked, Nyel cried out in shock, clapping his hands over his ear fins. The sound was so much stronger on the surface. He had to get out of this.

Nyel ran up the shore, his taloned feet sinking in the sand. Sopping grass squished between his toes as he fled the beach. He squinted through the rain, spotting the human shelter. It was a square-shaped building with a mighty tower that supported the sky. It took him a moment to find the entrance before shoving it open and closing it behind him. Instantly, the noise muffled, and he let out a sigh of relief.

He took in his surroundings, squinting in the dim light. The home was in a clear state of abandonment. No chance of running into humans here. The longer he stood, the drier Nyel's body became. A tingling sensation rippled across his skin—sharp, needling, like the prickling rush of blood when a limb falls asleep. He shivered as *Marvassa* took hold, his scales sinking into his skin and disappearing while fuzzy strings sprouted along his head. His tail retracted, shrinking smaller and smaller until it was gone.

Nyel steadied himself with one arm against the wall. His body was so heavy that even the simple task of keeping his head up was taxing. How did humans do this? How did they walk around without toppling over? Nyel needed his freakin' tail. Shifting his weight from side to side, he tested his balance and how it felt on his hips. Hunched over, Nyel cautiously took a step forward with his right leg.

Then his left.

Repeat.

Now, he was getting the hang of it. Maybe walking wasn't so ba—

Razor-sharp pain tore through his leg. He cried out as he fell, a fiery ache flaring in the soft tissue of his foot, as if he'd stepped on a sea urchin. Red spattered across the floor.

Blood.

His blood.

The scent exploded in his nose like he'd been splashed with it.

Nyel whimpered, bringing his foot closer to examine the wound. A clear piece of glass stuck from the soft flesh.

"Stupid humans. Stupid humans and their stupid pink skin and stupid soft feet," he grumbled through clenched teeth, pulling out the shard with shaking fingers. It hurt, and the wound wouldn't stop bleeding even once the glass was out.

He ripped off the now dry seaflax vest, which wasn't doing him any good anyway, and tore off a strip before wrapping his wound.

"Stupid, stupid, stupid," he mumbled, standing again, now with a limp. "As if walking wasn't already hard enough."

Nyel ran a hand through his (was it hair?) and watched much more carefully where he stepped. He made it to another door, this one leading to an impossibly tall staircase that went up and up and up.

This had to be the tower. He could probably see for miles from the top and find a comfortable corner to rest.

With no glass, preferably.

Driven by his exhaustion, the ache in his foot, and a pinch of curiosity, Nyel climbed. He'd had enough excitement for one day.

CHAPTER 4

ATREUS

THERE WASN'T TIME to douse the fire. No time to hide the evidence of his space being lived in. Atreus only had a second to grab the sharpened metal pipe and dive behind the curtain partition, heart in his throat.

How had he been so careless? He cursed himself; it was this damned weather. The rain always made him melancholic, and he let his head drift to another world.

The steps grew louder, with a slightly irregular gait as if the person climbing was hobbled on one side. He held his breath and watched through a slit in the curtain. When the door opened, it creaked loudly, the rusted hinges protesting. Lit by the flickering firelight came a hand—an arm, a face.

The young man was pale, almost alarmingly so. His dark brown hair lay in messy waves that curled around his ears. He appeared close to Atreus's age, though with a slighter build. His frame was lean, lacking noticeable muscle definition. This person didn't spend a lot of time doing physical labor.

Atreus knew all this with only a glance, reading the stranger better than any words on a page. The intruder stepped fully into the firelight, his bare chest exposed and his lower body covered in dried seaflax pants. He stooped as he walked, as if still grappling with his center of gravity, and Atreus knew instantly that this stranger was Mer.

Mer— and likely out of the water for the first time.

What are you doing on a human island, you dummy?

Atreus lowered the makeshift spear but kept it in his hands, just in case.

He watched the stranger for another minute, noticing the Mer's amazed expression as he took in every foreign object. His eyes were wide with awe, seemingly oblivious that a fresh fire meant somebody had recently inhabited this space. Atreus caught the glimmer of gold in those brown eyes. They shone like bits of mica embedded in the rocks along the island.

He couldn't look away.

When the stranger reached a cautionless hand to the metal bowl and yelped as it burned him, Atreus decided it was time to step out before he did any real damage—mostly to himself.

"Yeah, I wouldn't touch that," Atreus said as he revealed himself.

The stranger yelped again, losing his footing and landing hard on his rear, the seaflax pants crunching as he fell. "I— please... I don't.... I'm not going...."

Panicked eyes locked onto the sharpened rod in Atreus's hand, so he tossed it to the side with a loud clang.

"Relax. I'm not gonna hurt you," Atreus said in what he hoped was a calm voice. "Talk normally; we understand each other."

Despite trying to calm the boy, Atreus's heart was racing in his chest. Someone was here—a real person. He hadn't spoken to another person in months. But this wasn't a human—this was a being of the sea.

Like me.

It dawned on him that, other than his father, Atreus had never held a whole conversation with another of his kind.

"Oh. I didn't know we spoke the same as humans— I mean. Of course, we do." He let out a nervous chuckle. "Of course, we can understand each other. Why wouldn't we?"

Atreus rolled his eyes. "Smooth."

"W-what do you mean? This is, ugh, human language?"

He said it like a question. His lie was so poorly hidden that Atreus wondered if this idiot was that clueless or just a special kind of stupid.

"You're not human, and you're not doing a very good job hiding it." Atreus said, "What are you doing here, *sireno*?"

"Oh. I'm just y-y-ou know." The Mer could hardly speak as tremors ran down his body. His teeth chattered as he spoke.

"You have no idea what you're doing. Go back to the sea where you belong," Atreus bit out, annoyed at the intrusion. But he couldn't help adding, "Unless you have a good reason to be here."

He flinched internally at the shallow sign of weakness. The loneliness inside him escaped for a brief moment and opened the door for this stranger to stay.

It was pathetic.

"I can't. I-I have to s-s-stay a-away."

Atreus couldn't ignore his chattering. "You're cold."

"C-cold?"

"Yes. It's something humans have to deal with."

"Oh," the *sireno* said, goosebumps erupting along his arms and legs.

Atreus moved to his meager store of belongings and threw him a spare set of clothes.

"Put these on. They'll be big on you, but at least they're dry. You can sit closer to the fire—but don't touch it!" he warned.

"Right. I figured that one out," the stranger said, holding up one red-tipped finger.

When he stood, the seaflax pants nearly fell off him. They weren't meant to dry outside the water. Atreus averted his gaze, not willing to turn his back to a stranger entirely but allowing him privacy. Cloth rustled as the boy struggled to organize himself in foreign clothing.

Finally, he heard, "I don't know how to put these on."

"Legs in the two long holes, ignore the hole in the back."

"What's that for?" the Mer asked.

"A tail."

"But... we don't have one right now."

"Well, I never know when I might have to make an emergency dive. Don't want to tear my stuff," Atreus huffed, annoyed.

That's exactly what had happened. He'd dropped a pail of water onto himself, revealing scales instantly. With Leo seconds away from spotting him, Atreus leaped over the ropes and into the sea. His tail manifested with *Marvassa* and ripped his pants to shreds. After that, he'd painstakingly sewn a convenient human invention called 'velcro' to a hole in the back of all his pants. It kept the hole closed while he was in human form and adapted to a tail without ruining it.

"Right, okay, I got it. What about this one?"

Atreus turned to see the boy struggling to figure out the t-shirt.

"Here," Atreus said, holding it open and helping him work his way inside. The stranger's skin was cold to the touch. But also... so clear. Not a blemish. Not a single imperfection. It was pure, like the world hadn't yet had a chance to mark him.

Once he settled the boy beside the fire with a patchy blanket, he addressed him again.

"I'll ask again, *sireno*, what are you doing here?"

"You're a *sireno* too?" he asked, avoiding the question.

Atreus didn't know how to answer that but found himself nodding anyway. The boy sighed.

"That's a relief. I thought I'd run into a human."

"Well, what did you expect? You surfaced in human territory."

"I heard it was abandoned."

"It is. Well, besides me."

A million more questions burned in the boy's eyes, but Atreus wasn't ready to answer any of them.

"Are you going to tell me what you're doing here or not?"

"Oh, well." His hands twisted in his lap. "It's a long story."

They listened to the fire crackle in the bowl and stared at the embers as they dwindled. Atreus reached and added a fresh log, coaxing the fire to grow, much to the boy's amazement. He scooted further away as the heat intensified.

"I never knew it could be so pretty. The fire."

Atreus didn't say anything. He didn't know what to say. It'd been months since he'd spoken to another person, and none of them were Mer. His social skills were excruciatingly out of practice.

"I'm Nyel Veritani, by the way."

Atreus thought about that for a moment. "Your first name is weird," he said and cringed at how rude it came out.

Nyel nodded. "It's from far away. My dad insisted on it. My mom wanted to call me 'Raffi.'"

The fire gave a loud pop, making Nyel jump. He curled in the blanket, his teeth worrying the inside of his cheek. "I didn't catch your name."

"I didn't throw it."

Nyel tensed, tugging the blanket even tighter. "Can... can I get it now?" he asked cautiously, as though he were approaching a wolf eel with an attitude.

Realizing he was being a jerk, Atreus sighed loudly. "It's Atreus."

"And your last name?"

"Don't have one," he said too quickly and was glad when no follow-up questions came.

"Your name is strange, too," Nyel said.

"It's from far away," Atreus copied, which earned him the barest hint of a grin.

The tense, wordlessness they fell into after that was enough to make Atreus's skin itch. He fidgeted until his patience wore thin and stood, retrieving the remaining cans of sardines. He didn't feel like cooking anymore, and the lobster would be fine until morning.

"Here." He tossed the can to Nyel, who missed and picked it up from the floor. "Like this," Atreus said, showing him how to break the seal and pull open the metal can. Instantly, Nyel covered his nose with his hand and gagged. "What?"

"Is that— fish?"

"Sardines, yeah. Humans put them in these things and they last forever without going bad."

Nyel pushed the can away, still actively trying not to be sick. "I can't. Sorry."

"What's wrong with it?"

Nyel looked at him incredulously. "It's meat. You can eat this stuff?"

Atreus shrugged. "I prefer them fresh, but this is better than going hungry."

"I'll have to disagree with you on that," Nyel said, taking shallow breaths.

"Well, it's all I have unless you want to cook him," Atreus said, pointing to the lobster.

"I'll pass, thanks." Nyel watched him, and for the first time since he'd dropped the spear, Atreus thought he saw a flicker of fear in those eyes. "You said you were *Sireni*?"

"Yeah. And?"

"*Sireni*, don't eat meat."

Well, shit.

Atreus was painfully aware of how little he knew about Mer. He was more familiar with humans than his own species. He ignored Nyel's comment.

"You're from that village, right? Down the sandbank?"

"Yeah. My family and I live on the edge of Corallina, just outside the hijiki fields."

"Family?" Atreus hated how the word caught in his throat as he said it.

"Well, yeah. You didn't think I lived by myself, did you? I'm only eighteen springs."

I've been on my own since my thirteenth winter. And I have no idea how many years I've lived since.

"How many springs have you seen?" Nyel asked as though reading his mind.

"Twenty-two," Atreus settled on, though he had no idea. He opted for the higher range.

"And you're out here on your own?"

I didn't used to be.

"Yes. And I'm very comfortable that way," he lied. And, sensing more questions about his personal life, he redirected, "So what— you ran away from your parents?"

Nyel's jaw tightened, and he curled inward, tugging the blanket tighter. "I left my aunt, too. She's about to have a baby. She told me to come here and... wait it out."

"A cousin." Atreus mused, quickly getting swept up in the idea of it all. Nyel had parents. Two people to watch out for him and care about his well-being. He also had an aunt and a cousin on the way. A new life was coming into this world—more family.

"I wonder if she'll have a boy or girl, not that it matters as long as the baby is healthy—"

"Go back in the morning," Atreus cut him off, a bitter tang in his mouth.

"What? Why?"

"Because you don't belong here; you belong there, with your family, in that village with hundreds of other happy families like yours."

"You don't know a thing about my family."

"I know what all you *Sireni* are like. You're all the same, right down to the scales on your back."

No room for outsiders like me.

"You speak like you aren't one," Nyel said, not bothering to hide the suspicion in his tone.

Atreus glared. "Out. Tomorrow. I'm leaving early in the morning, and I don't want you hanging out here while I'm gone."

NYEL

Nyel couldn't believe his ears. This was the most presumptuous person he'd ever met. What made him the authority on Nyel's business?

When he limped up the tower's steps, he never imagined he'd find another Mer at the top. At first, Nyel thought he'd stumbled upon a human and was seconds away from having a sharpened piece of metal shoved through him. But Atreus immediately understood what he was and looked just as relieved as Nyel. Neither of them were expecting company this evening.

Though Corallina was a large settlement with hundreds of families spread over thousands of nautical miles, Nyel was pretty confident he would have remembered a name like 'Atreus.'

He'd never met this *sireno* before, and Nyel wasn't sure calling him a '*sireno*' was accurate either. Atreus was dodgy, and Nyel didn't miss the way he talked about the villagers with disdain.

Now, Nyel was getting kicked out.

And I just got warm.

But he wouldn't let the cozy warmth of the fire tempt him into begging. He had more dignity than that.

Nyel stood abruptly, dropping the blanket as he returned Atreus's glare.

"Why tomorrow? Since I'm such a nuisance, I'll see myself out now." As he turned to stalk away, he slipped on the material wrapped around his foot and fell.

"Sharks!" Nyel cursed, head spinning. He wasn't used to the sensation of falling and found that he didn't like it at all.

A gentle hand lifted his foot a second later, inspecting the wrapping. Nyel hadn't even noticed when Atreus dashed across the room to help him.

"You're hurt."

It wasn't a question.

"It's not your problem." Nyel tried to stand, but Atreus's gentle grip raised his foot, preventing him from moving. "Hold still," he commanded, resting Nyel's foot on his lap and removing the wrap. The wound immediately started to bleed again.

"There was human glass downstairs."

"Yeah, I know," Atreus said, a guilty look coming over his face. "Wait here."

He carefully laid Nyel's bleeding foot on the floor, returning a moment later with a stool, a bucket of what smelled like fresh water, and a dry rag.

"There's sand in your cut. Wash it out here, and I'll wrap it," he said, turning his back and preparing pieces of white cloth.

Nyel wanted to protest, but the deep incision in his foot pulsed in rhythm with his heart.

"Fine," he huffed, sitting on the stool and easing his foot into the water. It didn't sting as much as he expected, and he gingerly stuck both hands in, cleaning the wound with his fingers and flushing out the embedded sand. Though the water was likely made of rain, *Marvassa* changed him where the water touched. In less than a second, he was removing sand from a webbed foot with elongated talons.

"After you dry off, I'll wrap it and—"

Atreus stopped mid-sentence, his eyes wide at the sight of Nyel's transformed skin. He stared, mouth slightly open. Feeling self-conscious, Nyel finished cleaning the wound and pulled it from the water.

"What?" he finally bit out when Atreus continued to stare as he dried himself with the rag, and his skin returned to its human state.

"You're... it's you."

"Me?"

"Your scales. They're... green."

Nyel rolled his eyes. "Of course, they're green—mine and every *Sireni* in the ocean. Good job," he mocked.

Atreus ignored his jab. "No. Not like the others. You're unique; it's —" He tilted his head, thinking. "It's like jade."

"Yeah, I'm weird. My mom and aunt have it, too. So what?" A rush of heat flooded Nyel's face.

For a moment, Atreus looked like he wanted to say more but shook himself. "Never mind. Hold still."

Despite his sharp words and abrasive attitude, there was a surprising gentleness in the way those large hands touched him. Atreus dressed Nyel's wound with a clear, syrup-like liquid before wrapping it in clean white cloth. He pinned the end of the wrap closed with a metal clamp and inspected his work.

"Keep it dry for a few days."

His voice lost its bitter edge, and he still held Nyel's foot in his lap, staring at it as if the green scales might spontaneously return.

"Kind of hard to do in the ocean."

At this, Atreus lifted his head, and with him kneeling so close, Nyel got a clearer look at his features. His curls fell low, covering most of his forehead. His nose was wide-set, in proportion with his defined square jaw. A light dusting of freckles bridged over his nose, growing darker as they dotted down his neck and shoulders. But what made Nyel's gaze stick like barnacles on a rock were those eyes. Beneath thick brows were eyes unlike anything Nyel had ever seen. All *Sireni* had the same colored eyes: Brown. Boring. Bland.

But *these* eyes...

They shimmered like nacre, or the inner lining of abalone shells —but with an unsettlingly hypnotic green hue. Even the kelp in its most ripe state couldn't compare. Streaks of deep sea green and hints of turquoise blended together. As the firelight shifted, the colors transformed, undulating with a pearlescent sheen, like liquid glass in motion.

"You can stay," Atreus said, snapping him from his daze.

"Wait— what?" Nyel blinked rapidly and straightened. He hadn't realized he'd leaned in so close.

"Wait until the wound closes, then go. Before you leave, jam the front door closed with a stone."

"What about you?" Nyel asked because it sounded like Atreus was going to leave him alone in this tower.

"I have somewhere to be," Atreus said, finally releasing his leg and standing. He ran a hand through his tight curls, a motion Nyel suspected he did a lot.

"Where?"

"Nowhere," he said too quickly, and Nyel didn't miss the way his eyes flickered to the window. Then it clicked—why he'd never seen Atreus before, why Atreus was so familiar with human artifacts.

"You're going to the human town, aren't you?" Nyel knew he was right when Atreus's jaw set. "That's where you go, isn't it? Why, I've never seen you around before."

"You don't see me around because it's been made very clear that I'm not wanted," Atreus bit out.

Nyel recoiled. He had no idea what that could possibly mean.

Atreus made a frustrated sound like he regretted saying so much. "Forget it. Doesn't matter at this point; I've done well enough on my own. Tomorrow, I'm leaving. I'm going back to my life, and you're going back to yours. End of story."

Nyel sat frozen, his mind reeling.

Atreus waved a hand in front of his face. "Hello?" he called in irritation, but Nyel's gaze remained distant. He was caught in a whirlpool of thoughts and revelations.

Somehow, somewhere on human sands, Atreus had a life. A life outside of farming kelp or herding schools of goatfish. A life outside of arranged dinners with potential Bond mates. A life free from expectations and living exactly as his parents did—as his grandparents and great-grandparents. The same ebb and flow of farming, mating, and raising the next generation, only for the cycle to start again.

Yet Atreus didn't fit that mold. His life was made up of something else entirely. Nyel didn't know that was even possible. His chest tightened as a sickening thought took hold—Nyel knew so little of the world beyond the one he was raised in.

But here was proof that a different life existed. There was another way to experience the world. And now that Nyel knew it was there, he couldn't go back to the way things were—back to the sheltered community where he never belonged.

"Hello? Did you hear me?" Atreus snapped his fingers in front of his face.

"Take me with you," Nyel blurted.

Atreus huffed a laugh. "Absolutely not. It's a *human* town," he said, putting emphasis on the word. "It's too dangerous."

"You do it." Nyel countered.

"And I've been doing it since I was thirteen. I can read them—or at least the few I talk to."

"You talk to humans!?" Nyel said, almost leaping to his feet in excitement when the sting in his foot forced him to remain seated. "Isn't that dangerous? Don't they... you know..."

"Attack me?" Atreus finished. "If they knew what I was, yeah, they probably would."

"They don't?" And the scope of what Atreus was saying sank in.

"They don't know what you are. They think you're a human like them."

"Yes. And I'd like to keep it that way."

Nyel couldn't believe what he was hearing. Atreus was walking the razor's edge of life and death. One slip-up, one splash of water, one raindrop, and he'd be exposed. If he'd managed to keep himself hidden since he was thirteen, surely Nyel could do it. Right?

"I still want to see it." Nyel insisted, and he could almost hear Nephi's cautionary words in the back of his head.

"That's too bad." Atreus shot out. "Heal and go home."

Nyel was standing now, ignoring the pain in his foot. "Why not?"

"Because you're running from your problems, and I'm not gonna enable you. Go home and deal with it."

"You don't know what you're talking about."

"Don't I? Let me guess," he held up a hand, stopping Nyel from speaking. "Your mother or father told you to do something, and you don't want to do it. So, instead of handling it like an adult, you ran. Am I in the ballpark?"

Nyel didn't know what a *ballpark* was, but he sure as hell wasn't going to let this stranger talk to him like that.

"It's not that simple."

"Sure it isn't." Atreus rolled his eyes. Treating Nyel like a whiny child.

"You have no idea what you're asking me to do!" Nyel shouted.

"And you don't know how good you have it!" Atreus recoiled at his own words. "I-I..." he stuttered, but nothing came out.

A look of instant regret crossed Atreus's features, and that's when Nyel felt like an intruder—not for being in the tower but for uncovering a truth Atreus wanted to keep hidden.

"I'll leave first thing in the morning," Nyel said a moment later, sparing Atreus the need to explain himself.

Nyel wouldn't go home, though. Despite Atreus's words stinging his insides like the quill of a lionfish, he wasn't about to surrender so easily. He'd finally found the strength to stand up for himself and take control of his life. He wasn't about to back down now. He'd figure out where to go in the morning.

"Take the mattress," Atreus said, arranging his lumpy blankets beside the fire.

"The what?"

"The white soft thing over there," he gestured without looking. "It smells like smoke, but it's clean otherwise."

Careful not to irritate his newly bandaged foot, Nyel walked to the rectangular shape. It was soft and...jumpy? He didn't know how to explain it, but there was a definite bounce as he lay down. It did smell like smoke. Smoke and... something else. Like the storm raging outside, only softer. It carried a gentle hint of melancholy. Nyel pressed his face into the springy surface, letting this strange scent lull him into a pleasant calm as exhaustion crept in. The maelstrom of emotions Nyel had endured left him utterly drained. He couldn't remember the last time he'd been so tired.

The last thought that drifted behind his closing lids was of abalone shells glistening in firelight.

CHAPTER 5

ATREUS

ATREUS WAS THIRTEEN. His father left exactly sixty-seven days ago. Summer was in full swing, and the seafloor was full of crustaceans that kept his stomach full. He wouldn't taste the bitter tang of starvation for months to come, but he was already starved for something else. For company. For someone to talk to.

Atreus swam back and forth on the outskirts of the village, too nervous to go any closer and too lonely to go back to his tower. For the past two weeks, he'd been hiding behind stones near the villagers' homes, picking up bits and pieces of their conversations. To hear the voices of other living creatures. The inflection of a laugh or the hum of a mother's lullaby. Soon, it wasn't enough. And now he swam circles on the outskirts of a family sand-hut home, reciting his opening lines.

"Hi, I'm Atreus, and I live on the island…"

Too informal.

"Hello. I'm Atreus…"

That made him about as interesting as a sea slug.

It needed to be perfect. If what his father said about the villagers was true, he only had one chance to change their minds. His father's words rang in his head like a warning bell.

"Stay away from those Mer. They'll likely stone you the moment they see you."

"Why? Did I do something wrong?"

His father scoffed. "You exist. That's reason enough."

He never expanded more than that.

But sixty-seven and a half days of isolation broke through that barrier of fear. Now, he drifted outside the family home he'd watched for weeks—a mother, a father, and a boy. The boy was around Atreus's age, maybe a little younger, and much smaller. Most of the Mer in this village were small, with Atreus already nearly the size of the adults at thirteen.

"You can do this," he chanted, forcing himself closer to the home. "Just be polite."

Atreus was behind the house when his nerves got the best of him, and he stopped.

I can't do it.

He turned around, defeated, when he collided with a scaly body.

"Ouch!" a small voice yelped as Atreus's bulk pushed him through the water.

"Sorry!" he said, helping the boy from the sand. "I'm so sorry. I didn't mean to."

It was the boy who lived in the house. Atreus recognized him right away. He didn't look like the others.

"It's okay," he said, straightening his seaflax pants and picking up the long stick he used to herd the goatfish. When his eyes locked on Atreus, they widened. "You're not *Sireni*," he said with a mix of awe and fear. "What are you?"

"I don't know," Atreus said honestly and bit his tongue.

He felt like an idiot. The lines he rehearsed died in his brain. He should introduce himself. How did that go again?

"Wanna help me gather the goatfish?" the boy asked, snapping him from internal panic.

Atreus nodded stupidly, his out-of-practice words uselessly trapped in his throat.

"Here, hold this. They listen better when I wave it around." The boy handed Atreus a long, smooth staff made of seawood.

Before they reached the school of meandering goatfish, a figure dashed between them, shoving Atreus with unexpected force and yanking the staff from his grip.

The woman, her scales the same color as the boy—likely his mother—yanked her son close as if rescuing him from the jaws of a Great White. She was so alarmed that Atreus spun to see what was attacking them. It took him a moment to realize she was looking at *him*.

"What are you doing here?" she screeched, pushing her son away. "Get out of here! GO!" she shouted hysterically. Atreus backed away, arms raised in surrender. Her mouth set in a manic snarl, and he worried she would strike him with the staff.

"I—I wasn't doing anything wrong."

"You stay away from my son, away from this village, halfling mutt! Keep your *Skraith* away from us."

As the unfamiliar words tumbled from her mouth, Atreus watched the boy's slitted pupils constrict in alarm. He stared at

Atreus as though seeing him for the first time. As though seeing a monster.

Atreus's heart beat heavy in his chest, a sting of guilt eating away at his insides. Guilt for... he didn't know what. He didn't know what he did wrong, but he'd violated some rule, some law.

His crime?

He existed.

Atreus swam straight to his island, ran to the house, and buried himself under patchy blankets. He didn't stop crying for hours.

It was the first and last time he spoke to the Mer of the village.

Now, likely a decade later, Atreus stared into the fire, sleep impossible as the story of his isolation played over and over in his mind. The look of fear and disgust on the *sirena's* face was palpable. And even worse, it reflected in the eyes of her son.

Halfling. Skraith.

To this day, Atreus didn't know what those words meant. He'd never had another Mer to ask. But it was reason enough for him never to approach the Mer village again, even when he was only days away from starvation. He was quicker to approach the bloodthirsty humans than the *Sireni*. Luckily for him, the humans hadn't seen him as an abomination.

*"Only because you're hiding
in a shell of their skin."*

Atreus flinched at the whispering voice in his head. He poked at the fire more insistently, letting the floating embers distract him. He wished the sun would hurry and rise already. There was no chance of him sleeping, not with another person so close.

Too close.

Nyel hadn't so much as rolled over since falling asleep on the mattress. He slept soundly. Obviously, whatever issues he was dealing with wouldn't stop him from getting a good night's sleep.

Would he be so comfortable if he knew what I was?

Atreus had made a point not to dip his hands in the bucket Nyel used to clean his wound. It was better to let Nyel believe he was 'normal' and not well... whatever he was.

Does he even remember me?

No matter how many times Atreus wished he could forget, the precious minutes he spent with the jade boy remained permanently etched in his brain.

During the nights when his stomach was empty and his heart even more so, Atreus comforted himself by imagining what it would have been like if the boy's mother had never appeared. Would they have herded the goatfish together? Talked? What would they have talked about?

Since that day, Atreus held dozens—no hundreds—of conversations with the boy. His imagination supplied him with stories that would never be. And now, the subject of his daydreams slept only feet from him. Older, bigger, and with no memory of Atreus.

The sun wasn't up yet, but Atreus couldn't stand it any longer. He doused the fire (assuming Nyel wouldn't think to do so), grabbed his leather pack filled with extra clothes and food, and moved to leave the lighthouse. He paused with his hand on the door.

Nyel slept. Not a snore. Not so much as a heavy breath. Peaceful.

Atreus approached, using the *sireno's* moment of vulnerability to get a good look. Nyel's human body was as strange as his Mer. It was so unblemished that he almost appeared fake, like the marble statue in the center of town. But the wavy dark hair that fluttered with each breath was proof enough of his mortality. Atreus was tempted to stroke a finger across his pale cheek, just to know what it felt like.

Then he'd leave, and they would never see each other again.

*"If he knew the truth about you,
he'd run and never look back."*

Atreus retracted his hand and, without a sound, left Nyel alone in the tower.

He didn't belong with his kind. He belonged with the humans. He belonged in Baia Vita.

NYEL

THAT GREEN-EYED JERK killed the fire, and Nyel couldn't make another one. He woke up shivering, only to see he was alone in the circular tower room.

Atreus was gone.

Nyel's shoulders drooped. He shouldn't have been so disappointed; Atreus told him he was leaving. Still, part of Nyel hoped he would have stayed long enough to say bye.

"It's only polite," Nyel muttered to himself, rubbing his fleshy hands together. His human hands were more flexible than his webbed ones.

However, the more he pondered it, the more it bothered him. He got the distinct feeling that Atreus didn't like him very much.

Another shiver tore through him.

"Sharks!" he cursed, rubbing his arms up and down vigorously. He hated this part of the human body. Why did he have to fight against the air he breathed? This body was so frustrating. When he woke, it took him a moment to remember he wasn't underwater. The weight of himself was suffocating. With no water to support him, he was a sack of sand. He lay there, gasping for an embarrassing amount of time before he had the strength to lift his head.

Nyel observed his spindly fingers as he wiggled them. In less than a day, he'd learned more about himself than he had his entire life in Corallina. He'd learned that fire was hot, dangerously so. That humans had air balloons instead of gills. That his body needed heat to stay warm.

And now that he'd gotten a taste, Nyel wanted more. He didn't know it before, but now it was so painfully obvious. The missing piece in his mundane life. He was starving for something new— something his mind could latch onto—something to digest and learn.

Something different.

Nyel cautiously touched the metal bowl that once held the roaring fire. Though the flames were gone, the bowl was still warm. He sighed, letting his hands fall flush to the metal. One jump into the waves, and his body would no longer be so sensitive to the difference between hot and cold. He could return, apologize to his mother, and prepare to go on the Tideway with Chel. He scoffed.

No way.

From this height, Nyel could see the shores of the human land. Their settlement sat right beside the curve of the bay before climbing the hill.

Atreus is there.

Nyel squirmed as jealousy took root like a coral in stone.

What is he doing? Who is he seeing?

How could he have spent years in the company of humans without being gutted? Nyel wanted to know more. More about humans. How they worked, what they ate, and the way they socialized. For the first time in his life, Nyel dared to want *more*.

NEPHI

NEPHI GRITTED HIS teeth as he lost the trail for the third time. He'd have to double back to find it again. At this rate, he wouldn't have any fucking fangs left for how hard he was grinding them. Nyel's scent was faint in the water, but with a general idea of where he was going, Nephi found it. Yet the trail continued to go blank as his damaged scent receptors failed him again and again.

"Fucking damn it!" he cursed, kicking a fire coral where a piece snapped off and fell to the sand. He hadn't always been so useless. He didn't used to lose fresh trails. Back then, he was a predator. Back then, he was unstoppable. Back then...

Back then... It might as well have been only hours ago, with how vividly the images now flashed through his mind.

Opalescent fins. Moonlight reflecting off sky blue scales. Then... orange. So much *orange*.

The color alone was enough to send him into a rage. Overcome with the need to tear, to cripple, to kill—he tore apart his corallite victim. One branch at a time. He only wished the creature had vocal chords. He wanted to hear it scream, to cry out. Maybe its cries could drown out the ones that replayed in his brain.

Every.

Single.

Night.

If I had been faster. Stronger. Smarter. We could have escaped. I could have saved him.

The sudden memories made Nephi lose focus. His vision blurred, the edges turning red. He roared in frustration, tearing into the innocent animal piece by piece.

When his vision cleared, only the stump remained, and scavenger fish picked at the newly exposed flesh. Nephi panted, gills heaving, missing the taste of copper in his mouth as what remained of the bloodless animal floated around him. If anyone saw, they'd think he lost his mind.

Didn't matter. As a halfling, people made that assumption about him anyway. But now, after everything. Well... Nephi was beginning to think they were right. These days, he was like a torpedo hurling through the water. He was a mortar of repressed fire and wrath - ready to blow with the slightest spark.

He needed to get ahold of himself. Getting lost in memories wouldn't help anyone, least of all Nyel. A quick visit to the Veritani home told him that Nyel hadn't returned. Bianca was inconsolable while her sister and his father, Donato, tried to calm her. Donato noticed him peeking into the home but turned away and continued consoling his wife.

Just as well.

Nephi had no intention of talking to his father. Besides the green scales covering his torso, they had nothing in common. And Nephi was more than happy to keep it that way. He had no attachments to these people. Not Bianca, who hated him. Nor his father, who pretended he didn't exist. And not his half-brother, with whom he shared blood.

They never treated him like family, and why should they? He was a stranger. A living, breathing mockery of the Spirits. Cursed. When he returned to Corallina, fresh burns covering his body and barely clinging to life, they didn't even offer him a place in the home. Nephi slept beneath the sand hut —where the sandwinder slept. Only occasionally did they remember he was down there, wounded and too weak to move, and they'd set out a bowl of food as if he were a stray leatherback turtle.

Didn't matter.

Nephi didn't come here to be babied. He just needed a place to rest. To lie low and take care of his damn self. He was no good to the Pod wounded, and they moved too often for him to keep up in this state. Tariq ordered him to find a place to rest until he was ready to return—and like a fucking idiot, he went home.

Not my home.

But it was where his half-brother lived. And thoughts of Nyel continued to nag Nephi for hours. Since leaving Nyel at the sandbank, the idea of that dumb kid getting close to a human encampment made his skin crawl.

The idiot doesn't know what the hell he's doing. He has no idea what those land dwellers are capable of.

Nephi found the spot where they'd last spoken and followed the scent. In his prime, following a scent, even one a day old, would have been child's play. Despite resenting that side of himself, the *Sireni* were excellent trackers. Their enhanced sense of smell allowed them to detect even the smallest change in their crop. But with his sense of smell damaged and his right eye nearly blind, he struggled. Still, he followed the scent and, late in the afternoon, found that it led to a small island with a human tower perched at the top.

Of course he came here, even after I told him not to.

Nephi stepped from the waves, unflinching as *Marvassa* tickled his skin. He walked with confidence, upright with perfect posture. He'd spent many weeks in this form, hiding amongst the humans. Learning their secrets. Listening to their conversations. Watching. Waiting for the right opportunity to strike.

A spy amongst wolves.

But now he was marked by the human's sadism. Nephi cringed as *Marvassa* changed scale to skin, including the parts disfigured with burns. He examined his new body, seeing for the first time how these scars fared under the sunlight. They were just as distorted and disgusting as they were in his Mer form. He touched the side of his head; his dark brown hair burned off one side, and his ear crinkled to almost nothing.

"You're an ugly bastard in both bodies," he told himself as he smirked.

At least he wouldn't have to worry about the human females throwing themselves at him anymore. That was the part he hated most about his missions into human territory. The dance between male and female. The ritual of courting and mating. Humans were mad for it. It was their greatest weakness, an easy one for him to exploit. And when he learned that he was particularly attractive to the human females, it was almost too easy to infiltrate their defenses.

He got close enough to steal the needed information, then returned to the sea. He'd never actually bed any of them. Even the idea of lying with a human made him want to gag. They were filthy, oily, and smelled of the earth they lived on. It took years for him to master enough self-control to hide his repulsion. To smile instead of snarl.

They ate it up every time.

Now, with scars marring his once handsome features, Nephi would have to figure out a different way to infiltrate their ranks. It didn't matter. His job right now was to heal. That's what his commander said. He'd be back in the thick of the fighting soon enough.

Nephi shook off the remaining water droplets, letting the air fill his nose. His shoulders relaxed some. There were no humans here; by the looks of it, there hadn't been for a long time. He followed Nyel's trail to the lighthouse, pushed inside, and halted. The scent was strong now, mixed with the tang of iron.

Nyel was hurt.

Nephi raced up the tower steps.

The humans have him. Damn it, why didn't I stop him? The stubborn brat should have listened when I—

He charged into the lighthouse room, only to find it empty. Nyel's scent was strong. Fresh. He'd been here only an hour or two ago. Nephi was about to go down to find the fresh scent when another one made him pause. Another Mer. Male. There was something off about this one—something different. A scent Nephi hadn't encountered in a long time.

Another halfling.

Even more on edge, Nephi didn't bother with the stairs and shoved open a window. The tower stood resolute on the rocky cliff, the waves crashing against the stone. He jumped on the railing with ease, his balance perfect. He may be an ugly bastard, but he was still strong. Poised. A weapon itching for its next fight.

He jumped.

There was no hesitation. The wind howled past him, but he didn't brace—didn't tense. The height didn't scare him. He had done this a thousand times, and he would do it a thousand more.

The ocean rushed to meet him. At the last moment, he curved his body, angling just right—barely disturbing the surface as he slipped into the depths.

Marvassa took him, and he was a monster once more.

The swim to the human settlement would take him less than half an hour. That meant it would take Nyel twice that. And in this weather, the choppy current may have slowed his brother even more.

In typical early spring fashion, the sky remained in a perpetual state of indecision. Rain. No rain. Wind. Lightning. A constant whiplash of weather currents, shifting on the whim of *Pygon's* mood.

In the minutes he spent in the tower, the weather turned once again to an angry gray whirl of nature's forces. It was the perfect storm and a prime opportunity for an inexperienced Mer to get caught unaware.

Nephi shook his head, cursing the foolishness of youth. He'd never been so careless at that age. If he pushed himself, he might catch the dumb kid before he did anything even more stupid. Nephi kept close to the surface, where Nyel's scent was the strongest.

Moron. If a boat came by, he could have been spotted—

No sooner had the thought occurred to him than the sound of an approaching engine sputtered in the water. Nephi dove straight down, letting the depth hide his presence from the vessel's captain.

The boat listed harshly to its port side. Something was off.

Easy pickings.

He could sink this boat. Overpower it like a shark picking off the weakest swimmers in a school. But Nephi was alone. Here, he had no Pod to help him sink the human machine. To help erase the land-dwelling creatures that dared intrude upon their ocean home. The thought sent Nephi's blood to boil. And even now, knowing it was stupid— he was tempted to take the vessel on his own.

If nothing else, he wanted action. He wanted adrenaline, claws, and teeth. He wanted those land rats to recognize what they took from him. To *feel* it. The way he'd felt it every fucking second since.

The ghost of a hand rested on his shoulder.

"Patience, my love. The right opportunity will come."

Ludomir's voice rang in his head. Even in the confines of his memory, that voice calmed Nephi. It put his angry heart at ease, reminding him to take calming breaths and temper his rage. To push it deep. Hide it away. Stay in control.

"You are the master of your mind. Not the wrath that haunts you. Breathe, my love."

The ghostly presence slid from his shoulder down his arm, reaching for his hand.

His breaths came easier now. Nephi unclenched his talons, but as he reached for the phantom hand, he only found empty water.

The momentary calm was sullied as agony took its place.

His chest spasmed, unable to decide if the pain was rooted in longing, loss, or regret.

Or all three.

If only I'd been faster, if only I'd seen the signs. I wouldn't be burned, and Ludo would still be at my side."

Nephi clenched his jaw until it hurt.

It didn't matter.

None of it did.

Ludo was gone, Nephi was brutally scarred, and his Pod was waiting for him. Once healed, he'd return and offer himself for the most dangerous mission he could.

At least then, his death would mean something.

Nephi turned tail to follow Nyel's scent and ignored the distressed vessel when a powerful wave crashed above him. The screech of tearing metal pierced the water, only to be swallowed by the ocean's roar. The boat's engine gave a final high-pitched whine before it sputtered and died. When the next wave hit, the vessel capsized. Metal and debris fell into the water, littering the sea floor with more human waste. Among the life vests and fishing nets thrown into the sea was a shape Nephi was all too familiar with.

A human fell from the boat and landed with a dull 'whoosh' as it sank below the waves. Even from a distance, Nephi could tell this was a man, a young one at that. Yet his body remained motionless as it sank lower and lower. Likely knocked unconscious when the boat flipped. He would drown.

Serves him right.

Nephi was seconds from abandoning the dying figure when he caught a flash of blond hair. He whipped around, heart in his throat.

Blond hair twisted in tight ringlets—high cheekbones. Sun-kissed skin and a full lower lip, now turned blue with cyanosis as he sank.

He was dying.

Drowning.

My Ludo.

Instinct propelled Nephi into action, shooting through the water like a missile. He grabbed the young man under his arms, dragging him to the surface. A bell rang its death tolls as the boat took on water. Nephi avoided the floating debris, careful not to let his fins get tangled in the nets. Even now, with his head above water, the young man remained motionless in Nephi's arms.

"Breathe, damn it!" Nephi yelled.

Swimming with half his body above the waves was hard enough, and the raging storm made it almost impossible. He only had minutes before the boy in his arms would be lost forever. Precious seconds while his blood retained some oxygen to send to his brain.

"Fragile fucking creatures." Nephi cursed as he swam the young man to the capsized boat. It was completely upside down now; its hull pointed to the sky. It would take another quarter of an hour to sink. It was enough.

Using his talons to dig into the wood, Nephi dragged them onto the hull, laying the young man on his back. The rain pelted his head as he crouched over....

Ludo. My Ludo.

But that was impossible. Ludo was dead. Killed in the explosion, his lifeless body burned beyond recognition in the fire.

Yet here he was, lips blue, chest still and lifeless.

"Damn you, Ludo!" Nephi roared and tilted the boy's chin up.

With expert precision, Nephi placed his mouth over the boy's and blew, inflating the lungs in his chest. In rapid succession, Nephi began chest compressions, pumping five times before returning for another breath. Over and over, Nephi repeated the process, his compressions cracking the boy's ribs. If that is what it took to manually force his heart to beat, it was a small price to pay.

On the fourth round of breaths and compressions, the boy sputtered. Nephi rolled him to the side so he could expel the seawater from his mouth. The boy coughed and choked, white foam coming out in bubbly spurts. Color rapidly returned to his lips and cheeks.

Despite himself, Nephi relaxed.

Ludo continued to spit out water and— no, not Ludo. Not Ludo!

But even as he berated himself, Nephi couldn't look away. Even knowing what this person was, he couldn't bring himself to drag the boy back to the water and watch him drown. Even as the human's eyes opened and focused on him, Nephi wasn't even remotely tempted to slit his throat as he should have done.

As he'd done countless times before.

The young man's eyes fluttered, focusing on him. He didn't cry out. Didn't attack or show any alarm at the sight of a sea monster at his side.

He just...stared.

And that is when Nephi's illusions fell away. The human's eyes were yellow—the merciless eyes of a predator.

Ludo's eyes had been silver, like the calm before a winter storm.

Whether it was the sight of such a creature or the stress of nearly drowning, Nephi didn't know. Only that the next second, the human slumped to his side. Unconscious.

Pathetic.

Yet Nephi didn't leave him to perish. He'd already crossed that line the moment his scales made contact with skin. Instead, he positioned the boy against his chest so his head lolled on Nephi's shoulder. And with painstaking slowness, Nephi paddled them to shore. It took three times as long as it should have, but it was all he could manage with the relentless waves and swimming with only his lower half. He dragged the boy's unconscious body along the beach before letting him flop (harsher than necessary) to the sand.

"There," he bit out, lip curling. But in the same breath, his expression softened.

With his eyes closed, the boy could have been Ludo. Asleep on the beach. Peaceful. Ready to wake and offer Nephi a smile like he'd done a thousand times before.

He'd never see that smile again. All because of *their* kind. The humans. And now, he'd saved one. Because of his broken heart, weakness seeped into the cracks, and now he had saved the very thing he'd dedicated his life to destroy.

Nephi leaped into the water before his weakness could compel him to do more. As he halfheartedly searched for Nyel's trail, Nephi's mind was lost. He couldn't focus on the scent, his thoughts elsewhere. They were back on the beach, fixated on blond curls and amber skin. He clutched his head.

What have I done?

CHAPTER 6

ATREUS

Atreus couldn't repress the smile tugging at the edges of his mouth as Giovanni's voice boomed from the top of the stairs. He sang along with his favorite opera, the record spinning on a high shelf. And Atreus had to admit, the grizzly man wasn't half bad. He rounded the corner with a fresh stack of newspapers, giving Atreus a good-natured shove as he passed.

"Hey, watch it, old man, or I'll mess up the cut on this fish," Atreus said, holding the knife steady.

Giovanni chuckled, the sound vibrating through the room. "You better not, *ragazzo*, that's my best seller. And who're you calling old? I'm healthy as an ox."

"Uh-huh, whatever you say," Atreus mocked, earning him another shove as Giovanni took a spot beside him.

He wrapped the cuts of fish in paper and marked the price, still humming along to the music. The old fisherman's hands weren't as steady as they used to be, so he tasked Atreus with cutting the higher-value catches. Today, it was yellowfin tuna. The red meat was marbled with fat and oil and would fetch a high price.

But that would have to wait until tomorrow. Today, the doors of the Sleeping Whale *pescheria* were closed because of the severe spring weather.

Atreus considered himself lucky, though. The rain held off long enough for him to swim ashore, change into his human self, and approach the *pescheria* before the sky reopened. With the town square half flooded with an inch of standing water, most stores remained closed. Giovanni's fishery was no exception, so today, they busied themselves with cutting, packaging, and organizing the store.

"How was your winter? How's your family?" Giovanni asked, working alongside Atreus at the counter.

"Good. Cold, but what else is new?" he lied, feeling like he'd stabbed the scaling knife into his gut.

"Yes, it was cold here as well. Many harsh nights."

Atreus dared peek at the old man, his salt and pepper beard more salt than pepper these days. Despite Atreus's teasing, Giovanni was as muscled as the day they met, just a little more lined now. Giovanni's clothes were simple and clean and would be covered in fishy splotches by the end of the day. Yet one part of the old fisherman's attire always remained the same. A black shark's tooth rested high on his chest, strung with a thin piece of worn leather.

The tooth's black color resulted from fossilization, a concept

Atreus still didn't entirely understand. These teeth were common enough, but Giovanni's was a special specimen. The tooth was large without a single imperfection on either of its serrated sides. But more than its appearance, Atreus admired what it symbolized.

A black shark's tooth was bestowed on a young man once he reached a certain milestone in his life. It was a right of passage, the evolution into manhood, and it had to be earned. Simply growing up wasn't enough to earn the title. In Baia Vita, without the necklace, you were still considered a boy regardless of age. The symbol of status dangled from the neck of every man on the island. These necklaces were heirlooms, treasured far more than common coin. In most cases, fathers were the ones to bestow the title on their sons. Necklaces passed from father to son, some dangling from family necks for generations.

Exactly like the one Atreus now admired. Giovanni's father gave him that necklace after he navigated a wild storm, keeping the boat aloft and saving the lives of the crew. It was brave and noble, all attributes of a man worthy of a shark's tooth.

Atreus could never hope to achieve something so incredible.

"I was surprised to see you so early in the season. Doesn't your family need your help on the mainland?" Giovanni asked, snapping Atreus's attention back to the present.

Atreus's stomach twisted, but it didn't show on his face. This was his first lie. One he'd told for years, starting when he began working for the fisherman. It was how he explained his absence during the winter months and why he didn't live in town. A tall tale he wove as carefully as a gill net. No knots. No loops. No reason for anyone to suspect a thing.

Atreus was a factory worker on the mainland, helping his family during the harsher months of the year. But the summers were his, and he chose to spend them on the island. The island where he worked hard, earned his way, and never allowed himself to be a burden. Ever.

That was the story.

"No. They had plenty of help, so I left early. I couldn't wait to get back here," he said truthfully, which earned him a smile and a hefty pat on the shoulder.

"Well, this old fisherman is glad to see you. It's been too quiet with only me and Horace."

"It won't be quiet for long. The island always livens up in the spring."

"Only if this blasted rain goes away. The barge won't come in this weather." Giovanni grumbled as his hands continued to wrap and price cuts of meat.

The only way to get to Baia Vita was by merchant barge. Baia Vita, in and of itself, was a massive island off the coast of mainland Italy. Passenger boats refused the voyage to the island since there weren't enough tickets sold to make a profit. This left travelers with two options: make the trip themselves or catch a ride with the merchants. The barge visited the island monthly to deliver supplies and the occasional passenger. Besides its visits, Baia Vita was cut off from the rest of the world.

And the residents of the island liked it that way.

But the World War crippled the small island haven, and in desperation, many turned to more affordable resources from the mainland. The island lost some of its integrity. Bits and pieces of timeless tradition, uncorrupted by mainland ideas, were chipped away as more and more families reached for help in the wrong places or left.

Every time Atreus returned in the spring, more of what made Baia Vita special was gone.

"Even if the rain continues tomorrow, we have to open," Giovanni said as the downpour showed no sign of abating.

"Understood." Atreus agreed, though his throat went dry as it always did when the store was open on rainy days.

He'd have to make some excuse to do indoor tasks, and he didn't like shirking the harsher jobs on the docks. The island used to have half a dozen fisheries and outdoor stalls selling a wide variety of what the sea had to offer. The island's main source of income was fishing, after all. But after the war, only Giovanni remained. And so it rested on the shoulders of this tiny *pescheria* to keep mouths fed. It was the sole reason many families had food on the table at all.

They couldn't keep the doors closed for too long.

The Sleepy Whale stood as the last reminder of Baia Vita's glory days. Giovanni worked alongside the remaining fishermen in town to keep him well-stocked. This meant he rarely took his own boat to the seas unless there was a shortage, in which case, he'd fire up that clunky engine and fish the bay alongside the others.

Atreus recognized the simplicity of it all, the peacefulness of this life. He loved it. More importantly, he saw the love in the eyes of those who called Baia Vita home. But he also sensed the mourning as they clung to the old ways, helpless to the shifting times and the ever-increasing influence of the outside world. Atreus hoped that one day, the island could stand on its own and be as independent as it had been in the good old days.

What he would have given to see it.

"This will likely delay Marina's arrival," Giovanni said. "She will be happy to see you already here. That is, if you finally decide to stay with us."

Atreus anticipated this. The offer came at the beginning of every season and it never failed to make his chest warm inside.

"I have a place to stay, *Signore* Marcello. As always, I'm grateful for the offer."

Giovanni let out a disgruntled huff. "One of these days, *ragazzo*, I will convince you to live here for the season. I do not like seeing you travel so far each day."

"You can keep trying."

He let out a yelp as Giovanni flicked his ear. "And I told you to call me Giovanni. How many years has it been? I've known you since you were this big," he said, holding a burly hand close to the ground. "I've known you as long as I've known my Marina. I've watched you both grow up before my eyes, so *per favore*, spare me the formalities —yes?"

But she's your daughter. I'm a seasonal employee. A nobody.

"I'll try to remember," Atreus lied.

"Do you remember the day the letter came?" Giovanni mused.

Atreus nodded. How could he forget? It was the first and last time he'd ever seen the sea-hardened fisherman shed tears.

"A child I never knew." Giovanni went on, his voice settling in it's story-telling timbre. "She was nine years old. Too young to lose her mama. Too old to love a *Papá* she never met."

"Marina loves you to death," Atreus said.

"Now, yes. But then? She was like a lost kitten. Yet she accepted you right away."

Atreus's mouth twisted in a grin. Of course, a doting father would call her a kitten. To Atreus, she was more like a feral alley cat. However, she had clung to Atreus in those early days. Like glue, she wouldn't leave his side. Atreus didn't know it back then, but if not for his shadow, he would never have learned how to live amongst humans. He would have mistakenly outed himself a dozen times and either be forced to flee or be killed on the spot. Marina taught him without suspicion. In return, he helped bridge the gap between father and daughter. Though to this day, Atreus didn't know what exactly he'd done to make that happen.

"I do not know what I would have done without your aid," Giovanni said, marking a bundle of fish.

"You two would have figured it out, I'm sure," Atreus said.

"My point, *ragazzo*, is that I've known you as long as my daughter. So please call me Giovanni. When I hear *Signore* Marcello, I fear my mother-in-law has risen from the dead to haunt me."

Atreus laughed but made no promises. Calling *Signore* Marcello by his given name was too informal. Too close. Too exposed. It was for the same reason that Atreus committed to his second lie. The one that claimed he had a 'friend' on the island's far side where he stayed during the fishing season. The reason why he never accepted Giovanni's invitation to stay in his home.

The home in question resided right above their heads. The *pescheria* was a two-story building with a large first-floor storefront and Giovanni's living quarters above. Atreus had worked here since he was thirteen and never once permitted himself to go up those stairs despite the invitations.

He didn't want to admit it. To accept the truth that had settled in his heart long ago. This place, with its worn wooden walls, dim lighting, and fishy smell, had become more than just a place to work.

It became his home.

And homes, like people, could disappear.

Even worse than losing everything was knowing *he* was the reason it was gone. Knowing that he'd done nothing but burden those around him until they couldn't take it anymore... and left.

Atreus refused to let it happen again. He'd work hard and ask for nothing. Take nothing. Cease to exist when there was no longer a need for him. He'd enjoy his season of usefulness, then vanish when the winter winds came, waiting patiently for the day he'd be needed again—when he'd be allowed to come home.

Fingers snapped in front of him. "*Ragazzo*, did you hear me?" Giovanni asked with a chortle.

"No, sorry, what were you saying?"

"I was saying that if you were to stay, you could help Marina with preparations for the Festival—"

Giovanni was interrupted as the *pescheria* doors burst open despite the closed sign in the window.

"Have you seen Leo!?" the drenched woman called out, her normally neat blonde hair strewn in all directions.

"Emelia, what on earth are you doing in the rain?" Giovanni asked, halting his work and ushering the woman inside.

Emelia Tradi was the village healer, midwife, and pretty much everything short of a surgeon. Her old-time remedies kept the town healthy. She was poised and proper and exuded an undeniable warmth. She was also the mother of Atreus's best friend.

"Giovanni, *meno male che sei qui*. Thank goodness you're here. I've searched all over. Leofel—he took that blasted boat out. I told him not to go, but he's so stubborn."

"Has the boat returned? Have you checked the docks?" Giovanni asked, his voice ever calm.

"I haven't been able to look, this darn weather. Thomasso is already searching the beaches. I hoped maybe he came here, and—oh, Atreus, you're already in town?" she said, seeing him for the first time. "Have you heard from Leo?"

"I'm sorry, no *Signora* Tradi. I haven't seen him, I only arrived this morning."

Her bottom lip trembled. "Will you help me search for him? You'd know where he might be better than I would," she pleaded.

Atreus froze. No matter how much he wanted to search for his friend, he couldn't go out in this weather. Giovanni spoke, sparing him a reply.

"I'll go. Atreus, can you finish this yourself?"

"Yes." He had to resist adding "sir" to the end of that.

"Good man. *Andiamo* Emelia, let us check the docks."

And with the tinkle of the bell, they were gone. Leaving Atreus with nothing but the hum of the refrigerators and the pattering of rain on glass.

"What were you thinking, Leo?" Atreus mumbled as his steady hands continued to cut the delicate meat. The Tradis' boat was ancient, barely seaworthy, and had more problems than he could name. He'd lost count of how many hours he and Leo spent repairing it over and over again. And that idiot took it out in this weather.

Atreus wanted to blame Leo's pride like his mother did. But he knew the real reason: the financial pressures to provide for his large family. Though Emelia was still in her prime, Leo's father was far older—older than Giovanni by more than a decade—too old to work the nets. This left the responsibility of a mother and five younger brothers and sisters to rest on Leo's shoulders alone.

"If he had just waited for me," Atreus grumbled. He could have helped Leo earn some extra money. If Leo was so eager to work on the opening day of the season, that meant the winter had been harsh. Atreus couldn't imagine the pressure of so many young lives depending on him. He could barely take care of himself.

He was so lost in thought that he mistook the rapping on the back door for thunder. On the third round of pounding, Atreus looked behind him. Why would Giovanni come through the back? Could it be Horace? No, the old man was likely asleep upstairs. Then who?

Maybe it's Leo. Maybe he's hurt.

Quickly wiping his hands, he dashed to the back door, kicking aside some empty bait boxes. He wrenched it open.

"Nyel!?" Atreus couldn't decide if he was horrified or surprised. Maybe equal parts both.

"Hey," Nyel said sheepishly.

"What are you... how did you...!?"

The *sireno* had found a piece of plastic tarp and was holding it over his head like a poncho. His upper half was dry, but there was no hiding his soaked feet, which were currently long and webbed.

"You've got to be kidding me!" Atreus yelled, grabbing Nyel by the shirt and jerking him inside. "Don't move," he ordered, grabbing the nearest rag and bending to dry Nyel's transformed feet. Almost instantly, they changed, revealing human toes.

Nyel wrinkled his nose. "What in Spirits-blessed is that smell?" he asked, covering his mouth like he might gag.

"It's a fishery; what did you expect?"

"How was I supposed to know? I was looking for you."

"Do you realize how dangerous this is? Do you realize what could have happened if anyone saw you?"

Nyel narrowed his eyes. "Hence the tarp."

Atreus threw his arms up in the air, defeated. "How did you even find me?"

"I followed your scent," Nyel said, tapping his nose.

"My... my what?" Atreus had never heard such a thing. Humans sure as hell couldn't do that. Not to the extent Nyel was describing. "What are you, a bloodhound?"

"What's a—"

Atreus held up a hand. "You know what, it doesn't matter. What matters right now is getting you back to the ocean where you belong."

Nyel stood straighter. "I'm not going back. I already told you."

"Well, you sure as hell aren't staying here." Atreus was shaking. This was bad—so bad. How was he going to get out of this? Nyel knew nothing about the human world. He was literally a fish out of water.

A stupid fish.

"Okay. Okay, okay, okay." Atreus said, trying not to panic. He needed to think. "This is what we're going to do. You're going to hide back here. I'm going to finish my shift, and then I can sneak you out of here and get you back—

"—I'm not going back," Nyel insisted.

"—to the beach without anyone seeing. Yes. That will work. Okay." Atreus ignored him. "Right, you stay here behind the shelves and don't make a sound—"

"Atreus?" a voice called from the front of the store. "Who are you talking to?"

His heart sank. He didn't hear the bell. Giovanni was back.

I was talking to myself. That's it; nobody here at all.

His mind supplied him with excuses. No, that wouldn't work. If Giovanni came back here and saw Nyel, he'd know Atreus was lying. He couldn't lie (more than he already was). Couldn't risk breaking the trust he'd garnered for so many years.

Everything he'd built for himself flashed before his eyes. He could lose it all.

"Atreus?"

"B-be right there!" Atreus called.

In one fluid motion, Atreus shoved Nyel. The *sireno* yelped as his head smacked the wall.

"What are you doing?" he whimpered, then choked as Atreus shoved a forearm under his chin.

"You listen, and you listen good," Atreus growled, putting pressure on Nyel's throat, simultaneously silencing and pinning him. "This is my life you're playing with. You understand that? My. *Life.* These humans don't know what I am. And it better damn stay that way. Follow my lead and do exactly as I say. And whatever you do — Don't. Get. Wet."

Atreus took an extra second to glare into those wide brown eyes. The flecks of gold shimmered even in the artificial human lights.

"Because if you do, I will not take the fall for you. I won't sacrifice everything I've built to save you. Do we understand each other?"

He hoped that Nyel understood what he didn't have time to explain—should he be exposed, Atreus would not save him. He'd watch the humans tear him apart.

Nyel nodded, his skin losing what little color it had.

"Good."

And with his heart racing, Atreus stepped from the storeroom, motioning for Nyel to follow.

He was about to risk... everything.

NYEL

ATREUS'S SCENT WAS easy to follow. When someone was stressed, their scent changed and grew more potent. Following the invisible trail with his nose, Nyel detected the nerves that had rolled off Atreus as he walked down this same path only a few hours ago. He was likely worried about the rain, which, to Nyel's displeasure, started the moment his feet hit the sandy shore. Luckily, he found a torn piece of human plastic and draped it over himself. There wasn't much to be done about his bare feet, but there weren't any humans around. Evidently, they didn't care for the rain either.

The scent led him to the back entrance of a weathered two-story building, its wooden exterior showing signs of age. A wooden board hung with human symbols etched into it. Though Nyel couldn't read them, one carving vaguely resembled a whale taking a nap.

Whales don't sleep like that.

Nyel laughed to himself. He should have been terrified. He was in human territory, surrounded by land dwellers who would rip him to pieces if given half a chance. But fear couldn't compete with the raging excitement that pulsed through him as his feet touched the solid ground. Once the rain stopped, he would explore this place from top to bottom.

If my parents knew where I was.

He paused when an even scarier thought struck him.

If Nephi knew...

He shivered. Nyel was positive that Nephi's anger was more about hating humans than caring about his safety. Still, he didn't want to be on the receiving end of that resentment.

Careful to keep his fist covered, Nyel rapped his knuckles on the door. It took several tries before a lock clicked, and the door creaked open, revealing the source of the stress-infused scent. Dark, sparse freckles dotted Atreus's sun-bronzed skin, trailing down his neck and disappearing beneath the collar of his tattered charcoal shirt, which clung to his corded arms. His shorts were ripped in several places, and he held a towel in one hand as though interrupted mid-task.

Nyel wasn't sure what he expected. For Atreus to smile? Greet him? He wasn't expecting anything like, "Good to see you," but he didn't foresee the look of pure terror as Atreus's eyes widened and darted to his transformed feet.

"Nyel!?" he shouted, then lowered his voice, looking around nervously.

"Hey," Nyel said with a timid wave.

"What are you... how did you...!?"

Rough hands grabbed his shirt and yanked him inside. Nyel hardly noticed as Atreus frantically dried his feet. Because his nose was on *fire*. The smell of blood, guts, and flesh made his throat lurch and his stomach squirm. He was going to be sick.

"What in Spirits-blessed is that?"

"It's a fishery; what did you expect?" Atreus tossed aside the rag.

"How was I supposed to know? I was looking for you." Nyel confessed.

"Do you realize how dangerous this is? Do you realize what could have happened if anyone saw you?" Atreus kept his voice low, but the intensity made it feel like he was yelling. Nyel took a nervous step, aware of how much bigger Atreus was. But he wasn't about to back down. He'd come too far.

"Hence the tarp," Nyel retorted with as much snark as he could muster.

Atreus ran a hand through his curls. "How did you even find me?"

"I followed your scent."

"My... my what? What are you, a bloodhound?"

Nyel's curiosity sparked.

"What's a—"

Atreus held up a hand, cutting him off. "You know what, it doesn't matter. What matters right now is getting you back to the ocean where you belong."

"I'm not going back. I already told you," Nyel said, planting his feet for emphasis.

"Well, you sure as hell aren't staying here."

Atreus was really and truly starting to panic, and Nyel almost felt bad.

Almost.

Definitely not bad enough to go home. When a voice from the front of the building called Atreus's name, both of them froze.

Is that a human? Am I about to meet one?

Fear and excitement buzzed in Nyel's blood, but before he could open his mouth to ask any questions, Atreus shoved him into the wall.

His head bounced on the wood, and he cried out in surprise. But his cry was silenced as Atreus pressed his arm into his throat. He could hardly breathe. And when his attacker spoke, Nyel's body went cold.

"You listen, and you listen good," Atreus growled, leaning into him and cutting off more air. "This is my life you're playing with. Do you understand that? My life."

Nyel knew what he was doing was dangerous. But until this moment, he'd never considered what it would mean for the man pinning him to the wall. He was a liability, and Atreus wasn't prepared to take the risk.

He only made it this far by not taking risks.

"Don't. Get. Wet." Atreus ordered. It was less of an order and more of a threat. A promise that if Nyel messed up, Atreus wouldn't save him.

He was truly alone.

"I understand," he croaked before gasping as the pressure disappeared from his throat.

Nyel rubbed at it, taking deep breaths. Atreus made a jerking movement with his hand, motioning him to follow. Nyel would do as he was told. He had to trust that Atreus, after all his time spent in the presence of humans, knew what he was doing.

If Nyel wanted to stay here, he'd have to trust this aggressive stranger. And even then, it might not be enough.

ATREUS

His nerves were shot, and even though he put on his best casual face, Giovanni would see right through him. The old man had a way of seeing through his walls as though they were made of glass.

"Atreus?" Giovanni said, but it was more like a question.

"Yes, sorry. I was talking to my..." He hesitated. "Friend. He just showed up."

"A friend, you say?" Giovanni turned to inspect Nyel, "This is the first time Atreus has brought over a face I didn't recognize. It's your home he's staying in on the far side of the island, yes?"

Atreus bit his tongue when Nyel took way too long to answer, eyes wide.

Shit. He's freaking out.

"Yeah, I am," Atreus said when Nyel showed no signs of speaking. "Sorry, he's a little nervous."

"No need," Giovanni said, extending a hand, "Giovanni Marcello. It's nice to meet a friend of Atreus's."

Atreus had to shove Nyel in the shoulder to get him to respond. The *sireno* extended the wrong hand and pinched Giovanni's fingers before jerking his hand back like he'd touched a moray eel.

"Your name," Atreus said from the side of his mouth.

"Oh, I'm Nyel Viritani. N-nice to meet you too."

Giovanni looked between the two; his mustache pressed into a hard line. "What brings you here, Nyel?" He finally asked.

"I... uh... I wanted to see Atreus at work," Nyel said, then looked to him for approval.

"I'm afraid today is slow, given the rain. We will likely finish early, and you can return home."

"Where?" Nyel asked.

Atreus stomped on his foot as casually as he could and spoke over him. "Yes. Your house on the far side of the island. The one your parents rent for the summer."

"Oh— yes. That house." Nyel agreed with pained tears welling in the corners of his eyes.

For the second time that day, Atreus was spared from more impossible questions when the front door opened. This time, Thomasso, Leo's father, limped in with his walking stick.

"They have him at the hospital right now," he said, shaking the water from his cap. "Dr. Romano is with him. It doesn't look too terrible." His gravelly voice was a reminder of years spent smoking on the open sea, each word carrying the rough edge, as though the salt and smoke had permeated his lungs.

"And the boat?" Giovanni asked.

Thomasso's already slumped shoulders sagged even more. "Gone. Probably sitting on the sandbank by now."

"Le porgo le mie più sentite condoglianze. I am sorry my friend."

Thomasso waved him off. "Boats can be replaced. It's more important that my son is okay."

Atreus's brain spun like a broken compass.

Leo. His best friend. His best friend was missing in a storm. How could he forget so easily? Nyel's arrival completely threw all worry for Leo out of his mind. Those worries came rushing back to him now.

"What happened? Is Leo hurt?" Atreus asked, stepping forward.

"Oh, Atreus, it's good to see you, son," Thomasso said, squinting to see him better. "He has a big bump on his head and was cold as ice when we found him on the beach. Dr. Romano said he will be okay. He'll be by to visit you tomorrow, I'm sure."

Atreus relaxed. "Good."

"I better get back to the house. Emelia is with Leo, and I don't want the little ones alone for too long." Thomasso turned to leave, his walking stick clanking on the wooden boards, when Giovanni stopped him.

"Wait." He reached for the freshly wrapped yellowfin and placed ten pounds of it in a satchel. It was half their entire stock. "Take this."

Thomasso's watery eyes narrowed.

"For Leo," Giovanni added. "The red meat will be good for his recovery."

When the old man made no move to take it, Atreus raised his voice. "The docks will be busy this week. When Leo feels up to it, can you send him to us? I could really use the help."

Thomasso sighed, then nodded, accepting the satchel of food. "I'll pass the message to him."

"Thank you," Atreus said, sharing a knowing grin with Giovanni as he helped Thomasso shoulder the pack.

Without some exchange, Thomasso would have refused the food. So Atreus asked for help even though he could handle the work on the docks perfectly on his own. At least this way, the Tradi children would be well-fed while Leo recovered.

As soon as the door swung closed, he turned to his boss.

"I'll share my wages with Leo when he comes. I didn't mean to hire someone for work without asking first."

Giovanni shook his head. "Do not worry, *ragazzo*. You did the right thing."

Giovanni patted him on the shoulder, and Atreus felt like he would float to the ceiling. But that elation came crashing down when Nyel opened his dumb fish mouth. "Um. What's a hospital?"

"Nyel," Atreus spoke loudly. "Why don't you sit in the back and wait for me to finish? Huh?" He offered in a way that didn't allow for argument.

He shoved Nyel to the back and out of view before roughly sitting him down on a stool in the corner. "Don't ask questions in front of anyone but me. Got it?"

Nyel nodded, looking sheepish. "I was just curious."

"Well, you sound like an idiot," Atreus said but regretted it when he saw the hurt look on Nyel's face. He exhaled heavily. "A hospital is a place where sick people go to get better. There are trained people there called doctors who can cure sickness and fix broken bones and stuff. I don't know a lot about it."

Nyel's eyes grew wide. "That's amazing. Cure sickness? Like a healer?"

"Uh, sure."

"Wow." Nyel said in awe, "It's like magic."

"I'm pretty sure it's called science."

"What's science?"

Atreus rubbed his face with a groan. "I don't have time to answer all these questions. Sit here," he said, looking around and grabbing a stained book at random. It was an old fish encyclopedia. "Look at this. It has pictures."

He was about to walk away when Nyel took a sniff at the book like he might eat it.

"Like this." Atreus showed in exasperation, opening the book and showing him how to flip the pages. "Don't tear it."

"Oh wow!" Nyel gasped, flipping the pages with delicate fingers. "Oh wow!" he exclaimed again when he reached a page with an illustration. "It looks so real!"

Atreus couldn't help but smile at his wonderment. His wide eyes, gaping mouth, and flushed cheeks were... cute. He remembered the first time Marina showed him a book and was positive he hadn't been this excited. Nyel studied the pages as if he'd discovered a new world. Atreus left the *sireno* on the stool, confident he'd be occupied for at least a couple of hours.

Returning to their work, Giovanni said nothing for a while. They quietly wrapped cuts of fish while the record player sang in the background.

"Your friend is interesting."

Atreus stiffened but tried to shake it off. "He doesn't get out much."

"Hmm," was all Giovanni said, and Atreus wished he'd say more. But the old man was an expert on keeping his thoughts and feelings to himself.

"He, uh, is pretty sheltered." Atreus offered again.

"Reminds me a lot of you when you first arrived here."

Atreus tried to swallow past the tightness in his throat. He laughed nervously. "Similar upbringing, I guess."

They were close to finishing when Nyel's timid voice sounded. "Um... excuse me?"

Atreus whipped around, ready to tell him to go back to his corner when Giovanni spoke.

"What is it, *ragazzo*?"

"Um, I have a question, but," his eyes darted to Atreus.

"Can it wait?" Atreus asked through clenched teeth.

"It's not a worry; we are almost done," Giovanni said, tossing the soiled rag in the sink.

"I'll take it from here," Atreus said, inserting himself between the two and pushing Nyel to the back.

"What is it?" he whispered heatedly.

"What are these?"

Nyel pointed to the rows and rows of letters on the page. Atreus let out a sigh. "They're words. Human symbols make sounds and form words. The words we use to speak."

"So, the book is talking?"

"Sure."

"Wow." Nyel said, looking at the stained pages like they hid the world's mysteries, "I wish I understood what it was saying."

Giovanni's voice boomed from the front. "I can teach you a few letters," he offered, clearly eavesdropping.

"Really!?" Nyel asked, sliding past Atreus and to the front. "You know how to understand this?"

Giovanni laughed. "A little. Only the basics. If you want to learn more, you must ask my daughter. She can read, write, and spell like a scholar."

Atreus's gut twisted. He'd tried to read. Many, many times. No matter how hard he studied, the symbols on the page seemed to move before his eyes. Like the letters were dancing, taunting him with their hidden meaning. He was an idiot.

"Can you read?" Nyel asked him as though sensing his guilt.

"Uh, no. Not really. *Signore* Marcello has tried to teach me, but I'm pretty hopeless," he finished, hanging his head.

Giovanni bumped a shoulder into Atreus, his mustache quirking as he spoke. "Most of the men and boys on this island cannot read a word. We're fishermen, after all. And I've never seen anyone weave a net or repair an engine as quickly as you can."

Atreus couldn't force away his grin at the praise. "Thank you, sir."

"What did we talk about with the formalities?" Giovanni huffed, shaking his head. "Well, I say today's work is finished. Are you sure you don't want to stay the night?" he asked, "Your friend is welcome too."

Atreus's stomach went queasy at the idea of Nyel spending so much time in close quarters with humans. So many risks. So many chances to be exposed.

"No, we should go back to our—" A clap of thunder shook the room. Nyel let out a yelp of surprise, and the overhead lights flickered. The rain was coming down harder than ever.

They weren't going anywhere.

"You were saying?" Giovanni asked with a smirk.

Atreus clenched his jaw, his brows furrowed. He wanted to kick

Nyel, who looked like a child pleading for a treat at the market. The storm had set the wheels of fate in motion, and he was powerless to stop it. Shoulders slumping in defeat, Atreus deflated with a heavy breath.

"I'll prepare two rooms then," Giovanni said, a smug expression twisting his mustache. He left the shop and climbed the stairs to the second-floor house.

"For most of my life, I have lived by a set of rules," Atreus said quietly, his voice low enough that only Nyel could hear as he stared after his mentor. "Don't get too close. Don't expose yourself. Don't take risks."

Nyel said nothing, clutching the fish encyclopedia like a child would a teddy bear.

"Then you show up. And now I'm breaking every single one."

"Why so many rules? This human, *Signore* Marcello, he seems like a good person. I think he cares about you a lot."

Atreus spun on him. "You've been here a day. Don't act like you know anything," Atreus snapped. "Every second in this town is dangerous for us. One wrong move, and it might be our last."

Nyel dropped his gaze and said nothing else.

"Talk as little as possible," Atreus instructed before approaching the stairs. He'd watched this landing for over a decade. And for the first time, he placed a foot on the rickety step.

CHAPTER 7

ATREUS

IT WAS EVERYTHING he imagined it would be. Each step across the creaky floorboards echoed with memories. The furniture was primarily wooden, worn, and well-loved. The layout was simple: a kitchen on the left and a living space with a single couch and TV on the right. Straight in front of him stretched a long hallway that likely contained the bedrooms Giovanni constantly offered him.

The smell of the *pescheria* downstairs lingered faintly, mingling with the aroma of Horace's tobacco and fresh basil. It was cramped, old, and stuffy.

It was perfect.

Nyel was likely thinking the same thing as his head spun, trying to see everything at once. He opened his mouth to speak, but Atreus quickly covered it with his hand, stopping him from asking something stupid like, *What's a window?*

"Make yourselves at home, *fate come se foste a casa vostra.* Horace is already in bed for the night, so the space is ours," Giovanni said, tossing his leather gloves on the round kitchen table. "Dinner will be ready in an hour. You boys can choose your rooms—any on the left side of the hall are open. I've left some linens in the hall for your beds. You might want to crack a window, though; the rooms haven't been used in some time."

"Thank you, *Signore* Marc-" Atreus stopped when the old fisherman raised a thick brow at him. "Thank you, Giovanni."

His mentor smiled and pulled ingredients from the icebox. The moment the refrigerator door opened and the light inside came on, Nyel's feet practically floated closer, his mouth gaping in fascination. Atreus grabbed his arm and dragged him to the hall before he could cause a scene.

"C'mon," he said, rolling his eyes.

He opted to give Nyel the room farthest down, which was also farthest from any of the already occupied rooms.

"This place is amazing!" Nyel blurted the moment the door closed.

"It is," Atreus said shortly, even though he too was in awe. This was his first glimpse into what life at home looked like for humans. Or anyone, for that matter. He didn't consider his upbringing *homely.* But this place...

This is where memories are made. This is a place for family.

"Yeah," Atreus mused, "It's nice."

"I mean, did you see that giant white box? It's cold. And so much wood, how do they shape it? Oh my gills, I want to touch that dark green thing; I bet it's soft; how do they make those? And there is light coming from the top of the house. Light without the sun! And did you see the—"

Atreus let Nyel rattle off every mundane thing he'd seen, only half listening as he opened the window to air out the stuffy room. He found some fresh blankets in the closet and made Nyel's bed, occasionally giving names to the objects Nyel described.

The dark green thing - couch.

Cold white box - refrigerator.

Tan box with two antennae sticking out of the top - Television.

"It's even cooler when it's turned on," Atreus said regarding the moving picture box.

"I can't wait," Nyel said, lighting up like he'd found sunken treasure.

"You need to take a deep breath before dinner. And remember the rules? No questions in front of anyone. I'll answer them later."

"What if Giovanni asks me something? What do I say?"

"Let me do the talking. And don't worry—the old man is comfortable with silence."

That was one of Atreus's favorite parts about Giovanni—well, one of his favorites; he admired almost everything about that man. There was a certain stillness in the way his boss stood, a calm that suggested he was someone who observed more than he spoke. And the fewer the questions, the less Atreus was forced to lie.

By the time Atreus showed Nyel where he'd sleep and explained everything about using the bathroom (threatening him at least ten times to dry off completely before unlocking the door), the scent of fresh basil drifted down the hall.

"And what's the number one rule?" Atreus asked for the third time, blocking the *sireno's* way.

Nyel rolled his eyes. "Don't get wet. Don't ask questions. Don't be stupid - I'm not a kid, you know. I can handle myself."

"You're basically an infant when it comes to humans," Atreus said, pulling back the curtain, hoping for clear skies. The rain continued its merciless barrage with no end in sight.

"Even when it stops, I'm not leaving," Nyel said, reading his mind.

"Yes, you are."

"That's what you think."

Atreus glared at him, jaw clenched. The flecks of gold in Nyel's honey-brown eyes sparkled as he fixed his face with determination. His resolve, however misguided, was set. It was plain as day, and Atreus hated that a small part of him admired it.

Stupid fish.

Nyel would get them both killed. And even if Atreus survived, he could lose it all. Everything he worked his entire life to build. He'd be alone while Nyel returned with his tail tucked to a loving family. This *sireno* had to go before it was too late.

"*Ragazzo! Buon appetito!*" Giovanni's voice boomed from the kitchen.

Nyel stuck out his tongue rudely before ducking under Atreus's arm and darting to the hall. Atreus groaned, pressing the heels of his hands into his eyes.

This guy is going to be the end of me.

The kitchen was small and worn. Mismatched plates and chipped mugs sat on the table, remnants of dinners shared over the years in the cozy, rickety space. The scent of basil pesto and roasted chicken filled the air, mingling with the faint saltiness that seemed permanently embedded in the walls. Atreus's mouth watered as Giovanni served them generous portions. Only the soft clinking of forks on plates punctuated the quiet.

Atreus carefully interlaced the comfortable lull with safe topics of conversation. It worked for the most part. When Giovanni set a glass of water in front of Nyel, the *sireno* tensed. He stared at the cold, clear liquid like it might grow fangs and bite him. Smirking, Atreus reached for the glass and took a big sip. Nyel's eyes went wide in alarm, giving Atreus more satisfaction than it should. He winked, then went on with the conversation about possible repairs to *Signore* Cicco's boat.

"He's been overloading the weight capacity on those cables for years. It's no wonder that—" Atreus halted midsentence as he and Giovanni both turned their attention to Nyel, whose body suddenly lurched, stopping him mid-chew.

"Is everything alright?" Giovanni asked.

"W-what is this?" Nyel asked, prodding a pale strip of meat on his plate. Atreus groaned internally.

"It's chicken," Atreus filled in. "It is very healthy. Has lots of protein," he said through clenched teeth, communicating with his eyes.

Hearing the threat in his voice, the vegetarian squeezed his eyes shut and forced a swallow. Nyel shivered as the meat passed.

"So good," he said through a painful smile.

"What do you think about the new docks the mayor commissioned this year? They should be helpful at high tide." Atreus directed attention away from Nyel as the *sireno* meticulously picked out all the chicken from his pasta.

They talked back and forth until Giovanni let out a great sigh, reaching for the bottle at the center of the table.

"I fear those blasted ships will hurt our catch this year," Giovanni said as he poured himself his second glass of red wine.

"They aren't allowed to fish in the harbor. Right? That's protected?"

"Yes, but they've taken nearly everything outside the harbor, fishing the sea until it's bare. That is not our way. We take only what we need. They're taking it all. They pour their filth into the waters and have no respect for the life beneath. Soon, our Baia Vita will be empty."

Baia Vita - "The Bay of Life."

It provided for the people. In turn, the people only took what they needed and respected the sea—keeping it clean, nurturing it, and protecting it.

"Do you think—" Nyel cut himself off as Atreus shot him a glare.

"What is your question, *ragazzo*?" Giovanni asked politely.

Nyel looked from him to Atreus as though he were asking for permission. Atreus sighed and nodded, giving him the go-ahead.

"You said those ships are making the water dirty. Will that hurt the plants and animals under the water?

Giovanni huffed. "I can almost guarantee you it will. Waste like that is more than just dirty. It's poison."

"It's already happening," the *sireno* mumbled, almost to himself.

"What is?" Giovanni asked, his mustache twitching.

"The ships. The water. It's already making the kelp below the surface sick. Some people—I mean, animals are getting sick too." Noticing the other men's quiet shock, he added, "I heard that from a friend. He likes to dive and see stuff underwater. But not me! I- I hate swimming."

Atreus stiffened as the word 'people' slipped from Nyel's lips. This was getting dangerous—time to wrap it up.

"Maledizione!" Giovanni cursed, slamming his fork to the table. "I will have to speak to Mayor Gianfranchi about this, see if we can widen the island boundary, push those ships farther away." He sighed, and the sound was heavy. It was tired and worried. Atreus itched to take some of that burden. "I fear for our home, *ragazzi.*"

When the stillness stretched to painful lengths, Atreus rose without a word to clear plates.

Giovanni emptied his glass of wine in two gulps. "I will retire early this evening. This home is yours; please make yourself comfortable." He bid them goodnight, and Atreus hated how his massive shoulders slumped.

"Did I say something wrong?" Nyel asked the moment Giovanni's bedroom door closed.

"No," Atreus said. "He gets like this. We all do when we see what's happening to our island."

"Our?" Nyel asked.

Something in Atreus's chest twisted. "Theirs, the humans."

"This island doesn't belong to you.
You don't belong at all.
You're lucky to be here."

"I thought the ships were helping the humans. Turns out it's hurting them just as much as the *Sireni* in Corallina," Nyel mused.

"Something you'll learn is that there are good humans. And there are bad." He paused, considering his words. "And all of them are just scared."

Atreus cleared the kitchen, doing everything he could besides washing the dishes. Giovanni might come back while his hands were in the sink. He filled a glass full of water and walked Nyel to his room.

"Here," he said, setting it on the nightstand. "Human bodies need to drink. A lot. Practice until you can make sure the water only touches the inside of your mouth. You'll have to drink in front of humans at some point or another."

Nyel rounded on him. "You say that like I might interact with them for a while."

Atreus chewed his lip. "You've made it pretty damn clear I can't get rid of you. Not unless I want to make a scene, which I don't."

"That's right," Nyel confirmed, lifting his chin haughtily.

Atreus narrowed his eyes. "Don't tempt me."

"I won't," he deflated a bit.

"If you're going to linger, then you might as well learn the basics. I collapsed from dehydration once. We don't have to worry about it as Mer, but the land dwellers do. Practice."

Nyel lifted the glass, holding it with both hands like a child, but didn't bring it to his lips. His gaze fixed on the clear water as he readjusted his hold again.

"Sometime tonight would be nice," Atreus said impatiently.

"I don't know how," Nyel bit back.

Atreus rolled his eyes. "Here."

He guided the glass to Nyel's lips, which parted over the edge and allowed the water to slide into his mouth. Of course, it dribbled from the sides, running down his neck and into the collar of his shirt. Nyel sputtered, coughing and spitting.

Atreus chuckled. "Not as easy as it looks, huh?" He smacked Nyel on the back as he choked.

"I'll need more practice," Nyel said with tears in his eyes.

But Atreus hardly heard him. Something caught his attention. Transfixed him. Something that only appeared with the touch of water. A line of green scales ran from Nyel's mouth, down his neck, and onto his chest. The air grew still, and Atreus was suddenly reminded that this person, this male standing before him... was Mer.

Like me.

Of course, Nyel was Mer. That's what they'd been talking about all night. But there was something about seeing the transformation. Watching *Marvassa* touch someone else right before his eyes. The realization hit Atreus like an avalanche cascading down a mountain, burying him with the weight of the *sireno's* presence. He wasn't alone anymore.

Had he been lonely all this time? Even among the humans?

Atreus reached gently, tracing his finger up the line of green scales starting from Nyel's neck—his jaw—pausing at the corner of his parted mouth. The scales were cool to the touch, and as the water dried, they melted into flesh before his eyes. Nyel's skin was porcelain—perfect. Atreus traced a finger along his cheek.

Nyel's shuddering intake of breath had Atreus jerking his hand away, backing up like he'd been caught doing something indecent.

He cleared his throat. "Well, uh, goodnight. I'll get you in the morning, and uh... keep practicing," he said by way of parting as he closed the door.

Atreus paused outside the room, hand still resting on the doorknob. He had no explanation for what had just happened. That was unlike him—encroaching on someone's personal space. The awkwardness of it all made his stomach squirm uncomfortably.

But he didn't pull away.

Still, Atreus couldn't let his infatuation with the idea of another Mer being around lead him to forget basic manners. That was weird, and he knew it.

Atreus walked down the hall and flopped onto his bed, burying his face in the pillow and breathing in the homey smell. He was exhausted, and today had been... a lot. Even the incredible fact that he was sleeping in an actual bed for the first time in his life wasn't enough to dispel the unease that settled in him like a termite infestation, eating away at his wooden foundation of rules.

Don't get too close.

Don't get too comfortable.

Don't be a burden.

Know your place.

There were too many new things happening all at once. That was the only explanation for his behavior in Nyel's room. He'd return to his right mind after a good night's rest.

Still, the restive image of jade scales turning to porcelain skin consumed his thoughts until he finally fell asleep.

A YOWLING CAT jarred Atreus from arguably the best sleep he'd ever had. Sleeping in an actual bed designed for a human body was incredible. He'd be sorry to return to the lumpy pad in his lighthouse —because he was going back. He and Nyel were not staying.

Last night was a fluke.

The sound of the crying cat (maybe a small wounded animal?) scratched his eardrums until it was too much, and he rose. If he didn't already know what made that noise, he'd wish to put the poor creature out of its misery. Alas, Atreus was all too familiar with the sound now coming from the kitchen—not a dying creature, but Marina—singing. In her most elegant soprano, she forced songbirds into a life of mutism.

Giovanni's daughter, a few years his junior, must have arrived on the merchant barge early that morning (or late in the night) once the rains eased. He'd listened to that singing voice almost every day of every summer since he was thirteen. As a child, it was cute, but now that Marina was well on her way to womanhood, it was painful.

Atreus opened the door, rubbing the sleep from his eyes. He'd have liked to yell for the vocalist to knock it off, but this was her house—not his.

"Remember your place."

Nyel was already awake, dressed in the clothes Giovanni had lent him, and sitting expectantly on the edge of his bed.

"G-good morning," Atreus said, surprised to see the gold-flecked eyes so alert.

"Morning." Nyel's expression was placid. Way too awake for this early in the morning, but untroubled.

He doesn't look upset.

Maybe Nyel forgot about his awkwardness the night before.

"Time to eat. And I promise to warn you about any meat."

The *sireno's* shoulders relaxed. "Oh, thank the Spirits. I don't think I can force down another bite."

In the hall, Atreus reminded him for the millionth time, "Remember the rules."

"Follow your lead," Nyel said with an eye roll.

"And there is someone else here—"

"Atty!"

Atreus only caught a flash of thick, curly red hair before he was bear-hugged and nearly knocked off his feet.

"Oof— hey, Marina. Good to see you," he said, returning the embrace for only a second before easing her back to create some much-needed space.

"Oh yep, sorry. Not a hugger, forgot," she said, then promptly slapped him on the arm.

"Ow! What was that for?" He recoiled.

"I didn't get a single letter from you this winter - again!"

Atreus rolled his eyes. "You know I'm trash at that kind of thing."

"You could still tryyyy," she whined. "I'd have been happy with a stick-person drawing."

"I don't draw."

"Yes you do Atty, I've seen it," she said with hands on her hips.

"I do not, and it's Atreus."

"Do too," she said, sticking out her tongue. "And can you call me Rina? Pleeeease. I gave you a nickname; why don't I get one?"

"I'm not doing that."

Before she could argue, Marina finally noticed Nyel. "You

brought someone over? Atty, did you make a friend while I was gone?" She sounded like a proud parent.

"Don't call me that. And this is Nyel," he grumbled. "And I have plenty of friends."

"Sure," she said, extending a confident hand. *"Buongiorno!* I'm Marina Marcello."

Nyel took it (correctly, this time after he and Atreus practiced). "Nyel Veritani, it's nice to meet you. I've never met a female before— I mean-" Nyel scrambled and turned beet red. He sidestepped far enough so Atreus couldn't stomp on his feet. An urge Atreus barely resisted.

"A— what?" Marina said, eyes alight with curiosity.

Atreus would have been more worried if Nyel had said that to anyone else, but Marina was a special peach.

"He meant a woman as pretty as you," Atreus filled in. "He doesn't get out much."

"Awww, Atty, you think I'm pretty?" she said, pinching his cheek.

Atreus swatted it away. "Don't call me that. And I know you're basically a feral cat with red hair. You can't fool me."

She laughed, a sound much more pleasant than her singing voice. "You do know me. Anyway, come eat! *Papà* cooked way too much food."

She skipped to the kitchen, her bare feet slapping on the wooden floorboards and her voice resuming its call.

Nyel flinched.

"What?" Atreus asked.

The *sireno* lowered his voice to a whisper, his expression horrified. "When I heard it this morning, I thought the humans were killing our breakfast."

Atreus barked a laugh before he could stop himself.

Breakfast was eggs, bacon, sausage, and a mouth-watering *Fette Biscottate.*

Atreus usually skipped breakfast—oversalted canned clams weren't exactly an appetizing way to start the day—but he couldn't stop his mouth from watering at the sight of the meats covering almost every inch of the table.

Atreus restrained the urge to pile a mountain of food on his plate and only took a small portion. He directed Nyel to the *Fette Biscottate,* sliced bread with a sweet glaze.

"Antonio," Horace greeted from his designated spot in front of the window, "Good to see you again."

Horace, Marina's *Nonno* on her mother's side, was among the remaining men who served in World War II. Atreus hadn't been alive then, but the stories never failed to send shivers down his spine.

Horace was white-haired, with a bristly mustache and lined skin. He barely hobbled with his cane from one chair to the next. Still, his gap-toothed smile never failed to brighten the day of anyone who slowed down long enough to talk.

"It's good to see you too. And it's Atreus, *Signore* Finotto."

"That's right," he said, but Atreus knew he'd be reminding him all summer. "Maybe now that you've arrived, this *questo bestione* will stop moping around."

Giovanni huffed indignantly. "I do not mope."

"You've been rattling my rigging all winter with your sulking."

"Call it *sindrome del nido vuoto.* But now my empty nest is full," Giovanni said, extending his arms to the crowded breakfast table.

"*Grazie a dio* for that," Horace said, toasting his orange juice like champagne.

A black-coated and white-mittened feline leaped to Horace's lap, sniffing for scraps.

"Niccolo down!" Marina ordered, but for all the mind the cat paid to her, she may as well have been a fixture on the wall.

Atreus caught the way Nyel flinched at the creature's sudden appearance. "That's his cat," he explained. "A family pet."

"Uh-huh," Nyel said and continued to watch the creature as though it might target his lap next.

"He is always by my side." Horace wheezed through a cough. "Though he enjoys his nightly prowls."

"And you keep leaving your window open at night and letting the chill in," Marina scolded. "Then you wake up with a chest cold."

"But he cries so terribly when he's locked out, don't you *micino*?"

Niccolo purred, his milk mustache curved as though he were smiling. Atreus bit the inside of his cheek to keep from laughing at the way Nyel, not so casually, moved his chair further away from the rumbling creature.

"Gabriella, would you be a darling and bring your old grandfather his pipe?"

"Not at the table, *Nonno*. I'll bring it to you outside," she said as she set a plate of eggs in front of him, kissing his cheek. "And it's Marina."

"You look so much like your mother," Horace said, another phrase Atreus was used to hearing.

"I know, *Nonno*." Marina smiled fondly.

"Thank goodness," Giovanni commented from the stove, "I would have feared for her had she looked like me."

"Oh, *Papà*, you're as handsome as ever," she said, patting her father's shoulder.

"It is good to have my *Bambini* back home."

"Only one more semester of school, *Papà*, and then I'll be here forever. You'll get tired of me."

"Never," he chortled. "How I've missed your beautiful voice in these early morning hours. It fills my heart with joy."

At this, Atreus and Nyel shared a glance with barely repressed smiles.

Horace squinted across the round table as though looking from a great distance. "We have an intruder in our midst."

"Oh, sorry, this is Nyel, a friend of mine," Atreus said through a mouthful of pancetta.

"Hmmm." Horace narrowed his watery eyes. "A new young face." He inhaled dramatically. "I served in the twenty-fourth division of the *Marina Militara*."

"Here we go," Marina mumbled under her breath. They'd all heard this story.

A few times.

Per day.

Every summer.

For most of their lives.

Horace ignored his granddaughter and reached a trembling hand to the sleeve of his shirt, pulling it to reveal the number twenty-four tattooed in roman numerals.

"Wow," Nyel said, his tone sincere. "You fought in the huma—I mean the war?"

"Sure did, young man," Horace grunted with a proud smack on the table. His breakfast was forgotten. "The twenty-fourth fought on the fiercest ship in the *Marina Militara*. We called her *La Balena Foroce*."

Atreus tuned out the majority of the conversation. He'd heard it a thousand times—the ship's victories, the battles it had seen, until its inevitable demise when it finally succumbed to the violence of war, sinking to the bottom of the sea where it now slept. The *pescheria* was named the 'Sleeping Whale' in honor of the sunken warship.

As long as he kept the story true to its official series of events, there shouldn't be a problem. It was when Horace diverted into fiction that the problems began—

Horace reached for a framed black-and-white photo he always kept close by. "This was the twenty-fourth regiment, and this man," he pointed to a young man with a bright face, visible even in the grainy black-and-white photo. "That is me."

Nyel leaned forward in his chair as Horace's finger slid over.

"And this man beside me was my best friend, Kirill. And he was a Mer."

Atreus choked on his eggs.

"*Nonno*, what did we say about telling that story?" Marina warned, though there wasn't any weight in her words.

"How can I not tell the truth? Just because the papers refused to print it does not mean it didn't happen. *Uomo del Mare* fought in the war whether you kids believe it or not," he said, banging a non-threatening fist on the table.

"*Nonno*," Marina said in a pitying voice, "Mer do not exist."

"How can you say that when I have a photograph right here!" he said, shaking the small picture as though this settled the matter.

"That is a picture of a man, *Nonno*."

"They transform! Kirill looked like a man on land, but once in the water, he turned into a creature unlike anything I'd ever seen. He had scales blue as the darkest part of the sea and gills like a fish." He made three slashing motions on the side of his neck with a pointed finger.

"Oh, *Nonno*," Marina said, resigned to her breakfast.

"Kirill was my best friend, but as soon as the war ended, he took to the sea, and I never saw him again. All the Mer have hidden from us now." Horace stared at the picture with a sad expression. His fingers trembled as they traced over the faded faces, unfinished words lingering on his lips. "I often wonder what I said to make Kirill want to hide from me. I never got the chance..." He trailed off, lost in a past he couldn't change.

Atreus tried to keep his face neutral as his jaw clenched. Nyel looked from him to Horace as though to say, *Are you hearing this!?*

Atreus shook his head, telling him to keep quiet.

He had heard it. A million times told in a million different ways. All from the mouths of the old crowd—men and women who saw the war and lived to tell the stories. Horace wasn't the only one who spun tales of Mer, but those tales were becoming fewer and fewer as the oldest generation passed. Now, their stories were largely regarded as fiction—legends at best or delirious war stories born of trauma and drink at worst. One day, even Horace's stories would be gone from this world.

And the idea of Mer will vanish from humans entirely.

The thought was both sad and comforting. His species would remain in the confines of fiction, and that was for the best.

Better forgotten than remembered and feared.

Marina was ready to say more, but her father cut her off.

"Horace likes to entertain us with tales of the old days and how he remembers them. Now let's get to work." Giovanni said by way of ending the conversation.

"Good call. I have to get to city hall," Marina said, quick to clear her plate and race to the door. "I'll come find you later, Atty!"

"Don't call me tha—"

She was already out the door.

"Just like her mother. Never could sit still for more than a handful of minutes," Horace said with overflowing fondness.

"Will you tell me more about your friend later?" Nyel asked as Horace moved to return the picture to its place on the mantle.

Horace's face lit up. "Now, here is a young man who knows a

good story when he hears one," he said, clasping Nyel by the shoulder and shaking him. "Of course, *ragazzo*, anytime. Remind me your name again?"

While Nyel tried to get the old man to remember his name, Giovanni and Atreus helped him down the stairs and into his wooden rocking chair. Once settled with a pipe and a blanket over his lap, Horace wished them well as they made their way to the docks.

They crested the hill, and the view of Baia Vita spread before them. The sound of a ship's bullhorn tore through the air. A massive fishing vessel, only a speck in the distance, reminded them of its looming presence.

Atreus couldn't hold back the snarl contorting his face and the hiss rising in his chest. He had to force both reactions away, as humans didn't express themselves like that. But instinct had him wanting to bare his fangs and flare his fins at the intruder.

Stay out of my waters.

"To work, boys. With any luck, there will be some fish left over for us," Giovanni said with a defeated sigh.

Atreus wished there was more he could do.

CHAPTER 8

MARINA

MARINA TOOK AN exaggerated breath, tasting the salt in her lungs. The gulls squawked in the distance, their cries mingling with the gentle toll of bells swaying on old boats. She was home. After a long winter of stuffy corridors and grouchy professors, she was ready to stretch her arms and soak up every last drop of sunshine like a plant starved for light.

She didn't hate *Accademia di San Benedetto* for its rigid rules and the enforced 'straighten your back' etiquette. Marina hated how far it was from home. And how, even in a bustling city, she was alone.

City life had been her mother's dream, not Marina's. Gabriella blended effortlessly with the lively crowds and blue-blooded socialites.

Marina never did.

She never had the chance.

It was Gabriella's dying wish for Marina to finish her education on the mainland. And even though her heart longed for the island, Marina heeded her mother's last request. Her last words. The last sliver of acknowledgment that Gabriella had a daughter at all. Marina clung to it with all her might.

"My beautiful sunshine."

During the winters, Marina attended school, honoring her mother's wish. Even though living in a dormitory full of girls should have meant she was never without company, Marina was an outsider. From the moment her worn leather boots crossed the marble threshold of the dorm, her fate was sealed. She was an island girl from an unheard-of family with no social connections. She didn't belong among the elite. Her simple clothes and shore-line accent were enough to put off any potential friends, as though her low-class status were contagious.

They didn't know she had lived in a luxury condo in the heart of Florence, with a view of the *Firenze Duomo*, the Cathedral of Santa Maria del Fiore. They didn't know she wore simple clothes by choice, while her closet was packed with the finest creations Italian designers had to offer. They didn't know that the priceless piece of art hanging in the dean's office had been painted in her childhood living room while she crunched on *pane e Nutella* and watched cartoons.

They didn't know... anything. Because all her life, Marina wasn't allowed to tell anyone. And by the time she could, it was too late.

On the rare occasions her roommates invited her to the city, Marina lagged behind the group, uninterested in the lavish boutiques. She'd met most of the designers featured inside and didn't think they deserved the attention. When Marina spotted a print of one of her mother's paintings on a touristy t-shirt, she pointed to it and spoke before thinking,

"My mom had a fever when she painted that one."

The girl's high heels clicked to a halt.

"Your *mom*?" They burst into a fit of laughter.

"Didn't you know? Her *mom* painted that," another girl said, using air quotes.

"Oh, and I bet it's her *mom's* art in *Galleria degli Uffizi*."

"Why yes, of course. Right next to the Michelangelo."

They snickered again, heels clicking as they walked away. Marina trailed behind with her head hung low, wondering why she bothered coming at all.

Her mom really did have a fever while painting the ornate piece now cheaply printed on a t-shirt. She'd been so sick she could hardly hold the brush. Marina remembered it as if it were only a few days ago. But even if she shared those details, no one would believe her. Because there was no way Marina—with her simple clothes, fish-monger father, and quiet, unremarkable demeanor—was the daughter of the great Sofia Botticelli, the most celebrated painter of the modern era.

Of course, nobody knew that name was fake. That Sofia was Gabriella, and she liked tea over coffee. That she ate two pieces of toast every morning before work and loved to sing while braiding her auburn hair. That she had a daughter... one she'd kept secret from the world.

Marina shook away the memories of winter, centering herself in the sunshine and the smell of briny air. Not for a moment was Marina Marcello going to let old hurts dampen her spirits. No sirree. Right now, *Accademia di San Benedetto* was far away on the mainland, and she was in Baia Vita. Her home.

She breathed in again, shaking off the cold memories.

"The sun is shining, the gulls are singing, and I'm going to have the best day—"

"Hey, watch it!" A man holding a precarious stack of boxes hollered as she bumped into him, nearly knocking them over.

"Sorry!" she said, tripping out of his way.

He grumbled something as he stomped off.

Where was she? Oh yes.

"The sun is shining, the gulls are doing whatever it is gulls do, and I'm going to have the best day ever!"

She skipped to music only she could hear, red hair swaying in a world all her own. Because that is what Marina did. She smiled. She laughed. She brightened the room.

Her mother's words echoed in some far-off memory.

"My happy little sunflower."

City hall's weathered steps sloped from decades of feet climbing up and down. The Greek Orthodox pillars were purely decorative, as the cracks and warped plaster rendered them incapable of bearing any load. At least, Marina hoped not as she quickly darted beneath them in case they decided to crumble then and there.

Mayor Gianfranchi had a single secretary managing the ever-silent phone and a librarian who wiped the dust off ancient shelves on the upper floors. City Hall also served as Sheriff Fanti's police station for her and the island's only two other officers.

And that was it. The entire government of the island. Marina wondered what the mayor actually did besides organizing a few festivals a year.

Marina rang the bell on the desk with a sharp 'Ding!' and twirled around, enjoying the mosaic windows before ringing it again.

"I'm coming!" The librarian, *Signora* Brambani, shuffled over, the beads from her round glasses swaying. "Oh, Marina, you made it safely, I hope? The weather didn't slow you?"

Of course, everyone knew she was coming. *Papà* likely talked of nothing else for months, and it warmed her chest. "No problems at all, *Signora* Brambani. I'm here because the mayor sent me letters over the winter."

The old woman waved a dismissive hand. "Do you really think Jeremias Gianfranchi has that kind of penmanship? With his sausage hands? No girl, I wrote the letters; he signed the bottom."

"Oh, well, the letters said that you needed help?"

"Yes, my dear. *Signora* Marcialese just had a baby; it wasn't an easy delivery. She will not be able to organize the Bayallon for the kids this year. With your writing skills, I thought a bright young lady like you could lend us a hand."

Marina stood straighter. This is how responsible adults stood, right? She had to be grown up about this. If she got too excited, they'd think she wasn't taking it seriously. She took a steadying breath.

"Yes, yes, yes! Oh my gosh, yes!" she squeaked, clapping as she jumped. "Yes, oh, I'd love to! I already have so many ideas."

Signora Brambani hesitated, her smile tense. "Yes, well. Thank you for your... enthusiasm. Here is the route the kids will take this year. I trust you know how this goes."

"Yes, yes, yes!" she said too fast. "I loved the Bayallon when I was a kid. I'll make it extra special."

"Regular special is fine."

"I better get to work—bye!" Marina skipped off before the old woman could change her mind.

Yeah, she blew that. But the papers were in her hands, and that's all that mattered. She'd be the BEST event organizer the island had ever seen.

Her fondest memories of summers spent on the island were of the Bayallon. Towards the end of World War II, the residents of Baia Vita were given the chance to view the Olympics for the first time.

Until then, the island had never seen a television; instead, it got news through radio broadcasts. Recognizing the island's morale was at an all-time low, the mayor purchased five television sets. He set up the small box screens inside city hall, allowing residents to watch the Olympic events.

The arrival of the revolutionary TV, combined with the thrill of Olympic competition, brought smiles to the island for the first time since the war began. In honor of the island's favorite sporting event, they started their own tradition.

Children sixteen and under were invited to participate in the Bayallon at the end of every fishing season. With its vibrant festival, lively music, spirited dancing, and mouthwatering food, the Bayallon was Marina's most cherished event of the year.

And now, she would be a part of it.

Marina hurried down the city hall steps, stumbling on the last one before catching herself with a mumbled "oops" and a light giggle. She skipped toward the town square, humming a cheerful tune.

To have a good race, she needed a lot of racers, so the sooner she began advertising the event, the better.

She was inside *Signore* Ignasio's craft supply store, picking up paints and cloth to make banners, when a large group of women jostled in. Marina peered over a shelf to see several older women and perhaps one of their daughters chatting and perusing the shelves.

"I simply cannot go to my appointment in these rags. What do you think of this? It would make a nice skirt," one woman said, eyeing a plaid pink fabric.

"What are you, twenty years old?" another laughed.

"In spirit!"

"That would be more appropriate on your *younger* daughter."

The other woman scoffed, turning to her daughter. "What do you think, sweetie? I'm still young enough for this color, right?"

"Sure, Mom," but the girl wasn't looking at the fabric. Her eyes caught sight of Marina, and the rest of the women followed her gaze.

"Little *Signora* Marcello!"

They scurried over as Marina tried becoming one with the wall. She knew that girl. Her name was Anna, and she despised every breath Marina took. She had espresso eyes and matching straight hair, not unlike most of the girls on the island. And Marina knew them all—it was hard to avoid each other when they had spent every summer on the same small island since she was nine. Except Marina was the only one who left every winter. Marina was the only one to inherit a substantial sum of money. And it was Marina who received a very expensive education on the mainland.

So, in the eyes of all her peers, it was Marina who didn't belong.

She was *privileged.*

"So good to see you, dear. What do you have there? Making some summer clothes?"

"Oh no, I'm, uh, putting together a banner. I'm in charge of the Bayallon for the kids this year."

"Are you now?" the woman tittered. "Well, it is only right that Mayor Gianfranchi put you in charge; such a smart girl."

Marina smiled, trying her best to ignore the way Anna glared at her, as though she were a grouper Anna wanted to gut and toss overboard.

"I was just here to get some clothes for a new skirt; I have a doctor's visit later this week. Tell me you've heard of him," she said, likely as an excuse to talk about it.

"I'm afraid I haven't."

"Oh, my dear, he is—" she took a moment to catch her breath, "extraordinary."

"And that's putting it plainly," another added. The women chortled. Anna rolled her eyes.

"He opened the hospital at the top of the hill. Dr. Romano is a blessing on this poor island. Set my son's wrist in no time at all."

"And my daughter's new baby had the worst colic, but after seeing the doctor, she is sleeping through the night."

"He sounds good," Marina said, still trying not to make eye contact with Anna.

"Oh, he *is* good. And also good to look at," she said, then covered her mouth with a giggle as the other women slapped her shoulder.

"Nina, you're so bad."

"And I seem to have developed a terrible tightness in my chest," Nina said, forcing a cough from her mouth. "I have to get it checked." They tittered again.

"Mom, stop. He's closer to my age. I'm more likely to date him," Anna said with an eyeroll.

"Oh, let these old women have some fun," the mother said with a wave of her hand.

Her gaze fixed on Marina. "You know," she said, eyeing Marina up and down. "You're a young, beautiful woman. Why don't you go speak with him?"

"I... uh...." Marina stammered, heat creeping into her cheeks.

"Yes," the other woman agreed. "A young lady with your education would be a good match for an intellectual like Dr. Romano."

Marina's mouth went dry; Anna glared as if trying to infect her with scurvy.

"Mom, can we go already?" Anna complained.

"Oh, it was good to see you, dear. The Bayallon will be fantastic under your care."

They exited the store in a gaggle of giggles and loose fabrics. Marina exhaled a shaky breath.

That's all I need, to take the most eligible bachelor on the island off the market. I'll be on everyone's shit list.

Not to mention, educated though she was, a freakin doctor wasn't going to pay any mind to a daughter of a fishmonger.

But that's not all I am. I could have—

She halted.

Stop it. No more of this.

Marina left this kind of thing behind on the mainland. She shook herself and focused on the fabrics.

"I won't let Anna or anyone else dampen my spirits. Today's a good day - because I said so."

She pasted on a smile and resumed perusing the paints, returning to her nonsensical humming. While paying for the supplies, she struck up a conversation with *Signore* Ignacio about the best painting techniques.

The conversation was as easy as breathing.

Not only was Marina well-versed in the world of paints and canvases, but she *loved* old people. Talking to them gave her a boost of joy, like eating a sugary piece of hard candy. She could listen to their stories all day, and that's how checking out from a craft supplies store turned into a two-hour conversation about late Renaissance era watercolor.

Marina shivered, hugging her supplies close as she exited the store, Anna's glare leaving behind cold, hateful traces. It would have been fine if it were only the older women.

But her peers...

Marina couldn't shake the anxiety that had festered since she was a child. At school, she was the dumb island commoner, making her an easy victim of pranks and jokes. On the island, she was the privileged girl with an education, showing off her superiority every time she signed her name.

No matter where she went, Marina was as isolated as Baia Vita itself—an island surrounded by old fishing boats.

But you know what? She rather liked the old creaky fishing boats.

The older folks, especially those who were close to her father and grandfather, were always delighted to see her. *Nonno's* friends were some of her best friends, always good for a story of the old days. Because of them, she was a fierce chess player and knew Baia Vita's history better than anyone. She was proud of her home and cherished the traditions passed down from the old-timers. The very lifeblood of Baia Vita ran through their veins, and Marina only hoped that one day she might be as connected to the island's soul as they were.

Life hadn't been kind to many of the old crowd, yet they always harbored nothing but kindness for her. And in return, she listened to their stories even though she could recount most of them by heart.

"Aging is a blessing not everyone gets to experience," they'd tell her while rocking in their chairs. "You do well to take care of yourself, *Signora*. Surround yourself with good people."

And Marina had. Did she get lonely for people closer to her age? Sure. But she didn't need much. Her favorite person under the age of fifty was Atreus. Sure, Marina only had him during the summer months, and he worked long hours. But she'd steal him away before the festival; she was determined.

"Atty, I'm gonna put those steady hands of yours to work," she said to herself, picturing Atreus's large hand grasping the small brush. He was a far better artist than her, though he'd never admit it.

She'd ask him to help with the preparations. He'd argue and roll his eyes. She'd beg and say, "Pretty, pretty, please, with sardines on top!" He'd smirk and tell her sardines did not go on cupcakes, but ultimately, he'd agree.

Atreus was always like that—reliable. Every summer since she turned nine, he was there—her rock, her friend. She imagined that if she had a brother, it would feel a lot like him. Marina couldn't put her finger on it, but she got the feeling that Atreus understood what it was like to be an outcast.

And outcasts stuck together.

Marina squinted as something glinted in the noon sun, forcing her to shield her eyes. Only then could she make out the shiny new hospital building atop the hill, its massive glass front gleaming against the clear sky.

Every time Marina returned to the island, she found another of her favorite shops gone, replaced by a large, soulless chain store. The only welcome addition to Baia Vita was the hospital. She was thrilled when *Papà* wrote to her explaining that a rich doctor was building on their island. Not that the old-time remedies and midwives weren't great, but the people desperately needed professional medical care closer than a three-hour boat ride to the mainland.

The hospital's angular design, with its sharp lines and pointed rooftop, gave it an imposing presence. The front wall, made entirely of glass, reflected the sky, allowing light to flood the atrium. Despite its rapid construction, the building was of the highest quality. It screamed of wealth, and its modern design contrasted wildly with Baia Vita's terracotta tiles and rustic charm.

Marina thought it was an eyesore but a necessary one. It was the perfect place for the famous Doctor Romano to start his practice and help the island's people. She'd never seen him before, but if the village women's gossip was anything to go by, he must be even more impressive than *Signore* Cicco's record-breaking 177-pound amberjack.

Marina huffed, turning her head away.

So sorry for you, Dr. Fancy-Pants; this girl doesn't have a cough.

Marina rounded the corner into the square, just a few blocks from the Sleeping Whale, when a sudden commotion made her stumble. She knocked into a fruit stand, sending oranges tumbling across the cobblestones.

"What is going on?" she asked, bending to help the merchant recover her fruits.

People tossed worried glances toward the local gelato shop, yet nobody moved. Some were quickly packing up their wares, and others were locking doors. The yelling intensified, and when the sound of shattering glass cracked the air, Marina set her things on a bench and ran forward.

"Don't, *Signora!*" one of the onlookers called. "It's Vincenzo."

"And you think that scares me? Someone has to help," she hissed, causing the man to drop his head in shame. Marina burst through the gelato shop door, the bell clunking rather than ringing as though it'd been bent.

"You call this gelato? What am I supposed to do with this frozen cow-piss? Huh?" A dominant voice yelled above the chortling of his companions.

"*Spaciente, Signore*, this is our freshest batch," *Signore* Rossi said, his hand wrapped in a cloth stained with rapidly spreading red.

"Your freshest? So what, prepared last month?"

The groupies laughed again, their grunts empowering their leader's tirade. The emblem of the family they served—a roaring lion standing on hind legs against a bright purple sash—was emblazoned on their vests.

The Vincenzo family crest.

The leader in question wasn't the tallest or broadest of them. But he exerted an unquestionable power in the way he stood. The way he talked. All the way down to the small fortune he wore in every stitch in his suit. This man, with his gelled black hair, artistically styled scruff, and piercing blue eyes, was the heir to the Vincenzo Empire. A vicious war-profiteering family that, by the time the war ended, had lined their pockets with enough money to buy the country. They had hands in the government, the economy, and (though nobody spoke of it) the police.

Italy belonged to families like the Vincenzo's. All with power. All with fortune. All with influence. They were a poison. And now, Baia Vita - desperate from thirst, was drinking from their cup.

Their primary tormentor came from the man who stood before her. Somewhere in his late twenties, but with the presence of someone far older, he played with them like a cat might a limping mouse.

"Please, *Signore*, I'll offer a full refund," the shopkeeper pleaded.

"Do you think I need your coins? Do you think a Vincenzo needs your pennies?"

"N-no, I meant no disrespect-"

"How can you mean no disrespect while serving me this muck?"

"W-what can I do?"

Signore Rossi was almost in tears, and Marina watched in horror as the dark-haired man stood straighter, soaking in his victim's despair.

"What you can do is get this backwoods dairy farm out of *my* square to make room for a real gelato shop."

He raised his boot and crashed it into the glass display, sending shards of glass into every bucket of flavored cream.

"Alvise!" Marina yelled, shoes crunching on glass as she positioned herself between the two men. *Signore* Rossi cowered behind the counter, his face gone white as his entire stock of cream was ruined.

The leader of the troupe turned, his expression softening into one of pleased amusement. Alvise Vincenzo regarded her like one might a beloved dog they hadn't seen in a long while.

"Marina~" He purred her name with a velvet grin. "I worried the storm would delay you."

"And here, I hoped it swallowed you whole."

Alvise laughed loudly like it was the funniest thing he'd heard in an age. "Oh, how I missed your sharp tongue. Unfortunately, my yachts don't yield to trivial storms."

"Pity."

His eyes ran up and down her again, more slowly this time. She resisted the urge to cover herself. Marina was curvier than most, with wide hips and a well-endowed chest. But she was never ashamed of it - that was until Alvise looked at her like that.

He ran a tongue over his lower lip, eyes lingering on her bosom for too long. "How I've missed you."

"Get out of here, Alvise. You got your gelato; now beat it."

"Oh, this?" He gestured to the ruined buckets of colorful cream. "It can't be considered edible. Why don't you return with me to my estate in the valley? Yeah? I'll share some real gelato I've had delivered from the mainland."

"I'd rather drink actual cow-piss."

He tutted. "So un-lady-like. The women in my circles would never allow such unpretty words to come from their mouths."

Marina let out a mirthless laugh. "Women? You mean the caged peacocks wearing nothing but diamonds?"

Alvise grinned, showing too many perfect white teeth.

"Oh, they are not caged, my dear. Women line up at my door, hoping to be chosen and added to my—" he searched for the right words, "guest list."

"More like your collection."

"And I only collect the most beautiful."

He took a confident step forward, invading her space. So fast she couldn't smack his hand away, he grabbed her chin with strong fingers.

"And you, island mutt, can't hold a candle to even the ugliest of them. Shame these beautiful locks are wasted on a face like yours."

Marina twisted her head, teeth clamping together as Alvise barely yanked his hand back in time.

He laughed despite nearly losing a finger. "But that's what I like about you," he said, straightening his suit. "You have fire. And something in me stirs when you burn. I wonder what kind of blaze you'd make with the right touch."

"Go to hell," Marina growled.

"Only with you, my dear. Only with you." He leaned close enough for her to smell his cologne, which reeked of money. "My offer from last summer still stands. When you and your geriatric family are starving, my estate is always searching for a maid."

Before she could hit him, he pulled away. Alvise jerked his head, the movement a command for his groupies to follow.

"Oh," Alvise turned to the shop owner, who looked like he was trying not to pass out. "Consider this an eviction notice." His eyes slid over Marina one final time, "*Arrivederci*, my dear."

The door slammed shut, and the broken bell clattered to the floor.

CHAPTER 9

ATREUS

THE SMELL OF fish, salt, and sweat filled Atreus's nose as he lifted the heavy chum barrels from the dock and onto the bobbing boats.

"That should do, boys. Thank you," the toothless fisherman hollered, his boat puttering away.

Atreus took the moment to wipe sweat from his brow with the hem of his shirt. Luckily, his own perspiration didn't trigger the change. Summer was upon them, and the humid air wrapped around him like a second skin he couldn't shed. But he liked the work—no, he loved it. The burn in his arms, the strain in his back—it was proof that what he was doing mattered. That it meant something.

"Dante's boat is coming in," another worker hollered. Their brief moment of reprieve was over when Dante's boat docked, and they began unloading his catch.

"Any luck?" Atreus asked, lifting the lighter-than-usual barrel.

"As you can see, no. Not a good start to the season." Dante sighed, his sunburnt nose peeling. "And I was up by the rocks. That's usually good fishin'."

"Next run will be better," Atreus encouraged, but knew it'd likely end with the same disappointing result. After unloading the catch and resupplying the boat with chum, Dante was off again.

This went back and forth as boats docked, unloaded, and went out for another run. All of them returned with light catches, and the poor yield caused many to anchor down for the day, unable to afford the fuel to make another trip into the bay.

Atreus knew them all by name, both the boats and the men driving them. The same faces, but more lined now. Many had their sons aboard, teaching them the ways of the water. Yet even with young, eager faces, the air was solemn. This would be another short season, another hungry winter.

A bull horn sounded from the edge of the bay. The industrial fishing giants were only a speck on the horizon. The horn's vibrating boom was meant for them, a reminder of where their life source was going. Many of the men cursed at the dot in the distance. Others made rude hand gestures.

Atreus looked ashore to the only thing that could distract him from the darkening atmosphere. Nyel worked at a long metal table, sorting the barrels of fish in carefully marked bins. This was the job Atreus tasked him with, the one farthest from the water. Atreus spent years mastering how to walk along the ever-rocking deck without getting splashed. Just this morning, he watched Nyel almost stick his hand under the stream of a small fountain before Atreus snatched his wrist away.

"Oops," Nyel said, "forgot."

Atreus was going to have a heart attack. But despite the grisly and smelly work, Nyel didn't complain about his task. Sure, he had twisted strips of newspaper shoved up his nostrils, but he worked hard.

"Friend of yours?" asked a voice behind the adjacent barrel.

"Not really. But he's my problem, in a manner of speaking—Leo!" Atreus nearly dropped the barrel of sardines at the sight of his best friend.

"Took you long enough. I've been standing here for ten minutes."

"Sorry, I was distra—I wasn't expecting—what are you doing here?" Thick white bandages looped around Leo's head, flattening his bright blond curls. "You shouldn't be lifting that."

"Ugh, you sound like that pretty boy doctor," Leo said, lifting the heavier of the two barrels just to prove he could.

He was the same height as Atreus, though narrower in the shoulders. Atreus didn't like the way his tan skin lacked its usual glow.

"He probably has good reason for telling you to take it easy," Atreus said, lifting his barrel with ease.

"I'm fine. Anyway, Dad told me you needed some help at the docks, so I came right over," he said, then added, "And tell Giovanni thank you. For the food."

Atreus nodded. "So the *Vino Rosso*..."

"Gone," Leo said shortly, "she's completely sunk."

"There is no chance of getting her back? *Signore* Cicco has a crane mounted on his boat. We could try—"

"No." Leo cut him off. "After that storm, she's gone. The tide probably dragged her along the sandbank, where she's likely stuck in the rocks."

"I'm sorry," Atreus said, but it didn't feel like enough. Still, he couldn't stop himself from pressing his friend: "Why didn't you wait for me, Leo?" he said on an exhale, "I could have helped."

Leo snorted and genuinely sounded amused. "You? On a boat? You're kidding, right?" He laughed louder than necessary. "Oh, I can only imagine it, *Gatto* on the sea."

"Laugh all you want; you know I'd do it for you," Atreus said, shaking his head at the nickname. One he'd earned for his obvious 'fear of water' and 'severe lack of swimming skills.'

"I know," Leo said, dropping the barrel with a grunt. "That's what makes you a good friend." He looked like he was about to say more when his attention caught like a fish on a hook on something up the hill.

Atreus followed his gaze to where Nyel sorted through the last boat's catch, dropping one of the slippery bodies. Shaking his head, Atreus was about to tell him off when he paused, noticing Leo's expression. His best friend's eyes were glazed over, and color rushed to his cheeks.

"Who's that?" Leo asked breathlessly. "He's... really cute."

"Cute?" Atreus asked with a raised brow.

Leo shook himself, falling out of his trance. He put on his usual cocky grin. "You know." He waved a hand. "Like a puppy or something. Anyway, who is he?"

"No one," Atreus said, trying to turn away, but Leo caught his arm.

"Nuh uh, you aren't running from this. You make a new friend all on your own, *Gatto*?" He pretended to get choked up before wiping an imaginary tear from his eyes. "My Atreus is all grown up. Making friends all by himself."

"Shut up." Atreus hit his arm.

"No, but seriously, who is it?"

"I told you no one—"

"Hey!" Leo called, catching Nyel's attention. "I'm Leo!"

Atreus rubbed his temple; he was getting a headache. Nyel approached cautiously, eyes darting from Atreus to Leo.

"Relax, I don't bite," Leo said, flashing his award-winning white smile. "What's your name?"

"Uh... I'm Nyel," he said, sounding ridiculous because of the newspaper stuffed into his nose.

"Nell?"

He pulled the wads from his nose, sniffling as his airway cleared. "Nyel."

"Ah. Well, it's nice to finally meet a friend of Atreus. He hasn't stopped talking my ear off about you."

"Really?" Nyel asked, and Atreus hated how a hopeful smile played on his lips.

"Oh, sure. It's not every day that this stick in the mud brings a new face around. You must be something special."

"Um. I guess you could call us friends."

Atreus's chest gave a guilty twist. He hadn't been nice to Nyel; he knew that. But there was too much at stake, too great a risk. He couldn't afford to relax.

Still, that doesn't mean I have to be an ass.

"I'm sorry about your boat," Nyel offered with a sincere frown.

Leo stiffened a moment. "Nothing we can't figure out. It'll work out; it always does."

Atreus didn't miss the way his smile faltered at the end. The air grew awkward for a moment before Leo broke the stillness, his voice cheerful if not a bit strained.

"So, Nyel, how long are you staying? Will you still be here for the Baia Festival?"

"No," Atreus answered for him. "Sorry, we have other plans."

"Awww, come on, *Gatto*. You said that last year. I swear I'll drag you there myself. We're totally going."

"What's a festival?" Nyel asked.

Atreus shot him his best 'shut up' look but recognized the determined set to Nyel's jaw.

"What's the Baia Festival? It's only the best event of the year!" Leo said like an announcer might to a crowd. "Food, music, dancing, games—you name it."

Nyel's eyes grew brighter with every word. "I want to go."

"We can't make it," Atreus repeated.

"Don't be like that, *Gatto*. The three of us would have an amazing time. And that way, when Gloria Lorenzo invites me as her date, I have an actual excuse," he said, shivering at the girl's name. "She's been laying hints about as subtly as a lumberjack."

"Who?" Nyel asked.

"Just a girl who won't get off my tail. Been trying to let her down easy, but the ladies can't resist this face," he said, striking a cocky pose.

Atreus rolled his eyes. "Uh-huh, sure. You keep telling yourself that."

"Bringing a date is basically sentencing you to the gossip mill. I'll be avoiding that like the plague, thank you very much," Leo scoffed.

"I'm confused. Isn't a date a marker of the day?" Nyel asked with a quirked brow.

Leo laughed. "Good one, but no. It's not that kind of date. A date is someone you're interested in. You know, getting all romantic with. Being lovey-dovey until you make everyone around you sick," he said with a face like he'd swallowed an oyster that turned.

Nyel's brow pinched. "Do you have to bring one?"

"No. But my mom wants me to get serious. Says I'm plenty old enough to start thinking about a family. As though I don't already have enough on my plate." Leo said, his charm cracking for the second time.

Nyel nodded. "Yeah. I get that."

Atreus was about to ask Nyel what he meant, but decided against it in front of Leo. Instead, he turned to his best friend. "If your mom wants you to date so badly, why not bring Marina? She likes you well enough."

"No way. If I even look at her the wrong way, my family will never let me hear the end of it. You know how close our dads are."

"Is that a bad thing?" Atreus asked.

"Speak of the red-headed devil," Leo said, spreading his arms wide as Marina jogged to them, red hair bouncing. "What's up, curly-q?"

She snorted. "Pot calling the kettle black, don't you think, Leo? How's the head?"

Leo knocked on it with his knuckles. "Hard as ever."

"I don't doubt it," she said before turning to Atreus and Nyel. "Are you two ready to go?"

"Go where?" Atreus asked.

"I promised to show Nyel around town. You guys are almost done, right?"

Nyel looked at Atreus hopefully.

"No. Still have stuff to do," he said, turning away.

"Oh, stop being such a wet blanket, *Gatto*. We only have one boat left. I got this. You guys go," Leo said with a wave.

"You shouldn't be here at all. I'll do it." Atreus said stubbornly.

"Well, if that's the last boat, why don't I get a head start with Nyel, and you two finish up?" Marina offered. She took Nyel's arm. "Come on, there is so much to see."

"No!" Atreus shouted, making everyone jump. He couldn't let Nyel out of his sight—not for a single minute. What if Nyel stuck his hand in a fountain? What if he spilled a drink on himself? What if it rained? Atreus cleared his throat, "I mean... he can't..."

"Go already." Leo said, "I got this."

Atreus hated leaving his work unfinished, but with both Marina and Nyel's puppy eyes on him, he had no choice.

"Fine."

"Nice to meet you, Nyel; I'll see you at the festival," Leo said with a wink before turning to the dock.

"Onward!" Marina cheered, leading them to the main square.

With most of the day's work finished for the people of Baia Vita, the streets grew lively as children, no longer tethered to chores, spilled out to run and play. A few kicked a football around while others raced up and down the steep cobbled streets on rusted bikes. Voices carried across the square as people milled about, creating a comforting ambiance that put Atreus's worried mind at ease.

Marina showed Nyel everything from the cafés to the general markets. Atreus noticed she only showed Nyel the stores still owned by islanders, deliberately skipping over the chain stores with their flashy neon lights.

"Oh, and this is the heart of Baia Vita. Isn't she gorgeous?" Marina awed, stopping a few feet from the island's famous marble fountain.

Nyel's head tilted to the side, trying to make sense of the sculpture—the half-woman, half-fish creature that represented what humans believed to be a Mer. Nyel's hand clapped over his mouth, stifling a laugh as Marina continued to admire the statue's beauty.

Atreus caught his eye, understanding passing between them. All at once, Atreus couldn't hold it in and burst into a fit of laughter. Nyel lost his composure too, and they laughed until their stomachs hurt. Atreus had wanted to laugh with someone over the ludicrous fountain for years. Until now, he'd never had anyone to share it with.

A weight lifted in his chest, replaced with a feeling like birds taking to the sky.

"What's so funny?" Marina asked, grinning despite not getting the joke.

"Nothing, nothing," Atreus waved but couldn't help catching

Nyel's gaze again. The gold flecks in his eyes shone like sea glass in the dimming orange glow of sunset.

An unfamiliar warmth spread through Atreus's chest. It trickled from his heart and settled in his stomach. It took him a moment to make sense of it. But at last, as they recovered from their inside joke, he settled on what it must be. It was the quiet relief of being seen. For the first time in his life, there was someone like him.

Someone who understood.

Nyel smashed into his life like a crashing wave, unsettling everything Atreus had built and causing enough stress to streak his hair gray. But he'd also offered something Atreus never had before.

*"Don't get too attached.
He won't be around long."*

The voice whispered from a forgotten corner. The sound of it wiped the smile off Atreus's face almost instantly. He should have agreed with it. Every logical part of him screamed to get rid of Nyel as soon as possible. It was the safest thing to do. But for the first time, Atreus was tempted to keep him around.

"He'll leave you."

The disembodied sound reared its ugly head. The words slithered to the forefront of his mind, curling around his insecurities and squeezing tight.

"They always do."

Shut up.

"When he finally sees you for the freak you really are, he'll walk away without a second thought."

It spoke with a cruel certainty, dredging up every memory of loss, every scar left by those who had walked away before. Atreus's jaw clenched so hard his teeth hurt.

I know.

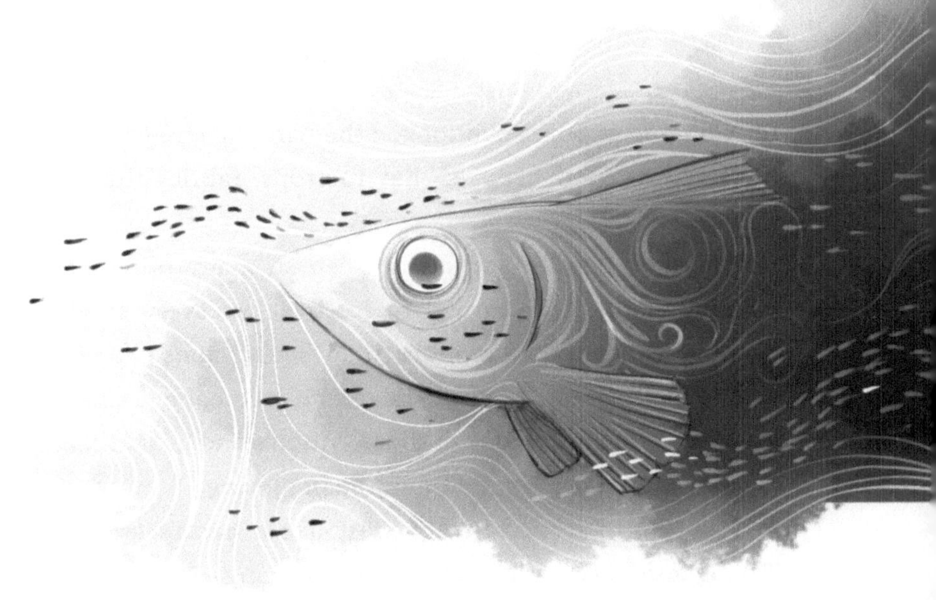

CHAPTER 10

NYEL

NYEL WISHED HE had about eight more eyes. When he'd first arrived in Baia Vita during the storm, the downpour was so strong he could hardly see anything. Now, as he, Marina, and Atreus walked through the town square, Nyel didn't blink for fear of missing something.

The buildings cascaded up the hillside, painted in a mosaic of bright colors—each one a vivid hue that contrasted yet harmonized with its neighbor. Warm oranges, soft yellows, and deep blues created a patchwork of vibrant life. Balconies lined with overflowing flower boxes overlooked the winding streets, while clothes-lines crisscrossed between flat rooftops, fabrics fluttering in the breeze.

Never in Nyel's life had he seen so many different things he couldn't name. He yearned to learn about every single one. But nothing frustrated him more than seeing those familiar human symbols etched onto signs or planks of wood above shops. He knew humans were able to look at those symbols and 'read' them.

I want to read. I want to know what it's saying.

The desire settled in his chest like a hermit crab in its shell. Taking residence with no intention of leaving.

Marina led them to the center of the square, where an ornate statue made of white rock stood high, surrounded by arcs of spouting water.

"This is my favorite part of the square. Isn't she beautiful?" Marina cooed.

Nyel didn't know what he was looking at. He cocked his head to the side, trying to get a read on it. Then the pieces fell into place.

Is this supposed to be...us?

He choked back a laugh, clamping a hand over his mouth. Nyel didn't want to seem rude, but when he glanced over and saw Atreus grinning, they shared a moment of understanding. They broke into a fit of laughter. Atreus's deep voice gained a light tenor. The sound was like the gentle 'whoosh' of sea foam lapping at the sand.

Then, as though the spell had broken, the light in Atreus's face went dim. He turned away from them, his smile disappearing and his expression growing cold.

Don't stop smiling like that.

Nyel wanted to coax that lightness to return.

"We'd better get going. Long walk home," Atreus said.

"We aren't staying at the Sleeping Whale?" Nyel asked, his voice pleading.

"No, we can't keep intruding. I already told Giovanni that we're going back to our place—"

"Nope! You're coming over for at least one more night," Marina interjected.

"Marina, we can't—"

"*Papà* is already making a big dinner for us. You wouldn't want him to waste all that food, would you?"

Nyel watched Atreus's thoughts war in his head before his shoulders slumped. "Fine. But this is the last night."

Marina fist-pumped the air, and Nyel couldn't hide his delight. He didn't want to sleep in the lighthouse again—that is... if he was still invited to stay with Atreus.

Or does he expect me to go home?

Nyel hadn't given it much thought. There was so much for him to discover that the status of his permanence faded into the background. But now it was front and center. And the answer couldn't be more obvious. Of course, Atreus wanted him gone. He'd made that clear from day one, and his coldness towards Nyel only solidified that fact.

I'm not going home. I can't.

Even if Atreus kicked Nyel out, he'd find another way to stay in the human town. Because somehow, in the turn of a tide, Baia Vita had captured Nyel's heart.

Nyel had never worked so hard in his life, nor had he been so happy. Sorting the stinky fish was hard work, and Atreus even let him on the docks to help with the nets after a while. His arms and shoulders hurt, and he felt the sun's bite on the back of his neck.

He wouldn't have it any other way.

They're probably worried about me.

Nyel shook off the thought. Maybe his mom shouldn't have pushed him so hard then. Anger still bubbled in his chest every time he remembered the last dinner at home—the way Chel looked at him with hurt in her eyes. The insistence of all the adults in the room. The way they ignored him completely.

Sonia was on my side. She always is.

Now, true guilt ate away at Nyel, even more so when he recalled Sonia's approaching due date. He promised to be there when the baby arrived.

"You alright, Nyel?" Marina asked.

"Oh yeah, sorry. Long day."

"*Papà's* famous *Ossobuco alla Milanese* will pep you right up."

Between Marina's puppy-eyed begging, Giovanni's persistence, and Nyel's quiet pleas, they eventually wore Atreus down and spent every night at the Sleeping Whale. Each night, he insisted it was the last time, and each night, they proved him wrong.

Nyel had already accrued a few meager possessions, which he stored in *his* room. Of course, he and Atreus paid a good portion of their wages for rent and food. Still, the arrangement nagged at Atreus. And for the life of him, Nyel couldn't understand why.

Evenings were the best part of the day. The food was ten times better than anything he'd ever eaten (especially the items with *sugar*). The lively chatter at the table filled Nyel with buzzing synchronicity he'd never experienced, even with his own family. He couldn't remember the last time he'd laughed and smiled so much over a meal.

Back home, meals were a time for his mother to grill him on responsibilities, for his father to avoid his gaze, and for his aunt to shoot him sympathetic looks. But here, around the circular table that rocked on uneven legs, the air was alive. He listened to Horace's stories about the human war and, more particularly, about his Mer friend. Nyel was fascinated with the human perspective of their kind, even if nobody believed the old man.

No matter how fun the conversation or how good the food was, Atreus's mood remained damp. Nyel wanted to talk with him and hear him laugh again. But no matter how much he and Marina tried probing him into the conversation, Atreus remained stoic.

Clearly, Giovanni and Marina want him here. Why doesn't he just accept it and relax?

Nyel pondered this as he made his bed for the night. Giovanni helped him and Atreus acquire more clothes from families who no longer needed them. They were ratty and had holes, yet Nyel folded them as though they were made of coral silk.

As he lay in bed, he admired the empty bookshelf with his belongings. He had three possessions now, two of which he'd bought using the money he earned—all on his own. A sense of pride surged in his chest.

The first item was the fishing encyclopedia Atreus gave him on his first day. He found himself flipping through the pictures most nights, trying to find meaning in the assortment of symbols the humans used to read. The other item was another book, but the pages were blank. Marina wrote his name on the blank pages, and Nyel had practiced the strokes for hours. The last item was a small bundle of charcoal pencils.

Next time, I'll try one of those colored pen things.

His lids grew heavy after a large meal of pasta and cheese. A knock on the door roused him, and he blinked awake.

"Come in?" he said like a question, sitting up when Atreus entered his room. "Oh hey. Everything okay?" he asked, feeling more alert.

Atreus closed the door quietly behind him, his shoulders tense. "We need to talk," he said, shoving his hands into his pockets and fixing Nyel with a steely gaze.

"What about?" Nyel asked, trying to sound light. He'd anticipated this. But a part of him had hoped it wouldn't be so soon.

Here it is; he's going to tell me to beat it.

"Why did you run away from your family?"

Nyel hesitated, the question catching him by surprise. "Uh, why?"

Atreus shrugged. He shifted from foot to foot and wouldn't look at him for more than a second. "Trying to understand, I guess."

Nyel remembered something Leo said at the docks. "Is what Leo said true? That you talk about me and that we're, you know..." He hesitated. "That we're friends?"

Atreus sighed, rubbing the back of his head. "Leo never lets the truth stand in the way of a good story. But let's not get ahead of ourselves. I need to get you figured out. I can't handle any more surprises right now."

Nyel didn't miss the way Atreus avoided answering his question.

"My parents, well, my mom is trying to send me on a Tideway. She believes it'll encourage a Bond. She wants me to settle down with this girl, Chel, or any *sirena*. And I just..." He shook his head. "It's not for me. Or maybe not right now. I don't know, but I couldn't stand to go through with it."

Atreus stared at him like he'd grown a second head. "What the hell is a Bond?"

Nyel's mouth actually fell open. "You're kidding me, right?"

But before he could explain, there was a knock at the door, and Marina rushed in. "Oh, good. You're both here," she said, her nightgown swaying as she glided inside.

"Why do you bother knocking if you're going to come in anyway?" Atreus grumbled. She ignored him.

"I need you both tomorrow after work. Atty, you have the steadiest hands, so you'll write the words on the banner." She held up a hand when Atreus went to complain. "I already wrote it on paper. You only have to copy it. And Nyel, would you mind cutting fabric to make flags? I want to line the path for the biking portion with colored flags so the kids know where to go."

The three of them spent the remainder of the evening discussing plans. Marina talked, Nyel listened, and Atreus rolled his eyes so much Nyel was sure they'd get stuck in the back of his head.

"Oh, don't you huff. It'll be fun! I have so many paints and brushes; you'll love it."

"I'm vibrating with excitement," Atreus said in the most deadpan voice he could muster.

Marina flicked him on the ear. "Party-pooper."

Atreus grabbed the nearest pillow and smacked her with it. "Dork."

Nyel burst out laughing at the spectacle.

"What's so funny?" Marina asked, blowing hair from her face.

"You two, it's just... I didn't grow up with siblings."

A guilty knot twisted in his gut at the thought of Nephi. Despite sharing blood, they were virtual strangers.

He was never around; what was I supposed to do about it?

"Oh yeah, it's loads of fun," Atreus said sarcastically, putting up a hand to block an attempted pillow-snipe from Marina.

"Here. Get in on this," Marina said, tossing Nyel another pillow as she stalked towards Atreus, a wildcat grin on her face.

"Whoa, whoa, what is this? Ganging up on me? I call foul," Atreus protested, backing into a corner and holding his pillow like a shield.

"Show no mercy," Marina said like a battle cry.

All three of them were red-faced and disheveled when Giovanni burst through the door, looking thoroughly annoyed. "Are you toddlers? Spare me, *per favore*; it is the middle of the night."

"Sorry, *Papà*," Marina said through a curtain of tangled red hair.

"Sorry, we didn't mean—" Atreus was cut off as a well-timed pillow smushed into his face.

"Got 'em!" Marina cheered, pumping a victory fist into the air.

Nyel slapped a hand over his mouth, unsuccessfully covering his snort. Giovanni shook his head and grumbled something about getting too old for rowdy children before leaving.

"There you go, getting me in trouble," Atreus hissed, but he was smiling.

"Oh, don't be a baby."

"What did I tell you? A feral cat, this one," Atreus said, wiping curly strands from his eyes.

Nyel paused, almost doing a double-take when Atreus's gaze caught on his as though by accident. With his face flushed and a smile tugging at his lips, Atreus's eyes shone like nacre shells. They glistened with an untamed energy that promised... something.

"We should go to bed," Atreus said, breaking the connection. Nyel dropped his head, heat creeping into his face.

"See you boys tomorrow!" Marina singsonged, twirling on a single bare foot before leaving the room without closing the door.

Atreus rolled his eyes, following after her. "Night," he said shortly, but before he disappeared, Nyel called out.

"Atreus?"

"Yeah?" He stilled.

"I'm—" Nyel's throat was dry. "I'm really happy to be here."

"Yeah. Alright," Atreus said after some consideration.

"You're not going to, I mean, you don't want me—"

"If I was going to chase you out of here, I would have done it by now," he said with a teasing lilt.

Nyel's shoulders relaxed. "Really?"

"Really," he said, and to Nyel's relief, it looked like he meant it. "Night."

"Night," Nyel replied as the door clicked shut.

He turned off the light and rolled onto his side. The last thing he saw imprinted behind his eyelids, lingering like a vivid, unshakable dream—the image of abalone green eyes and a reluctant smile.

"You two, go ahead. I need to stretch for a minute," Nyel said, pressing his hands into his lower back and arching. The three of them had been bent over the stupid banner for hours, but Nyel had to admit it looked great. Atreus had an incredible knack for penmanship, and the words flowed evenly across the cloth. He'd even added a variety of ocean creatures in bright golden paint.

Atreus halted, paint cans perched dangerously in his arms.

"I'll be fine," Nyel assured him. "I'm just going to stretch my legs along the beach for a second. Plenty far from the water."

"Atty, let's go," Marina whined.

Atreus hesitated before saying, "If you're not back in fifteen minutes, I'm coming after you."

"Aye, aye, captain," Nyel said with a salute, a human gesture he'd grown fond of.

"Atty, hurry up!"

"I keep telling you not to call me that," Atreus said, joining her. Nyel couldn't help but laugh as they bickered all the way up the hill.

The beach was empty, and Nyel took off his shoes, sighing as the sand ran between his toes. That was one human custom he absolutely hated. Shoes. Nyel had to force his feet to stop where the water kissed the sand. After almost two weeks away, a sharp pull tugged at his stomach, one calling him back to the waves.

The tides.

The ebb and flow of all life.

An eternal dance he was inexplicably tied to.

Nyel resisted the call. He'd promised Atreus he wouldn't go into the water. But if this insistent tugging continued, they'd have to sneak away for a swim at some point. Soon.

Nyel strolled around a massive black boulder, running his fingertips over the cold, smooth surface. With Baia Vita blocked from view, the temptation for a swim came again.

He missed the flow of water through his gills. He missed the weightlessness. Spirits, he missed his freakin' tail. Nyel laughed at himself. Maybe someday, there would be a world where he could have both his newfound human life and his old life as a Mer.

Nyel sighed, shaking his head at his own wishful thinking when he sensed it—the presence of another. His skin prickled, alert to the change, and the once ordinary quiet now felt charged, heavy with something unseen.

Before he could whip around to face the intruder, a hand clasped over his mouth, and a thick arm pinned him to a muscled chest. The stranger lifted Nyel off his feet.

"Finally, you little shit." Nyel kicked and was about to bite his captor when the stranger said, "You're going home right this fucking second."

"Nephi?" His voice was muted through the hand.

His brother released him, and Nyel whipped around. He'd never seen him as a human before. Nephi was tall, probably taller than Atreus. He had a stocky build and deep complexion several shades darker than Nyel's, and though their hair matched in color—Nephi's was straight and clipped short. But it was his scars that seized Nyel's attention, a grim testament to the violence his brother must have endured. The entire right side of his body bore the marks, twisting the skin in a way that looked even harsher without fins to soften the effect. His right eye, clouded and milky, was even more haunting in this human form.

"What are you—? How did you—?" Nyel checked around them, ensuring they were alone. "Have you been following me?"

Nephi made an irritated growling sound in his throat. "For fucking days. This is the first time you haven't been glued to that Mer bastard's side."

"What do you want?"

"You're coming home. Your parents are worried sick. They're so worried, in fact, that they actually acknowledged my existence and asked me to bring you home."

"You talked to them?"

"Yeah. Your mommy is a mess. And dear ol' dad played the 'father' card on me as though he has any right. But I was looking for you even before they asked."

"Why?"

"Because you're a stupid brat that has no idea the dangerous game he's playing."

Nyel stiffened. "You don't know anything, Nephi. I've been doing great."

"You're a whiny kid who threw a fit. And now you're running around like a wounded fish in a tank of sharks. It's only a matter of time before they catch your scent."

"You don't know a damn thing!" Nyel yelled, shocking himself. He dropped his voice to a whisper, "You don't know anything. And I'm doing just fine. Why do you care anyway? Don't you have somewhere to be? Where you've been all these years?"

Nephi nodded. "Yes, I do, actually. But I can't go until I get my dumb half-brother home. And to answer your questions, I don't care. I don't give a rat's ass about your parents' wishes either."

"So why then?"

Nephi hesitated for the briefest moment. "Don't like to leave a job unfinished."

Nyel scoffed. "Sure. Whatever, Nephi."

"So you gonna come home or stay until a human sticks a gaff through you?"

"None of the humans know what I am. I'm careful. I have a job, a place to live, and…and I've made friends," Nyel said, listing his accomplishments like a petulant child. He hated the way he sounded.

Nephi laughed. "Oh yeah? And how well do you know these friends? How well do you know that bastard that you follow around like a puppy?"

"Don't call him that. Atreus is a good person."

"But it's true, isn't it? It takes one to know one. And I know a bastard-born when I see it."

"What are you talking about?"

Nephi smiled, his white teeth too perfect for his mean expression. "Haven't seen it, have you?"

"Seen what? Spit it out already, Nephi. I don't have time for this." Nyel snapped, but with every breath, his stomach sank lower.

"His Mer form. You haven't seen it."

It wasn't a question this time. But a statement. A true one.

"So what?"

Nephi nodded like his mind was made up. "You'll change your tune once you've seen it. Mark my words."

Nyel opened his mouth to argue when the sound of nearby voices made him jump. He hissed, ducking further into the boulder's shadow. "We can't be doing this here."

"When you've learned the truth, I'll be here to take you home."

"I'm not going home, Nephi; you can't force me."

Nephi raised a brow. "Wanna test that theory?"

Nyel took a step back. "Okay, maybe you can, but I'll just run away again."

"Trust me, you'll never walk these shores again after you see it."

In the blink of an eye, Nephi's body moved with inhuman speed and dove into the waves. Nyel waited, but he didn't surface again.

NEPHI

AT FIRST, KEEPING tabs on his brat brother was somewhat enjoyable. Sneaking around, remaining out of sight, gathering information. That's what Nephi was good at. It didn't hurt that Nyel spent a lot of time on the docks, where a particular human frequented. A human Nephi saved. He'd discarded the bandages around his head, showing off a full head of curls. Nephi hated the way the golden locks were identical to the ones he'd run his hands through so many times. Right down to the rogue curls that poked out behind his ears.

It's not him. It's not him.

Nephi knew that. So why did he abandon the watch on Nyel to stalk this look-alike?

But the fun was over when his father, Donato, approached him while he rested under the house with the sandwinder.

"I need you to bring your brother home. What he's doing isn't safe."

"Get him yourself," Nephi snapped without bothering to roll over.

"Bianca and I aren't comfortable with *Marvassa*."

"Oh well, Spirits forbid you be uncomfortable."

"I'm asking you as your father, Nephi."

Blood surged like molten fire through his veins, flooding the hidden vessels beneath his skin. In an instant, Nephi's fins flared wide, tripling in size—the legacy of his RaMaa mother written in every vein of crimson. The membrane along his back and tail expanded like the crest of a sailfish. Their surface glowed with the heat of his blood, pulsing in time with his rage-fueled heart.

The sandwinder yelped in alarm and scurried away.

Nephi rounded on his father like the Kraken disturbed from sleep.

"You have no right to call yourself a father," he spat so close he blew water into Donato's face.

Donato retreated, his scales cast in red as the sun passed through Nephi's flared fins. Nephi relished the fear in the old *sireno's* eyes. It was delicious and so deserved.

That's right. Cower from the monster you created.

"If not for me, then for your brother. He's done nothing to hurt you," his father said, even as he shrank away.

Nephi wrinkled his nose in disgust. "You're pathetic. Fine, I'll get him, but don't forget," he hissed, flaring the spine on his tail, making himself twice—no, three times—larger than his sire. "You owe me, and one day, I'll make damn sure to collect."

He held so much power over this pathetic excuse for a Mer. Nephi was a force of nature— an imposing display of brute strength. His frame was wide, every muscle honed and taut. He was built to overpower, to crush, to dominate.

At any second, he could end this *sireno*. And he wanted Donato to know it. *Needed* him to feel it—to understand, deep in his bones, how powerful Nephi had become. And not just Donato. They all needed to know it. To know what an incredible monster he was.

Let them fear what they never tried to understand.

With a final glare, he swam away, leaving his father frozen in dread at the thought of what this monster might one day demand of him. Of course, Nephi had no intention of cashing in on this *favor*. But knowing the idea would ferment in his father's head and keep him up at night was reward enough.

Nyel was done pissing around in human territory. Time to come home. But as Nephi stalked his oblivious brother, there wasn't a single opportunity to grab him. Nyel stuck to that Mer's side like glue. And in turn, the other Mer kept an annoyingly close eye on Nyel. Even when the Mer's back was turned, Nyel was too surrounded by humans for Nephi to make a move.

Days passed, along with any shred of patience Nephi had left. The moment Nyel was alone on the beach, he pounced.

"Finally, you little shit."

He expected some resistance from his brother but not outright refusal. It didn't matter; once Nyel realized the kind of company he was keeping, he'd turn tail and run. They all did once they knew the truth.

The second Nyel figures out who he's been wasting his time on, he'll go running home, and I can finally get the hell out of here.

It was time to confront the other impostor among these humans.

Nephi yanked an oversized coat from a clothing line. What better way to blend in with the locals than to wear their clothes? Normally, he wouldn't have bothered and remained in his shirt and pants, but the scars on his body posed a problem. He was too noticeable now. Conspicuous. He couldn't allow anyone to make a note of his presence.

In and out, just like always.

But it had been a while since Nephi infiltrated human territory, and he found himself ducking behind walls as a group of fishermen passed in the early morning light.

Make this quick, damn it. Then you can get back to the Pod.

If he died among his brothers and sisters, fighting for his home, for his people - at least, then it would mean something.

Not if.

When.

When he died.

Nephi understood that there would be no return trip. And he itched to fight until his final breath. He'd die on the front lines.

Like my Ludo did.

But he sure as hell wouldn't let a human get the better of him in this grimy fishing village. That wasn't his fate.

Dodging groups of fishermen, Nephi made his way to the docks. A steady stream of men starting their boats filled the air with tolling bells, clanking metal, and groaning engines. He took a deep breath through his nose, filtering out the smell of oil and fish. He found the foreign scent soon enough.

Nyel's Mer companion, Atreus, was already working alongside the humans. The other men had taken off their shirts and tucked them into their pants, but Atreus remained the only one still wearing his.

Like that's gonna keep the water off you. One slip-up is all it'd take for them to gouge your eyes out.

But he supposed this was the razor's edge a halfling was forced to walk. All because of what he was. Nephi could scent Nyel further up the hill, likely doing his 'job.'

A lamb playing at being the lion.

Nephi waited for Atreus to separate from the other men before he moved. Keeping his hood up and face low, he stalked forward. His steps were sure, and within seconds, he was on the Mer. He bumped his shoulder into Atreus hard, knocking him off balance.

"Oh, sorry—" Atreus started, but his voice cut off when Nephi's bruising grip tightened on his upper arm.

Bending to his ear, Nephi whispered, "I know what you are— sea monster. If you don't want to go for a swim in front of all these humans, you'll meet me by the rocks in three minutes."

With a final brutal squeeze, he shoved Atreus aside and disappeared into the narrow lane, shadowed by the swaying clotheslines.

Now, Nephi leaned comfortably against the black stone, relishing the scent still lingering in his nostrils. It was fear. When Atreus heard his threat, the stench of it rolled off him in waves. Nephi savored the smell. It came off everyone he ever encountered. He was used to it—expected it even. It made him feel powerful.

He was a halfling mutt. Deranged, angry, and dangerous. Cursed with *Skraith* inside him, if such a thing existed to begin with. Maybe that was the source of his rage? In the end, it didn't matter; Nephi knew who he was, *Skraith* or not.

If they only see a monster, then I'll be the worst monster that ever breathed.

The sound of shifting sand alerted him to Atreus's presence. He breathed in deeply, the scent of fear strong in the air.

That's right. You should be scared.

"Who are you?"

Nephi stepped lazily from the stone, lowering his hood and sizing up this Mer. He looked strong. They'd be evenly matched if it ever came down to a fight. But that was in a fair fight. And who said Nephi ever fought fair?

"Someone that knows all about you, Atreus."

He basked in the way the other male stiffened at the sound of his name.

"How did you—"

"Nyel told me. He's awfully fond of you. Seems to think very highly of you."

"You know him?"

"We are," he paused, "distant relatives."

"What do you want with him? With me?"

"It's time for him to stop playing house with predators and come home."

"He won't go. I've tried."

"He will. Once he learns the truth." Nephi let that ominous phrase hang in the air for a moment, extracting every last bit of tension. He watched as it settled over his opponent like a chain. "Why haven't you shown Nyel your Mer form?"

"W-what?"

"Is it because you know he'll run away? Just like everyone else in your life?"Atreus's jaw clenched so tight Nephi could practically hear his teeth grinding. A thrill shot up his spine.

Maybe I'll get some action after all.

His body itched for a fight. For claws and teeth.

"That's why you're all alone, isn't it? Why the *Sireni* shun you? Why you have chosen to throw your lot in with the enemy?"

"I—I don't—"

"But of course, the *Sireni* in Corallina weren't the first to cast you out," Nephi smiled wickedly, showing off the canines he so badly wanted to sink into flesh. "Your parents abandoned you first. Isn't that right?"

He saw Atreus's movements as though in slow motion. The set of his feet, the lunge in his knees, and the cocked shoulder. Nephi dodged his punch with unchallenged ease, redirecting Atreus's momentum with an elbow to the back. Atreus fell face-first in the sand but was up again in seconds, trying for another strike. This time, Nephi dodged, gripping his wrist and bending forward, throwing Atreus's bulk clean over his head. He heard Atreus's breath knock free of his lungs.

"You're strong. But untrained. You fight like a human."

Atreus wiped sand from his mouth and stood warily. "How do you know all this?"

Nephi considered how to answer, taking his time. With hands in his pockets, he waded into the surf until he was waist-deep. With deliberate slowness, he lifted his tail, fanning out his bright red fins.

"Because I'm like you. A mutt. A bastard child nobody wanted. A halfling." When Atreus appeared confused, Nephi sighed, feeling bad for the man. "They abandoned you and didn't even bother to tell you why. How cruel."

"Tell me what!?"

"That you're a freak. A mix between two species that should never be. An abomination. You should have been killed as a babe, but like me, somehow you survived. We are born with *Skraith* inside us, slowly driving us mad. And now we live like outcasts."

He lifted his tail, admiring his scales as they glistened in the early light.

"The green comes from my *sireno* father. And the red comes from my mother, a *Ra-Maa* woman. Mixed colors like these are the easiest way to spot a halfling. But to someone with more training, it's possible to identify by scent alone. That's how I figured you out."

Atreus swallowed hard, and Nephi could see the wheels turning in his head. Answers he'd likely searched for his entire life. All thrown at his feet in a flash.

Poor bastard.

But it was better to learn the truth and hurt than to remain oblivious.

"Now you know why they left. And why you've been hiding yourself from Nyel. This is the shame we bear."

"I'm... a halfling."

Nephi nodded. "You are. From your scent alone, I can tell you carry *Rusalki* blood; the rest is unfamiliar to me."

"And I have *Skraith*?"

"An evil spirit that lives in your body. Your mind. The punishment for your continued existence. Humans might call it a demon."

Atreus shook his head. "I don't know what that means. I don't know what any of it means."

"If you continue to live hidden among your enemies, it won't matter. To them, you're human, and it's in your best interest to keep it that way. But if a Mer saw you, well…" He tilted his head. "I trust you've already experienced how they react."

Atreus's freckles stood out against skin drained of color, his hands clenching and unclenching like he didn't know what to do with them.

"So you're saying… if Nyel sees—"

"He'll come home in an instant. Halflings are sick. Cursed. Driven mad by the *Skraith*. We're demented, twisted beasts. The deadliest Mer in the sea."

Nephi flourished his tail a final time before splashing out of the surf. The water evaporated quickly in the blazing sun. *Marvassa* took away his scales in seconds.

"I'm not mad." Atreus's voice shook.

Nephi laughed. "I used to say the same."

Atreus glared at him. "I'm not," he said more firmly. "And I've never attacked anyone."

"Not yet." He loved the way Atreus paled further. "Show him what you really are. You'll see that I'm right. I'll be waiting for him when he runs."

"Atreus!"

Nephi stiffened as an unfamiliar voice approached.

"Atreus, where'd you go?"

A figure jogged to them, feet light on the sand. Nephi's eyes widened, and his breath caught in his lungs. He tried to pull air through his gills but realized he had none and inhaled sharply through his nose.

It's him.

All the days he'd followed Nyel, Nephi secretly hoped to run into *him*—the human with curly blond hair, amber skin, and a full lower lip. For a second, it was Ludo who jogged to him, all vibrant smiles and alive with each footprint he left in the sand.

The dimples are the same.

Once again, the illusion was broken when the young man turned his eyes to Nephi. They were yellow, not silver.

Not my Ludo.

Yet no matter how much he told himself that, visions of this human continued to haunt Nephi. And now he was right in front of him.

Don't panic. He doesn't know who you are.

Nephi was in his Mer form when he saved the boy and was likely written off as a delirious dream. Despite himself, Nephi pulled up his hood, hiding the right side of his face.

"Hey, Atreus, I've been meaning to talk to you, but if now's a bad time…" The human glanced at Nephi with curiosity.

"Leo, I'll meet you at the docks in a minute," Atreus said, his voice stern as he watched Nephi for any signs of an attack.

His name is Leo. Leo. Ludo. Leo. Ludo.

Even the names blurred in his mind. Without a word, Nephi turned on his heel and stalked away. He'd said what he needed to say. Now, he had to get the hell out of there before he did something he'd regret.

Damn you, Ludo.

But it wasn't Ludo's silver eyes now burrowing deeper and deeper into his psyche.

"Leo," he said out loud, tasting the name. It was so similar yet different. Acid bubbled in his chest. How dare a human take the face of his Ludo? How dare a human with such striking similarities breathe the same air? How dare he show his face to Nephi after all he'd lost?

Maybe I'll have him before I go. Or maybe I'll drag him to the ocean floor where he belongs.

CHAPTER 11

LEOFEL

L EO'S HEAD THROBBED as his eyes struggled to blink into focus. The sterile scent of antiseptic filled the air, and the faint hum of machinery droned in his skull. The harsh white lights and beeping monitors only heightened his disorientation.

It took him an hour of pestering the nursing staff before the pieces finally clicked, and he remembered how he'd ended up in the hospital. But when the memories returned, they were a blur of wind and waves and... scales.

"You signed the AMA?" Dr. Romano asked for the third time.

"Yes, can I go already?" Leo barked. He'd already spent too much time in a hospital bed.

"I don't recommend it."

"Yes, hence the AMA. Against Medical Advice. I get it."

"Don't strain yourself. If you start to feel dizzy or have a lapse in memory, come right back."

"Sure," Leo said, knowing he'd do no such thing.

The pretty boy doctor was annoying as hell.

As he descended the hill, the smell of rain still lingered in the air, though the storm had passed. The storm that took the *Vino Rosso* and nearly took his life. Leo bit the inside of his cheek hard enough to draw blood. He wouldn't cry over a stupid boat. But the *Vino Rosso*, with her rusted hull and failing engine, was like a second home. He grew up on that boat. She'd provided for their family since before he was born. And now, because of his stupidity, she was at the bottom of the bay.

"Idiot!" Leo yelled, kicking a garbage bin, sending its contents everywhere. He regretted it instantly as a wave of dizziness washed over him. He crouched among the garbage in case he passed out, but bending so suddenly sent razors through his side, his broken ribs screaming in protest.

Breathe, you moron. You'll figure this out.

But the words remained as empty as the waste bin that lay at his feet. What was he going to do? Without the *Vino Rosso*, how would they make enough to live? To pay for the home? For fucks sake, they would eat through their savings in less than a month on food alone. Feeding a family of seven wasn't cheap.

You'll figure it out. Come on, think.

Yet his fuzzy brain couldn't work past the panic surging in his chest. They'd starve. They'd lose the house. Then what? Then... what?

Leo coughed hard. It was chest-deep and torture on his sore

lungs. Every ragged breath was a reminder of how he'd nearly drowned. He remembered how badly it'd burned, as though he'd breathed in molten rock instead of seawater. Residual terror still bubbled in his veins at the slightest suggestion of storm clouds on the breeze.

He didn't want to die. That became abundantly clear as death stared him down, trying to intimidate him into submission. He was terrified. But before he was forced to kneel before death's blackened robes, someone dragged him to his feet.

Hands clutched him, pulling him through the heavy water. A smooth mouth pressed to his, parting his lips and breathing air into his lungs.

He shouldn't have remembered those details. Leo was knocked out cold the moment the *Vino Rosso* tipped over, her derrick striking him in the head. Yet every detail played before him as though he were an onlooker, watching himself drown in the bay. Leo didn't know if it was his imagination filling in the gaps or what some might call an out-of-body experience, but he remembered everything.

Almost everything.

He touched his lips, trying to unlock more. But his rescuer remained a blurry mass in his mind. When he returned to his body, he had a single fleeting image: a face with scales, green as emeralds and crimson fins catching the rain.

Then he was in a soft white bed with an annoying doctor telling him not to push himself.

"I'm losing my mind," he said with a hysterical laugh.

Leo didn't have time for this. Didn't have time for fantasies induced by a near-death experience. Still, he couldn't stop thinking about the creature that saved him.

"You got lucky," he said, picking up the trash and righting the bin. "Now, forget about it."

Leo opened the door to his childhood home, reminding himself that he promised to fix the lower hinge, which creaked in protest.

"Ma?" he called, listening for the ever-present patter of feet from his younger siblings. The pattering increased in speed, and he was surrounded by four heads with bobbing curls.

"MA!" his sister Annetta yelled, "Leo is home!"

"Leofel Tradi!" his mother said in her no-nonsense voice, hands on her hips, apron stained with red sauce. "You are not supposed to be out of the hospital."

Leo waved dismissively. "I'm fine, Ma," he said, kissing her grumpy face on the cheek. "Where is Dad?"

"He said he had a meeting with some friends. But do not change the subject, child of mine. Did Dr. Romano discharge you?"

"Of course," Leo said with one of his flashiest smiles. "Perfect bill of health." He kissed her head again as she sighed.

"Oh my boy, what am I going to do with you?"

"Leo, is the *Vino Rosso* really gone? Did she sink?" Caterina asked, her clumsy hands grabbing his shirt.

Leo picked her up. "Yes, *sorellina*. She's gone. I'm so sorry."

"Gone? What do you mean gone?" Edgar asked, frozen at the base of the stairs. "We can't get her back?"

Leo could hardly look at Edgar's devastated face. At eleven and the next eldest son, he was expected to start helping Leo on the bay. He'd spoken of nothing else all winter, and Leo had even begun teaching him the basics on the docks. Now though...

"I'm sorry, Edgar. But we can't get her back. There is nothing left to save."

Edgar's face turned red, and his fists clenched. "This isn't fair. It was finally my turn."

"I'm sorry Edgar, you know I—"

"It was finally my turn to help, and you ruined it! Ma told you not to go out in the storm, and you didn't listen. The *Vino Rosso* is gone because of you!" Edgar stomped up the stairs with glassy eyes.

"Edgar Tradi, you come apologize this instant!" Emelia shouted but was answered by the sound of a slamming door. She looked ready to chase after him, but Leo stopped her.

"It's okay, Ma. Let him blow off some steam."

Caterina's lip trembled as she squeezed his shirt. She screwed up her tiny face and hugged Leo around the neck. "I'm glad you're okay."

Caterina and Muerello wrapped around him in a tangle of arms and tears.

"We thought you drowned," Annetta said. At thirteen, she was old enough to understand the gravity of losing the *Vino Rosso*.

"No, lil' sis. I'm alright." He bent low, kissing each one of their curly heads and wiping stray tears.

"What are we going to do now?" Maurello asked in his innocent voice.

The question sent a pang through Leo's stomach, and his head throbbed worse than ever. His mother saved him from answering the terrifying question.

"Upstairs! Chop chop, baths and brushed teeth. I'll come tuck you in, and I better see butts in bed."

The little ones protested, and only after Leo promised to read a bedtime story did they climb the stairs like a pair of pups.

"Ma, I'll get them bathed, then come back and finish the dishes," Annetta said.

"Take a break, sis. I got it," Leo offered.

She gave him a thankful smile before disappearing up the landing. He knew the house was still standing because she'd stepped in while he was gone.

"It's late. Shouldn't Dad be back?" Leo asked once she was out of earshot.

Emelia waved him off. "He might spend the night at Cicco's."

Leo gritted his teeth. He knew what that meant. His father would be too drunk to come home.

"Right," Leo said, going to help with the dishes just for something to do.

Emelia grabbed a towel and dried as he washed. "Give him some time, and he'll come back."

"Right," Leo said again.

This happened every time things got hard. His father ran to one of his old war buddies and drank until he passed out on their couch. Every time they lost something, anytime money was so tight it choked them like a noose—Thomasso ran.

It was never for a long time. For one or two days, he'd drink away his woes in the company of friends. After he was done, he'd return home and help carry the burden alongside his wife and son. Still... Leo never got to run away. Leo never got to take two days or even two hours to throw a fit.

"Not that he does much anyway," Leo mumbled, but his mother heard him.

"Leofel," she said harshly, and that was enough for him to bow his head.

"Sorry, Ma. I'm just... I'm just tired," he settled on because he couldn't tell her what he was actually feeling. He couldn't tell her that the storm that nearly killed him hadn't gone away. It'd moved from the sky and into his chest, where it continued to rage and tear him apart.

His father did all he could at his advanced age. The man walked with a cane, for heaven's sake. Thomasso met Emelia later in life and had Leo when he was already well into his forties. Now, with four more mouths to feed and a spinal injury that left him hobbled, Thomasso had no choice but to retire from the sea—leaving Leo to provide them with food. With a home. With the clothes on their backs.

"Go to sleep. I'll finish," Emelia said, and Leo noticed the dark circles under her eyes. But he understood the offer for what it was. She needed to be alone for a while.

"Night, Ma," he said, kissing her unkempt hair.

She gave him a curt nod, and he knew neither of them would sleep tonight.

THE NEXT MORNING, Leo rose to the smell of seared fish, garlic, and olive oil. It took him twice as long to dress since every time he bent, his head spun so badly he had to pause for breath. Leo inspected the wound on his head and replaced the crusted rags with clean ones. It was red and messy, and the stitches were sharp and easy to see. He'd have a scar, but his hair would cover it in time.

"Idiot," he said to himself in the mirror. He should never have gone out into that storm.

When he came downstairs, a thick slab of red tuna sizzled in the pan. The smell made his mouth fill with saliva.

"Where did you get that?" he asked, inspecting the cut of meat. It was thick and full of marbled fat—a premium cut.

"Giovanni sent Thomasso home with it."

Leo didn't miss the stiffness in her voice, and his shoulders tightened. They were already depending on the good nature of their friends to eat. How had they already become so desperate?

"Smells good," he said.

Once it finished sizzling, he took the smallest cut for himself, letting his growing brothers and sisters take the bigger slices.

Leo had his boots pulled on when Emelia called from the living room.

"Giovanni said he could use some help on the docks this morning."

Leo nodded; he was already going there. He would not let a gift like that go unpaid.

"I'm going there now—" His voice caught in his throat like he'd swallowed a handful of sand. His mother was in the living room, scissors in hand, cutting long strands of hair from Annetta's head.

"What are you doing?" Leo gasped, watching as gorgeous curls fell to the floor. Unshed tears brimmed in Annetta's eyes, her fists bunching up her dress.

"Locks like these go for a high price. They make wigs out of them on the mainland," his mother replied, stone-faced.

Annetta held his stare with desperately fragile determination as if she were holding herself together with fraying seams.

"I offered," she breathed as if the words physically hurt.

Emelia stopped cutting, resting a sorrowful hand on her daughter's shoulder.

He couldn't take this.

Couldn't stand there a second longer.

Leo stormed out the front door, slamming it so hard he probably broke the only working hinge. He couldn't bear to look at his sister's face as her hair was cut just so they could eat.

How had he failed them so terribly?

The world spun, and he fell to one knee, bracing himself with one hand on the side of the house.

Breathe.

He had to focus. He had to get his banged-up head on straight and figure this out.

Had to... had to...

Green scales. Red fins. Slitted pupils stared down at him as rain traced cold paths down his cheeks.

No time for that.

But even as he chided himself, Leo couldn't force away the memory. Hallucination? He didn't know. He didn't know anything anymore. His chest was going to split in two—rip right down the middle, his organs exposed for the gulls.

A flash of green scales.

A crest of fins the color of blood.

Slitted eyes.

The image should have been terrifying.

Yet memories of the creature calmed something inside Leo. It made him feel safe.

He forced the image away as he stood, and his head swam. Leo braced against the wall, taking a moment to compose himself. But he didn't rest long before forcing his legs to move in the direction of the docks.

EVEN AS LEO caught sight of his long-time friend, relief hit him like a fresh breeze on a hot day. Atreus looked the same as ever, and if there was anyone in Leo's life he could confide in, it was his best friend.

He snuck behind Atreus, hoping to make him jump, when his friend's gaze locked on something further up the hill. Leo followed his stare, seeing an unfamiliar figure working at the sorting tables.

"Friend of yours?"

"Not really. But he's my problem in a manner of speaking —Leo!"

Leo laughed, getting the exact facial expression he knew Atreus would make.

"Took you long enough. Been standing here for ten minutes."

"Sorry, I was distra—I wasn't expecting— what are you doing here?"

Leo lifted the barrel of mackerel beside Atreus as they made their way up the hill.

"You shouldn't be lifting that," his friend scolded. Leo rolled his eyes even as his ribs ached.

"Ugh, you sound like that pretty boy doctor. I'm fine."

Atreus didn't look convinced as they climbed the narrow path, the sound of puttering engines and gulls squawking serving as background noise. Of course, Atreus had heard about the *Vino Rosso*, but Leo didn't want to discuss that. He didn't want to talk about how stupid he'd been to go out in that storm, how lucky he was to be alive.

He was about to poke more fun at Atreus's suggestion to help him on the boat when the figure at the sorting table finally came into focus.

Leo dropped the heavy barrel with a harsh smack on the cobble path. "Who's that?" he breathed.

The boy had a slim build and short, wavy hair the color of pine bark. He moved with a clumsiness that reminded Leo of a toddler learning to walk but in the body of an adult. His skin was fair and would likely burn in the sun. He should have looked silly with newspaper strips shoved up his nose, yet...

"He's... really cute," Leo said on an exhale before he even realized the words came out of his mouth.

"Cute?" Atreus asked with an arched brow.

Leo cleared his throat, forcing his gaze down.

Get ahold of yourself.

He blamed his head injury for letting the words slip. "You know, like a puppy or something. Anyway, who is he?"

When it was clear Atreus wasn't going to give him an answer,

Leo went ahead and introduced himself. Nyel's voice matched him perfectly—light and airy. Leo had to hide the goosebumps that snaked down his arms when Nyel said his name.

They talked briefly, and Nyel seemed genuinely interested in attending the festival. But his friend, in typical Atreus fashion, was determined to be a wet blanket and tried to get out of it. Luckily, Marina's arrival saved Leo from making even more of a fool of himself. The red-headed wonder took the two men, leaving him alone to finish the work on the docks.

He needed the breathing room.

Of course, today. Today, of all days, is when he'd show up.

Leo hadn't reacted to another man like that in... well, a very long time. The last boy he'd crushed on had been Pacco PiaCheli. They were childhood friends, and when they got older, Leo had to sort through a tangled mess of feelings. And when Pacco kissed him for the first and last time, Leo recognized what he was. There wasn't a doubt in his mind where his heart lay and what he wanted. And, news flash, girls weren't on the list. His mother would be broken-hearted, and as for his father—Leo didn't have to consider it. That reality didn't exist for him; he had too many responsibilities. Too many beating hearts depending on him.

All they need is for their eldest son to come out as a sodomite.

That would likely be the final nail in the Tradi family's coffin—the same coffin Leo was desperately trying to keep them out of. No, even if relationships were on the table, the world would never accept him. Real men liked women. A man who wanted to be with another man? There was no doubt in Leo's mind that he'd be considered "less than," and that was putting it lightly.

Pacco kissed him and was gone. The PiaCheli family left Baia Vita for the mainland in the hope of finding work. Leo never saw or heard from him again. And that was fine by him. He didn't need the distraction. Didn't need to add temptation on top of everything else he was dealing with. He refused to allow Nyel to become a problem for him. Even if Nyel returned his desires, even if he wasn't the sole provider for his family, Baia Vita would never accept it.

And Baia Vita was his home, whether Leo liked it or not.

Maybe on the mainland, they think differently.

He quickly shook himself, picking up a heavy load of fish, allowing the burning in his back and dizziness in his head to distract him. Ideas like that were pointless. Baia Vita was where his family was. Where he was needed. There wasn't any room for fantasies about another life. This was the hand he'd been dealt. Now, he had to play.

"Play with a deck missing half the damn cards," he mumbled, grunting as he set down the heavy load.

He'd figure it out.

He had to.

MOST OF THE fishing boats docked early for the day. The catches were so meager they couldn't justify the fuel for more than a couple rounds of netting. It was just as well; the *Vino Rosso* would never catch another fish in her life. Probably best she was now resting at the bottom of the sea rather than witnessing the fall of Baia Vita.

We're disappearing.

And Leo's family would be the first to vanish.

As the sun dipped behind flat rooftops, Leo rounded the corner and heard a familiar gravelly voice. But before Leo could call out to his father, a second voice spoke. Leo ducked behind a wall, listening hard.

"You've made the right choice, *Signore* Tradi."

"I hope our working relationship remains fruitful for us both, *Signore* Vincenzo," his father wheezed.

Leo's heart dropped, and if he had not already been leaning against the stone, he would have wobbled.

Vincenzo?

No. His father didn't just...

Leo darted from behind his corner, needing his eyes to confirm what his ears told him. And there they were. His father, worn like an old piece of leather, leaning heavily on his cane with bloodshot eyes. And standing above him like a vulture ready to descend on the dead was Alvise Vincenzo. He wore black pants and a halfway unbuttoned white collared shirt that revealed a thick gold necklace resting on his smooth chest. His piercing blue eyes caught Leo like a fish in a gill net.

"The mighty fisherman joins us," he greeted Leo. "Your father has made a very good investment."

Leo turned to his dad. "What have you done?"

Thomasso Tradi looked on the verge of collapsing as he opened his mouth to speak. "I've taken out a lease on a new boat with *Signore* Vincenzo. We've come to an agreement."

No.

No. No. No.

Leo wanted to shout at his father, to beg him to take it back. But the triumphant twist at the edge of Alvise's mouth told him it was too late. What was done was done.

"I'm sure you'll have much better luck on one of my boats than your last—vessel," he said like he hardly considered their rust bucket worthy of the title.

Leo's throat tightened. He knew what this meant. And so did his father.

Alvise sauntered to him, shoes too shiny in the dim light. He leaned close as he passed. "I'll be seeing you around a lot more, my pet."

And he was gone, leaving Leo alone in the alley with his father. Seconds ticked by like hours.

"Why?" he rasped, his eyes stinging. "You know what that man is."

"I'm sorry, Leofel. But it's what we have to do."

Leo knew this was their last option. He knew that, given time, he'd likely have come to the same conclusion. Still, he hated his father for it. Hated him for being so old. For leaving the burden of a large family resting on Leo's shoulders.

His thoughts must have shown on his face because when his father spoke again, his voice was more hoarse and broken than ever. "You probably hate me, and I cannot blame you. And if you ran away from all this, if you took the next barge to the mainland and never looked back, I also wouldn't blame you."

Leo had to swallow the profanity that rested on his tongue. He locked onto the black shark tooth hanging from his father's neck. The tooth itself wasn't extraordinary, but his grandmother had woven the leather into a beautifully braided cord. What did his father do to deserve that honor? Leo never heard the story, no matter how many times he'd asked for it. Probably because it was so underwhelming, his father was ashamed.

And now, here Leo was, definitely old enough to be considered a man, yet no tooth rested on his chest. Had he not earned the right to have it around his neck? Was providing for their family since he was big enough to hoist a net not enough?

And now, his spineless father had the gall to suggest Leo would abandon them.

"How dare you?" Leo hissed. "How dare you even say that?"

The image of long curly strands falling to the floor pierced his brain like an iron poker. Leo turned away, intending to stomp home and lock himself in his room. He paused.

"Don't come home. Stay with *Signore* Cicco again tonight. Make sure to drink enough for me, too." He walked away, leaving his father behind.

All night, blue eyes raked over Leo's body, appraising him like a pig at auction. The memory alone staved off sleep, dread rooting itself in every layer of his skin. Alvise tried once or twice before to coax Leo onto his 'guest list.' His collection of human pets who frolicked around his estate, wearing jewels and silks. Leo didn't know if it was his golden hair or the unique shade of his eyes; all he knew was he'd caught the attention of the most dangerous man on the island.

Instead of giving him the shark-tooth necklace, his father helped Alvise slip a jewel-studded collar around Leo's neck.

Now, all he could do was wait for Vincenzo to pull on the leash.

WHEN SLEEP FINALLY ACCEPTED him in its hold, Leo dreamt of dark water and flashing lights in the sky. Of crunching metal and sinking into the abyss.

Smoke-filled eyes.

Green scales.

Claws and fangs.

Leo gasped awake, sweat rolling down the side of his face.

It'd been over a week since the accident, and still, he woke every morning this way.

I need to talk to someone about this. Get this idiotic idea out of my head.

There was only one person he could rattle off his nighttime delusions to. Leo quickly dressed, not bothering with the bandages on his head. He hardly felt dizzy anymore and didn't care if anyone saw the stitches. What Leo needed was to talk. For someone to tell him he was being crazy and put these visions of sea monsters to rest.

Was monster even the right word?

He didn't understand what his dreams were telling him. But *monster* didn't feel right. Because when he lost himself in that otherworldly face, Leo wasn't scared.

"Nyel, is Atreus around?" Leo hollered up the hill to the sorting bins.

"I saw him walk to the beach, probably taking a break. Everything, okay?" Nyel shouted back, and Leo snorted in his effort to hold back a laugh. Nyel had the newspaper stuffed up his nose again, and he sounded like a duck with a head cold.

"Yeah, it's all good, just want to talk to him."

All week, Leo had done everything in his power to stay away from Nyel. But the odd jobs he'd managed to scrape usually involved dirty work on the docks; thus, he and Nyel saw a lot of each other.

He was kind.

Kind in an innocent way that called Leo in, like a lighthouse beacon guiding his ship to port. There was something about him. Maybe his eyes? The golden flecks mixed in a background of honey brown were familiar in a way Leo couldn't explain.

He tried not to ponder it as he searched the shoreline. Finding Atreus's footprints in the sand, he jogged, spotting his friend right away.

"Hey, Atreus, I've been meaning to talk to you," Leo said, then spotted a second figure. A dangerous tension pulled at the air, and the wind fell still between the two men as they stared off at one another. The stranger was tall and built like a warhorse. A hood covered the majority of his face, but Leo was able to spot one detail —a single milky eye.

"Leo, I'll meet you at the docks in a minute," Atreus said, and the warning in his voice only made Leo plant his feet. He wasn't about to leave Atreus with this guy, whoever he was.

But it didn't come to that because the stranger turned on his heel and was gone behind the rocks in seconds.

"What the hell was that about?" Leo asked, unable to shake the palpable heaviness in the air.

"Nothing. What's up?" Atreus asked, letting out a too-long breath as though he'd been too afraid to release it.

Leo didn't bother to push. When Atreus wasn't ready to talk about something, nothing Leo could do or say would get him to budge. The man could hold a secret.

"I, uh, just wanted to vent some stuff. It's stupid, and you're obviously busy."

"No. No. Let's sit. I could use a distraction," Atreus said, plopping in the sand.

Leo joined him. "It's really dumb."

"But you're going to tell me anyway."

"Yeah. Yeah, I am."

Atreus waited, ready to listen.

"Do you believe in, like, sea monsters?"

"Sea monsters?"

"Well, kinda." Leo tried to piece together his memories and paint a cohesive picture. "Not like underwater dragons and shit, more like —sea people?"

"Mermaids?"

"I think?"

"Like the statue in the square?" Atreus offered.

"Not exactly, but kind of?"

Leo didn't know what he expected from his friend, but watching Atreus drop his head in defeat wasn't it.

"What?"

"Nothing. It's just... man, I can't catch a break."

Leo didn't know what he meant by that so he continued.

"When I got caught in that storm, and the *Vino Rosso* capsized, I was thrown into the water, and I... I think something saved me. Someone?"

Leo recounted the series of events exactly as he remembered them—or at least as he believed he remembered. At this point, he wasn't sure what his mind was making up to fill the gaps. Then, he told Atreus about his dreams. "And well, that's it. Stupid, I know."

"It's not stupid, but..." Atreus paused, carefully choosing his words. "You went through something and you're trying to make sense of it."

"I'm not making this up," Leo pleaded.

"I never said you were. Your mind can play tricks on you. You're still processing."

Leo rubbed the stitches on his head. They were healing, thank god, but Leo didn't think he'd ever get used to the tightness on his scalp.

"You're stressed, Leo," Atreus said. "Let this vision, or whatever it is, go. You've already got enough on your plate."

"It's hard to let go when it feels so real."

"Real or not, it's not doing you any good. I'm saying it's a lot for you to handle right now."

"And I'm handling it just fine," Leo snapped. He groaned and rubbed his eyes with the heels of his hands. "Sorry."

"No need."

Atreus was a good friend, better than Leo deserved. Still, Leo hated that Atreus knew just how dire his situation was. Hated the way his friend's eyes narrowed with pity. Hated that the boy he'd known since he was ten years old never once offered to take him to the mainland in the winter.

That's not what this is about.

Atreus released a long sigh. "Leo, if you need some help, my wages are more than enough for my needs—"

"Stop," Leo interrupted. "Just stop."

Atreus chewed his lip but said nothing else.

"Be straight with me," Leo said, turning his body to face Atreus fully. "Do you think I'm crazy? Do you think I'm losing it?"

"I never said you were crazy, Leo; you're taking on too much—"

"Do you think it's all in my head? The... the creature I saw?" Even as Leo asked, he dreaded the answer. How could something that felt so real be a dream and not a memory? How could he still smell the creature's briny scent? Feel the cold press of its scales? Taste of ocean spray on his lips...

A flicker of indecision flashed in Atreus's eyes, but it vanished in less than a second."It's in your head, Leo. Let it go."

Leo relaxed back into the sand, head bent low. "You're probably right," he said, though he couldn't keep the defeated inflection from his voice.

Atreus reached over and shook him. "Hey, it's gonna be alright. You hear?"

Leo nodded. "Yeah. I hear you. Thanks for listening."

"That's what friends are for, right?" Atreus said, slapping him on the shoulder.

Leo stayed on the beach even after Atreus returned to work. Soon, he'd be back on the water, on a new boat, doing what he did best: working the bay and providing for his family. He didn't think about what Alvise expected in return. He couldn't. Not yet. That reality would surely come for him all too soon.

Instead, he let his mind wander as the waves lapped at the sand. The sea foam collected at his feet, and he watched the bubbles pop until nothing remained but a milky swirl.

Merpeople don't exist.

Atreus said exactly what Leo needed to hear.

Yet, a small part of him had hoped for a different answer.

CHAPTER 12

ATREUS

Atreus lay on his bed, eyes open, staring at the bedroom ceiling. The wooden boards were warped, creating gaps between them. Some of the gaps were host to old spiderwebs, their owners long gone. He wondered where they went. If they had big spider families to return to. In all likelihood, they were dead, leaving behind nothing but a few cobwebs.

"You should have been killed as a babe."

That's what the stranger on the beach said. That was the fate of those born like him. A mutt. An unwanted bastard child.

"Halfling."

The word sliced through him, making the corners of his eyes burn. All his life, he'd been plagued by the same question.

Why?

Why did he and his father live separately from others?

Why did the villagers in Corallina hate him?

Why did his father ultimately leave?

Atreus never got the answer; never knew why he was so hated. But in a span of seconds, all those questions were answered— thrown at him with about as much care as a butcher tossing fish guts.

He rolled over, tearing his eyes away from the abandoned web. The bed felt hard despite the mattress. He had the urge to sneak out, run to the beach, and dive into the waves. He'd never gone this long without *Marvassa* changing him.

"Unmasking the freak hiding beneath human skin."

The voice sneered, using its words like a blade; it was dissecting him, peeling away Atreus's defenses to expose the raw truth he feared others would see. That Nyel would see.

It'd been more active since his world was turned upside down.

Reminding him.

Taunting him.

"He left because you're nothing but a disgrace. You should've been snuffed out as a baby—every breath you take is a waste."

Shut up!

Atreus slammed the pillow over his head as though that could silence the voice. But there was no escaping the cavities cracking open in his mind.

> *"Nyel will leave you.*
> *Just like everyone else."*

Atreus took calming breaths, trying to fight away the rising panic. Would Nyel leave? Atreus had made efforts to be nicer to him. But was that enough?

> *"Of course not. A few sweet*
> *words could never mask*
> *the stench of you."*

The memory of his first encounter with Nyel came back with full force. The one when they were children. Nyel's expression was permanently scarred into his mind, no matter how hard Atreus tried to blink it away.

"Halfling Mutt! You keep your infections away from us!"

That's what Nyel's mother had yelled. Back then, he didn't know what it meant. Now he did. And so would Nyel.

I'm not mad. I'm not crazy. I'm not dangerous.

Atreus chanted the words in his mind over and over.

> *"Are you not?"*

It mocked him, its tone dripping with sadistic glee.

> *"Are you not mad?*
> *With me in your head?*

Am I the Skraith in your soul?"

Shut up.

No matter how hard Atreus tried to silence it, the voice berated him all night. Just as it had countless other nights since his father left.

When things were good, it went quiet, and Atreus could almost forget it was there. But the moment his defenses crumbled, it returned.

It always returned.

Atreus rolled his left shoulder, trying to work out the pain in his back.

He imagined the old scar tissue tugging and pulling his skin. Puncturing his muscles. Scraping against bone. It throbbed despite the wound being a decade old. It was a phantom pain, all in his head. It was nothing but a scar on his back now. Yet tonight... it hurt. It hurt, and Atreus was half convinced that if he rolled over, his sheets would be stained with blood.

ATREUS WALKED through a field of wildflowers, their glow harsh and white against the surrounding gloom. The light wasn't warm or inviting—it was cold, so bright it hurt to look at for long. Their eerie luminescence was the only thing that existed in the endless void. No stars. No horizon. Just oppressive darkness. The diamond-shaped petals stirred a sense of nostalgia Atreus couldn't catch. He stepped around them carefully, unable to crush even a single bloom, as if breaking one would shatter the fragile glass casing of memories he wasn't ready to face.

But something wasn't right.

With every step, the air grew heavier. A prickling sensation crawled up Atreus's spine, and his heart pounded in his chest. He tried to shake it off, focusing on the glowing petals. The buds swayed to and fro, though there was no wind. The feeling gnawed at him as he sensed movement beneath his feet—something below.

He glanced back, knowing he'd see nothing. The nameless flowers danced innocently under his gaze. Still, he felt it. The ground pulsed beneath him as if something deep down was stirring. His steps quickened, fear bubbling in his throat.

Suddenly, the earth trembled.

A soft rumbling, like a beast shifting beneath the soil, sent the flowers quivering. Atreus broke into a run, his feet slamming into the soft earth as the ground beneath him rippled with every stride.

The rumbling grew louder. Faster.

He felt it, whatever it was, chasing him—hungry, savage, unseen, and terrifyingly close. His legs pumped faster. Each step felt more uncertain, the ground growing softer, threatening to give way.

The glow of the flowers was no longer comforting. It illuminated the terror—the closeness of the thing below, the thing that would soon drag him under. He tried to scream, but the sound died before it left his lips.

A crack split the ground. The earth shifted violently as something below finally caught up, ready to pull him under.

Fleshy white vines burst from the soil, reaching for him. Their thorns cut into his skin as they coiled around his ankles, dragging him through the wildflowers. Atreus cried out, his fingers clawing at the petals, ripping them from their roots. For a moment, they shimmered in defiance—beautiful and useless—before the glow faded, the petals turning black and crumbling to ash in his fingers.

They never offered any help.

They didn't back then.

They didn't save *her*.

And now, they would do nothing to save him.

The vines tightened, winding around his calves, thorns digging deeper with every pull. The ground split, revealing a yawning pit.

It was going to take him. He couldn't escape. He couldn't breathe. He couldn't—

The voice came, low and menacing, like an echo from the earth.

"You are mine."

"ATREUS! ATREUS, WAKE UP!"

It wasn't the sinister voice from the pit. It was...

The whispering tide.

The sighing swell of water.

The gentle murmuring of the sea.

It pulled him away from the blackness.

"Atreus!" It was louder now, more urgent. "Wake up!"

Atreus shot up in bed, drenched in sweat, heart racing so fast he might choke on it. His hands flew to his ankles, frantically searching for the fleshy white vines, expecting the sharp sting of thorns. But his fingers only met smooth skin.

No vines. No thorns. No blood.

Atreus blinked rapidly, disoriented, still half in the dream, running from the tendrils. His breath came in ragged gasps, his body trembling as the nightmare refused to release its hold. He barely noticed Nyel kneeling beside him, brow furrowed, his hand resting on Atreus's shoulder.

"Atreus."

Soft as the gentle hiss of seafoam. Churning currents. Rippling waves. That voice, saying his name, banished the last of the nightmare. He looked into Nyel's micah-filled eyes.

"Are you okay? You were thrashing really bad."

Atreus dragged a shaky hand over his face, trying to grasp some semblance of composure. "A bad dream. That's all."

Nyel's hand rested steadily on his shoulder, the touch grounding, even as he likely felt the faint tremor running through Atreus's body.

"You were thrashing so loud. I thought someone was—" He hesitated, his grip tightening as if to reassure himself Atreus was still there. "I thought someone was hurting you. For being a Mer. I was afraid it was all my fault."

"Then why the hell did you rush in?" Atreus rasped.

"Well, I—I couldn't just let them... I wasn't going to let someone hurt you."

Atreus stilled as Nyel's words slowly sunk in. Nyel believed someone had come to kill him for being Mer. Yet Nyel had come to save him, ready to throw himself into danger. A lump tightened in Atreus's throat.

And I told him I would watch the humans tear him apart if it came to it.

Atreus looked up, meeting Nyel's gaze for the first time. Nyel's face was earnest, his hair tousled from sleep. Atreus's usual annoyance and irritation for the *sireno* was absent. Instead, he felt something warmer, something far more unsettling.

"I'm fine," Atreus muttered, though his voice still trembled. "It's just... it was nothing."

"It didn't seem like nothing," Nyel said, his hand sliding from Atreus's shoulder to rest on his arm.

Atreus's first instinct was to pull away, to shrug off the concern and retreat from the contact. He wasn't a *touchy* person. But something stopped him. There was a warmth in Nyel's touch, a comfort that Atreus hadn't expected. It had been so long since anyone saw him this vulnerable...and chose to stay.

The room was silent, save for the steady rise and fall of their breathing. Slowly, Atreus allowed himself to relax, sinking back against the pillows. He didn't pull away from Nyel. Instead, he found himself studying the young Mer's face illuminated by the yellow glow of the street lamp leaking through the window—the lines of worry etched into his smooth skin, the earnest concern in those eyes.

"I know you said we were friends, but..." Nyel's voice was barely above a whisper. "I know you want me gone."

Atreus hesitated. He had wanted that—he'd spent days trying to push Nyel away, to shake off the burden of him. But right now, with Nyel sitting beside him, his presence felt like anything but a burden.

"I did," Atreus admitted.

Nyel's eyes widened, a flicker of hope sparking at his use of the past tense. "I'm not here to make your life harder," he said genuinely. "I just... I didn't want to be alone either."

For the first time, Atreus wondered if there was more than one type of 'alone.' That, even surrounded by family, Nyel was isolated. Suddenly, Atreus didn't feel annoyed, didn't feel the urge to push the *sireno* away. He felt something else—something he couldn't quite name. Maybe it was trust.

"Thanks for waking me," Atreus said gruffly, "I'm good now."

Nyel's hand lingered on his arm for a moment longer before he pulled away, a soft smile tugging at his lips.

"You don't have to thank me," he replied. "As you know, I'm not going anywhere."

And for once, Atreus found that he didn't mind.

"ATTY, ARE YOU LISTENING?"

"Huh?"

Marina rolled her eyes. "I said lift it higher; the left side is crooked."

"Oh, right."

Atreus was practically sleepwalking. He didn't sleep again after the nightmare woke him, making him sluggish on top of being distracted. He lifted the banner higher.

"Perfect. Nail it right there," Marina instructed, and Atreus did as he was told. They were hanging the banner the three of them painted for the Bayallon sign-ups. Tonight, when the festival was in full swing, kids would flock to sign up for the race. Marina put a lot of time and effort into making sure the display was perfect. The least Atreus could do was pay attention.

"Good?" he called once the nail was in.

"You got it. Come down and help me with the rest."

Atreus descended the ladder just as Nyel ran to join them, a stack of fliers in his arms.

"We have some leftover. What should I do with them?" Nyel asked. Marina had sent him all over Baia Vita to hand out fliers to local businesses, reminding them of the Bayallon and encouraging kids to sign up.

"Start handing them out!" Marina clapped.

"Like, randomly?"

"Yep! Anyone and everyone needs to hear about this. This is gonna be the best Bayallon in years." She pointed to a man sitting on a bench, reading the paper. "That guy right there, go get 'em," Marina said, shoving Nyel in his direction.

"I'm not sure that's—" Atreus began.

"I'll stay in town, promise," Nyel said with a reassuring smile and took off.

The *sireno* had grown more confident in his time on the island, and Atreus wasn't as nervous about letting him go off on his own. Still, he liked to keep Nyel close. He'd grown used to his company and—

"He will leave you.
Like they all do in the end."

"Nyel's really good at this sorta thing, isn't he?" Marina said.

"Huh?"

"Are you even awake? What's up with you today?"

Atreus shook his head. "Nothing. Didn't sleep."

"Well, which is it?" she demanded, hands on her hips.

"Both. Neither. Anyways, what about Nyel?"

She eyed him but continued. "Well, look at him! He's so excited. Honestly, I'm glad he's around."

They watched as Nyel approached person after person, giving them a flier. Every single one of them walked away with a flier and a smile.

"Yeah, he's great."

"Sounds like he's sticking around too. He feels like he belongs here, you know? Like he was our hidden missing piece."

"He does," Atreus managed to say through the tightness in his throat.

"I wonder if he's got anyone."

Atreus's neck stiffened so quickly it sent a sharp twang through his spine. "He has a girlfriend," he blurted.

Marina turned to him, one eyebrow raised. "I meant I wonder if he's got any family. He doesn't talk about it much."

"Oh," Atreus said, unable to look at her.

"And how do you know he has a girlfriend?"

"He's mentioned something. I don't remember exactly."

It wasn't a complete lie. He remembered Nyel mentioning his parents trying to set him up with a girl. But that didn't explain why he jumped to tell Marina.

"Right. Well, anyway, I'd better get some chairs. Hopefully, I'll be stuck at this booth for a while taking sign-ups."

She skipped away, leaving him to watch Nyel go from stranger to stranger, looking more at home than Atreus ever had.

A jolt of clarity shook his chest as he finally pieced together the nameless feelings that paraded in his chest every time he thought of the *sireno*. He'd been alone for so long that he'd forgotten what it felt like to want someone to stay.

And now, he was finally admitting it to himself.

I...don't want him to go.

CHAPTER 13

ATREUS

The sky blushed with molten hues as the sun set over Baia Vita. The island stirred, coming alive with an energy that buzzed in the air like the hum of cicadas. Strings of lanterns criss-crossed the square and stretched between buildings, their flickering light dappling the cobblestones in hues of amber and crimson. The golden glow climbed the hill to illuminate the island's only wind-mill, its weathered blades turning lazily in the summer breeze. Laughter spilled from every corner, carried on the scent of roasting hazelnuts and citrusy wine. Booths and stalls lined the square, each overflowing with an array of treasures: meats glistening with juices, candies wrapped in jewel-bright paper, fruits so ripe their sweetness mingled with the aroma of sugar-filled pastries. Other vendors sold handmade soaps, glittering jewelry, and finely stitched clothes.

A kaleidoscope of colors and sounds wove together in a timeless tapestry. Boisterous melodies from fiddles and accordions tangled in the cool evening breeze as dancers swirled, their skirts snapping like waves against the shore. Children darted between booths, sparklers crackling in their hands, their sticky fingers leaving traces of frosting on their clothes. The laughter of old folks, already deep into their wine glasses, rose above the music, blending with the rhythmic stomp of feet.

Baia Vita wasn't just alive—it was a symphony of hearts beating as one. The very sands spoke, and they all said the same thing.

We are here.

For one night, everyone could forget about the fishing vessels that prowled outside the bay. For one night, they could forget about their dying town and just be. Atreus wanted nothing more than for this feeling to last all season.

Normally, Atreus would spend this night in his lighthouse, barely catching the distant echoes of music. But tonight...tonight he would be here, amongst the people, the humans that permanently took up residence in his heart.

Even if he'd never be one of them. Never feel the lifeblood of the island flow in his veins. Not like they did.

"An imposter."

"Are you coming?" Nyel urged by the front door. He was buzzing, waiting about as patiently as a pup on a lead. "The sun is down; that means it's started, right?"

An irrepressible grin intruded on Atreus's lips, despite his best efforts to force it away.

They'd dressed in their 'nicest' clothes, which meant the ones with the fewest holes. Atreus was in a cream long-sleeved button-down and tan dress pants. Nyel sported a short-sleeved orange collared shirt that he left unbuttoned to reveal a white undershirt with blue jeans that were obviously too big for his slight frame.

"Coming, coming," Atreus said, reluctantly slipping on his shoes. He and Nyel walked side by side, the music growing louder with each step.

"Oh wow," Nyel said breathlessly as the lights glistened in his eyes.

Even for Atreus, who was familiar with human celebrations, it was overwhelming: the sounds, the lights, and the mouthwatering smells.

"Look, look!" Nyel dashed to the nearest stall, mouth open at the tiny ornamental glass animals.

"What's that?"

Atreus barely caught up when Nyel was off again. The crowd jostled around them; nearly the entire island's population gathered in the main square.

"Hey, wait up," Atreus called as sardine-packed bodies separated them. He lost sight of Nyel and was about to call out when a light pressure wrapped around his wrist.

Atreus froze, his gaze snapping to the point of contact before tracing the arm to a face radiating joy so loud that it cut through all sound, all sense, until it was just... him. Nyel held Atreus—steady and unbothered, as if it were the most natural thing in the world.

"Come on, slow-poke," Nyel said, dragging him to the booth selling candied strawberries.

Atreus followed, overwhelmed by the sensation yet unwilling to pull away, drawn forward by the quiet comfort in Nyel's touch.

They went from stall to stall, Nyel's hand sliding from Atreus's wrist and cupping their palms together to prevent them from being separated. Atreus hardly noticed the goods for sale. He was captivated by the awe in Nyel's eyes, the way they lit up with every new discovery. The light caught the golden flecks, shimmering like coins tossed into a fountain.

Atreus couldn't look away.

The crowd thinned as they moved through the square, finally stopping at a stall selling fruit tarts. He was still holding Nyel's hand.

It's so much smaller than mine.

Atreus ran his thumb along the delicate digits before he realized what he was doing. He let go quickly, but Nyel was too engrossed in the tarts to notice. He spoke to the woman behind the booth.

"Which one of these has *sugar* in it?"

Atreus grinned at the befuddled expression on the woman's face.

"Here, you'd like this one," he said, picking a peach tart from the bunch and placing it in Nyel's hand. He also bought a strawberry tart and placed the paper-wrapped treat in his pocket. Handing the woman a few coins, he led Nyel to a nearby bench to enjoy his treat.

Only when they were seated did Nyel stop admiring the delicate cup of custard and fruit.

"I have coins. I could have bought it."

Atreus waved a hand. "You'll get the next one. Take a bite."

Nyel brought the tart to his mouth and bit into it. His shoulders slumped, and a flush crept into his cheeks. "Mmmm, it's so good," he said through a full mouth. "Here, try." He held out the tart.

Atreus's first instinct was to crinkle his nose in disgust at the sickeningly sweet treat. But with Nyel holding it out to him, the offer lingered between them like an unfinished cadence, and he was tempted to lean in and take a bite.

But he cleared his throat, swallowing. "I'll pass."

"You don't like sugar?"

Atreus shook his head. "Not a sweets kind of guy."

"I don't know how you've been here so long and don't like it. Sugar is my favorite human food."

Atreus chuckled as he stretched his legs, hating how his toes felt trapped, like they were encased in a coffin. He really hated shoes.

"Why did you buy the second one then?" Nyel asked through a mouthful.

"For Marina. I can guarantee she's so busy at her booth, she won't get to see much of the festival. She deserves a treat for all the work she's putting in."

"That's so nice of you. I didn't even think about that," Nyel praised.

"It's in my best interest to keep that girl happy. Otherwise, she drives me nuts."

"I think you just have a soft spot for her," Nyel teased. "Who knew you were such a softie?"

"Okay, let's not get carried away. She's my boss's daughter. I like to stay in her good graces," Atreus said, even though the idea hadn't even crossed his mind when he made the purchase.

"Whatever you say," Nyel said, shoving the rest of the tart in his mouth.

They continued moving up and down the rows, keeping their coins to themselves except for a little glass turtle that Nyel couldn't resist.

"I want one of those. I see all the fishermen wearing them." Nyel said, pointing to a stall selling fossilized shark's teeth.

"It's not something you can buy for yourself," Atreus said with a hint of longing.

"Why not?"

"Someone has to give it to you. It has to be earned."

"How?"

"It's different for everyone. Traditionally, it's passed from father to son."

"Oh." Nyel admired it a moment longer, and Atreus sensed he wanted to ask more questions, but a booth with bright neon lights stole his attention. "What does that one say?"

Atreus squinted at the sign and recognized the 'B' as the first letter, but couldn't make fins or tails of the rest. He took a guess based on what lay behind the ticket counter.

"It says *Bocce*. It's a game."

Atreus guessed as much since behind the sign were several strips of grass surrounded on three sides by wooden boards. Two girls played on the strip nearest to them, and the balls clacked against one another with a soft 'crack' followed by either cheers or groans.

"I wanna play," Nyel said.

"Go ahead, dear. The last pair just finished," said the old woman managing the game. She handed Nyel a bag filled with *Bocce* balls before returning to her needlepoint.

"C'mon, I'll show you," Atreus said, once again smiling at Nyel's confused expression.

He divided the balls into three groups: Nyel was green, Atreus was purple, and the single white ball, the *pallino*, stood alone. Atreus tossed the *pallino*, and it rolled to the center of the course.

"Alright, so here is the basic idea," he began, showing Nyel how to toss the ball onto the grass. The goal was to roll as many balls as possible close to the *pallino*. The person with the balls closest to the *pallino* was awarded points before the board was reset. Having your ball hit any of the wooden barriers disqualified that ball from play. Atreus explained the strategy of trying to hit the *pallino* closer to your balls and knocking the opponent's balls out of the way. "You got all that?"

"I think so," Nyel said, taking an interesting stance. He stood ramrod straight, holding the ball high above his shoulder.

"You're gonna throw it off the strip doing that," Atreus said, stopping him before he hurt someone. "Like this."

He crouched over Nyel, cupping the hand with the ball and guiding it closer to the ground, helping him adopt more of a bowler's stance.

"Now bend your knees a little. There you go. And it's a gentle toss. Go back and forth a few times. Get used to the weight," he said, making the motion along with Nyel.

"G-got it."

Atreus leaped away as Nyel's breath shuddered against his chest, the warmth of his back lingering like a brand. He cleared his throat. "You got it. Go ahead."

Nyel lobbed the ball, and it rolled within an inch or two of the *pallino* before coming to a halt.

"That's a point!" he cheered. "Right?"

"Only if I don't knock it out of the way, but yes." Atreus took his ball and copied the move with an easy throw, knocking Nyel's green one away. "Now I canceled yours out."

Nyel glared. "Oh, that's how it's gonna be."

They went back and forth, making points and canceling them. In the final round, Nyel's last throw knocked one of Atreus's balls away from the *pallino*, bumping it into the border and disqualifying it.

"I win! Take that," Nyel cheered.

"Beginners' luck," Atreus teased.

"I don't know; that looked like pure technique to me," a voice said from behind them.

Leo jogged forward, his partially unbuttoned dress shirt loose-fitting with the sleeves rolled to his elbows. There were dark circles under his eyes, but few would notice because of the brilliant smile acting as a mask.

"Mind if I play the victor?"

"Go ahead," Atreus said, stepping aside.

As Leo picked up his first ball, a woman with a group of curly blond kids walked past.

"Good luck, Leofel. Don't be too late."

"You got it, Ma," Leo said, waving to Emelia. Atreus did a double-take, certain that Leo's sister had much longer hair than the last time he saw her.

"Your name is Leofel?" Nyel asked.

"That's the full name. But only my parents get to call me that," he replied with a wink.

"I like it. It's pretty."

Leo smiled. "How about we make a bet? If you win, you can call me by my full name. Deal?"

"And if you win?" Nyel asked.

"I'm sure I can come up with something."

Atreus clenched his fists, resisting the urge to point out that Leo never offered to let *him* use his full name.

Why does it matter?

He shook off the unbidden irritation and watched the match from the side.

"I'm game," Nyel said. "Don't expect me to go easy on you."

"Oh, I'm counting on it," Leo said, flashing his signature smile.

Atreus didn't care for the way Nyel returned the gesture. The game took far too long, filled with endless high-fives and snarky trash talk. Neither pulled too far ahead in points, despite Nyel tossing his ball out of bounds twice. Atreus suspected Leo was intentionally missing points, and that irritated the hell out of him. After what felt like the entire night, the game finally ended, with Nyel winning by a hair.

"Great game. You're a natural," Leo said, patting Nyel on the shoulder.

"It was fun. Thanks for the match, Leofel," Nyel said, emphasizing the full name. "Are we only allowed to play during the festival?"

"Not at all. We can play anytime." Leo said, again touching Nyel's arm, "My folks have an old beat-up set behind the house. Come by sometime for a rematch."

"Hey, Nyel, didn't you want to see the booth selling belts?" Atreus interrupted.

"That's a good idea. Half my pants don't fit, and I'm tired of using the rope to keep them up." He pulled up his too-big jeans for emphasis.

"I'll tag along," Leo said, and Atreus bit the inside of his cheek as he quickly fell to the back, the other two taking the lead and talking animatedly.

On their way, they paused at Marina's Bayallon booth but could only manage a quick wave as she was swarmed by kids eager to sign up.

"Looks like a good turnout. Should be a fun race," Leo remarked.

"I can't wait to see it. Especially the 'bike' part. I've never been on a bike," Nyel said.

"Never been on a bike? Well, I'll have to do something about that," Leo said, his hand once again finding its way to Nyel's shoulder.

And for the first time in his life, Atreus wanted to smack that smile off his face. When they arrived at the booth selling leather belts, it quickly became clear that Nyel was far too short on coins to afford one.

"It's okay," Nyel said, noting the price. "I'll save up, and the rope works fine for now."

"I'm sorry you couldn't get one. Did you get anything else cool?" Leo asked.

"Yeah, check this out." Nyel pulled the small glass turtle from his back pocket and held it in the palm of his hand.

"How pretty. Let me get a closer look." Instead of taking the turtle, Leo cupped Nyel's hand, bringing it close to his face. "That's a neat one. Good find."

"Right? I like the way it sparkles inside."

"I just remembered something. You two keep going," Atreus said, his voice harsher than he intended.

He didn't wait for a response before shoving through the crowd, earning a few displeased glares. He had to get away from those two. What was wrong with him? Why was his best friend pissing him off so much?

And why does he keep touching Nyel?

It shouldn't matter. They were simple gestures. Humans touched to communicate all the time. So why did it make Atreus want to hit something?

Nyel doesn't owe me a damn thing. He isn't obligated to spend all his time with me.

But with the chance of Nyel leaving, Atreus wanted to keep the *sireno* all to himself.

Which was stupid.

"He'd sooner trust a human than a halfling."

Atreus ground his teeth, his feet wandering wherever they wished. He hardly noticed that he'd left the square and was pacing up and down random backstreets. But he couldn't shake the truth. Nyel was perfectly at ease among humans now.

"And yet he'd turn and run from a freak like you."

"Stop talking."

"You're mad. Talking to yourself like that.
What would Nyel think?
Maybe that stranger was right.
Maybe I am your Skraith."

"Shut up!" Atreus yelled, nearly tripping as his shoe sank into the damp sand. He blinked, the faint glimmer of moonlight illuminating the gentle push and pull of the water. Without thinking, he'd walked to the beach, his subconscious taking over, trying to lead him home.

Atreus kicked off his shoes, letting the cool sand soothe his bare feet. He had no reason to be this upset.

You're being stupid.

This time, he didn't know if it was 'the voice' or himself thinking the words.

It didn't matter.

He wasn't sure how long he stood on the shoreline—maybe only a couple of minutes or more— maybe he'd go to his lighthouse after all. Maybe he was better off alone—

Maybe I'm not meant to be with my own kind.

"You've always been an outcast.
It's in your nature."

What if I don't want to be alone anymore?

"It's not possible.
They'll hate you.
Fear you. Despise you."

Nyel doesn't hate me.

"Because you're a liar."

I'm not a liar.

*"You've been living a lie since the
moment you stepped on this island.
You'll always live in the shadows."*

Stop it. I don't want that.

"It's too late to change the tides of fate."

You don't know that.

*"Oh, but I do.
I know what you are, Atreus.
For I am you, and you are me."*

I'm nothing like you. I don't think like you.

*"You are me.
A freak.
A mutt."*

I'm not.

"Halfling. Bastard. Monster."

Stop it.

THE WORDS ECHOED, bouncing in a chasm of his own making, distorting and multiplying until they became a horde—a macabre choir whose sole purpose was to inflict insurmountable pain.

"It's your fault.
It's always been your fault.
You ruin everything you touch."

"STOP IT!" Atreus screamed, clutching his head as he dropped to his knees in the sand. The voice beat against his skull like a creature trying to claw through tissue and bone.

"PLEASE JUST STOP!"

BASTARD
Nobody wants you
FAILURE
disappear
VERMIN
DISAPPEAR
Defect
SCUM
Freak
SCUM
ALONE
Monster
SCUM
YOU'LL DIE
SKRAITH
HAVE BEEN
MUTT
ALONE
KILLED
SHOULD HAVE BEEN
FAILURE
SKRAITH
ABOMINATION
FREAK
Freak
MUTT
MONSTER
BASTARD
ALWAYS
ABANDONED
BRAT
KEEP YOUR SKRAITH AWAY
MUTT STAY ALONE
FILTH
AWAY
VERMIN
SCUM
ALONE
FROM US!
MONSTER
WANTS YOU
Defect
NOBODY
SCUM
STAY AWAY
SKRAITH
ALONE
DISAPPEAR
Freak
DISAPPEAR
Freak
MUTT
SKRAITH
ALONE
DEFECT

"Atreus?"

NYEL

Nyel knew this night would stay with him forever. The festival was a whirlwind of sights and sounds, a world so vibrant and alive it made every celebration he'd known before pale in comparison.

Everywhere he looked, something called for his attention, leaving him dizzy, unsure which way to run first. But more than the stalls of goods and food, the festival was about the people. For the first time since his arrival, Nyel saw who the villagers of Baia Vita truly were. The heavy lines on the fishermen's faces had softened, their defeated voices replaced with laughter, their weary sighs gone with the empty nets of yesterday. Baia Vita was more than just an island—it was a people, a way of life. And tonight, as their hearts beat in time with the push and pull of the tides, they were allowed to just *be*.

Men and women spun in the square and cheered over carnival games while children ran underfoot, screeching with delight. Nyel was sure he'd never seen this much joy in Corallina, even when their crop yields were good. His people, the *Sireni*, were too scared.

Scared of the world. Scared of the humans.

Maybe scared of themselves.

He thought of his parents, terrified to let *Marvassa* change their bodies.

They're missing so much.

With a pang, Nyel wished he could bring Sonia here. She'd love this. Guilt twisted his insides at the memory of his aunt.

The baby will be here soon.

Nyel should be there for her as the baby's due date approached. He should go back and tell his parents the truth—explain that he couldn't live the life they had so carefully laid out for him. That his existence couldn't revolve around a Lifebond and nothing else. He snorted, already imagining his mother's response.

"You only say that because you've never experienced it. You'll take back those words once you find the right girl."

But would the right girl ever come? He and Chel were very close, yet Nyel felt nothing. No sparks. No blossoming of light. Empty.

Maybe I'm just not built for a Lifebond.

The reality of being mate-less would kill his parents, with no hope of grandchildren. And even he had to admit, the idea of spending the rest of his life alone was depressing. Nyel wanted it—to have someone. But maybe not yet? Whenever he tried to settle with the idea of becoming Bonded, something always felt... off.

Maybe I'm just broken.

He jerked himself to the present, shoving the rest of the peach tart in his mouth. The sweetness made him giddy and more than a little buzzed with energy. He wanted to see it all. If this festival only happened twice a year, he wouldn't miss a second of it.

"What does that say?" Nyel asked, pointing to a bright green neon sign as he and Atreus explored the square.

"It says *Bocce*. It's a game."

Atreus had to explain the rules twice before Nyel finally got the picture. As he lined up his first throw, a hand grabbed his arm, stopping him mid-motion.

"You're gonna throw it off the strip doing that. Like this."

Suddenly, Atreus's chest pressed against Nyel's back. He guided Nyel to arch lower, bending with him as they swung their arms back and forth, testing the ball's weight.

"There you go."

Nyel felt more than heard the words as they rumbled through his back, down his spine, settling somewhere in his stomach.

"G-got it," Nyel stammered, overwhelmed by the scent flooding his senses.

The scent reminded him of the sky after a storm—crisp, charged, and alive—as if *Pygon*, the Spirit of the Sky, had swept through with torrential winds, washing away the old and welcoming the new. The comparison made Nyel's head swim, amplifying the strange, jittery feeling coursing through him.

At that moment, Atreus leapt back, and Nyel was both relieved and disappointed by the loss of contact. He blinked, forgetting that they were in the middle of a game.

Focus, you weirdo.

When Nyel landed his first roll directly on the board, a smirk twisted his lips.

"Lucky shot. Let's see if you can do that again." Atreus said, lining up his throw.

Nyel forgot to follow the ball as it flew through the air. He was too focused on Atreus's face. His friend was... off. The entire night, Atreus was like one of those human toys called a Yo-yo. Smiling and enjoying the festival for one minute, then tight-lipped and distant the next. As though he were constantly being reminded of something heavy.

We all have something heavy weighing us down.

But this felt different. Atreus was definitely bothered.

When Leo showed up and joined the game, Nyel thought for certain that his presence would lift Atreus's spirits. They'd known each other for years. How could Nyel compare to that? He was certain Atreus still half-hoped he would leave Baia Vita and never come back, a thought that made him sadder than he cared to admit.

However, Leo's presence only seemed to darken Atreus's mood, and Nyel couldn't understand why. Leo, or rather, Leofel, was perfectly pleasant the entire evening. The three of them should have had a great time.

So why?

"I just remembered something. You two keep going."

Before Nyel could ask him where he was going, Atreus pushed his way through the packed crowd.

"What's his problem?" Leofel asked, releasing Nyel's hand with the glass turtle.

"I don't know," he said, tucking his treasure in his pocket. "Should we go after him?"

"No. Atreus is a guy who likes his space. Just leave him to it; he'll come around." Leofel said confidently.

Nyel wasn't so sure. But wouldn't Leofel know better? Still, the nagging in Nyel's mind told him to go after Atreus—that this was something only *he* could help with. That right now, Atreus needed a fellow Mer.

Or maybe Nyel was kidding himself. Maybe he was searching for a deeper friendship, a deeper connection that simply didn't exist.

"Hey, wanna go try the darts? I bet you'd be good at—"

Leofel stopped mid-sentence as two burly men approached. They stood out from the crowd, seeming to part the tide of bodies without effort. People cast worried glances over their shoulders, hurrying away.

"You know what, I'll meet you at the darts in an hour," Leofel said, his charming tenor going serious.

"Are you sure?"

"Yeah, yeah," he said, trying to be casual, but Nyel saw the increasing worry in his yellow eyes. "I'll meet you there."

Before Nyel could say anything else, Leofel met the two men a few yards away. The music was too loud for Nyel to catch what they were saying, and a moment later, Leofel was herded away from the square—one man leading, the other pushing at his back. The interaction left Nyel uneasy as he stood alone, palms sweating, unsure of what to do.

Leofel had it handled. Nyel had no right to interfere in his business and would likely just get in the way. There was still so much he didn't know about humans. But there was a non-human he *could* help.

Nyel didn't hesitate this time. His gut told him to go after Atreus. Worst-case scenario, he'd tell Nyel to go away.

It took him less than a minute to lock onto Atreus's scent. It was distinct among the human scents of earth and oil. It was alive with shifting winds carrying the musky tang of rain. There was a wildness there, like the charge of an open sky before a crack of thunder. The scent clung to Atreus as if he'd just stepped from the swirling torrent —raw, brooding, and ominous. Nyel couldn't help but breathe deeper, the sensation both rejuvenating and suffused.

He zigzagged through the alleys until he reached the beach, where discarded shoes lay scattered and footprints etched a path in the sand. Nyel kicked off his own shoes, but a distant yell cut through the ocean's steady song of waves and foam, making him freeze.

Heart pounding, he dashed forward, following the sound until he spotted a lone figure kneeling in the sand. Atreus's shoulders trembled, his head bowed as fingers tore through his gorgeous curls, yanking hard enough to make Nyel flinch at the sight. Crumpled and unmoving, Atreus looked as though the weight of the world had driven him to his knees.

"Atreus?" Nyel called, quickening his pace, alarmed.

The sound of his name startled Atreus, snapping him out of whatever episode he'd been experiencing. He stood abruptly, swaying as if dizzy. As Nyel cautiously approached, Atreus stiffened but didn't turn. Nyel shivered, rubbing his arms up and down as he stood beside him. The air turned frigid this close to the sea, and he wished he'd brought a jacket.

"Atreus... what's going on? You've been off since yesterday."

Atreus said nothing, but Nyel knew he'd heard as he watched the muscles in his jaw flex.

"Please. Just talk to me."

So many moments passed that Nyel was convinced Atreus would continue ignoring him. But when he spoke, it sounded like a dam breaking, his voice spilling with pent-up frustration.

"How would you know if I'm off? You barely know me. We're practically strangers." The words were spoken softly but sent a biting cold through Nyel's chest.

"I... I just..." Nyel sighed. "I thought I did. Sorry."

Atreus let out a ragged sigh of his own. "Don't be. I haven't made it easy."

"No. You haven't."

A pause.

"I don't know how," Atreus confessed, tilting his head to the sky in self-deprecation.

That wasn't true. Atreus could be open; Nyel had seen glimpses of it. Moments so rare they burrowed into Nyel's brain like drops of water carving their way into stone. A flash of mirth as they laughed at the fountain, the flush of cheeks as Marina accosted him with a pillow, the half-hidden grin as Giovanni complimented his work. It was there. But Atreus held himself back, damning up his feelings like they were something shameful and unsightly. He built a wall around himself, shutting out everyone—just as he had with Leofel, Marina, and Giovanni.

And now me.

"I think you're scared."

At this, Atreus rounded on him, his shoulders stiff and his fists clenched.

"Can you blame me? I risk my life every time I step on this island. Every time I work at the docks. I'm risking everything *constantly*." The exhaustion in his voice sounded like a rope pulled taut for too long, fraying and ready to snap.

"You don't have to." Nyel steeled himself. If they were going to talk about this, then he would say everything on his mind. He faced Atreus, looking into those intense eyes. "These humans care about you, whether you want to admit it or not. Marina adores you like an older brother, Leofel looks up to you, and Giovanni pretty much considers you a son."

Nyel might as well have slapped Atreus in the face for the appalled expression he now wore.

"How can you even say that?" he breathed with fracturing restraint.

"Because it's so freakin obvious! They care about you; I'd even go so far as to say they love—"

"Stop," Atreus barked, silencing him. "You don't know a damn thing. You've been here a couple of weeks and think you've got this all figured out, do you? Well, news flash: humans don't adopt sea monsters into their families. To them, we're a myth, and if that illusion ever breaks, they'll hunt us down like animals."

Nyel shook his head. "You don't see the way they look at you."

Whatever mirror he's looking in isn't sending back the right picture.

Nyel wished he could replace Atreus's warped self-image with the one Giovanni saw, the one Marina and Leofel saw.

Or the one I see.

"You're full of shit." Atreus laughed mirthlessly.

Nyel stiffened. "Well, if I'm so full of—that, why even bother with me? Why haven't you forced me off this island? You could do it. You know you could. Chase me into the sea. Force me to leave and keep Baia Vita all to yourself. So why haven't you?"

Atreus let out a shaky breath with measured control.

"Because," he said slowly, "I let myself get used to you."

"Then why do you keep pushing me away? You want me here, or you don't, Atreus, which is it?"

Atreus flashed him a venomous glare, abalone eyes blazing. "You're making that decision very easy right now."

Nyel huffed, throwing his hands up in exasperation.

"There it is again. Pushing me back. Like you push everyone back. Those people care about you, Atreus. They care, and if you'd just let them see—"

"Let them see what I am!?" Atreus yelled so loudly that Nyel jumped. "Let them see the monster that's been working alongside them, walking the streets while their children play?"

Nyel set his jaw. He wouldn't back down.

"Horace has already seen a Mer. He won't stop talking about it. It wouldn't be that big of a shock."

"I hate to break it to you, but they all think he's crazy."

"Maybe. But that doesn't mean they wouldn't accept you—"

"How could the humans accept me when my own species pushed me away!?" His voice echoed against the rocks. "How can *anyone* care about me when my own kind call me a FREAK!"

Atreus shoved off the sand and ran. Ran into the water and disappeared beneath the surf. For a moment, Nyel stood alone, mute with shock. He was frozen in place with nobody for company except the twinkling stars.

When Atreus rose, his clothes hung in tatters, shredded by razor-tipped fins. They flared, the moonlight accenting every curved spine. His body was big, much larger than it had been as a human. A mosaic of scales sparkled in the light, glistening off the water.

Mixed scales.

Halfling.

Nyel's breath caught in his throat as a wave of dizziness struck him. No. No, no, no. This couldn't be happening. It just couldn't. How had he gone so long and never—?

Atreus stalked closer, talons curved, tail swishing. Nyel barely resisted the urge to run, keeping his feet planted until Atreus stopped— barely a breath away. Nyel clenched his fists but couldn't stop the tremble of fear rocketing through his body. He was at the mercy of Atreus now.

At the mercy of a halfling.

"How can the humans accept me when my own kind call me a bastard?" Atreus whispered, and Nyel scented his breath. It was the same scent of an oncoming storm. No, not oncoming. The storm was here, and Nyel could anchor himself and weather it or run.

"I'm a mutt. A halfling abomination because of who my parents were. Cursed."

Atreus's voice went so quiet that Nyel could barely hear him over the waves.

"How can I let anyone in, when everyone before... left?"

Abalone eyes locked with his, and Nyel witnessed the fracture inside them—a chasm stretched over a decade long and deeper than a broken heart.

A shattered spirit.

Nyel saw the resignation in those eyes. The defeat. Atreus had already accepted that Nyel would cast him out. Would leave him.

Nyel remained like a pillar of marble. Frozen, for one, two, three seconds.

He doesn't get to decide the way I see him.

Nyel sloshed into the lapping waves, his steps unsteady as feet turned to claws. Yet his resolve remained firm as he threw his arms around Atreus's middle. The water soaked his clothes and clung to his legs, but he didn't care.

"You don't get to push me out," Nyel breathed, voice steady

despite the wild beating of his heart. He buried his face in Atreus's chest, refusing to let go. "Not this time."

ATREUS

HE DIDN'T KNOW what to do. One moment, Nyel looked ready to bolt; the next, unwavering arms wrapped around him. Atreus flinched in shock. Never expecting this—not the embrace, not the warmth, not the refusal to walk away.

"You don't get to push me out. Not this time."

Atreus's arms lifted in surprise, hesitating mid-air, and several moments passed before he allowed them to descend. He held Nyel's petite human form to his middle, hardly believing this was real.

"I'm not going to run away." Nyel pulled back enough to stare up at him. "I'm not going to do that. So get that idea out of your head."

Atreus couldn't swallow, couldn't feel the waves lapping at his ankles. All he felt were warm arms and the solid pressure of Nyel's body against his.

When was the last time anyone held him like this? Touched him? He couldn't remember.

"I was wrong," Nyel continued, and it seemed the words couldn't come out fast enough once he started. "I was so stupid and wrong and.... I'm sorry. I don't care what you look like. I don't care who your parents were. It's all so freakin stupid."

Atreus realized with a start that Nyel was close to tears.

"There is nothing wrong with the way you are, Atreus. Nothing.

I'm so glad I got to meet you, to see the *real* you before I saw the color of your scales."

His breaths were heavy, and Atreus felt their brush of warmth.

"I'm ashamed of the way I was raised to think. I might have missed this. I might have missed you."

Nyel shook his head, face buried in Atreus's chest.

"I hate to think that. I hate it." He squeezed tighter, his voice a whisper nearly swallowed by the waves. "I'm so glad I got to meet you."

This was the last place Atreus ever imagined he'd find himself tonight, with Nyel squeezing him like he might melt into the sea, begging for his forgiveness.

"Y-you're..." He cleared his throat. "You're not scared? You don't think I'm dangerous?"

The memory of Nyel's mother flashed behind his eyes—the revulsion on her face, the way she shielded her son from him. From a monster.

Nyel shook his head, face still buried in Atreus's torn shirt.

"No. You're not dangerous. You're kind and generous to a fault and so freaken down on yourself—" he took a shuddering breath. "It's my fault. Mine and all the *Sireni*. I'm so sorry."

Atreus didn't know that a few select words were all it would take to evaporate years of pain and self-loathing. Of course, it didn't all go away, but a significant weight in his chest eased.

"It's just one sireno.
The rest of them will never accept you.
You're a freak."

The voice hissed loudly, eager to get its words in.

But with Nyel holding him like this—like he meant something, like he was someone worth holding onto—it was easy to push it away.

He's enough. Even if it's only him. Nyel is enough.

Atreus didn't trust himself to speak. With a shuddering exhale, he returned Nyel's embrace, his massive webbed hand covering half the *sireno's* petite back. They stayed like that, silent, until Nyel finally spoke.

"Oh. I'm sorry—I forgot you're not big on hugging. I didn't mean—"

But as he tried to pull away, Atreus's arms tightened instinctively, pinning Nyel to his chest.

Don't let me go...not yet. Not yet.

Without hesitation, Nyel wrapped his arms around Atreus again, mindful of the sharp spines along his back, and pulled him closer—closer than they had ever been before. It was as though they'd bridged a gap. An unspoken distance neither had dared to cross until now. At that moment, it didn't matter what separated them: their differences, their fears, or the barriers they'd built. All that remained was this closeness.

"Can I ask you something?" Atreus asked after a while.

"Anything." Nyel pulled back just far enough for Atreus to look into those gold-flecked eyes. The side of the *sireno's* face was damp where it rested against Atreus, a patch of green scales glinting on his cheek. Slowly, Atreus lifted his hand and brushed his index finger over the smooth, shimmering surface.

Nyel's breath hitched as he repeated, "Anything."

"Can I see you? In the sea?"

Nyel smiled at him, finally letting go. Atreus had to resist the urge to pull him back. Without preamble, Nyel dove into an oncoming wave, disappearing for a few seconds before emerging. He appeared almost silver under the moonlight, his jade scales catching the glow with every ripple of the ocean's surface. His fins deepened into a rich azure, their edges fading into the blackened night. Nyel lifted his tail, the fins soft and elegantly curved, flowing gently with the water instead of ending in harsh barbs.

"I didn't realize how much I'd miss this," he said, waving his tail back and forth.

Atreus moved his tail closer, comparing the two. They were so different.

But... Nyel said he didn't mind. He sees the parts of me I'm most afraid of—the pieces I've spent my whole life trying to hide. And he's still here. He's not running.

Atreus still didn't dare let himself believe it. He half expected Nyel to flip on a dime and tell him to get away.

But he didn't. In fact, Nyel did the opposite and moved closer, his voice going quiet.

"I wish the *Sireni* would take the time to get to know a halfling. The way things are, it's... not right."

Nyel lifted his tail, running it against Atreus's. The smooth edge grazed his scales in a touch so fleeting it could have been an accident —if not for the way it lingered. Atreus's breath stuttered, his body trembling at the contact. The touch was strangely intimate, like the gentle pass of fingertips tracing across bare skin. The warmth pooling at the base of Atreus's neck spread down his spine all the way to the end of his tail.

He was utterly unmoored, and that's probably why his mouth kept going.

"I only learned about it less than a day ago: that I'm a halfling. I knew something was wrong with me, and that's why the *Sireni* drove me off as a kid. I just never knew why."

Nyel's tail stilled, and Atreus was left breathless at the loss of its caress. "You said they drove you off?"

"It was a long time ago."

Nyel dropped his head, face averted. It took Atreus a moment to recognize the sound of muffled sniffling.

"Hey, don't... don't do that." Atreus reached out, gently taking Nyel by the chin and tilting his face toward him. Before he could stop himself, he wiped away a tear with the back of his index finger. "I don't like it when you do that."

Nyel let out a hysterical sort of laugh. "What? Cry? You've never seen it."

"And I never want to."

Their eyes met, and something happened. Or took shape? The air shifted, and Atreus felt as if an invisible current coiled around his ankles, tugging him toward the sea. Radiance flickered, like fractured sunlight through cresting waves, making him blink—but the glare didn't fade. Something warm pressed against his core, seeking entrance. It was alive.

Atreus had no control, no will to keep his chest from cracking open, letting in that strange warmth. It was as though the cage guarding his heart unlocked, spread wide and exposing the delicate bead of light that was...him. His pulse thudded heavily in his ears, and the distant echo of song rang louder and louder as the entity moved in— a whale's hymn.

And then, he saw it—or thought he did. A golden thread looped in the air around them. It shimmered, twisting and dancing before his eyes. The hair on the back of his neck rose as a shiver tore through him, heart pounding and ears filled with whale song. His fingers twitched at his sides, aching to reach out.

But just as this...thing. This alive warmth almost touched the light inside him, it pulled back... and was gone.

The glow, the warmth, the connection—it vanished like brittle glass snapping under pressure, leaving Atreus reeling. He staggered inwardly, the absence of it striking him like the air had been knocked from his lungs. His chest ached with a hollowness he couldn't name, and tears welled in his eyes, hot and stinging, blurring the sight of Nyel, who was now hastily wiping his eyes.

For a moment, Atreus just stood there, swallowing against the lump rising in his throat.

What... the hell was that?

Had Nyel felt it too? For a brief moment, he was tempted to ask.

That golden thread, that... feeling.

Or was it only Atreus foolish enough to believe in something so fleeting? Who'd felt like he was on the edge of something, only to watch it slip through his fingers like sand?

The ache twisted as though he'd been struck by a devil ray's barbed tail. The ocean continued to move around them, indifferent to the loss he could still feel echoing in his bones. Yet as he wracked his brain and blinked away the sting in his eyes, Atreus couldn't name what it was he'd lost. He bit down on the trembling in his jaw, grinding his teeth.

What... just happened to me?

Nyel took a moment to compose himself, wiping at his eyes repeatedly before letting out an embarrassed chuckle. "Ugh, I'm a mess. It's been a lot."

Atreus cleared his throat, shaking himself. "Yeah. A lot."

"Where did you learn about it? That you were a halfling?" Nyel asked, still pushing at the wetness in his eyes.

"A stranger. I didn't catch his name. He was a Mer—another halfling like me. He told me that if I showed myself to you, you'd leave. He wanted you home—a relative of yours."

"Nephi."

"What?"

"His name is Nephi. And he's my brother. Well, half-brother."

Half-brother sounded a lot closer than 'distant relative,' as Nephi had called them.

"I take it you don't have a good relationship."

Nyel shook his head. Atreus didn't have to think too hard to guess why.

"I need to fix it—all of it. I'll do it in front of my parents if I have to. There is nothing wrong with Nephi, besides the fact that he's an incurable jerk," Nyel added under his breath. "But it isn't his fault our dad had an out-of-species relationship. He hasn't done anything wrong."

"He's expecting you to run home."

Nyel huffed. "Well, then he's in for a surprise. But I am going home."

Atreus jerked his head, tail splashing.

"Not to stay," Nyel added quickly, "to make things right. I'm going to tell them everything."

"I imagine that will be a fun conversation."

Nyel laughed with a nervous hiccup. "Yes. Super fun. They won't take it well, but I don't care."

"Even when you tell them you're hanging out with a halfling?"

Atreus knew Nyel's parents would react poorly to the news. They'd tell him Atreus was dangerous. That Nyel was an idiot for being so close to a monster. Would Nyel listen to them? They were his parents, after all. What if they convinced him Atreus really was a freak? What if they persuaded him to stay home?

"Especially then," Nyel said, and Atreus took comfort in the determined resolve in his voice. Nyel faced him, mouth set in a severe line. "I'm on your side, Atreus. Please believe me."

Atreus averted his gaze, unable to hold its intensity. He nodded.

"Say it."

"Say what?"

"That you know I'm on your side." The look on Nyel's face told Atreus he was dead serious.

"Why?"

"Because sometimes you have to hear things out loud with your own voice to believe them."

Atreus took a deep breath. "I know you're on my side."

"And that you know I'll be there for you."

Something twinged in Atreus's chest, and he had to resist the urge to rub it.

"I know you'll be there for me."

"And that I'm the best *Bocce* player that ever was."

The tension in the air popped like a balloon, and Atreus barked with laughter. "Don't push your luck. And I demand a rematch."

"Wanna get your tail kicked again that badly? I guess I can do that," Nyel said with a mischievous smirk.

"You're so—"

The sound of gunfire cracked in the sky, drowning out his words. Nyel yelled, and Atreus grabbed him, ready to drag them into the waves and away from the firing shells. They'd been spotted. They—

Lights exploded across the sky in flashes of blue and purple, followed by a dull 'boom.' The display disappeared in a whisp of smoke and the sound of crackling popcorn.

"Nyel, look!" he said, pointing to the sky with one webbed hand while the other remained wrapped around the *sireno's* shoulders.

Fireworks flew, blasting the air before fizzling into a dazzling display of color and light. Bursts of amethyst and iris exploded, followed by smaller pops of magenta and orchid.

Nyel's mouth fell open. It opened and closed a few more times before the words finally made it out on an exhale.

"It's you. Those colors. It's you, Atreus. It's... beautiful," he whispered, the brilliant lights reflecting in those honey-brown eyes.

And in that moment, Atreus didn't hate the color of his scales.

CHAPTER 14

LEOFEL

Her name was *Pesce Pagliaccio*. The Clown Fish. Leo gritted his teeth as a well-dressed man handed over the keys, leaving him staring at the shiny new vessel bobbing in the harbor. It was as though Alvise wanted to remind him what a fool he was. How stupidly dependent Leo had become. The keys burned in his palm. The boat was perfect—better than perfect, the newest model on the market with every luxurious upgrade imaginable.

The hull was crafted from sturdy wood, painted in a crisp white with orange accents that gleamed under the sun. Its powerful

229

inboard motor promised a smoother, faster ride even in choppy waters. The deck was wide and open, perfect for hauling in large nets or working with lines. It was practical and efficient, yet with thoughtful details like polished brass fittings and leather-wrapped controls. It was more than a boat; it was a statement.

He wanted to sink it.

But then his family would go hungry. He had to do this. Leo fished on the *Pesce Pagliaccio* for nearly two weeks, cutting through the water faster than any other boat on the bay. Despite his meager catches, Leo still caught significantly more than the other fishermen in the village because of his vessel's strength.

Each night, he docked the boat, bracing himself for the inevitable —a man in a dark suit arriving to escort him to the Vincenzo estate in the valley. Yet day after day, catch after catch, nobody came. No summons, no demands for payment. Nothing happened.

Maybe Dad is taking care of it?

Leo didn't dare hope, and the lack of correspondence unnerved him. The only thing that helped was losing himself in the harsh work of casting nets, setting traps, and towing lines. He loved the work and relished the familiar burn in his back after a hard day. This is what he knew, what he was good at.

I won't let them starve.

Yet as the sun set and the night of the festival approached, a nagging worry settled in the back of his mind. When would the axe finally fall? And would he be able to survive its cut?

Despite his nerves, Leo was determined to enjoy the Baia Vita festival. This was the celebration of men like him, who made their livelihood on the sea. It celebrated those with salt on their skin and sand in their boots.

Regardless of that damn shark tooth necklace.

Leo dove headfirst into the celebrations, dismissing all worries. Tonight was for fun, and he wouldn't squander that.

"Mind if I play victor?" Leo asked, watching Nyel and Atreus finish a game of *Bocce*.

Nyel was good, but more than his accuracy, Leo found himself admiring the set of his shoulders and the way his arm swung from his slight frame. He'd done everything in his power to avoid Nyel, to ignore this irritating attraction. And for the most part, he'd succeeded—keeping his distance, steering clear of those big brown eyes and shy smiles. The never-ending gloom hanging over his head was enough to numb his desires, a constant reminder that he had far bigger problems to face.

But tonight? Tonight was about having fun, so what harm was there in a little self-indulgence? Leo allowed himself to joke and laugh with Nyel, hopefully moving from 'friend of a friend' to 'friend.' Atreus was on edge; that much was obvious by the way he continuously ground his teeth. He'd known Atreus long enough to read him like a book, and Leo wasn't going to let one of his sour moods ruin this perfect night.

"Did you get anything else cool?" Leo asked after Nyel was unable to buy the belt he wanted. Leo had the insane urge to purchase one for him. Of course, that was stupid when they were only one bad fishing day away from going hungry. Still, the desire was there.

"Yeah! Check this out." Nyel said, pulling out a glass sea turtle.

"Cool, let me get a closer look at that," he said, lifting Nyel's hand to his eyes. He admired the glasswork on the ornament, and Nyel's hand was soft in his.

What would he say if he knew the thoughts in my head?

Leo couldn't get a read on Nyel. But the newcomer showed no interest in the women on the island, so that gave him some hope.

"I just remembered something. You two keep going," Atreus said suddenly and disappeared.

Leo watched his bunched-up shoulders part the crowd. "What's his problem?"

"I don't know," Nyel said, "Should we go after him?"

Leo shook his head. "Nah. Atreus likes his space. Just leave him to it; he'll come around."

When Atreus was in one of his *moods*, Leo learned a long time ago to let him cool off.

"Hey, wanna go try the darts stand? I bet you'd be good at—"

Leo's voice caught in his throat as two men in leather coats strode toward him. Emblazoned on their chests was the emblem of a golden lion roaring against a backdrop of vibrant purple and black. Alvise's men—finally here to collect.

"You know what, I'll meet you at the darts stand in an hour," Leo said, trying to put himself between Nyel and the men.

"Are you sure?"

"Yeah, yeah, I'll meet you there," he said, waving Nyel off, even though his heart pounded against his ribs like an inmate trying to escape its cell.

"*Signore* Vincenzo wants to speak with you," one of the men said, his voice monotone.

"Can it wait until after the festival?"

In answer, the man shoved Leo forward, taking up position behind him while the other led the way. They didn't go to the valley; rather, they ducked into a nearby alleyway. Stacks of old crates, rolls of spare wire, and cracked water buoys piled along the sides. It was dark except for the distant flickering from the festival lanterns, splitting the darkness into thin strips of light.

"I was wondering when you'd come to visit me. The Clown Fish isn't for free, my pet." Alvise leaned casually against the brick wall, his appearance exuding the effortless elegance of old money, like aged wine and worn velvet.

So, his father hadn't dealt with the payments. Of course not.

How could Leo even let himself believe his father did anything? He'd signed the contract and left Leo to deal with the mess.

"Leave it to Leo; he'll figure it out," his father said over the dinner table when Emelia worried about funds for shoes.

Because Leo always did.

Bile surged up his throat, and he worked to keep his voice even.

"Of course not *Signore* Vincenzo. I'd hoped you and my father had an arrangement, but I see I was wrong. I'd be happy to discuss one now." His voice was light. Polite. No hint of the rage inside. Or the fear.

"And how will you make the payments? You can hardly feed that rat pack as it is."

Leo's neck muscles tightened. "I am ready to discuss an arrangement that will satisfy both parties."

Alvise's mouth twisted into a feline smile. "I was hoping you'd say that. Satisfaction is a rare commodity in my circles. Money bores me." His eyes roamed up and over Leo's body. "What I crave is beautiful things at my feet."

Leo's stomach turned as he imagined them—Alvise's so-called 'guests,' preened and polished like exotic birds in gilded cages, admired but never free to fly. He wondered if Alvise clipped their wings or if they were too terrified to use them.

Alvise approached him, his ice-shard eyes making Leo feel naked. He smelled of rich cologne and musk—undeniably masculine—yet it stirred nothing in Leo.

"Yes. Beautiful things. At my feet."

He grabbed a section of Leo's blond hair, twisting it in his fingers, the strands gleaming like threads of gold in the light. With a silver flash, Alvise brought the knife down, cutting the golden lock. Leo yelled, stumbling back, but rough hands restrained him.

Alvise held the golden lock, bringing it to his nose. He inhaled deeply, eyes closing. "Yes, this will do. It's too bad the red fox doesn't have a face as pretty as yours."

"You stay the fuck away from me," Leo hissed and immediately knew he'd made a mistake.

His cheek slammed into the cobblestone street, and a boot buried itself in his gut. He gasped, but no sound came out as air was forced from his lungs.

"None of that, my pet. I see you need more training. Get him up," Alvise ordered, and Leo was lifted, hanging limply between the two brutes.

"Look at me, my golden boy."

Leo kept his gaze on the ground. A moment later, a fist made contact with his cheek, sending a flash of white-hot pain through his skull, rattling his teeth.

"Look at me."

With tears brimming, Leo lifted his head, meeting that arctic gaze.

"When I say look at me, you say—?"

Leo couldn't keep the tremble out of his voice and hated himself for it. "Yes, *Signore* Vincenzo."

"When I tell you to come to my estate, you say—?"

"Yes, *Signore* Vincenzo."

"And when I tell you to use my given name and to get on your knees, you say—?"

Leo's jaw didn't move as he ground his teeth, scarcely releasing the words. "Yes, Alvise."

"Good boy." He tickled the tip of Leo's nose with the strand of hair.

Leo fell as the grunts dropped him. He barely caught himself and slumped against the brick wall, hugging his middle. They disappeared around the corner like predators after a kill, knowing full well they'd be back for more.

Leo reached up, feeling the shortened piece where a long curl had been. He fought back the sting in his eyes.

Fuck.

MARINA

ATREUS HAD OUTDONE himself with the banner above the booth. Not only were the letters spaced evenly and perfectly straight, but he'd also drawn several sea creatures along the edges in bright gold paint. It still baffled her that, despite his immaculate penmanship, he couldn't read a single one of the words he'd so beautifully written. When she'd asked him about it, he said the words "swam around," whatever that meant.

But as Marina watched him carefully paint the golden sea creatures, painful memories rose to the surface, twisting her heart until she felt physically ill. The way the bristles slid across the canvas, leaving marks that would remain forever, reminded her of a permanence she'd never known. It was too much.

After a while, she couldn't take it anymore. She left Atreus to finish on his own, masking her pain with a practiced smile and a nonchalant performance. Not a flicker of unease showed as she walked away, shoulders steady, masterfully hiding the hurt churning quietly beneath the surface.

Still, she'd been right to put him to the task—the bright banner did its job.

When the flood of kids hit her booth like a scurry of chattering squirrels, Marina could barely catch her breath. One moment, she was overrun, struggling to collect forms and fees; the next, the crowd thinned as the kids dispersed, drawn like moths to the bright stalls selling cakes and candies.

Marina counted the forms for the third time, tallying up the numbers. There were more young kids this year than she'd seen in the past. Her heart sank; they had zero chance of winning, going up against teens as old as fifteen.

"We should separate them into groups based on age. What do you think, *Nonno? Nonno?*"

Her grandfather sat in his rocking chair, eyes closed, mouth gaping. When she shook his knee, he snorted. "*Che succede!* I wasn't sleeping."

"Sure, *Nonno*. Did you want to go see the festival?"

"I can see plenty from here. You go enjoy, I'll guard the booth."

Marina very much doubted it since there was a one hundred percent chance he'd fall asleep again, but it seemed all the kids who would sign up this year already had.

"You're okay by yourself?"

Niccolo slinked around the corner, his tail wrapping at the edge of the rocking chair before gracefully hopping onto Horace's lap. "I am not alone. Niccolo is good company."

"He sure has a lot to say," Marina said, scratching the cat behind the ears. His purring was so loud, she half-expected him to rattle right off *Nonno's* lap. She kissed her *Nonno* on the head. "I'll be back in a bit."

He waved her off, and when Marina glanced over her shoulder, his eyes were closed, mouth open, with Niccolo swatting at his white beard. She laughed and made her way to the center of the merry-making.

Marina wound her way through the stalls, trying to spot Atreus. He'd been off, and she hoped the festivities lightened his mood.

She was quickly distracted by a stall selling women's clothes. Marina admired a yellow sundress on display. The stitching practically yelled the word *libertà*. She imagined wearing it on a bright morning sunrise. Free as a sunflower in the breeze.

The older women would call it revealing, but Marina gravitated to the open-shoulder cut. It would fit her perfectly. Yet, as she looked, the price warded her away. They weren't struggling for money—not with her mother's inheritance tucked away in a bank in *Firenze*. Marina used part of it to pay for her schooling, but with just one semester left, half the original amount still remained.

But her *Nonno* was old, and every rasping cough felt like the tick of a bomb. He might need medical attention at any moment, and Marina was ready to use everything she had left to help him. Her father would swallow his pride when it came to *Nonno's* care, even if he refused to accept her funds for anything else.

With her future uncertain and *Nonno's* coughs worsening, there was no room to spend on frilly dresses—even if they would make her boobs look phenomenal.

She was admiring a pair of silver earrings with a blue stone carved to resemble a fish scale when the edge of her sandal caught on a beam beneath the booth. It hooked her leg, and she fell.

Marina grabbed at the table but only managed to wrench the black display cloth as she toppled. Something hard collided with her back, and as Marina landed on the stone, she realized it was another person—who was now also on the ground.

"Marina, you cow!" a female voice screeched.

Anna, the same girl from the fabric store, glared as sticky orange liquid splattered all over her shirt. The man on the ground held an empty cup, and it didn't take Marina long to piece together what had happened.

Man holds drink —Marina knocks into him —man spills drink—

Anna's dress is ruined. A beautiful domino effect of chaos. Marina's specialty.

She didn't bother apologizing to Anna, instead addressing the man. "Are you okay? I'm so sorry."

He turned, and despite the orange splatter on his cream cotton shirt, he smiled as if being knocked to the ground by her was the highlight of his evening.

"It is no problem. Accidents happen." He straightened and offered his hand. Marina's gaze lifted from the tragedy staining the man's shirt and then to his face. She blinked.

Is he... real?

Standing before her was the most gorgeous man she'd ever seen, his dazzling smile so bright it made her wonder if she should worry about getting sunburned—or maybe gorgeous-man-burned? Whatever it was, this man radiated it. An aura was definitely exuding from him, and Marina was quickly getting overwhelmed. This man was not from Baia Vita. There was an air of refinement that floated around him like a barrier between him and everyone else.

He was tan, with a tasteful amount of manicured scruff framing his jawline. His dark brown hair was long, reaching the tips of his shoulders. It waved with enough messiness to be considered windswept without being untamed.

"Are you hurt?" he asked as she found her feet.

"Just my butt and my pride. Nothing major," she said, wiping her hands on said butt.

He laughed, and it was so relaxed that Marina almost forgot she'd nearly concussed the man.

Anna clicked her tongue in disapproval. "Of course, you'd make a mess. For god's sake, when do you return to that preppy school?"

Marina didn't look at her. Couldn't. Shame forced her chin down, her fingers twisting in knots. She mumbled something akin to, "I'm sorry."

"Well, 'Sorry' doesn't fix my dress, does it?"

"It's a fruit-based drink. It'll wash out," the man said, checking his own ruined shirt.

"I'm so sorry. I can wash it for you if you'd like. I'm used to getting stains out of clothes," Marina offered.

"I'd rather tear this dress apart and make curtains out of it before handing it over to you," Anna spat.

It'd probably look better that way.

Behind her, the woman with the jewelry booth began slowly picking up her wares.

"*Oh mio Dio*, no, let me," Marina said, bending low, "*Per favore*, sit. I'll do this."

The old woman gave a relieved nod and waddled to a seat as she held her lower back. It was a few seconds before Marina noticed the man crouching beside her, picking up the delicate silver earrings.

"You don't have to do that. It's her mess; let her pick it up," Anna snapped.

"I don't mind," he replied.

"You don't have to kneel in the dirt with the likes of her."

At this, the man looked up, flashing Anna a wide smile, but Marina sensed none of the searing warmth this time.

"Why don't you go home and take care of that stain? I think we are done here."

Anna gaped at the obvious dismissal, shooting Marina a glare before stomping off.

Great. Just great.

"I am terribly sorry for her behavior. She was rather rude," the man said, finding matching pairs for the scattered earrings. His hands were steady and delicate with the fragile ornaments.

"I'm used to it. Anna doesn't like me much."

"Anna? So that was her name," he mused.

Marina quirked a brow. "You were on a date with her and didn't know her name?"

He grinned flirtatiously. "I only met her tonight. And I am terrible with names, honestly. Speaking of which, might I get yours?"

"You didn't hear Anna yelling it?"

"I'd like to hear it from your lips if you don't mind."

Marina didn't know why that made her pause, and she definitely didn't know why she was humoring him. Yet she found herself granting his request.

"Marina Marcello."

"Marina," the man purred, "Now that is a name I won't forget."

"Why is that?"

"Because it's beautiful."

Marina was at a loss for words. No man had ever complimented her like this before. Feeling completely out of her element, she remained silent, unable to muster even a simple "thank you" or a follow-up question.

I'm such a weirdo.

She could practically feel Anna's scoffing judgment. Anna would have said something nice in return, maybe giggle and twirl her hair. Bat her eyelashes with pouty lips.

But that just wasn't Marina.

Silent, Marina continued fixing the woman's booth, apologizing ten more times as she set everything back in place. The final pair of earrings—the ones she'd been eyeing—were carefully placed on the table. The blue fish-scale stones sparkled with opalescent reflections. They were stunning, and Marina was always on the lookout for something to distract from her flaming hair.

But she really shouldn't.

"Well, see ya," Marina said awkwardly and turned to disappear into the crowd. She'd only made it ten steps when the barest touch graced her upper arm.

"Wait."

She raised a brow at the man, his dark eyes imploring. He gestured to the festivities.

"I see no reason why we can't enjoy this together. What do you say?"

"Don't you want to change?" she asked, eyeing his shirt.

"I kind of like it, actually. Gives it character."

"You look like you got drunk and sloshed on yourself."

"Like I said, character."

Marina laughed. "That's one way of putting it. I can still wash it out if you'd like."

"No need." He held out an arm. "Walk with me instead?"

Marina hesitated. This was weird. She should get back to *Nonno*.

"One pass around the square," he begged.

Marina had ruined this guy's date. Not to mention his shirt. One pass couldn't hurt. Lips pressed tightly together, Marina relented, taking his arm.

They walked through the bright stalls of carnival games and fried foods, but Marina took in none of it. She watched her feet, trying her best to avoid the eyes bearing into her like daggers. But there was little chance of that when her bright red hair stood out like a flamingo in a flock of pigeons.

They'll see me. With him.

They'll see her on the arm of arguably the most gorgeous man Marina had ever laid eyes on. The rumors would fly. For something like this, she worried the girls would seek revenge. Anna especially. Marina shivered, remembering the pranks and jokes her roommates pulled on her all winter.

Please just let this night end.

"This song is one of my favorites. Can I persuade you?"

Before she knew it, they were at the edge of the square, feet away from whirling figures and swishing skirts.

"Oh no, no, no, no, no," she said, backing away with her hands raised as though she were being held at knifepoint. "I don't dance."

The man cocked his head, his stupidly-perfect hair swaying on the night breeze. "Is that so?"

"You witnessed just how good my coordination is," she said, still backpedaling. "So did your shirt."

"Don't worry about the shirt. And the perfect cure for *not* doing something is practice. Wouldn't you agree?"

"But I—" Marina eyed the crowd. They were moving so fast, so synchronized with the beat. "I'm sorry. I can't."

"Hmm," he said, bringing his hand to his chin in contemplation. "Let's try something."

Without a word, he led Marina to a secluded courtyard tucked a few alleys away from the bustling square. Here, the music softened to a distant hum, replaced by the gentle trickle of the fountain. The moonlight bathed the space in a cool, silvery glow, a striking contrast to the buzzing yellow lantern light that flickered in the square.

"How about this? Nobody around." He placed her left hand on his shoulder and took her right. "May I?" he asked, his opposite hand hovering beside her waist.

"U-uh-huh," Marina stuttered and tried to keep her breath even as he placed his palm on her waist, hardly making any contact at all.

"Listen, bringing me away from the crowd still isn't going to protect your toes."

"Lucky for me, I've lost feeling in all ten toes," he said, taking a step backward and leading her into a simple four-step sequence.

"Liar," she snorted, following his lead.

She managed through half the song before stomping on his foot. "See, I told you I'm no good at—"

He pulled her in tighter, his hand sliding from her waist to the curve of her back.

"You're doing beautifully. Let's go again."

"Okay," was all she could say past the hummingbird tempo in her chest. He led her through several more sets, and Marina didn't even notice when one song ended and another began. She was only aware of her gliding feet, the warm pressure on her back, and the flush in her cheeks.

With a delicate twirl, they ended the final song, coming to a standstill as the last note lingered in the air.

"See, I told you it only takes practice."

Marina was panting. "I guess there's still hope for me."

"Have more faith in yourself, my dear," he said, his words like a caress.

He brought her hand to his lips, and Marina hoped her gasp went unheard as a chaste kiss ghosted across her knuckles.

"Until next time, Marina."

As he released her hand, he pressed something small into her palm before turning down the alley and fading into the night. Marina stood in a daze for an embarrassingly long time before inspecting the gift in her hand. Inside a thin cotton pouch tied with a bow were the blue opalescent fish-scale earrings. Her stomach twisted as she realized she never asked for his name.

NYEL

IT FELT LIKE NO time at all before the fireworks ended, the last sizzle of light and sound fading into a starry sky. The silence settled heavily in their ears.

Nyel was reeling, and he couldn't tell if it was from the explosions in the sky or the onslaught of sensations that had besieged him in the span of a breath. Something had happened—or tried to—but whatever it was felt incomplete.

Nyel ducked his head and squeezed his eyes closed as twirls of golden light zigzagged across his vision, likely remnants of the overwhelming emotions temporarily blurring his sight. That's all they were—nothing more. And the feeling? He had no explanation.

Yet, deep down, in the quiet corners of his mind, a tiny ember of thought sparked to life, whispering to him.

He knew. He knew. He *knew.*

"Well, that's the end of my favorite shirt," Atreus said, examining his shredded dress shirt.

"You can't fix it?" Nyel asked, knowing Atreus to be very adept with a needle. Or really anything with his hands.

"No. It's a goner."

He tore the fabric off himself, the back completely shredded by his barbs. They dried on the beach, regaining their human selves. Luckily, Nyel's clothes were baggy on him to begin with, so with the addition of his rounded fins, his shirt only stretched. His pants, however...

"I think my pants are a goner," Nyel said, facing Atreus, embarrassed at his likely exposed rear.

"I can fix that—just a bit of velcro, and it'll be hardly noticeable. For now, though," he said, handing Nyel his torn shirt, "tie this around your waist to cover it."

"Thanks," he said, blushing as he tied it to hide himself.

Only then did Nyel realize just how shirtless Atreus was. He'd never seen him with this much bare skin before. Even when the other men shed their *camicia*, Atreus always kept himself covered. Was that why it caught Nyel off guard now? Why did his gaze keep drifting to the sculpted ridges of Atreus's abdomen? Even when he realized he was staring, Nyel couldn't tear his eyes away.

"We should get back," Atreus said. "After the fireworks, things usually close up."

"Right." Nyel forced himself to turn around.

What is my problem?

When they arrived at Marina's booth, they only found Horace asleep in his rocking chair. Niccolo cowered under the blanket around his legs, likely spooked by the fireworks.

"*Signore* Finotto? Sir?" Atreus gently shook the man's shoulder.

"Gabriella?" he wheezed, blinking back to reality. "Oh, Antonio. I've been watching the booth for Gabriella. She should be back soon."

Nyel had to resist a laugh.

"I'm here!" Marina's voice called as she jogged to them. She was rather flushed despite the night being cool. "And it's Marina, *Nonno*."

Horace smiled. "You look just like your mother."

"I know *Nonno*. Ready to go home?"

"Yes, it's time for this old man to be in a proper bed."

As they helped Horace to his feet, Nyel noticed a pretty gleam of color below Marina's ear.

"Are those earrings?" Nyel asked.

"You never wear jewelry," Atreus said, squinting.

"And you never walk around half-naked. I guess we're all trying new things tonight," she quipped with a wink.

"Did someone give you those?"

"Don't ask questions you aren't ready to hear," she teased in a sing-song trill. "And what happened to your shirt?" she asked before spotting it tied around Nyel's waist. She eyed them with a raised brow.

"Don't ask questions you aren't ready to hear," Atreus mocked, mimicking her tone.

"You *ragazzi* keep me young," Horace said with a sleepy smile from between their bickering.

Nyel was about to follow them to the *pescheria* when his stomach sank with sudden realization.

"Have any of you seen Leofel?"

When neither Atreus nor Marina had seen him, Nyel's worries grew. He was supposed to meet him, but after the fireworks, Nyel completely forgot.

How could I blow him off like that?

"I'll meet you guys at the house, okay?" he said, turning toward the carnival games. He thought he heard Atreus call after him but ignored it. The stretch of booths lined with games was empty now, save for the vendors packing up for the night. Nyel spun, worry eating at him like barnacles on a ship's hull.

Nyel ducked around a vacant stall when a glint of golden curls hooked his attention. Leo wandered aimlessly from corner to corner, as if he had no particular destination in mind.

"Leofel!" Nyel called jogging to him. "Hey, sorry I didn't meet with you. I got caught up, and then the fireworks, and..." Nyel gasped, his hand covering his mouth.

Leofel's face was a mess. One eye was swollen shut, and a smear of blood streaked from his lips to his cheek, where he'd wiped it.

"Leofel, what happened—Oof!" Nyel made a startled sound as the air knocked from his lungs.

Leofel embraced him like a drowning man. He squeezed Nyel, his head bent, his mouth so close that Nyel could feel his shuddering breath.

"Hey, are you okay?"

It was a stupid question. Of course, he wasn't okay, but Nyel didn't know what else to say. After a moment, Nyel returned the embrace, rubbing his hands up and down Leo's back in what he hoped was a comforting gesture. Leo shuddered again.

"Please. Don't tell anyone," he breathed.

And he was gone, ducking into an alley, leaving Nyel cold, concerned, and confused.

CHAPTER 15

NEPHI

"What do you mean you're staying?"

Nephi glared at his naive half-brother. It was the first hot morning of the summer, and the parka was sweltering. He wanted to tear it off, but his swollen scars kept it firmly in place.

"I mean exactly what I said; I'm staying," Nyel said with conviction.

"With him? Didn't you see what he is?" Nephi shouted, jerking his head to Atreus standing close by.

Nyel chewed his bottom lip.

"I did. And it doesn't matter, Nephi. I don't care that Atreus is a... a halfling," Nyel said, his voice hesitant. "I know what kind of person he is. That's enough."

Heat rose high in Nephi's head, and his stomach filled with acid. He went for a laugh, but it came out as a growl. "So glad a stranger is what convinced you halflings are more than mindless beasts."

Nyel had the sense to look ashamed.

"I was wrong, Nephi. I was completely wrong about halflings, especially about you. You've been hanging around the island to keep an eye on me, and all I've done is complain. I'm sorry."

Nephi didn't mention that the prospect of running into Ludo—Leo tied him to this town more than his brother.

"What now? Halflings aren't monsters? Just like that?" he accused, snapping his fingers.

Nephi noticed Atreus flinch at the word monster. The other male was silent for most of the conversation, but Nephi was acutely aware of the way he hovered behind Nyel like a bodyguard.

Protecting him from his own brother. How ridiculous.

"I actually met Atreus!" Nyel shouted, his voice pleading. "I got to know him before I learned what he was. There is no difference between non-mixed and mixed blood. And with you, I..."

Nyel's gaze paused on the right side of his face. It was a fleeting look but enough for Nephi to catch, even with one working eye.

"All you see is this," he said, pointing to the mutilation.

"That's not what I said."

"You didn't need to."

"I didn't—don't know who you are, Nephi. Growing up, you were always gone. And every time you came back, you were more and more—" He took a deep breath. "You scared me."

"That, coupled with mother dearest's attitude telling you I was the monster hiding under your bed? The one she said would come get you if you didn't eat all your sea prunes?"

Nyel grimaced. "Don't pin this all on her—or me, for that matter. You didn't try Nephi—not until now, and I still don't understand why you even bother."

"I don't like to leave things unfinished."

"So you've said. But I've made my choice. I'm staying."

"What do I tell mommy-dear?"

"I'll talk to them. About my choice and about you."

At this, Nephi stiffened. "What about me?"

"That they are wrong. All of Corallina is wrong. I was wrong. You aren't what we made you out to be."

Nephi shifted, uncomfortable, wishing Nyel would say something he could be angry about. "And what if that's not good enough? What if they still demand you come home?"

"I won't go."

"And what's stopping me from tying you up and dragging you back?"

At this, Atreus raised his shoulders, fists clenched. He side-stepped in front of Nyel. "Try it," he growled.

Nephi's body responded, taking a fighting stance out of instinct. He'd love a good rumble in the sand. "You sure you want to try that, Bluey? Remember last time?"

Atreus didn't back down, which made Nephi want to slam him into the sand all the more.

"Stop it, both of you!" Nyel placed a hand on Atreus's shoulder. "This isn't helping."

"What the hell am I supposed to do then? Leave you in this human death trap?" Nephi pressed.

"You could come with us?" Nyel offered, but it came out like a question.

"Nyel, what are you doing?" Atreus hissed, his attention never leaving Nephi.

"He's my brother."

"He's also a murderer."

"What—!?" Nyel's gaze darted between Atreus and his brother, disbelief warring in his eyes.

"How do you think he got those burns?" Atreus accused, jabbing a pointed finger. "He's been fighting humans—probably killing them, if his lack of respect for the living is anything to go by."

"You don't know that. It could have been—"

"How many Mer do you know who can build a fire?"

Nyel's mouth snapped shut in defeat.

Nephi grinned, showing off his longer-than-usual canines.

So my reputation precedes me. Even this far south.

"It doesn't matter. He isn't doing that anymore," Nyel insisted.

Not by choice, Nephi thought.

"This is a chance for a fresh start—for all of us," Nyel said, addressing them both. "Let's start this over."

"Not likely," Nephi said, full-heartedly ignoring the small prickle of hope in his brother's words, tamping it down with decades of bitterness and rage.

Here was the chance to make amends, to fix burned bridges, and to quell the rage that took permanent residence in his heart. But the injustices of his life flared, and the rage returned. Hot. Familiar. Safe.

"I'll stick around until you either see sense or the humans kill you. Fuck if I care which happens first." Atreus let out a low hissing sound in his chest. "Or maybe this monster will finally snap." Nephi grinned maliciously. "What do you think, bastard-born?"

Nyel wasn't fast enough to stop Atreus this time, and Nephi was ready. The Mer attacked, learning from their last encounter and keeping his feet firmly planted.

Clever fish.

But with a solid base and feet stuck in the suctioning sand, Nephi's opponent was top-heavy. It was too easy to dodge his human-learned punch and headbutt his chin.

Nephi loved how the other males' teeth clashed as he slammed his jaw shut, sending him toppling to the sand. A wave broke over the beach, half submerging Atreus as he stood. When he found his feet, he was taller, broader, and with flared fins.

That's it. Show me your Mer.

Atreus dove, moving faster than before despite his size. A stray claw sliced through Nephi's parka, shredding it in a burst of puffy white cotton. The tattered fabric hung like a rag, exposing his scars.

"Come at me, fucker!" Nephi roared, his glee uncontained.

Nyel shouted something, but Nephi ignored him, eyes locked on his opponent. He could have dove into the surf and transformed, but where was the fun in that? It'd be too easy. He preferred the disadvantage.

"What do you say? First to draw blood?"

Atreus responded with another dive at Nephi, claws raised. Nephi dropped to the sand, rolling on one knee and landing a perfectly timed punch to Atreus's lower back. Atreus balked, his entire lower half momentarily numb. All Mer had a conjunction of nerves right at the base of the spine, above the tail. And Nephi loved using it. Atreus stumbled as he tried to regain control. It was all the time Nephi needed. He spun, swinging his boot into his opponent's rib cage.

But as Atreus fell to the sand, he flung his tail, slashing Nephi's cheek with a barbed fin. Nephi recoiled, feeling warm, sticky blood dripping down his face. He touched it, admiring the beads of red on his fingertips. Maniacal laughter exploded from his throat.

"Well done. Barbed fins, what a weapon. But if you actually knew what to do with them, I'd be cut to ribbons by now."

Atreus stood as though to strike again, but Nephi held up a hand.

"I honor my word. You've bested me." His gaze lingered on the single blood-tipped barb on Atreus's tail. "By a scratch."

He took a second to admire the Mer's body. Nephi's Mer form

had advantages, but he was a defensive creature, bulky and built to withstand blows. Atreus's body, with its size and array of natural-born weapons, was an offensive attacker—a predator.

Someone worth keeping around, Nephi mused.

He turned to his brother, who was whiter than before. His eyes followed the thin stream of blood running down Nephi's neck.

"I will not be a part of your delusional life with these humans."

If my Pod were here, we'd burn this island to the ground.

"But I'll be close."

As Atreus dried and regained his human form, he hissed in frustration at his tattered shirt; only his pants had survived the change.

"Damn it. Leo gave me this," Atreus lamented.

Nephi was half tempted to ask about the human—about Leo—but he held his tongue.

"Spar me again sometime, Bluey. If the humans don't kill me, I'll likely die of boredom," Nephi said, turning his back to them. He kicked off his boots and tossed aside what was left of his coat.

Diving into the surf, Nephi felt the shallow mark on his cheek knit itself together, the salt of *Spuragin*—the Spirit of Tides—healing his wound. He crested the surface, showing off his crimson fins before diving below the waves and away from the beach.

NEPHI SWAM THE PERIMETER of Baia Vita, noting its rocky cliffs on one side and the bay on the other. A sandbank wrapped the edge of the island, stretching like a crescent moon, protecting the inhabitants from ships. At the tip of the crescent sat a mini island with a single lighthouse at its peak.

Nephi couldn't explain it, but an unsettled energy hung around

Baia Vita. This place had hardly seen any conflict, yet clashing species walked its shores. Corallina, a hidden village, lay below the waves. Right under where these humans fished. How had they managed to remain separate while practically on top of each other?

In the north, Mer and humans lived leagues apart. Oceans stretched between settlements, and yet they sought out one another to fight. The proximity made Nephi's scales itch from the strangeness and the need to paint these white beaches red.

He thought of Tariq and Dema. Of Giselle and... and Ludomir. What they could do to this place. What they'd done to countless other coastal towns just like this one. The victory it would bring to the Mer.

"We are children of the sea. And we will keep our Mother pure of mankind's touch. By the salt, we are born, and by the depths, we will fall."

Nephi could hear Tariq's voice as he recounted their mantra. It felt more like a prayer. They followed its words, eliminating the parasite one human body at a time. But then...

The fires of hell tasted flesh. Molten agony as scales melted into muscle. Heat so vicious it tore him apart. And the scream... the last scream.

My Ludo.

Nephi was too weak to finish the job. But after they saved him, the rest of the Pod laid waste to that human village. Usually, they only targeted the boats and fisheries. But after everything—after losing one of their own—Nephi wished he could have heard the dying squeals of the humans as they were slaughtered like swine.

Not even the little ones were spared.

Yet the revenge wasn't enough. Not nearly enough to satisfy the boiling rage inside him. He wanted to kill. To take from the humans what they'd taken from him. Baia Vita was helpless. Pathetic in its blindness.

It would be too easy.

He could find his Pod and bring them here. He was tempted. He was…

Nephi paused, realizing where he'd found himself. It was the same secluded beach where he'd left Leo's unconscious body. The human he'd saved when he should have watched him drown.

His heart twisted as he recalled that day—the day he'd acted completely opposite of what he believed. The day emotion and heartache drove his actions rather than his conviction. The day he'd let weakness seep through the cracks Ludo left behind.

He loathed himself for it.

Nephi swam to the surface, wading through the waves until he was on the sand. The beach was on the cliffside of the island, with no way for humans to spot him unless they came around the corner. Still, he made sure no prying eyes were watching before he ascended. He pulled on a hooded sweater he'd stolen from a first-floor balcony and stashed in the rocks a few days earlier. It was damp and smelled of human detergent, but it would do. It was about double his size, and he didn't care for the piss-yellow color, but thieves couldn't be choosy.

As he dried, he let his stubby human toes dig in the sand, wrinkling his nose at the useless appendages. Human's were so damn fragile.

He remembered Leo's unconscious body, lying lifeless on this very beach. Someone found him and fixed him up. Nephi hated the fact that, if not for him, that boy would be dead. He hated even more that a small part of him panicked at the idea of losing him.

A sniffling on the other side of the rocks made him pause, tuning to the sound. Nephi listened to the barely repressed sobs, wondering how a human's pathetic life could possibly be worth crying about. Curiosity won out as he stood up and stalked to the rock's edge, peering to the other side.

Inju, the Spirit of war, must have heard Nephi's desire for blood.

Or maybe *Dahest*, the Spirit of life and death, had placed an offering before Nephi as recompense for the life he'd lost. Because sitting in the sand was a familiar curly blond head with bloodshot yellow eyes.

As he approached, his pupils constricted into slits. This human's life now rested in his hands. And not even the Spirits could stop what was about to happen.

He pulled up his hood, tightening the strings to hide his face, forcing his eyes to relax into circles as he approached. Nephi made himself known, kicking sand as he walked.

When Leo spotted him, he quickly turned his head, wiping at his eyes.

"Sorry. Thought I was alone."

Even his voice...

Nephi wanted to howl in rage as the boy's eyes flickered between yellow and silver in his mind.

"What're you doing here?" Nephi asked, but suspected he knew the reason.

Leo shrugged. "It's a long story."

Nephi remained still, his reticence prompting the boy to continue.

Leo sighed. "I guess this is the place where things stopped making sense. Anyway, my life has kinda gone to shit recently, so if you don't mind, I want to be alone."

Nephi forced back a grin, ignoring the dismissal. "And you think this beach will help?"

"Nothing else has."

Nephi sat a few feet from him in the sand, gazing at the horizon, but his attention was painfully focused on the human on his left. Leo didn't argue. Either deep down, he wanted the company, or he had no fight left to protest.

It would be over so quickly. My hands around his throat. Finish what I started.

"I'm Leo, by the way," he offered, startling Nephi out of his fantasies. He didn't offer his name in return, so Leo continued. "You were talking to Atreus on the beach a few weeks ago."

"What if I was?"

Leo shrugged again. "That's none of my business."

"How'd you know it was me?"

"I recognize the eye," Leo said, making a circular motion around his own.

Nephi pulled the sweater tighter, hiding the right side of his face. He turned to make some rude remark, but it died in his mouth.

Leo looked at him, *really* looked. And he didn't cringe. His gaze didn't linger on Nephi's ruined eye or the scars still visible despite the hood.

He just... looked. As though Nephi were as common as a scallop. It was surprising.

"It's fucking hard to ignore," Nephi replied instead, forcing his gaze back to the horizon.

"I bet."

Nephi was like a sail on tenterhooks. Strained to the point of snapping. His insides were being pulled in all directions at once. He could end this. End this persistent itch in his brain. Kill the boy and be done with it. Leave this Spirits-forsaken island.

He's here. He's exposed. And he's mine.

Nephi wanted to grab Leo, to break him. To feel the brittle snap of bone beneath his grip, to see the light drain from his eyes. To reduce him to nothing but a crumpled heap. To tear him apart...

PIECE

BY

PIECE

However, as Nephi sneaked another glimpse, he knew he was too late. Someone else had already started chipping away at this human. It was written all over his angled body. In his red eyes, his dark circles. Painted in the sickly color of his skin.

"Why are you sitting here crying?" Nephi asked harshly.

Who did this?

He needed to know.

He needed to punish whoever hurt Leo because if anyone was going to break this human—*his* human—it would be him.

Nephi couldn't pinpoint when Leo became his. Maybe it was the first time his life fell into Nephi's claws. It didn't matter. Leo belonged to him. His right. His obsession. His prey.

My Ludo.

"Does it matter?" Leo responded. "And I wasn't crying."

Nephi's nose wrinkled, and the beginnings of a growl rumbled in his chest.

"Awfully defensive for someone hiding on a secluded beach, definitely *not crying.*"

"Awfully nosy for someone who won't even give me a name," Leo snapped, "or completely show his face."

Nephi grinned, leaning back on one hand and sinking into the sand. His prey had teeth.

And he liked it.

"Anyway, it doesn't matter. It's nothing I can't handle. For now, at least," Leo said, tossing a stone into the waves.

"So it has the potential to get worse. Is that what I'm hearing?"

Leo swallowed hard. "Yes. But it won't come to that."

"Don't be so sure," Nephi crooned.

"You have no idea what we're talking about."

"Oh, but I know that things that can get worse usually do."

"That's pessimistic."

"It's realistic."

Neither could hide the amused smiles that spread across their faces. Leo let out a soft chuckle.

"Wise words coming from a fucked up stranger on the beach."

Now it was Nephi's turn to laugh, and when he did, it felt like a thousand sea birds diving from the cliffs.

Untethered by the world.

"You don't know the half of it. Though fucked up is a pretty good way of putting it."

"So, does this fucked up stranger have a name or what?"

"No, he doesn't," Nephi snarled, then softened as he added, "but he does visit this beach a lot."

Leo nodded. "I'll keep that in mind."

And instead of watching Leo's lips turn blue as he choked the life out of him —Nephi watched the color return to his cheeks as he smiled.

CHAPTER 16

NYEL

"T HAT'S NOT FAIR. I've been outside just as much as you," Nyel complained, holding his forearm beside Atreus's. He was pasty by comparison.

"You're pale enough to scare off the fish," Atreus teased as Nyel shoved him.

"Ha ha," he deadpanned. "At least I'm not getting sunburnt anymore."

"Way to look on the bright side, Marshmallow."

"Are we doing nicknames? *Gatto's* already got his," Leo hollered

261

from the deck of his boat. Atreus and Nyel unloaded his cache as the shiny new vessel bobbed along the dock.

"What does that even mean?" Nyel asked, taking the tray of squid that sometimes got caught in the nets.

"Don't ask—"

"It means kitty cat," Leo called, "because Atreus is so scared of the water. It's been years, and he still won't get on the boat with me. I've stopped trying."

Nyel exchanged a meaningful look with Atreus.

"Well, I guess I can be *Gatto*, too, since I won't go anywhere near it either."

"Aw, come on! Nothing I can do to tempt you? One loop around the bay?"

"No thanks," Nyel said, earning an approving nod from Atreus.

Since their conversation with Nephi, he was more determined than ever to make Baia Vita his home. At least for the fishing season. After that? Nyel didn't want to think about it. If he was going to stay, he needed to be more cautious. And if Atreus, in all his years here, had never gone on a boat, neither would he.

"I don't want to be called Marshmallow. Even though they are delicious."

This made the other two laugh as they finished emptying Leo's catch. They wished him luck as he ushered the boat into the bay again. With all boats out working the bay, the pair had a moment to sort the fish before the next rush returned. They tagged the bigger catches with a handheld 'clicker' that punched a colored ribbon through the gills.

Nyel winced in sympathy as he stapled a heavy sea bass with Leo's black tag. Now, even if there were a spill, this fish wouldn't be mistakenly thrown into someone else's catch. The smaller ones were dumped into a barrel of ice with the vessel's name painted on the side. Nyel frowned at the scratched-out letters. *Vino Rosso* was no more, crossed out and painted over with the name *Pesce Pagliaccio*. He couldn't read either of the names, but he knew the letters corresponded with the names of Leo's old and new boats.

"He's in the same boat as the rest of them," Atreus said, following Nyel's gaze. "No pun intended."

"What do you mean?"

"I know you're worried about him. So am I. Everyone is fighting the same battle. There aren't enough fish in the bay anymore."

Nyel's shoulders slumped. "I just worry. With the new boat and…"

And how beaten he was the night of the festival.

It'd been almost a month since the festival, and Leo's face showed no signs of trauma. But Nyel couldn't forget the way Leo trembled. Atreus should know, and Nyel was tempted to tell him. But true to his word, he said nothing. Leo never broached the subject again.

"We're on week seven of the season. The catches are at a record low. It's… It's going to get ugly come winter. Families will either go hungry or be forced to leave."

Atreus didn't have to say it; Nyel could hear it in his voice. Baia Vita was on the verge of becoming a ghost town—abandoned and lifeless.

"I wish there was more we could do to help."

"There's nothing we can do. Right now, we need to put our heads down and work," Atreus said, tagging a red snapper and laying it in a tray of ice.

But that wasn't true.

There was something they could do. As Mer, there was so much they could offer this place. The idea continued to fester in Nyel's brain long after they'd delivered the day's catch to the *pescheria* and settled on the upper floor for dinner.

Nyel pushed the marinated tomatoes around his plate, his mind too busy for food. Horace was deep in another one of his war stories, in which his Mer friend Kirill infiltrated enemy lines from beneath the water. Nyel had heard this one a few times and still loved it, pushing for more details about Horace's Mer friend with each retelling.

"He was a witty son of a bitch. Always had something smart to say." Horace laughed, then let out a series of frightening coughs.

"That's enough exciting stories tonight, *Nonno*. Let me help you to bed," Marina offered, setting down her fork and rising.

"Thank you, Gabriella. Make sure you leave my window cracked so Niccolo can come in. I don't know where he gets off to at night."

The cat, usually by the old man's side like a shadow, had recently started vanishing at night and returning in the early morning. The feline was as congenial as a well-worn blanket on a quiet evening. He never hissed or spat. Never scratched or pinned back his ears.

That was... unless a certain someone walked within ten feet of him.

Nyel was that someone.

The feline only had eyes for Horace, tolerated everyone else, and harbored a special hatred for Nyel, no matter how many fish scraps he'd offered under the table.

"*Nonno,* you shouldn't leave that window open at night," Marina said. When the old man produced a heart-wrenching puppy face, she groaned. "Fine, okay, you win," she relented, supporting his shaking frame out of the chair and down the hall.

When she returned, Marina and Giovanni engaged in a steady conversation about her plans for the Bayallon at the end-of-season festival. Giovanni worried that the village would be too out of spirits to get excited about the event.

"I'll have to work extra hard to make it special!" Marina said with her usual upbeat attitude.

Atreus remained quiet, ever the wallflower. But Nyel couldn't keep his exploding thoughts contained any longer.

"I have a question," he blurted, making everyone pause.

"Go ahead," Giovanni said, gesturing to him with his fork.

Nyel cleared his throat. "What if...What if there was a way to help the fishermen?"

Atreus's fork paused halfway to his mouth as he stiffened.

"We are all ears, *ragazzo*," Giovanni said cordially. "Though I believe all avenues have been exhausted. We've tried everything. There is no competing with those damned ships."

"What if there was a way to herd the fish away from the ships and into the bay? Into our fishermen's nets?"

Nyel could practically hear the alarm bells going off in Atreus's head, but he ignored him. This was important, and Atreus needed to hear it.

Giovanni let out a big belly laugh. "What, like sheep? I'm afraid this island doesn't have underwater sheepdogs. Fresh out," he joked.

But Nyel wasn't joking.

"Let's pretend we did, though. Do you think it would help?"

Giovanni took a sip from his wine. "I'm sure it would, *ragazzo*." He smacked his lips loudly, finishing the glass. "To have a young mind like yours. I admire your creativity. It's an interesting fantasy to consider. But I'm afraid a fantasy nevertheless."

"Yeah, I know. I was just curious."

He remained silent for the rest of dinner. Nyel scarcely closed the door to his room for the night when Atreus yanked it open.

"What was that? What the hell are you doing?"

"You know exactly what I'm doing. The Mer can help—"

"Shshsh!" Atreus hissed, darting his head to the hall before closing the door. "I thought we were past this. You're being reckless."

"It's not reckless. It's a solution, Atreus. Can't you see? We can help each other."

Nyel sat at the edge of his bed, crossing his legs, hoping Atreus would do the same and calm down. He didn't.

"You're out of your mind. It'll ruin everything. Realizing there are sea monsters on their doorsteps will only drive the humans off the island. We'd be speeding up its end."

"Not if the fish come back. It's the lifeline of this place, and it's dying. We can fix this! And we aren't monsters, Atreus. We're Mer. So get that out of your head."

"I know we're Mer I'm just saying—"

"Do you?" Nyel rounded on him. "Do you know that Atreus? Because sometimes I don't think you do. You don't stop being Mer just because no one sees you."

Atreus's eyes went hard on him, narrowing as the faintest hiss sounded in his chest.

"I am aware," he said through clenched teeth, "What I'm trying to say is that they will only see us as monsters. People don't change overnight."

"I did."

Atreus chewed his cheek, and Nyel pressed on.

"I changed my mind about you. About halflings. All it took was for me to get to know you."

"Fine. But you're one person. An entire village can't get to know me well enough to justify what I am."

"They already do!" Nyel leaned forward, the words pulling him towards Atreus. Begging him to understand. "How can you still not see it? These people, all of them, they already love you. You're a pinnacle of this community. They *rely* on you."

Atreus shook his head, and Nyel knew he'd failed. It would take a cataclysmic event for Atreus to finally believe him, to see what only took Nyel a few weeks to see.

"It would never happen."

"You said this island is desperate. Maybe desperate enough to accept the help of Mer?"

Atreus pinched the bridge of his nose, pacing the room. "Fine. Let's say, by some unholy miracle, the humans accept us. You think the two of us can herd entire schools away from those ships? I hate to break it to you, but two of us swimming back and forth won't be enough."

"The *Sireni* in Corallina will help."

Atreus scoffed. "Sure."

Nyel's face turned pink with indignation. "They will. I'll talk to them. They're being hurt by the ships, too."

Nyel vaguely remembered Chel's father mentioning something about the kelp dying the day she came for dinner.

"The ships are polluting the waters. Corallina is losing crops because of them."

"How much?" Atreus prodded.

"A—a few acres. I think. I don't remember." Nyel cursed himself for not paying more attention to the conversation on that fateful day. Granted, he had other things on his mind.

"A little crop damage isn't enough for them to break age-old tradition. They won't reveal themselves. They won't accept a union. They can't even accept one of their own if their scales don't match up."

"I'll talk to them," Nyel tried to sound stronger than he felt. "I promised Nephi that I'd talk to my parents about halflings. And I will. I just... need more time."

Atreus sighed, falling into Nyel's desk chair.

"You see how many things are against you? How many ways this idea of yours could go wrong? It can't happen, Nyel. Drop it."

"Against me? Not us?"

Atreus's jaw set, and Nyel had his answer. Despite growing close, the words Atreus growled into his ear all those weeks ago were as true today as they were then. If Nyel were to get caught, Atreus wouldn't come to his rescue. Wouldn't risk his dwindling way of life.

Nyel dropped his chin to his chest. "Right. I'm on my own."

"Don't pin this on me," Atreus said, rising to his feet again, his face growing red.

"And who am I supposed to pin it on?" Nyel retaliated, voice rising.

"I don't care. But don't go blaming me because I won't follow you off a cliff. You're telling me to jump with no wings, and I'm not buying it."

"I'm telling you to trust me!" Nyel yelled.

The sound of a closing door in the hall startled them both.

Nyel stepped off the bed, stopping only inches from Atreus. When he spoke, it was barely above a whisper.

"I'm telling you to trust in the way these people care about you."

Atreus's nostrils flared, his curls flopping as he shook his head. "You're delusional."

"And you're scared. You hide like it's the only way you know how to breathe."

They held each other's stare, neither willing to break the connection first. Nyel was sure he could hear Atreus's teeth grinding together as the muscles in his jaw bulged.

"We're done here."

Atreus stomped from the room without another word.

Nyel flopped onto his bed, slapping a pillow over his face and yelling.

"Atreus, you freakin idiot!" He pounded his fists on the mattress, wishing he were hitting some sense into Atreus's thick head.

Why can't you see it? Why can't you see the way everyone else sees you?

Even as the words rang in his mind, a new kind of heat surged to his face—one that had nothing to do with his frustration. Coupled with the feeling of wiggling fishtails in his chest, Nyel didn't know what to make of it—only that these feelings were growing steadier and steadier by the day.

"You're a dummy," Nyel whined into his feather pillow. Those angry green eyes would keep him awake for hours.

ATREUS

ATREUS FOUGHT THE URGE to slam the door to his room. If he threw the wooden door as hard as he wanted, he'd topple the entire damn *pescheria*.

Where does he get these ideas? Mer and humans? Me?

Atreus couldn't sit still and kept running his hands through his tangle of curls. At this rate, he wouldn't have any hair left. Nyel was...

"Gah!" he cried out, hitting his toe on the bed frame.

"As if you have any value to begin with."

Atreus snarled. He had nothing to say to the disembodied call in his mind. The single thread connecting him to the madness Nephi spoke of. The *Skraith*. Atreus didn't fight it this time.

Because he believed it.

The moment the humans saw what he was, it wouldn't matter that they knew him. Wouldn't matter that they'd broken bread with him, that he'd watched their children grow and weathered storms by their side. All of that would wash away like footprints on the sand the moment his scales appeared.

They won't allow it.

It was too much for him to comprehend, let alone accept. He thought of Giovanni. Would his face twist in disgust? Flare with rage? The idea made Atreus want to lean over his bed and vomit on the floor. That is what he stood to lose—everything.

Why can't Nyel understand that?

In all honesty, despite the proof, Atreus still couldn't wrap his mind around the fact that Nyel hadn't left. Their secluded minutes on the beach, under the light of the fireworks, felt like a dream— something he would have imagined on those lonely nights in the lighthouse. Yet it'd happened. And Nyel saw him.

Could I get lucky enough to be accepted twice?

Atreus doubted it, and he didn't need the voice in his head to tell him that.

Still, how did this always happen? How did he always end up fighting with Nyel? With the one person in this world who accepted him?

"You're messing this up," he hissed, the sound building in his throat before descending into his chest. It was like a massive serpent was coiled where his heart should be. Atreus forced calming breaths through his lungs, silencing the sound. He waited, making sure no one heard. The hiss was unnatural to humans. He couldn't remember the last time he'd let it slip.

Man, I'm losing it.

He continued pacing.

"Keep this up, and he'll leave for sure."

The voice purred, excited by the idea of Atreus alone and miserable.

"I know!" he yelled in the empty room.

Atreus didn't have a clue how to navigate his feelings around Nyel. One moment, they were laughing and joking; the next, Atreus was irrationally upset whenever Nyel's attention was diverted. At times, like now, he was so frustrated with Nyel that he could hardly stand it. And this all happened within a single day.

Before Nyel showed up, his life was consistent. His days were predictable and safe. He more or less understood how to navigate the maze of human emotions. How to navigate through the lies he'd built around himself like a shield. Yet, even knowing that— Atreus couldn't bring himself to wish Nyel was gone. In fact, the idea sank a leaden stone in his stomach.

And if he wanted the *sireno* to stay, he had to fix this. Soon.

"WE'RE CLOSING the bay for the day. Everyone's boats are docked. With quiet waters, hopefully, we can coax some of the fish to return."

It was the first thing Giovanni said to him when he rose for breakfast the next morning.

"No one is going out today?" Atreus asked, dumbfounded. In all his years working the docks, he'd never seen Baia Vita halt the fishing for even a second of daylight.

"I got word from Leo. He and some of the younger men are going door to door to spread the word."

They sat in oppressive quiet, Giovanni's gaze so unfocused that Atreus wondered if he was seeing anything at all.

"Do you think it'll help?" Nyel's voice startled him as the *sireno* approached from behind. "*Signore* Marcello?"

"Huh?" Giovanni reacted much too late. "Sorry, *ragazzo*. Will it help?" He exhaled loudly. "That is the question. I do not know. But what else can we do? There are simply no more fish left for us."

"Well, I'll just have to take the boat and go scare those big ships off now, will I?" Marina said much too loud for so early in the morning.

Giovanni pulled his daughter in for a half-hug. "That wouldn't do my *Bambani*. Your beauty would only draw them nearer."

"Or she could start singing for them. That'd scare them off," Nyel murmured so only Atreus could hear. Atreus choked on his eggs in his haste to stifle the sudden burst of laughter.

"What are you two *idioti* laughing about?" Marina glared.

"Nothing, nothing!" Nyel said, patting Atreus on the back as he choked.

There, he did it again. Somehow, even when things were grim, Nyel made him laugh.

Nobody had ever been able to do that before.

Atreus thanked Nyel and remained determined to do better—to be better—for this *sireno*. For this male who had the uncanny ability to make him smile all through breakfast.

With the docks closed, Atreus and Nyel had nothing to do. Marina busied herself running errands and preparing for the Bayallon. Atreus wondered what she could possibly be spending so much time on. It was a silly relay race. Yet Marina was elbow-deep in paint, banners, and other crafts whenever he saw her.

With the day free and Marina shooing them out of her 'creative space,' they found themselves walking aimlessly down the beach. The docks were upsettingly quiet. No tolling bells or hollering men. No '*Bongonrio's*' called in greeting. Only the gulls cawed above, and even they seemed irritated with the break in routine.

Then an idea struck him.

"Hey, do you wanna go for a swim? Maybe check on the lighthouse?" Atreus offered.

Nyel tilted his head to the side, eyebrows scrunched. "How have we never done that before?"

"Well... I was doing my best to stay out of the water in front of you," Atreus admitted.

"Oh, right." Nyel grabbed his wrist, dragging him to a private stretch of the beach covered with large black boulders. "There's no need for that anymore. Let's go for a swim. My skin's been feeling itchy all over."

Atreus felt it, too—the call of the sea after many days on land.

They ducked behind the black stones and, when they were sure nobody was around, kicked off their shoes. Atreus removed his shirt since his barbs would destroy anything on his back. Luckily, both their pants were altered to accommodate the tails.

Nyel dove into the water, jade scales shimmering to life as his thick, curved tail beckoned Atreus forward. "Come on!"

Atreus walked to the water's edge but stopped suddenly as if he'd reached the end of a leash.

What if it was a fluke? What if the night was dark enough that he didn't get a good look? What if he changes his mind?

Panic coursed through Atreus.

"*Get away. Don't show yourself.*
He'll be disgusted with you.
Half-breed."

It didn't just speak—it *taunted*, each syllable carefully chosen to unravel him further.

Atreus was convinced this was no ordinary voice. It was a demon. A curse. A punishment for his existence, a living reminder of everything that made him unworthy. The *Skraith* knew this, and it reveled in it, fanning the flames of his panic with every venomous word.

Atreus's heart raced, pounding against his eardrums so forcefully it felt like they might burst, flooding his brain with blood—drowning him in the very essence that marked him as a mistake.

He couldn't breathe; the air stuck in his lungs like sap. His vision tunneled to a single point of surf. He couldn't do it. He couldn't...

"Atreus?" He hardly registered the tight grip on his wrist, pulling him to the present. "Atreus, breathe. It's okay."

A gentle hand ran up and down his spine, encouraging the blood to flow, the nerves to fire, and the lungs to expand.

"There you go. You got this."

Another hand rested on his chest as it rose.

"Breath in. And out. In. Out."

The gentle pressure on his chest guided his steady breathing, helping him focus on the flow of oxygen in his lungs. It took several breaths before Atreus realized the hand on his chest—and the one gliding up and down his spine—were webbed.

The smooth scales on the palm of Nyel's hand were soft, cool to the touch, and...

Atreus could only describe it as a salve— soothing balm for a wound split open, bleeding freely. Normally, the blind panic would have left him paralyzed for hours. Yet now, all it took was a touch—Nyel's touch—to calm him.

"You with me?" Nyel asked, and Atreus looked at him. The *sireno* boy he'd met all those years ago. Jade scales. Black-tipped fins.

He's beautiful.

Atreus cleared his throat, shaking the buzz from his head.

"Yeah. I —" He swallowed. "I don't know what happened."

"Here."

With deliberate slowness, Nyel took both of Atreus's hands in his. Human hands clasped with Mer. Nyel walked backward into the surf, taking Atreus with him, never breaking eye contact.

"I won't think differently of you, Atreus. Not for a second."

Atreus let himself be pulled into the surf. *Marvassa* washed over him, and he was Mer once more. Nyel didn't stop walking backward until the water covered their heads, and they floated above the sand. The entire time, he never looked away.

"Your eyes are the same," Nyel said.

Warmth spread through Atreus's chest. He examined himself, noting the different tones of blue and purple on his body, with lighter shades of mauve flecking his fins.

"Betcha I can beat you to the island," Nyel teased.

"Wh-what? I don't—"

"Ready, set GO!" Nyel yelled before Atreus finished and was off like a sailfish on the hunt.

"That's cheating!" Atreus called, thrusting his tail and matching Nyel's speed. By the time they reached the beach, Atreus was leagues ahead. He made a show of waiting as Nyel trudged up the sand in defeat, panting for breath.

"What took you so long?" He smirked. "I was about to take a nap while I waited."

"Har har," Nyel said, shaking his fins like a dog. "It would have been better if you did. I'm exhausted. And hungry."

"There are still a few cans of sardines in the lighthouse," Atreus offered, just to see the disgusted look on Nyel's face.

He laughed, brushing sand from his pants, having already returned to his human form. He was refreshed, like *Marvassa* exfoliated layers and layers of dead skin.

"What is that?"

"What is what?" Atreus asked. His good mood dimmed when he realized what Nyel was pointing at.

"Your back, on your shoulder. I didn't notice it earlier."

Atreus averted his gaze and rolled said shoulder, feeling the familiar tug on his skin. "An old scar. It was a long time ago."

That should have been it. They should have moved on. But the way Nyel watched him, scales dissipating into skin as he dried, dark wavy hair appearing over fins, Atreus was too mesmerized to walk away. Too enraptured by Nyel's pinched brow and the slight down-turn of his mouth.

Concern for me.

"Let me see."

Atreus should have said no. Should tell him it was none of his business. So what compelled him to turn around, giving Nyel full view of his bare back? Of the history written in his skin?

Gentle fingertips brushed over the swollen wound below his shoulder plate—a circular scar, puffy, white, and dangerously close to his spine.

"A puncture wound," Atreus said, his voice tight as another pass of Nyel's fingers sent a shiver through him.

"It looks painful," Nyel whispered.

"It was," Atreus said without turning around.

At thirteen, it was the most pain he'd ever endured. And even though he knew it was impossible, the wounds still throbbed from time to time—a phantom pain. But the weight of knowing who had inflicted it had cut far deeper.

He could feel Nyel's quiet curiosity, probing for answers.

"Let's check on the lighthouse," he said, shrugging off the touch and climbing the beach without further comment.

Not that. I won't talk about that.

The lighthouse lay exactly as Atreus left it over two months ago. He carefully stepped around the shards of glass, cautioning Nyel to do the same. The rusted stairs groaned like a wounded beast as they climbed. He cleared the landing and— he was thirteen again— hungry, isolated, alone.

"The way you deserve to be."

"Doesn't look like anyone has been here," Nyel observed, snapping Atreus out of his childhood.

He cleared his throat. "Yeah. Little dusty, though."

"It just needs some air," Nyel offered, cracking open a few of the windows and welcoming a pleasant ocean breeze.

Atreus watched him move from window to window. A few weeks ago, the latches would have stumped him. Nyel was adapting to human ways quickly, much faster than Atreus had. It was as though he was destined to be part of their world from the beginning. Loved by both humans and Mer.

"And neither will ever love you."

"I need to check on some things," Atreus said, cutting off the intrusive voice. "Are you okay to hang out for a bit?"

Nyel made an affirmative noise, sitting at the window's edge, admiring the view. Atreus busied himself by taking stock of his possessions, which, now that he'd lived so long at the *pescheria*, he realized was mostly old garbage. He propped the mattress on its side for some ventilation when a sharp static sound made him spin.

"Sorry," Nyel apologized, jerking his hand away from the dial of an old transistor radio. "I thought these things made music."

Atreus smiled. "They don't make music, but they do play recordings." He knelt beside the small rust-colored radio. "You have to fiddle with this dial, then this one." Atreus tuned the radio, working through the screeching static, catching a mumbled voice here and there before an upbeat family of instruments vibrated through the speaker. He patted it. "*Voilà.*"

A man's voice boomed, his hearty base harmonizing with the instruments in a powerful vibrato. Even through the raspy radio, there was no denying that the man sang with all his soul. The words tumbled from him in a musical story of long summer days and a beautiful woman who stole his heart.

Nyel hummed along, picking up the melody. He stood abruptly, shoving his stool aside and clearing a space in the lighthouse.

"What're you doing?" Atreus asked as his belongings were shoved against the walls.

Nyel didn't reply until he was finished, then turned and held out a hand. "Dance with me."

Atreus furrowed his brows. "I don't know how."

"Perfect. Neither do I," Nyel said, his voice so light and easy that Atreus found himself reaching for the outstretched hand before he even realized it.

"I really don't, though," he repeated, clasping Nyel's hand, unsure what to do.

"It goes like this. I think." Nyel placed his free hand on Atreus's opposite shoulder. "I watched the humans do it at the festival. And your hand goes here," he added, guiding Atreus's other hand to his waist.

Suddenly, the room felt impossibly small, as if he and Nyel were being crushed together by invisible walls. Atreus couldn't help but notice the gentle slope of Nyel's waist beneath his palm, even through the fabric.

He jerked away, the closeness overwhelming.

"This is stupid," he said, stepping back, his heart hammering.

"Oh, c'mon," Nyel begged. "I want to dance at the next festival. How am I supposed to learn without practice?"

A new tenor voice sang through the speaker, accompanied by a furious violin, making Nyel's face light up.

"This song is perfect for it! Please, just for a minute?"

Atreus sighed, rubbing the back of his head roughly. "Ugh, fine."

Reluctantly, he resumed his place, stepping close again, though the proximity still felt suffocating. His heart thudded in his chest as his hand once again found Nyel's waist. The space between them seemed nonexistent, and he was painfully aware of every point of contact.

Then came Nyel's scent. He smelled of the sea, but... different. Not the salty tang of the ocean breeze wafting through the window. It was more soothing than that. Clean notes of seagrass mingling with the brightness of sunlit water breaking through the surface. It filled the space between them, carrying the wildness of the open sea and something warmer, something alive. It settled over Atreus like a tide, pulling him deeper than he intended to go.

"Are you even listening?" Nyel said, glaring up at him with gold-flecked eyes.

"Huh?" Atreus said stupidly.

"Pay attention. Step back with your left— no right, and I'll follow."

They stumbled through the steps, bumping knees and stepping on toes more than once. Both kept their heads down, watching their feet and laughing each time they mixed up their rights and lefts.

"No, your left, my right," Nyel said through a fit of laughter as they moved in what could be loosely described as dancing. And, with something akin to grace, Nyel stepped out of their two-step, twirling beneath Atreus's arm. That was until their fingers twisted, and they clashed elbows.

Both men pulled back, sucking air through their teeth and rubbing their funny bones.

"We're not ready for advanced moves like that yet," Atreus said, rubbing the joint.

"I bet it looked cool. Before we hit each other, at least," Nyel said, grimacing through the discomfort.

"We both look like complete idiots, I can guarantee," Atreus said, then worried it came out too harsh. But Nyel laughed with a nod.

"Okay, again. I know what I did wrong."

Atreus didn't hesitate this time, growing more comfortable with each step. Before they knew it, the sky turned a deep shade of orange, and both of them were sweaty. But Atreus had to admit they'd improved.

"We'll put those humans to shame at the next festival," Nyel said, chest heaving. They'd picked up the pace as their confidence grew, their bare feet gliding on the wooden floors without a single crushed toe.

"We'll see," Atreus said. "Let's get some air."

They opened one of the windows wider, stepping out onto a narrow landing that looped around the lighthouse. It wasn't meant for people to walk on, though Atreus had been doing it for years.

Nyel let out a long sigh as the wind cooled their skin. The radio music turned to something slow, the woman's alto voice singing powerfully in a minor melody. There was a soft 'thump' as Nyel closed his eyes and leaned his head against the glass.

Atreus gazed at the horizon, at Baia Vita in the distance. It was a view he'd seen hundreds of times. Now, his eyes were drawn to the *sireno* at his side.

His friend.

With a pang, Atreus realized that's what Nyel was to him. The word didn't settle right in his stomach, like that time he'd tried to eat kelp.

I need to get ahold of myself.

Still, his errant thoughts ran away with him no matter how he resisted.

Leo was a friend, Marina was a friend, Giovanni was a mentor, and Horace was an elder he respected. All those titles felt right for the people he'd assigned them to. Yet *friend* didn't fit Nyel. He stared at the *sireno*, contemplating this. With his eyes closed, Nyel looked entirely at peace as the ocean breeze blew his hair. The dark, wavy strands danced over his forehead. For the first time, Atreus noticed how long his lashes were.

He's beautiful like this, too.

Again, he was overwhelmed with the same stuffiness he'd felt inside the lighthouse—that suffocating feeling of being too close. Their proximity was all at once something he was too aware of. His breathing sped up.

Nyel's arm bumped into his. "You okay?"

"Mhm," Atreus said quickly, returning his gaze to the horizon. "We should head back."

"Wanna race again?" Nyel offered halfheartedly.

"I don't think it's good for you to be humiliated twice in one day," Atreus teased, earning a soft punch to the arm.

"You're lucky I'm too tired because those are fighting words."

"Next time, then."

"Next time," Nyel agreed.

And the certainty that there would be a next time made Atreus's heart skip. There would be many next times—just him and Nyel. Despite the stuffy feeling he couldn't explain, the idea didn't bother him one bit.

"Think we could make this jump?" the *sireno* asked, peering over the edge.

"That's not a good idea, Ny," Atreus cautioned. "I've done it, but I've been here a long time, and... what's with the face?" Atreus asked at Nyel's odd expression.

"You called me Ny."

"Oh. Sorry, I didn't realize. I can stop—"

"No! I like it. Nobody has ever called me that before."

Atreus didn't know what to do with that information, but it made something in his stomach flip.

"Well, let's take the stairs this time, Ny," he added, making the *sireno* smile.

"Lead the way."

CHAPTER 17

MARINA

S HE DID IT. Marina finally did it. It took her all freakin' summer, but it was done. The only thing left to do was dot some I's and cross some T's.

Marina had completely revolutionized the Bayallon.

Instead of having children from all ages compete together, leaving the younger ones with zero chance of winning, Marina devised three separate courses for different age groups. The little ones had a kiddie course with a small running and swimming section. They were too small to ride bikes, so instead of biking, their final event would be a wagon pull, where the parents pulled their child in a wagon and raced for the finish line.

The middle age group would participate in all three events but with a lowered difficulty level, leaving the older kids with the hardest course. With no little ones to worry about getting in the way, the course she'd planned would kick their snarky teenage butts. They had to pedal their bikes all the way to the top of the valley, circle around the windmill, and then race down a brutal, steep slope to reach the square for the finish.

"There are going to be some tired kids on the island by the time I'm done with them," Marina said proudly. The excitement was building to a boiling point. Townsfolk had seen her making preparations, and she could hardly leave the *pescheria* without being peppered with excited questions.

It would be the Bayallon of the century.

She didn't have much for prizes for the kids, though. Funding from the mayor's office had been non-existent. She would have loved to offer a brand-new bike as the prize for the older kids, but that would leave nothing for the rest. Instead, she put together simple baskets filled with candies and treats from the mainland—exotic delicacies for these island kids.

After tying the bow on the final basket, she decided to walk the kids' course one more time and check for any hazards. As she cut through a narrow alley between two tightly pressed buildings, hushed voices made her pause.

Marina peeked around the corner and immediately recognized one of the two figures: the gorgeous man she'd danced with at the season festival.

It's him.

Her heart leaped to her throat so fast she almost choked on it. His long, wavy hair was as immaculate as she remembered, though this time, his clothes were more casual. He leaned heavily over the second figure, a young, pretty blonde woman with pink cheeks. Marina ducked behind a corner, listening hard.

"My-my name is Leigha," the young woman said with a bashful flutter of her lashes.

"Leigha," he purred, "now that is a name I won't forget."

"Wh-why?" she asked breathlessly.

"Because it's beautiful."

Marina held back a snort as the familiar line made the other woman's knees go weak.

"Until next time, flower," the man said, lifting her hand to his lips before leaving her red-faced and starry-eyed.

The flash of hurt that tightened Marina's chest was gone in less than a second. Sure, she'd been swept away by this stunning man. Who wouldn't? Sure, she let herself fall into a fairy fantasy. Sure, she'd imagined running into him again a thousand times in a thousand different ways. And sure, watching him put the exact same moves on another girl hurt. But her shock vanished within seconds, replaced by mirth.

Marina couldn't resist the pull at her lips as she followed the man through another alley, winding through a few paths until they were alone.

She called out, "Your delivery was a little off. Slow it down next time. Really lean into the 'because it's beautiful' line."

The man turned to her, and the moment their eyes met, Marina was immensely satisfied to see a flash of panic in his. It was gone in a wink, replaced by a devilishly charming smile.

"You think? I'll keep that in mind for next time."

"Who knows, maybe one day you'll actually remember one of their names."

"Who says I don't?"

Marina guffawed with a very unladylike snort. "Sure. What's mine?"

She could practically see the smoke coming from his ears as he searched his memory for her name. He sauntered closer, taking her hand in the most sickeningly chivalrous motion she'd ever seen.

"What does a name matter when its owner is as radiant as you?"

And stupidly enough, for half a second, those dark brown eyes almost had her in their snare again. But she'd learned her lesson and wasn't about to let her heart be played with like a cat with a ball of yarn. She wasn't here for this man's amusement, whoever he was.

Quickly, her mirth turned to anger as her face hardened.

Who does this guy think he is?

"Nice save. I almost believed you," she said, jerking her hand back before he could place a kiss there. She spun, ready to leave him in the dust. So when his steps quickened, and she found him keeping pace with her, irritation reared its ugly head.

"Oh, you must at least credit me with that bracelet I gifted you. I'm sure it complements your pretty wrists so nicely."

"Bracelet?" Marina raised a brow.

"It wasn't a bracelet?" He thought momentarily before snapping his fingers. "Earrings. That's right. I gave you earrings, the ones you knocked off the table like a stumbling oaf."

Marina's jaw fell open, and she increased her pace. The man was undeterred, his long legs keeping close.

"Do you lure in all your conquests with pretty things? Or are your pretty words usually enough?"

"A healthy dose of both," he said with so little remorse Marina wanted to kick him in the shin.

She shook her head. "You're unbelievable."

"Why, thank you."

"That wasn't a... Don't you have better things to do? Other innocent girls' feelings to play with?"

He checked an imaginary watch on his wrist. "Not right now." He checked it again. "Though I am booked out this evening."

The audacity!

"Well, I have things to do, and spending my day with an egotistical jerk isn't on the list."

She marched down another lane, fists clenched, half-expecting footsteps to follow. But when she turned to tell him off, he was gone.

Serves him right.

Yet deep down, she'd wished he'd followed. If only to tell him off some more.

"Well, this is one girl who knows your tricks," she muttered, jaw tight as her cheeks flushed. "And I am *not* a stumbling oaf."

She glanced back one last time—just to prove it—then promptly rammed her shin into the edge of the marble fountain. She pitched forward, shoes splashing into the shallow water as she scrambled.

She caught herself, nose-to-nose with the Mermaid at the center, in what was nearly a very undignified first kiss.

"Well. Better you than anyone else." She muttered, checking to see if anyone saw.

Across the square, three old ladies outside the gelato shop were staring, spoons paused halfway to their mouths.

She groaned under her breath, sloshing from the fountain with as much dignity as she could muster.

"Stupid idiot with his stupid pretty face. I'm gonna kick him next time I see him," she grumbled all the way to the *pescheria*.

CHAPTER 18

NYEL

Nyel wanted to talk to his brother, but Nephi was like a shadow—there one moment and gone the next. Anytime Nyel tried to get close, the figure hovered at the edges of his vision before vanishing. Days would often pass without a single glimpse of his half-brother. Yet inevitably, Nephi would slink back into the periphery, like a stray alley cat—always lurking, unseen but ever-present.

"I just want to talk," Nyel grumbled after another failed attempt to catch his brother, watching the hooded figure dart around a shop and vanish.

It was obvious that Nephi wasn't going to make this easy. Maybe he didn't want a relationship with Nyel. Maybe there were too many years of damage. Too much pain to overcome.

That won't stop me from trying, Nyel thought with determination as he watched Atreus and Leo return to the docks while he remained at the sorting tables.

Nyel didn't mind the slimy work, and he'd finally stopped needing to stuff newspaper up his nose. But he couldn't help the longing in his chest as he watched Leo and Atreus descend the hill and pad toward the floating docks, where fishermen waited for fresh bait or to unload a catch. Atreus was barefoot as always, which Nyel thought was risky—one stray splash could trigger *Marvassa*. But he trusted Atreus knew what he was doing; he'd been doing it all his life, after all.

Leo was helping at the docks today rather than fishing himself. Nyel sensed he was eager to get away from the nets for a while, and watching him simultaneously work and joke around with Atreus solidified his suspicions.

From his vantage point, Nyel watched as Atreus nudged Leo with his elbow, almost sending him toppling into the water.

"Watch it!" Leo barked, stumbling but catching himself on a wooden post. "If you weren't such a *Gatto* I'd shove you in just for that."

Nyel's shoulders stiffened at the playful yet detrimental threat. But Atreus didn't appear concerned.

"You know the rule," was all he said with a good-natured smile as they lifted a heavier crate of bait together.

"Yeah, yeah. You've only reminded me a million times. My pinky still remembers." Leo said, but rather than being angry at the memory of his broken finger, he smiled fondly.

Atreus told Nyel that early in their friendship, he'd set the foundation of his 'water phobia,' earning himself the nickname *Gatto*. But Leo liked to push his limits, especially when they were young, and had tried dunking Atreus in the fountain despite the warning. Long story short, Atreus came out of the altercation perfectly dry, while Leo ended up with his head in the fountain and his pinky finger snapped in two.

Safe to say they'd settled on a healthy understanding after that. Atreus was *Gatto* - which meant no water.

Still, watching him and Leo shove at each other on the ever-shifting planks of wood made Nyel's stomach twist with worry. With the tolling bells of the boats now far in the bay, Nyel could hear the pair's conversation.

"Ugh, I hate low tide. Always brings that nasty smell." Leo said, scrunching his nose.

"I don't mind," Atreus said, organizing a pile of buoys and fishing line.

"Don't mind, huh? But wait till you get a whiff of this," Leo said, pulling off his shirt and throwing the sweaty cotton with the proficiency of a fisherman casting line. It smacked Atreus square in the face.

"What the f—Leo!" Atreus barked, peeling the cloth off him like it was toxic. "That smells like it's been marinating in bait and regret."

"Regret? That's the smell of a hardworking man," Leo shot back with a grin.

Atreus shook his head and tossed the shirt to Leo with far less enthusiasm. Both of them looked up when Nyel broke into a fit of laughter. Leo waved, and Nyel waved back, but when his eyes met Atreus's, the other Mer quickly averted his gaze, pretending to fuss with the already neatly stacked ropes.

Nyel returned to his work, though his mind strayed from sorting sardines. Occasionally, he glanced up, watching the pair deep in conversation.

Leo hadn't put his cotton tee back on. He was lean, narrower in the shoulders, but Nyel knew his frame was deceptive—his muscles honed from years of hard labor. His sun-kissed skin was smooth, not a freckle in sight, with only the faintest tan line suggesting he spent most of his hours on the boat without a shirt. Nyel wondered if Atreus might follow Leo's example and remove his. It was a hot day, after all—it wouldn't be unusual.

But he didn't. Yet that didn't stop Nyel from remembering a time when Atreus's skin was on display.

Flashes of their night on the beach surfaced in his mind: Atreus, with his finest button-up reduced to rags, draped over his torso. Even in the dim light, Nyel would've had to be blind not to notice the sculpted ridges of Atreus's body. Each muscle was perfectly toned, balanced against his broad shoulders. Freckles dusted his skin like the starry sky. Nyel found himself wondering just how far they went. Did they... go all the way down?

"You need to come with me."

"Sharks!" Nyel yelped, jumping and sending a tray of sardines clattering to the ground. He scrambled like someone caught doing something indecent, though there was no way his brooding half-brother could read his thoughts. Still, the evidence was plain as day, glowing red on Nyel's face as he struggled to gather the slippery fish.

"Spirits, Nephi! What was that for? Don't sneak up on me like that."

"You need to come home," Nephi said, another stolen jacket covering his scars.

"What are you—? I've been trying to talk to you for days, and now you decide to—"

"It's your aunt. The baby is coming."

Panic seized Nyel's stomach. Had he been gone that long? How had so much time passed so quickly? On the heels of panic came guilt. He hadn't thought about his aunt nearly enough in the passing weeks—Sonia, who was always on his side.

"Ny, what's going on?" Atreus jogged up, his eyebrows pinched.

"I have to go," Nyel said, spinning around, only to find Nephi already gone.

"Going? Going where?"

"I have to go home. My aunt, she's— I promised I'd be there," he said, every second ticking like a bomb.

The docks were unusually busy this morning. The fishermen were eager to get on the water, yelling for bait and supplies. But he couldn't stay.

"I'm sorry," Nyel said and darted in the direction of the beach.

"Ny, wait!"

Atreus followed him, and somewhere in the distance, he faintly caught Leo's voice calling, "*Gatto*, what are you doing?"

But Leo was far behind now.

Nyel had to get to the beach.

He had to get home.

NYEL SCARCELY CHECKED the beach to ensure he was alone before diving into the waves. A second later, Atreus was beside him, dark blue and purple scales matching his pace with a few easy strokes of his barbed tail.

"Ny, what're you doing?" he asked but didn't try to stop him.

"My aunt is having a baby. I promised her I'd be there."

Corallina was a shorter swim than he remembered, and Atreus followed Nyel to the outskirts of the village. They reached the landing of the sand-hut home, gills fluttering for breath. Nephi beat them there; his red fins flared with irritation.

"Took you long enough. From the sounds of it, you're right on time."

Nyel heard it too. The labored cries of his aunt as she endured contractions. He pushed open the wooden door, nearly slamming his tail as it closed behind him.

"Sonia, Sonia, I'm here!" Nyel yelled.

A moment later, his father emerged from the back room, his eyes widening in alarm at the sight of his son. He looked older now, the years showing in the harsh lines around his mouth. How had so much changed in such a short time?

"Nyel?" he croaked.

"Yes, I'm here. Is Sonia okay? Is there anything I can do?"

"N-no. Your mother and a few other *sirena* have it handled. It shouldn't be long now—"

The water vibrated with the high-pitched wails of a babe. Tears brimmed in Nyel's eyes. His tail drooped, and his shoulders fell. He'd made it.

"Can... can I?"

His father nodded, allowing Nyel to swim into the other room. Inside, Sonia lay under a shellweave blanket, her scales pale and her eyes bloodshot. But the smile on her face was more radiant than Nyel had ever seen.

"Sonia?"

She spotted him, and fresh tears broke free from her face. "Nyel. I knew you'd come."

Nyel approached slowly, hardly noticing the two *sirena* and his mother busy with a small bundle on the other side of the room.

He took Sonia's hand gently in his. "I promised I'd be here," he said, pressing a kiss to her knuckles. "Sorry, I'm late."

When his mother turned, she held a tiny bundle wrapped in a

soft coral silk blanket. From one end, a short green tail peeked out, the tip still curled. Baby Mer were always born with their tails curled tightly from months spent in the womb—it would take several hours for the muscles to relax and straighten completely. The sight was a reminder of just how new this little life was.

His mother froze at the sight of him. "Nyel!? When did you—?"

Nyel raised a hand, stopping her. "Later, Mom. I promise."

Bianca looked like she wanted to get into it then and there, even with an infant in her arms. But she composed herself, gently handing the bundle to Sonia. His aunt took the swaddle, and more tears mixed with the water. Nyel peeked over her shoulder.

"She's beautiful," he said, admiring the plump face of his new cousin.

"She looks like him," Sonia gasped, a sob catching in her throat. The babe in her arms didn't share their jade hue but was the spitting image of her father, Nyel's late uncle Santé. She resembled the other *Sireni* of the village, with moss-green tones around her eyes. The markings curved gracefully around her finless head, forming a pattern like a crown.

"What's her name?"

"Sabella," Sonia said, kissing her daughter's head. "It's what he wanted."

Nyel squeezed her shoulder. "You've done an amazing job."

She pressed her lips together, fighting off the lingering waves of grief. "He's here. The Opikun would have brought him for this. I know it."

Now Nyel had to fight off the sting in his eyes. "I think you're right." He kissed her gently on the forehead, hoping she could feel how loved she was.

He didn't know if his uncle Santé was with them, but if anyone could sense his visiting soul, it would be his mate—bound by a Bond that transcended the planes of the living and the dead.

"Okay, Sonia, we need to get you cleaned up," one of the *sirena* said. "Nyel, let's leave it to the women, yes?"

Nyel nodded. "I'll stay long enough to see you again," he promised before joining his father in the main room. A few minutes later, his mother and the other *sirena* entered.

"She's resting," Bianca announced.

His mother thanked the other two women and closed the door behind them. And it was the three of them: Mother, Father, and Son.

"I know we have a lot to talk about," Nyel began.

"You're sure as sharks we do!" his mother bristled, her fins standing on end.

"Bianca, please. Sonia needs the quiet," Donato said, urging his wife to calm down.

She lowered her voice, though the manic energy remained. "Start talking," she hissed. But before Nyel could open his mouth, she cut him off: "Do you know how worried I've been? I swear I've aged a decade. Are we not enough? Was I such a terrible mother? Do you hate me so much you'd rather live with those land creatures?!" she said hysterically, her volume rising with each word.

Again, Donato placed a calming hand on her arm, quieting her.

Nyel waited patiently for his mother to finish, and when her words finally ran dry, he said softly, "I don't hate you, Mom. I never did, and I never will." He searched for the words he'd rehearsed a thousand times, but they evaded him. "I couldn't go on the Tideway with Chel. I don't love her, Mom."

She huffed. "You didn't even try."

"It would never have worked. You never asked me what *I* wanted. Nobody even discussed it with me, and when everything started happening so fast I... I had to get away."

"Well, forgive me for knowing what is best for my only son," she whined. "And to think you'd go so far as to risk death to avoid your mother. I'm such a sea witch."

Nyel took a calming breath.

"Mom, that isn't what I said. Don't put words in my mouth. I didn't plan on going to Baia Vita. It just happened. I met a Mer who's been living with them for years. He showed me how to do it safely. I've started a life there, Mom, and I love it. I'm not leaving."

For the first time in his life, his mother looked too shocked to speak and Nyel took the opportunity to continue.

"And there is another thing I need to say. But we need to invite in some Mer before I start. I'll get them."

Without waiting for permission, Nyel opened the door, letting himself outside, happy for the walls separating him and his parents for a moment. Like he'd suspected, Nephi and Atreus were nearby. Nephi sat with his usual bored expression, picking at his talons while Atreus scratched a very excited Ripple under the chin.

"He likes it right behind the antenna," Nyel said, showing Atreus where. The sandwinder made a low groaning sound before kicking all three legs on his left side.

"I've never seen one," Atreus said, mimicking Nyel's movement, which caused the beast to roll over for belly rubs. "What is he?"

"He's a sandwinder, and his name is Ripple. You can visit him anytime. He loves the attention." Nyel said, knowing full well he was stalling.

The flat ends of the sandwinder's antenna reached for Atreus and began running up and down his torso with unnerving dexterity.

"Uuh, what is it doing?" Atreus asked, frozen in place.

Nyel laughed. "It means he likes you. He's getting a good look."

"Isn't that what the four eyes are supposed to do?"

"They're virtually blind. He's getting a good look through the electric signals in your body. That's how he herds the fish, by sending invisible waves through the water and gathering the school. It leaves patterns in the sand when he does it, hence the name."

"I'm honored," Atreus said as the pad of one appendage wiped over his face. "I think."

"Ripple is a good boy," Nyel said, patting a chunky webbed foot. "Sandwinders have been herding schools for the *Sireni* for generations. But there aren't that many around anymore. We have the only one in all of Corallina."

"That's too bad," Atreus said, pushing away an antenna that was starting to make its way up the leg of his shorts. "How is your aunt?"

"Good. I have a baby cousin. Her name is Sabella."

"That's amazing. Congratulations."

Nyel looked to his half-brother, who did his best to pretend they weren't there. He didn't offer any congratulatory words.

"I need both of you to come with me. We... It's time for a talk. It's long overdue."

At this, Nephi raised his head, his expression skeptical. "Really?" he asked sarcastically.

"Yes, really," Nyel snapped, "I said I wanted to, and there is no better time than the present. C'mon."

Nephi floated to him, looking about as happy as a molting shrimp.

"Why me?" Atreus asked, "Isn't this between family?"

"That's a stretch," Nephi said, but went quiet as Nyel shot him a look.

"You're part of this, Atreus. You're the one who showed me the world I want to live in. You're also a halfling. And..." The words were heavy on his tongue. He forced them out anyway. "You're important to me."

"Guh, stop stalling, and let's get this bullshit over with," Nephi said, pushing Nyel to lead the way.

Nyel bit his lip as he took in the horrified expressions on his parents' faces when Atreus and Nephi swam through the door.

"What? Forgot what I look like, *Dad*," Nephi snapped, accenting the last word with cruelty.

"What is the meaning of this?" Bianca's posture was tense, like Nyel had allowed a Great White into their home.

"Mom, Dad, we need to talk. I've figured some things out—about us, about everything—and the truth is, we've been wrong."

His parents said nothing as their gazes continued to dart between the three of them.

"Everything we've been told, or invented, about halflings is wrong."

Nyel let that sink in, and he could have sworn he heard a muffled, "Oh shit, he actually said it," from his half-brother.

"W-what do you mean, dear?" Bianca asked.

"The rumors, the stories, all those nasty things *Sireni* say about halflings—it's wrong, Mom. I don't know when it started, but I know when it will end. And it's now."

"What rumors, dear?" she asked innocently, eyes darting.

"Oh, don't pretend," Nephi cut. "Don't pretend like you haven't treated me like a bastard-born monster that might ruin your perfect life."

Both Bianca and Donato flinched, and the room went still, the water going stagnant with razor-sharp tension.

"Well, what did you expect me to think?" she finally snapped, her voice shrill. "You come back every three or four years with nothing but scars. No explanation."

"I don't owe you a damn thing, let alone an explanation," Nephi hissed.

"Mom, we never even tried to understand." Nyel pleaded.

"Well, excuse me for trying to protect my family from all of this," she gestured at Nephi— covered in burns.

"Alright. If all of *this* is your excuse, then what about him?" Nephi said, jerking his head towards Atreus.

"I don't even know who that is," Bianca retorted.

"This is Atreus. He's the one I told you about," Nyel said. "He's the one who taught me how to live safely on Baia Vita. He's my friend."

For a moment, Bianca said nothing; then her eyes went wide as she gasped. "I remember you."

The water shifted as Atreus's tail swished behind him, nerves billowing.

"What do you mean you remember him?" Nyel asked, looking from Atreus to his mother. "Have you two met?"

The look on Atreus's face made Nyel's stomach churn, a nauseating wave of guilt washing over him. Despite being the largest in the room, his friend looked impossibly small—shrinking under the weight of something Nyel couldn't fix.

"Atreus?" he asked, but his mother cut in.

"Oh, it was years ago. He came by while you were doing chores. Of course, I did the right thing and told him to go away, given what he is. I wasn't about to let anything happen to my baby."

"Is that true? We've met?" Nyel asked, appalled that he hadn't remembered. That Atreus hadn't told him.

"It was a long time ago," Atreus said.

Bianca huffed. "I wondered where you went after that. Seems you threw your lot in with the humans. Well, I guess that's for the best, given what you are," Bianca commented off-handedly.

"What he is!?" Nyel shouted, rounding on his parents. "Do you even hear yourself? Atreus is kind and generous to a fault. He's honorable and has worked himself to the bone to survive all because Corallina cast him out." He lowered his voice, unable to keep it from shaking, "Because *we* cast him out."

Nyel fell silent, grinding his teeth as tears of frustration spilled over. He wanted to bolt. To run away from all of this, just like he had with Chel all those weeks ago.

A webbed hand rested on his shoulder, and he met his brother's gaze. Nephi gave him an encouraging squeeze, and that small gesture was enough to push Nyel to continue.

It was the first time Nephi had ever been anything other than angry toward him, and that flicker of warmth from his cold, standoffish brother stoked a fire in Nyel's chest.

Don't stop now. Say it all.

"I met Atreus before I learned what he was. And when I found out, it took me about three seconds to realize we've been wrong. There is nothing wrong with halflings. They aren't sick, they aren't mad, they're just like us. Mer."

"Son, they aren't like us. Their blood is mixed," his father said, speaking for the first time. "You're young, and it's easy to get swept up in the excitement. But mixing blood is dangerous. The Spirits have warned us of the *Skraith*—"

"HA!" Nephi burst. "Oh, that's rich coming from you. And you think the punishment of mixing blood rests on the child's shoulders? The child who had no choice?"

"I'm not saying what I did was right. But what's done is done."

"Yeah. I exist. Fucking whoops, right?" Nephi said, a hysterical edge in his tone.

"Nephi, stop." Nyel placed a hand on his brother's chest. "Let me do this." Once again, Nyel was shocked to see his brother back down. He faced his father, more than a little disappointed by his reaction. "I don't care what you think, Dad. I know that there is nothing wrong with halflings. They're like us. End of story."

Silence stretched in the small room, its weight like sinking stones. Finally, Bianca inhaled sharply.

"If you want to live like an outcast, there is nothing I can do. I tried so hard to make things better for you, to give you opportunities I never had. I wanted better for you," Bianca huffed with frustration. "But I can see you'd rather spit in my face."

"Mom, that's not what—"

"If that's what you believe, fine," she interrupted, her voice now trembling with the threat of tears. "I guess I have to live with the fact that my little boy is going to get all kinds of ideas in his head. If you've found some kind of life on human land, there's nothing I can do to stop you. You're an adult now," she said, the regret in her voice unmistakable. "But I want you to know that every minute you're in that landwalker den, I'll be aging tenfold from worry. Who knows? Maybe when you finally manage to visit, I'll already be in *Thalaren*."

Nyel supposed that was about as good as he was going to get.

"Thank you, Mom," he said, doing his best to ignore her masterful guilt-tripping.

"But you'll visit us more often? Stay every once in a while?" she pleaded as though her acceptance could bind him back to her.

"I will make an effort to see you all more. Especially Sabella."

"Good, good." She rubbed her hands together uncomfortably. "And you two, seeing as you have taken care of my son all these weeks, I guess it's safe to say you won't hurt him now."

"I wouldn't be so sure," Nephi grumbled, then let out a stream of bubbles as Nyel elbowed him in the gut. "But no, I won't hurt him. Pain in the ass or not, he's my brother."

It probably wasn't healthy to feel such a wide range of emotions in such a short amount of time. Hearing Nephi call him his brother, not half-brother, was enough to make Nyel's eyes sting for an entirely different reason.

"I would never. Even back then, all those years ago, I never wanted to hurt him," Atreus said, his voice soft.

"Okay then. When Nyel comes for his *very regular* visits to us, both of you are also welcome." She looked like she'd bitten into a spoiled sea prune as she said it, but she said it. And that was enough.

Donato was still visibly uncomfortable, and for a moment, Nyel worried he would raise his voice in protest. But as usual, he never challenged any of Bianca's decisions.

"Well, if that's it, I'm leaving," Nephi said, swimming for the door. Their father reached out, almost touching his son's burnt arm but stopping an inch short.

"I didn't mean to say that you deserved the blame."

Nyel watched with bated breath as Nephi stared down at Danoto as though their father were nothing more than slime.

"Yet you were the first to abandon me," he hissed before darting out the door, his crimson fins flared so high they carved grooves in the ceiling.

Nyel approached his father. "He needs time, Dad. A lot of it."

Donato nodded, though his expression seemed distant. When he spoke, his voice was low and weary. "The heaviest burden you'll carry is regret—choices made in haste, without thought. If I can offer any wisdom, it's this: follow tradition, do what's expected, and don't fight the will of the Spirits. Go against them, and you'll find nothing but misery. When I was young, I didn't listen; I was rebellious and overconfident. I met Nephi's mother and—"

"Don't you dare speak of that sea witch in my home!" Bianca snapped loudly, arms crossed, and looking pale in the face.

Nyel balked. He'd never heard his father string together so many words in one breath. Let alone *those* words. In all his life, he'd never once heard him mention Nephi's mother. Who she was, and how Nephi came to be. But one thing was for certain. There was regret. And the reminder of that regret came in the form of Nephi. His own flesh and blood.

For the first time, Nyel felt the embers of anger flicker in his chest. He'd always brushed off his father's Unbonded history, choosing not to dwell on it and giving him the benefit of the doubt. After all, his father had been a perfectly good dad to him, right? But now, watching this wrinkled *sireno* all but disown his own flesh and blood—refusing to accept the consequences of his actions—Nyel began to see a clearer picture of the man before him.

How could his father say such a thing? Sure, Nephi was flawed, but he was also a victim of circumstance. If he'd been offered the same love and acceptance Nyel had, things would have been different. Watching his father so blatantly deny his son only deepened Nyel's understanding of Nephi's rage.

One thing was for certain: Nyel would never regret calling Nephi his brother.

As though to remind him of his presence, Atreus gently brushed his tail against Nyel's. Nyel tore his gaze from his father, too overwhelmed by the flood of emotions to come up with any more words. He needed to get out of here for a minute.

"I'm going to say bye to Sonia and Sabella. Meet me outside?" he said, offering Atreus an escape.

"Sure," Atreus nodded, darting to the door, but not before exchanging a lingering look that sent Nyel's already aching heart into a frenzy.

When Nyel entered Sonia's room, he didn't even open his mouth before she spoke.

"I heard."

He sighed, the strain of the last hour making him feel like he was sinking into quicksand. "I know you're going to tell me it's dangerous and that—"

"Nyel honey, hush," she said with a tired smile. "Oh, hush. You don't know a thing. Am I worried you're spending time on a human island? Yes. A hundred times, yes. But do I have confidence that you've worked things out? Also, yes."

Nyel let a tired grin take over his face. "Atreus has really helped me. He's been living with them for years."

"He sounds sensible. I hope the next time you come to see us, you'll tell me more about him?"

"I will. And you're okay that he's a..."

"Halfling," she finished for him. "That doesn't bother me, Nyel."

"It's just that, when Nephi arrived, and Uncle Santé—" he trailed off, unable to finish.

"Nyel, I don't believe Nephi's arrival had anything to do with my mate's passing. *Skraith* or no." Her voice was firm. But the stiff set of her jaw made Nyel question the truthfulness of her words. Still, she was standing by him, and that was enough.

"Okay," was all he could manage.

"Nyel?" she said, her face softening.

"Huh?"

"I'm proud of you."

This time, he couldn't hold back the sting in his eyes. He wiped at them, feeling utterly drained. He didn't know if they were tears of joy or exhaustion.

IT TURNED OUT HIS MOTHER wasn't ready to let go of him yet, and after much back-and-forth, Nyel agreed to stay for a couple of days and help with the baby.

"You sure?" Atreus asked outside the sand hut. Nephi was already gone, and Nyel suspected that after all that, they wouldn't be seeing him for a while.

"Yeah, just for a few days. I think Sonia needs someone to talk to who isn't my mom."

"Right." Atreus stared at his webbed toes, kicking them idly in the sand.

"What is it?" Nyel asked, though Atreus wouldn't meet his gaze.

"I didn't know it was like that. I knew you had a family, but I wasn't expecting…"

"It's not all sugar and sea prunes," Nyel said dryly.

"You could put it like that," Atreus replied, his tone softening. "I'm sorry I misjudged you before."

"When you assumed I was a spoiled brat running from a perfect life?" Nyel asked, knowing exactly what Atreus had thought of him.

"Well. Yeah. Sorry, Ny."

"It's complicated. But they're my family. And I've got a baby cousin and an aunt who need me for a while."

"Understood. But before I go, I wanted to ask you something."

"Sure," Nyel said.

"Back there, your mom said something I didn't understand."

"Yeah?" Nyel stretched the word, waiting for it like an oncoming punch.

"What is *Thalaren*?"

It was so unexpected that a flurry of bubbles escaped his gills as Nyel laughed.

"That's so random. How do you not know—" he stopped mid-sentence. "Sorry. I shouldn't laugh. I forget sometimes that you don't know these things. Just because I've known about it since birth doesn't mean…well, I shouldn't assume. Sorry. You probably felt the same way when I asked about the refrigerator."

"It wouldn't have been so annoying if you didn't keep opening and closing the damn thing."

"I needed to know if the light stayed on after it was closed!" Nyel defended through a grin. "But to answer your question, *Thalaren* is," he chewed on the words. "I guess it's a place? It's where our souls go when we, you know, die."

"Oh," Atreus said with a raised brow. "The context makes more sense now."

"Yeah. Mom likes to bring up her impending departure to *Thalaren* anytime I do something she doesn't like."

"Humans have a word for that. But I don't think it's a belief they practice a lot on Baia Vita."

"Neither do we," Nyel said, shrugging. "It's just something we say. Like calling to the Spirits. You know?"

Yet, as the words left his mouth, they felt wrong. Back in the house, his father had been more pious than Nyel had ever thought him to be.

Atreus shook his head. "I really don't, but I'll take your word for it."

They floated there, the silence thick with the weight of words both wanted to say but couldn't. Atreus's presence was like an anchor, tethering Nyel and keeping him from drifting off course. He didn't want him to go.

"Ny?"

"Yes?" Nyel said too quickly, perking up.

"If you aren't back in two days, I'm coming to get you."

Something about the way he said it made Nyel's heart thud heavier. "You will?"

"Yes. You don't belong here, Ny. You belong in Baia Vita with—" Atreus hesitated. "With all of us," he finished.

A small wave of disappointment rippled through Nyel's chest. "Yeah. Thanks. I'll be back," Nyel promised.

"Nyel!" his mother's shrill voice cut through the water.

"I better get to that before she comes to get me," Nyel said, wanting to spare Atreus from another heavy interaction.

"Don't be too long," Atreus said with a parting wave.

"I won't be."

As Nyel settled into his old bed for the night, his mind replayed their final exchange on a loop—replayed it with the words he'd wanted to hear.

You belong in Baia Vita with me.

THE NEXT MORNING, Nyel was shocked to see Sonia upright with baby Sabella asleep in her arms.

"Should you be swimming around like that?" Nyel asked with concern.

"We *sirena* are made of tougher stuff than you males," she said with a wink, handing him the babe. "Hold her for a second, will you? I want to help with dinner."

Nyel held his baby cousin; her squishy face contorted in an irritable expression. Dark, mossy green scales bordered her eyes before cresting onto her forehead like a crown. The fins on her head would come in when she turned two, and the rounded crest on her tail wouldn't develop until she was closer to his age.

"Hey there, baby girl. I'm your cousin," he said, gently bouncing her in his arms. A tiny hand reached out, wrapping around his finger, and in that moment, he was a goner. This precious new life had him in a chokehold, and he knew there was no going back. Sabella fussed, and he pulled her close, remembering that Mer infants needed tight, enclosed spaces, especially before their eyes opened. She settled and resumed snoozing in his hold. He couldn't wait for her eyes to open and see him, but that was still at least a week away.

Voices from the main room had Nyel swimming over to investigate. His entire body stiffened when, in the room, floated none other than Chel.

Immediately, Nyel's angry gaze darted to his mother.

"Are you serious right now?" he hissed in a heated whisper, trying not to wake Sabella.

"Nyel, calm yourself," Bianca said with an eye roll. "Mr. Ernesti came to talk with your father, and Chel wanted to see you."

He wouldn't put it past his mother to arrange another 'courting dinner' the day he came home, but that didn't appear to be the case, and he relaxed.

"Right. Sorry." Nyel said more to Chel.

"While your fathers are talking, why don't you two take a second to catch up? Here, give her to me," Bianca said, taking Sabella from his arms and practically shoving them out the door.

Nyel sighed loudly, a stream of bubbles tickling his gills. "Chel, I'm—"

"It's okay, Nyel," she interrupted, her voice soft as a passing tide.

"Is it, though? The last time I saw you, I busted out of the house like a rogue barracuda and left you alone with our parents."

She smiled sadly. "Yeah. That sucked."

"I'm sorry. I didn't know what else to do."

They swam to the goatfish pen, watching Ripple patrol the school, his antenna working to keep the fish in line.

"It did hurt my feelings. We've always been good friends, but a part of me still hoped it would lead to something more one day."

Nyel glued his gaze to the collection of orange fire coral climbing the side of the house. Someone had broken the branches off several of the poor creatures. He analyzed them, unable to look at her.

"After that day, I realized that's all we were. Friends, and that's okay, Nyel."

"Really? Because I'm pretty sure, according to my mother, it's a sin."

She laughed. "No, it's not. Sure, I cried a little, but I'm glad we can still talk like this. I'm glad we're still friends."

She reached for her tail and twisted in a cutely nervous gesture. Nyel laughed internally as he pictured a human running their fingers together. It was the same motion, yet so different.

"I'm glad we're still friends too. I wasn't sure," he confessed.

"Of course we are, silly. But I never realized how much pressure you were under. I should have seen it sooner."

"Doesn't make it right. What I did. I'm sorry, Chel."

"Apology accepted. Plus, it all worked out. I've been seeing Wyll."

"Wyll? From the farm on the north side?"

"That's the one. It's been going really well."

"Chel, that's amazing. Wyll is a good guy. He comes from a good family. I'm sure he will make you happy."

The mention of Wyll brought a flood of familiar images to Nyel's mind. Wyll's family was known across the region for their pristine oarweed fields, cultivated with care and precision for generations. They were hardworking, close-knit, and fiercely loyal to each other. If Chel was looking for stability and kindness, she couldn't have chosen better.

"I think so, too," she said, blushing. "And that's why what happened is okay. We wouldn't have made each other happy."

It hurt to hear her say it, but it was true. It would have been a match made out of obligation and tradition, not love. And a Bond? Nyel doubted one could have ever taken hold between them—not when he didn't love her.

"Have you—you know—with Wyll?" he asked awkwardly.

She shook her head, long green fins swaying. "No, not yet. But it's been going so well. I'm sure a Bond will click any day now. It's just a feeling I get."

Nyel reached for her hand, giving it a single quick squeeze. "That's awesome Chel. Wyll's a lucky *sireno*."

They swam around the cage, rounding the back of the house, when they spotted both their fathers talking. Nyel couldn't hear what they were saying, but both wore concerned, heavy expressions. Their tones were urgent, mouths moving fast as though time were running out.

"What is that about?"

"You haven't heard?" She shook her head. "Of course you haven't. You've been on the land. Which is crazy, by the way, but I'm not here to lecture you on that."

"So what's going on?"

"The kelp is dying."

Nyel gawked at her, positive he heard her wrong. "What do you mean it's dying? We're in the middle of growing season; it should be booming."

Chel's shoulders sagged, and he noticed for the first time her wavegrass dress hung loose around her frame.

"The kelp is getting sick."

"A pest?" Nyel asked, immediately wondering if it was something the goatfish could eradicate.

"We thought so. Your family's school has been working overtime, going from farm to farm, trying to fix this. But nothing is working. My dad says it's not a pest. It's the water."

"Water?"

"Those human ships. When they pass, they leave behind something. Like a black cloud, it dissipates in the water. It's killing our kelp. It is not just ours; all the farms are losing crops by the day. People are getting sick, too. Nobody's died yet, but..."

Nyel couldn't believe this. He knew the ships were a nuisance—their giant propellers creating noise that carried for leagues. But this? This was an epidemic.

"What is Corallina doing?"

"What can we do? We're trying our best to stop it. Some of the farms are resorting to harvesting early, even though the kelp isn't ready, just to preserve some food."

Nyel cringed. Unripened kelp was bitter and caused painful stomach aches.

"Have there been shortages?"

"A little. Right now, we're worried about feeding ourselves, let alone the other villages that depend on us. It's about to get a lot worse. And winter isn't even here yet. Some families are talking about leaving the bay."

Nyel's heart sank. *Sireni* were not deep ocean dwellers. Their kind, from the beginning of forever, had always lived in the abundant, warm, shallow waters where the rays of the sun reached the sand. In deeper seas? Open waters?

"They won't make it. If they leave, they'll either starve or be picked off by predators."

"What choice do they have?"

Before he could argue, Donato clapped Mr. Ernesti on the shoulder and exchanged parting words.

"I better go. We're going to harvest early, too. It'll taste vile, but food is food." Her shoulders fell miserably as she said it. Nyel hugged her before watching her and Mr. Ernesti disappear into the blue waters.

The ships were killing his people. Killing his village. And there was nothing they could do to stop it. Nyel realized with a desperate ache in his heart that he might lose both the places he'd learned to call home.

CHAPTER 19

LEOFEL

"D AMN IT!"

Leo kicked the net with frustration. Three tiny fish were all that accounted for his morning catch, and one was already dead. He stomped on their worthless corpses.

"Damn it, Damn it, Damn it, DAMN IT!"

He crushed them until they were nothing but chum beneath his boots. Leo collapsed to the deck, back against the guard rail, holding his head in his hands. The net brought up less and less fish every day. Pretty soon, even with the advantage of a new boat, it wouldn't be

313

enough. How was he going to explain to Edgar that they'd have to return the boots they'd just bought him? How would he explain to Annetta they'd have to sheer her curls again? Right when they finally started to grow back. How would he... how would he...

How would Leo bear this torture for the rest of the season? And likely the next. And the next. For the rest of his life, he'd be a slave to his master.

Alvise had called him into the valley six times now. Or was it seven? Leo lost track of the days spent on the estate. Lost track of the hours he spent on his knees, doing nothing. Leo didn't understand the game Alvise was playing with him or what reaction he hoped to get. Each time Leo was called to the estate, Alvise commanded him to kneel in the center of the room, hands crossed behind his back, and wait.

People shuffled in and out: businessmen, maids, butlers, and other members of Alvise's 'collection' of beautiful things. All of them wore the Vincenzo sigil in one form or another, a golden lion rearing over a sash of purple. It appeared over and over. First as a necklace, then a vest, or emblazoned on a suit pocket—all markers of ownership.

All Alvise's property.

They walked past Leo without a word. He may as well have been a piece of furniture. No one acknowledged him, not even when Leo's pleading eyes searched for theirs, begging for help. They didn't want the same fate.

He knelt on the biting cold marble floors until his knees went numb, and his arms ached from holding them behind his back. Leo learned early on that even the slightest shift in position would catch Alvise's attention. The Lord of the estate immediately commanded Leo to resume his uncomfortable stance.

"Or do I need to bring my guards in?"

Leo shook his head, crossing his arms obediently.

"Good boy," he said before returning his attention to the pile of paperwork at his desk.

Leo spent those hours counting the black speckles in the marble floor—spots scattered at random, like flecks of ash immortalized in stone. He began memorizing the number on each tile. The one beneath his left knee had ten. The one to the right had only three. The tile where the corner of Alvise's desk overlapped had sixteen. He counted them again and again, a quiet ritual to pass the time and dull the stabbing pain in his knees.

If kneeling on the cold tile until his legs went numb was Alvise's idea of payment for using the *Clown Fish*, Leo could endure it. The humiliation outweighed the pain—but he'd bear it. He'd do anything. Each time he was summoned, he knelt on the same tiles, counted the same black speckles, and left feeling a little more numb than the time before. Whatever game Vincenzo was playing, Leo was certain he hadn't seen the worst of it yet.

And it was Alvise's most recent summons to the valley—the one that forced Leo out of bed in the dead of night—that finally pushed him to his breaking point. The call came suddenly. Leo jumped out of bed when a furious knocking shook their house, waking everyone inside. One of Alvise's men demanded he come to the estate. Leo only had time to pull on his boots and shout some incoherent excuse about the boat to his parents before rushing out.

Alvise was in a rage, hurling chairs across the room and shattering porcelain china against the walls. Glassware crashed to the floor, splintering into glittering shards as he yelled at anyone and anything in sight. Something went wrong with a shipment. Or was it the title for a new commercial shop in the square? Whatever it was had sent Alvise into a tailspin.

"You!" he shouted when Leo rounded the corner to the office, the guard hurrying away. "Get your worthless ass here NOW!"

Leo rushed forward and was met with a ferocious slap to his face.

He barely caught himself with one arm, the unyielding marble floor jarring his bones.

"Did you think you could postpone this? That making me wait would delay our midnight rendezvous?"

"I—I didn't."

But it was pointless to try and defend himself with words. All he could do was endure the blows.

"Did I imagine how long it took you to arrive? Are you calling me an idiot?"

"No *Signore*. Never."

Leo had the sense to stay on the floor.

"On your knees. Now."

Tremors shook him as he assumed his position, mentally preparing for the endless night.

"Stay," Alvise ordered as though he were a dog. "And if you so much as move an inch"—he seized Leo's chin, jerking his head, his fingernails leaving imprints in his cheeks—"you'll regret it."

Alvise dropped his face and turned off the light, slamming the door closed and leaving Leo alone in the dark.

Leo hung his head, grateful for the black, empty space; it let him pretend the tears running down his face were drips leaking from the ceiling.

When Alvise returned, Leo couldn't tell whether he had been alone for hours or minutes.

He heard a click, and light flashed like another slap to the face. His eyes squeezed shut, burning from the sudden glare. At the sound of footsteps, he forced himself to look through a squint—just in time to see his tormentor stride into the room, holding a jockey's whip. A new kind of fear struck Leo's heart.

Alvise was freshly bathed, clean-cut, and drowned in musky cologne. If it weren't for the man wearing the scent, Leo might have liked it.

The whip pressed against the underside of his chin, lifting his head and forcing Leo to meet icy eyes. The strap hadn't struck him—yet, Leo shivered as though it had. It tapped against his cheek as Alvise let out a disapproving 'tut.'

"So close. So much wasted potential. You could be the prize of my collection with the right care, with the right training."

The whip slid across the crest of his nose, where a fresh sunburn stung.

"Too much time in the sun brings out these blemishes and darkens that pretty skin. It's a pity."

Leather glided along his cheek, resting at the curve of his jaw where he sported a thin pink scar.

"And this," Alvise shook his head like someone had scratched his prized car. "A permanent blemish on what could have been the prize jewel of my collection."

When the touch of leather disappeared, Leo hung his head, neck aching with strain. The moment his chin dipped, white-hot pain cut his arm, forcing him to reach out and catch himself.

"Did I say you could look down!? Hands behind your back!"

Leo complied, lifting his head but keeping his eyes tightly closed. He didn't trust the tears not to fall again.

The barest touch of fingertips stroked his cheek with dishonest tenderness.

"Open your eyes, my pet. I want to see you."

Leo did, and tears spilled from the corners in a steady stream of misery. His tormentor considered him for a moment, head tilted to the side.

"Better. You're learning. I like my pets to be trainable. Even though you'll never be the most brilliant gem in my collection, you will kneel and obey, as is expected of all my possessions. Still, your scum-of-the-earth upbringing might prove advantageous for me. I'm sure I'll find other uses for you besides cladding you in my silks."

Alvise paced in a wide circle around Leo, his footsteps deliberate and slow.

"I always had an eye for beauty, even as a child. But as I quickly learned, it was as much a gift as it was a curse."

He slapped the whip in his palm with a loud 'smack,' and Leo flinched. Alvise either didn't notice or enjoyed Leo's display of fear as he continued his predatory circling.

Leo kept his head up and tried to count the dots on the tiles. Ten. Three. Fourteen. He counted them again and again, grounding himself, refusing to let the fear take hold.

"Fine things, expensive things, bored me by age twelve. What was the point of jewels and silks if a mere snap of my fingers brought them to me on a silver platter? Where was the pursuit? The joy in the chase? The thrill of discovery? The *satisfaction* in laying claim. No. I set my eyes on something far more difficult to acquire."

Alvise paused somewhere behind Leo's back. Sweat beaded down his temple. He felt like a rabbit waiting for the mountain cat to pounce. Tied in a snare of his own making.

"People, my dear pet, are the most beautiful things in all creation. But finding examples of this perfection was akin to searching for a diamond amongst polished quartz. I found there were a lot of *fake* beauties in the world. Of course, as in all things I endeavor to do, I perfected the art and brought my diamonds home. As you can see, my collection has grown nicely. But where to keep my precious possessions? Surely they had to exist in a place as divine as themselves."

Alvise rounded on him, crouching so they were eye level, his arctic gaze burning into Leo like dry ice.

"Do you know a place like that? A place with white beaches and crystal waters? Where the land is lush, and the hills are painted with white clover in the spring?"

He leaned even closer, and Leo caught the hint of something sour on his breath.

"Tell me, pet, where might I find a place like that?"

"H-here. *Signore* Vincenzo."

Alvise nodded. "You're absolutely right. After years of searching, I've found the paradise my beautiful things deserve. But can you guess what happened as soon as I found this place?" His voice rose dangerously. "I found it overrun with vermin!"

The whip cracked on Leo's arm in the exact same place it landed before. He whimpered but didn't dare move. Alvise resumed his pacing, this time faster.

"And, of course, as my luck would have it, the good times of over-powering my enemies with sheer force are behind us. Now, we have to do things with a certain amount of *raffinatezza*—finesse, as my grandmother says. It seems the Bracaleone line is reforming their image."

He grumbled as he said it, as though the idea of simply over-throwing Baia Vita with guns and violence was his preferred method.

"No matter. As the Bracaleone heir, I will bide my time. I'll wait for Ginerva and Assura to meet their maker, then restore the Vincenzo name. I am nothing if not adaptable."

He hummed to himself, pondering his own genius.

Leo fixed his attention on the tile beneath Alvise's boot. Five dots.

"So what do I do in the meantime? I bring my family's fishing empire to your shores. I starve your bay, crumble your shops, and undercut your prices with stores of my own. And once the locally owned businesses are gone, I raise my prices—choking the last of the local filth. Warfare is waged just as effectively with coin as it is with bullets. Baia Vita will be mine soon enough."

Leo was going to be sick. He couldn't listen to this.

Alvise's voice suddenly doubled in volume as though he were announcing his plans to an audience.

"And what do I find among the dirt? Not one, but *two* diamonds."

He stopped in front of Leo again, squeezing the whip in both hands.

"One was easy enough to acquire but dulled from lack of care," he gestured to Leo. "And the other..." Alvise twisted and squeezed the leather until his knuckles turned white. "The other continues to refuse me. My usual bait doesn't tempt the red fox; no, she's too smart for that." He smiled as though the challenge excited him. "If only her face matched those beautiful tresses. How that color robs me of sleep."

Alvise considered Leo now, slapping the whip once again into his palm.

"But if she were here, on her knees, poised and obedient — maybe. Maybe I can break her into something more palatable. Chip away at that infuriating pride to find my diamond."

Leo ground his teeth together, crushing the words he wanted to shout. Marina would never bow to this man. She was strong.

Stronger than me.

Leo only hoped she could escape this monster before he found a way to break her.

"I digress," Alvise hummed, lifting Leo's chin once again with the leather rod. "What do you think? Will you stay with me when this island becomes mine?"

Before Leo could come up with a response, he was gagging as Alvise forced a thumb into his mouth, pressing down on his tongue.

Only then did Leo notice that Alvise wore a silken bathrobe, its folds tied gracefully around his waist. Leo had been so preoccupied with the whip that he hadn't considered the implications. Now, with his mouth open and a hungry look coming over that arctic face—Leo knew.

Alvise removed his thumb, smearing spit on Leo's lips.

"When I say, come to my estate, you say?"

"Yes, Alvise."

"When I say get on your knees, you say?"

"Yes, Alvise."

"And when I tell you to open your pretty mouth, you say?"

"Y-yes Alvise," Leo all but sobbed.

"Good boy."

NEPHI

"What the hell am I doing?" Nephi groaned to himself as he settled into his temporary shelter for the night.

The ground was too exposed, and the water too far from where he needed to be. Why he needed to be here in the first place, Nephi had no fucking clue. But here he was, curling into his lean-to on a human rooftop. A few pieces of wood, an abandoned crate, and a tarp made up one of the more comfortable shelters he'd managed while scouting human territory. What made the makeshift hut a bit less miserable was the black four-legged creature that curled up beside him.

Every night.

"Get fucking lost. I don't have anything for you." Nephi tried shooing away the feline. It didn't yowl or beg like other alley cats; instead, it watched him with poised interest.

"Go home!"

The glowing orbs continued to stare at him expectantly. He couldn't sleep with the little creep watching him like that.

"What do you want from me?"

As though finally given permission, the white-mittened cat leaped gracefully from its perch, flicking its tail at Nephi's nose. It curled against his side and began a surprisingly loud chorus of rumbling purrs.

And thus, their nightly ritual was born. Each evening, as the village quieted, the cat—whom Nephi had begrudgingly grown fond of—appeared like clockwork. It was clear the cat had a home, given its glossy coat and well-fed belly. Why it chose to bother him every night was anyone's guess.

Nephi was annoyed at first, muttering under his breath about how he wasn't running a damn hotel, but he never shooed the cat away. There was something oddly comforting about the soft purring that filled the rooftop silence. He told himself it was the warmth the feline brought on cold nights or the way it kept the birds away. The creature was useful—nothing more.

"You're just using me, aren't you?" he grumbled as the cat pawed at his makeshift blanket before settling in. And yet, when its small body curled tightly against his, Nephi felt his eyelids growing heavier.

When Nephi woke, his little shadow was gone.

He began yet another day of tailing Nyel, gathering intel for reasons he couldn't explain, and wandering around the outskirts of Corallina.

He chuckled to himself as he watched Nyel drop a heavy fish tray on his toe and hop on one foot like an idiot.

"Serves you right," Nephi said into the fishcake he'd swiped from a vendor down the block. He couldn't find anything with a hood after ruining the last sweater, but the leather jacket he stole this morning hugged his shoulders perfectly. Nephi might even say he looked sharp.

He promised himself to take better care of this one. But stealing from the locals and watching Nyel play human wasn't even close to the pace of life Nephi was accustomed to.

He was bored.

I should be back with the Pod.

But the memory of Nyel standing up for him made Nephi pause. It was the first inkling of a familial bond he'd never dared hope for. For the first time in his life, he wanted to try. And that, in and of itself, was a miracle. Because Nephi never once had the desire to try for anything.

He simply was.

Nephi watched as Atreus came to his brother's rescue, lifting the heavy tray. They were laughing. And the sight made something in Nephi's chest ache. He was so distracted by the display that he failed to sneak off before being spotted.

Nyel caught sight of him and waved with a genuine smile. Another pang sparked through his chest, and Nephi wasn't sure if he liked it. He'd never get used to it—the idea that someone was happy to see him.

Maybe my dumb little brother isn't half bad.

He shoved the rest of the fish cake into his mouth and flipped Nyel off. Nyel tilted his head in confusion, hesitated for a moment, then mimicked the gesture with a bright smile. Nephi snorted as Atreus quickly grabbed Nyel's hand and shoved it down, no doubt hurriedly explaining what it actually meant.

The white sand and blue waves were picturesque. If not for his own disfigured form ruining the scene, it would have been perfect. Nephi was glad when footsteps approached him on the isolated beach, and a moment later, Leo sat a few paces to his left.

"Nice jacket," Leo said by way of greeting.

"I think I'll keep this one for a while," Nephi replied, admiring the cuff.

"Pretty sure I've seen the exact same one on *Signore* Livici's son."

"Give him my thanks."

Leo scoffed but said nothing else.

"It's kind of a bitch in this weather, though," Nephi said, fanning himself with his collar. "It doesn't breathe very—what the hell happened to you?" he gasped as the human's face came into full view.

Leo's tone of voice and physical presence were completely out of sync. While he sounded fine, a single glance revealed that he was anything but fine. Both Leo's eyes were two huge bruises. Angry red welts ran along his cheeks and down his neck. Nephi assumed the wounds continued down the rest of his body—the tell-tale signs of a whip.

"Oh, this?" Leo pinched a strand of hair. "I got a haircut; thanks for noticing."

Nephi shook his head in disbelief.

Even when he's obviously been through hell, that mouth of his...

After a moment, Leo exhaled sharply. "Not gonna say anything else?" he huffed, his slouched posture betraying his strain.

"What is there to say? You look like shit."

"I don't know why I came here expecting anything from you."

"If you want someone to hold your hand, then this beach isn't for you," Nephi said callously.

"Nobody's ever held my hand. I pull myself up every fucking time."

"Yeah? And how's that working out for you?" Nephi probed.

"It's fine. Everything's fine. I have it under control." Leo's voice was solemn.

Nephi brushed a stray bit of dark hair from his eyes; he'd need to cut it soon.

"So, that thing you were telling me about—the one you said couldn't get much worse than it was—did it get worse?"

Leo's fingers gripped the sand like he could strangle it. "Yeah. And I don't need an 'I told you so.' I'll be a pessimist like you next time."

"Realist," Nephi corrected, "and what else did you expect coming from a fucked up bastard like me?"

Leo snorted. "Touché."

They listened to the waves ebb and flow; Nephi matched his breaths with the rhythm of the sea.

"Don't let this beat you," Nephi said, catching himself by surprise. He felt Leo's gaze on him but couldn't bring himself to meet it. His throat tightened as he spoke again, the words more firm this time. "Whatever it is, you need to come out on top."

Because nothing is allowed to break you before I get the chance.

"I won't. I'll endure it. Like I always do."

Nephi nodded, satisfied with his answer. "Good."

Nephi liked this human. Liked his fighting spirit. Not unlike another fighting spirit he once knew. Maybe he'd keep this human around. Maybe he'd leave Baia Vita and let this one live. But one look at those golden curls, the seamless glide of his amber skin, and the way his thin upper lip dipped just right—Nephi knew that was impossible.

He'd *have* this human. He'd have him and watch him shatter like glass. Feel his blood drip between his talons in a crimson rain.

"Who are you really?" Leo asked, breaking the stillness. "I never see you around town."

"A phantom."

Leo let out a mirthless laugh. "At this rate, I'm inclined to believe you." He took a handful of sand and watched it slide between his fingers. "Especially on this beach."

"Tell me about it—why you come here."

"You'll think I'm crazy."

"You assume I don't already think that."

Leo took a deep breath. "I'm pretty sure a sea monster saved me from drowning and left me here on the beach. There, see? Crazy."

Nephi chewed the inside of his cheek. He'd been hoping for a bit more than that.

"You don't look surprised," Leo said after a moment.

"Nothing surprises me."

"Really?" He shifted. "Not even this?"

Nephi's palm was up, and he snatched the pebble from midair before it hit his head.

Leo whistled. "Impressive. How did you know I would do that?" he asked, and Nephi was glad to see some of the darkness in his eyes gone.

He preferred him this way: engaged, alive.

Ripe for picking.

"You're predictable."

"How so?"

"Because you're human."

Leo rolled his neck, working out a knot in his muscles. "Aren't we all?"

No, my prey. We are not.

CHAPTER 20

MARINA

"Remind me again why we can't do this when the sun rises?" Atreus complained for the tenth time, smacking the torch against his palm until the bulb came back to life. It was a moonless night, and without the flashlight, Marina couldn't see her own hand in front of her face. The group paused, waiting for the beam to return before continuing.

"I want the kids to be surprised." Marina rolled her eyes even though none of them could see it. "Obviously."

"And they wouldn't be surprised if we did this during the day?" Atreus's voice grumbled in the dark somewhere to her right.

"Where is the fun in that? They will see us putting up the flags, and all the mystery will be gone. It's like *Babbo Natale* on Christmas morning."

More curses flew as the flashlight sputtered.

"What is *Babbo Natale*?" Nyel whispered somewhere lower on the path.

"I'll tell you later," Atreus hissed. "And why do we need this stupid thing anyway? I can see just fine." He finally smacked the torch back to life and handed it to Nyel.

"Um, because it's pitch black, Atty. We don't all have cat vision like you."

She thought she heard something like, "Don't call me that," but then again, maybe she didn't. They resumed their hike, the steep path doing a number on Marina's calves.

"Are you sure you aren't being too harsh on them?" Nyel asked as they climbed the hill, all three of them breathing hard. The hill crested high over the bay before dropping into the valley of private properties. At its peak stood an old windmill that groaned as the rotors spun in creaking circles.

"This is the course for the older kids. They can handle it. You're just out of shape and kind of a crybaby," Marina said, skipping to prove her point.

Nyel mumbled something along the lines of, 'You're the crybaby' before she rounded on him.

"Are we going to complain or finish this? And lower the light! Jeez."

"Sorry," Nyel said, lowering the beam.

Nyel and Atreus were kind enough to volunteer their time to help Marina set up the course for the Bayallon.

Which was the day after next.

And, maybe volunteered was the wrong word. Marina might have pestered Atreus until he finally caved to her will. She was very persuasive.

"You could have just asked for help," Atreus said as they climbed. "I would have said yes. You didn't have to barge into my room in the middle of the night like a squawking seabird—ow!" he yelped as Nyel silenced him with a stomp on the toes.

"Thank you, Nyel, for defending my honor," Marina said, smiling to herself.

Even she had to admit, her morning wake-up call had been one of her better performances. She really hit those high notes like a professional. Maybe she should try musical theater? She hummed her made-up tune.

The Bayallon's a comin',
The Bayallon's a comin',
Oh, won't you help me, please?
I'm begging on my knees,
The Bayallon's a comin' and I need some voluntee's
The Bayallon's a comin',
Oh yeah
Ooooooh yeah

"I heard you the first time!" Atreus yelled, rubbing the side of his head. "Again, you could have just asked."

"Yes, but you are missing the key ingredient in my plan."

"Oh yeah? What's that?"

Marina twirled until she faced Atreus and booped him on the nose. "My way was ten times more fun."

"I liked your song," Nyel laughed as they climbed the hill.

"Thank you!" Marina said with an exaggerated huff.

She heard a grumbled "Suck up" from Atreus.

They placed different colored markers at key points along the course. The oldest kids would follow the red flags, which they now carried up the hill. Or rather, Atreus carried the heavy box, Nyel held the light, and Marina tied red flags to fence posts, trees, and anything they could use as a landmark.

"I can't believe the festival is tomorrow night. It feels like the summer barely started," Nyel commented, aiming the light at a branch.

"Yeah. Feels too soon." Atreus agreed, and the melancholy in their voices made Marina's heart squeeze.

The docks were not a happy place to work. As the remaining days in the season dwindled to single digits, the people of Baia Vita resigned themselves to the prospect of another harsh winter. Catches were scarce, and Marina's stomach tightened every time she passed the empty shelves in the *pescheria*, where tubs of melting ice sat by the door.

But she wasn't about to let their sodden situation ruin the event she'd been preparing all summer. No. This was the end-of-season festival; this was the Bayallon! It was time for the town to rally behind their kids in a day of sportsmanship and fun—none of this messy depressy stuff.

"I don't have the energy for your whining."

"I'll be at the studio, don't wait for me."

"I can't stand your sulking."

Marina's breath caught in her throat, choking on her mother's words as they echoed through time.

"There's my happy girl."

"I oh-so-love it when you smile."

"Come here, my sunflower."

Marina stretched her lips, lifting her cheeks until her eyes squinted ever so slightly. Her fingers brushed against her dimples, confirming by touch alone that this was the right smile—the one she could summon on demand. The one she'd spent hours perfecting in front of the mirror. The one her mother wanted to see.

I'll be the happy one. I'll be the sunshine. I'll be what Mom needs.

Marina shook herself, snapping out of the memory. She clapped her hands loudly.

"C'mon, you two! No moping! Where is that energy!?" She made a yipping sound, pumping her fist into the air.

"It's too early for energy."

"It's called manifesting, Atty."

"Manifesting can happen when the sun is up. And I told you not to call me that."

"I tOLd YoU nOt To CalL mE tHaT," Marina mimicked. "And when will you call me Rina?"

"When Niccolo grows wings and flies."

"I'll have to arrange a meeting with the seagulls then," Marina replied.

This earned her two strained smiles as both boys half-laughed.

I'll take it, she thought, trying to infect the boys with her positive attitude. However forced. It usually worked, but this morning, they were a special type of droll.

"So what do you boys plan on doing after the season is over?"

When she was met with nothing but the sound of leaves rustling in the night wind, Marina turned to find them exchanging a glance. "Wrong question?" she asked, cursing herself. She'd done it again, stepped on an invisible nerve.

"No, I just haven't figured it out yet," Nyel confessed.

"Will you stay with family like Atty does?"

"I'm not sure," Nyel said, avoiding her gaze. "What about you?"

"I have one more term of school before I graduate. Then I can stay in Baia Vita year-round."

She couldn't wait to be done; no more heartless dorms with heartless roommates—just her, the sea, and the people she loved.

"Is school where they teach you to read and stuff?" Nyel asked.

"Yep. I'm lucky that my mama left me some money so I could go. Not many of us from the island do."

"Yeah. That's really cool," he said, and she didn't miss the longing in his voice.

"You know, there is a program to help people learn the basics. If you're interested."

"What do you mean?"

Marina waved a hand. "Basic stuff. Reading, writing, and math. Some science. It's just surface-level material. It's only one term, but that's plenty of time to give you a foundation."

"Is it expensive?"

"Not as expensive as going full-time like I do." Realizing she sounded pretentious, she added, "The country is trying to increase its literate population, so they're making this program more available for everyone. I think it's great!"

"But let me guess, it's on the mainland," Atreus chimed in.

"Well, yeah, that's where I go to school," Marina said matter-of-factly and, once again, somehow managed to say something wrong as Nyel's shoulders drooped.

"That's too bad," he said miserably.

"You don't want to see the mainland someday?" Marina asked. Given Nyel's curious nature, she was sure he'd enjoy the adventure.

"It's not in the tides for me." Nyel finished tying a flag. "How many more of these?"

"Not too many. We're almost at the top."

They reached the peak, and Marina had to admit it was a tough climb. Sweat trickled down her back and under her boobs. She leaned heavily against the water well, lifting the hem of her shirt to wipe her brow.

"C'mon, I'm right here!" Atreus yelled, shielding his eyes with one hand and turning away.

Marina dropped her shirt. "Oh, don't be such a baby. They're just boobs."

"No, they're *your* boobs, which is ten times worse," Atreus said, his face still turned in self-defense.

"What's wrong with my boobs? I think they're rather nice. Nyel, are my boobs weird?"

"Don't ask him that!" Atreus yelled, and Marina snorted a laugh.

"Can we not talk about—you know—*that*?" Nyel's timid voice interjected, and just from the sound of it, Marina knew he was beet red.

"Yes, please. New subject," Atreus begged. "Marina, why are we here?"

"We'll set up a water station here. Can't have those kids passing out from dehydration."

"And you thought the top of the hill was a good spot for it?" he complained, setting down the now empty bin of red flags.

"Would you rather carry gallons of water up the hill? I didn't think so," she said, squeezing the handle attached to the well. "All we have to do is make sure this puppy works, and we're done here. Nyel, can you shine the light?"

Nyel did before pointing the beam down the black hole. The light never reached the bottom.

"How deep is this thing?"

Marina shrugged. "Don't know. Wanna jump in and see?"

"No, I think I'll pass," Nyel said, taking several cautionary steps backward. "I'll hold the light from here, thank you very much." He stood a few paces downhill.

"You're no fun," she whined and gripped the handle.

As it turned, the gears squeaked in protest. It hadn't been used in some time, but that was precisely why Marina needed to make sure it worked.

"Little help?" she asked after only managing a couple of rotations.

Atreus took over, managing the crank easily. Soon, a smooth wooden bucket came into view, brimming with crystal-clear water.

"Is it safe to drink?" Nyel asked.

"Of course it is. The farmers in the valley use this well every day. That is, they used to."

Marina missed the farms and the families who left when the land was sold. The imported produce from the mainland didn't taste as good as the crops grown in Baia Vita's soil. Now, the rows of vegetables and fruit trees were gone, replaced by luxury mansions and gated grounds.

She scooped a handful of water and brought it to her lips, enjoying the crisp, clear liquid. At least the water was the same.

"It's perfect. Try it!"

She lifted the bucket, but the old wire handle snapped in her grip. Marina fumbled, the weight throwing her off balance, the bucket slipping from her grasp.

Nyel yelled as ice-cold well water soaked him from head to toe. The flashlight cracked to the ground, the bulb sputtering out. They were thrown into pitch blackness, leaving only the sound of the wooden bucket rolling down the hill.

"Shoot, Nyel, I'm so sorry. Are you okay? Where is the damn light!?"

Marina grappled for the torch, her hands searching cobblestone until the metal cylinder rolled into her palm. She smacked it, clicking the button several times before the light returned.

"It didn't hit your head, did it—?"

The words died in her mouth as Marina lifted her gaze to Nyel.

No.

Not Nyel.

Illuminated by the yellow beam, the creature that stood before her was unmistakably *not* her friend. It was green with scales and fins covering its skin. Its eyes were slitted, and talons lifted in the air in panic. The exact gesture Nyel had made moments ago. It even wore Nyel's clothes, except now a thick tail swept across the ground, swishing in the leaves.

"I...I..." Marina stuttered, both too afraid and too utterly shocked to move. The light trembled in her hand, and she was suddenly terrified of being left in the dark with this thing.

Bits of *Nonno's* stories echoed from somewhere in her brain as she searched for an explanation. His stories about the man who transformed in the water. It couldn't be true. It just couldn't.

But no matter how hard she denied it, Marina knew what this creature was. She lifted a shaking finger, pointing at its chest.

"Uomo del Mare."

ATREUS

THE BUCKET TUMBLED through the air in a drawn-out, surreal sequence, and by the time Atreus's brain registered what was happening, it was already too late. His useless hands grasped the air as the bucket fell. The water splashed Nyel, soaking into his hair and clothes, and within milliseconds, *Marvassa* had him.

The light died, and Atreus begged for it to be broken. He scrambled for it, ready to throw it into the trees, but Marina got there first.

"Shoot, Nyel, I'm so sorry; it didn't hit your head, did it?"

He should have grabbed her. Forced her face to the ground. Kick the torch from her hands—anything to prevent it. But Atreus's feet were trapped in cement.

"I...I..." Marina stuttered, all color draining from her face in an instant.

Atreus locked eyes with Nyel. His pupils were paper-thin slits—fear emanating from every cell in his body.

Yet...

The color of those eyes remained the same, the golden flecks ever present in the beam of the artificial light.

He'd warned Nyel of this. He'd told Nyel this could happen. But months of living so comfortably weakened his guard. Atreus had been too complacent. Too carefree. And had enjoyed Nyel's company far too much. And now, he was paying the price.

For a second, Atreus was tempted to point along with Marina and cry out in alarm—anything to save his place, anything to save the life he'd built.

It's not too late. I can fix this.

But the words died in his throat. He couldn't do it. Couldn't betray this *sireno*. Couldn't turn his back on someone he'd only met a few months ago—someone who became a pillar in his life without Atreus even realizing it.

He stepped toward Nyel, prepared to stand by him, defend him, and, if needed, go down with him.

But those honey-brown eyes locked with his, stopping him midstep. They widened slightly, and with the faintest shake of his head, Nyel sent a clear message.

Don't.

Atreus snapped to action, pulling Marina to him in a protective stance.

"Get out of here!" he shouted at the monster, at his friend. "Go back to the sea where you belong!"

He hoped the pleading in his eyes was enough to tell Nyel that he didn't mean a word of it. Nyel dashed into the trees, his tail dragging in the undergrowth as he disappeared in the dark. With any luck, he wouldn't run into any more humans until he dried. Atreus gripped Marina, who had gone weak at the knees.

"Get up. We have to get home. Don't say a word," he breathed, guiding her to her feet. He didn't have to say it, though. Marina was in shock, and during the entire walk home she only managed to look more pale. The cool blue of early sunrise brought no relief as they marched down the hill in terrified silence.

Once they were in the *pescheria*, Atreus was glad to find the house empty, with Giovanni and Horace likely on the first floor opening the shop. He ushered Marina to his room, closing the door behind him.

He set her on the edge of the bed, resting a comforting hand on her shoulder.

"Can I bring you some water?"

She said nothing, which was even more terrifying coming from her.

"Marina, talk to me."

Her hazel eyes were wide, and she wasn't blinking enough. He shook her.

"Hey. Stay with me. You're okay. We're home."

"What was that, Atty?"

"It…" Atreus couldn't finish. The lie he'd so easily committed to for almost a decade stuck like tar in his mouth. He didn't want to live like this anymore—in the dark, completely on guard.

And now… without Nyel.

Because unless the truth came out, the life he and Nyel had shared this summer was gone.

"Let me get you that water," Atreus said, needing a moment to compose himself.

What would he say to her? Would he ask her to keep it a secret? Would he lie outright? Would he gaslight her into believing it was all in her head? The options played before him as he filled a glass from the tap and returned to her.

"Here, drink."

She took it but didn't bring it to her lips. He sighed and pulled up a chair to sit across from her. He knew what he had to do, and his heart already hurt from the loss.

He'd miss this.

Atreus took the glass from her hands and set it on the nightstand, scooting forward until their knees almost touched. He took both her hands in his, squeezing them and placing a gentle kiss on her knuckles.

"Marina, you know I care about you, right?"

She nodded.

"You know I'd go through hell and high water for you? Right?"

She nodded again.

"You're," he fumbled; he wasn't good at this. "You and I both know I see you as more than just a friend." Realizing, he quickly added, "Not in a weird romantic way. No offense, but- ew."

Finally, she laughed, though it sounded a bit hysterical. "Gee, thanks."

"You know what I mean," Atreus said, trying to refocus, "It's more like—"

"Family," she said so quietly he almost missed it.

"Yeah. Like that."

His heart hurt so much. He wanted to go back to this morning. He wanted everything to go back to the way it was supposed to be.

"And you know I wouldn't do anything to hurt you or Giovanni or Horace or—"

"What are you trying to say, Atty?" She clutched his fingers.

He let out a defeated sigh. He was hopeless. Better to show her.

With deliberate slowness, Atreus took the glass from the nightstand, and with one hand still clasped in both of hers, he tipped it.

Marvassa took him, and a second later, Marian held a much larger, webbed, and taloned hand between hers.

She stiffened, turning to stone before his eyes.

"It's still me," he whispered and couldn't help the plea in his voice.

She didn't respond.

"It's always been me. I just... never let you see it."

She nodded again, and he worried she wasn't breathing.

They sat so long that Atreus's hand dripped dry. About a minute later, his human hand rested between hers once more. But her posture didn't relax.

"So *Nonno's* stories..." she mumbled.

Atreus nodded. "All true. Probably," he said with a half-hearted grin. "The old man likes his stories."

She didn't smile back.

"After the World War, Mer decided it was best to stay hidden," Atreus explained.

"There are more?"

Atreus nodded. "Yes. An entire village in the bay. That is where Nyel is from."

Now, she was blinking too much—processing, letting the truth sink in.

"Where are *you* from?"

"I'm complicated," he said, deciding it wasn't time to share his sob story.

"And you eat..."

Only then did Marina's fears truly dawn on him. Of course, she'd heard the stories—not the ones Horace told at the dinner table, but the ones whispered in the bars. The cautionary tales told by sailors. Legends and myths. Places where facts and fiction swam together in a tapestry of truths and lies. She was scared. She had every right to be.

"Fish, Marina. We eat fish. Actually, only me. Nyel and all the Mer in the bay are plant eaters only. I swear. You've seen the way Nyel picks all the meat out of his food."

She nodded, though it was automatic.

"Marina," Atreus squeezed her shaking hands. "You have the right to ask me anything right now."

She swallowed hard but remained silent. It was so uncharacteristic of her that the hairs on his arms raised.

"If everyone knew—I couldn't stay here. I'd have to go, and so would Nyel," Atreus begged.

"So... nobody else knows."

"Only you."

Marina yanked her hands back, unable to bear touching him any longer. It was sudden, and her eyes widened as if she had only now realized what kind of monster sat in the room.

Atreus's chest fell.

"Atreus, I— I need some time. To think."

Or time to alert everyone else.

"Of course. Nyel and I will crash somewhere for a few days. We'll come back to help with the Bayallon. Tell your dad we had some urgent news from family or something."

She nodded. "Sure."

With nothing left to say, Atreus stood to leave.

Marina's tear-filled words stopped him. "Would you have told me eventually?"

Atreus said nothing as he looked at the human he'd come to cherish.

Marina took a shaky breath. "Would you have told me? If Nyel didn't get wet and I didn't see anything, would you have told me someday?"

Atreus knew the answer, and guilt ate away at him as he said it. "No."

Marina nodded like she'd expected this. "Right."

"I'll see you later, Marina." He forced a smile and stepped out of the room, out of the *pescheria*, hoping it wouldn't be the last time. His heart sank when he realized that Marina had called him by his proper name.

Atreus never thought he'd wish to hear that awful nickname again. But as his feet sank into the white sandy beach, he wanted nothing more than for Marina to call him Atty.

NYEL

NYEL PACED THE LIGHTHOUSE'S circular room, back and forth, his bare feet taking him nowhere. He'd run his hands through his hair so many times it was a miracle it hadn't fallen out. Alternate realities played on repeat in his mind. He should have been paying more attention, watching more carefully to avoid the spill— knowing Marina was an incurable clutz.

Shouldn't have stood so close.

Should've.

Could've.

Would've.

All the things he wished he'd done differently ran through his mind with no other purpose except to torture him.

I've messed everything up. I've ruined everything. And Atreus...

It was only a second, but Nyel saw it. A step forward. Atreus coming to take his side. It warmed him, the feeling almost enough to drive away the raging panic in his chest.

Almost.

He was about to give up everything for me.

But even as much as Nyel wanted Atreus to run to his side, he couldn't let that happen. Couldn't let Atreus throw away everything he'd built. Signaling for Atreus to stay back was the right call.

Still...

Now, he was alone. Now, he'd have to face this reality by himself. Options played out before him like one of those moving picture things that played on the TV.

He could return to Corallina, back to his old life, where his mother would likely revert to her old ways, and by this time next year, he'd be Bonded to a nice *sirena* with a baby on the way.

He could live in the lighthouse. He'd be alone, with no friends and no work, nothing to keep him going. Would Atreus visit him?

Maybe he could find a new human town? But that was too risky. The only reason he'd made it so long in Baia Vita was Atreus's help. He had no chance of carving out an existence for himself in a different human village. Plus, he doubted there were many human villages like Baia Vita.

All options left him paralyzed and anxious.

"What do I do, what do I do, what do I do?" He tugged his hair uselessly.

As the hour-long minutes ticked by, regret sank in his stomach. He began to wish he'd let Atreus take his side, even if it made him a terrible person.

Nyel startled when groaning metal echoed up the staircase. He couldn't remember falling asleep. As the clanging steps grew closer, he huddled under the blankets, hoping whoever it was wouldn't see him. With the black-out curtains drawn, it was dark inside the tower despite it being only midday. The door opened. All was silent.

"Ny? Ny, are you up here?"

"Atreus!" Nyel sprang from his hiding place and wrapped his arms around Atreus's middle, burying his face in his chest. "Atreus, I'm so sorry. I'm such an idiot. I tried, but I—"

"Hey, hey, it's not your fault," Atreus said, holding Nyel close and rubbing slow circles on his back.

Nyel didn't know when he'd started crying, but it was like all the nervous energy he'd paced into the floors was leaking out of his eyes.

"It was an accident, Nyel. Nobody's fault."

"You managed to go years without an accident. And here I go, messing everything up after a few months."

"I've been lucky. And I talked with Marina. I showed her what I was. She saw it, Ny."

Nyel leaned back but couldn't see Atreus's face in the dark.

"W-why would you do that!?"

"Ny, it's—"

"She *saw* you?"

"Let's get a fire going and talk, alright?"

Nyel wanted to argue, but the way Atreus's hand pressed against his back, guiding him to the fire pit, made the words die before they could fully form.

Somehow, Atreus managed to start a fire in the pitch blackness, little cinders casting their space in orange light. Watching the embers grow from a dim sparkle to filling the hearth did wonders to calm Nyel's strained nerves. He inhaled the scent of burning wood, letting the occasional pop of sparks crack away the tension in his spine.

"You're really good at that," Nyel complimented, sitting close to the bowl of dancing heat with his knees tucked to his chest and hands outstretched.

"Been doing it a long time," Atreus said, tossing more sticks. "There's enough wood in here for a few days."

Nyel inhaled a deep breath, the question coming out on a sigh. "Why did you show her? I—"

I protected you from that.

Atreus took a minute to answer. "Watching you run off, as I shouted at you like you were some kind of mon—" He swallowed hard. "It didn't feel right. It only took a walk down the hill for me to realize I wouldn't be able to live with myself. So I did what needed to be done."

Warmth swelled in Nyel's chest even as he knew it shouldn't.

"How did she take it?"

Atreus threw in another log, harsher than necessary, sending up a flock of sparks like frightened seabirds on the beach. "About as well as you can imagine. But she didn't attack me, so I guess that's something."

His voice was laced with vinegar. The same bitterness coated Nyel's mouth. He didn't want to talk about this anymore, but there was no getting around it.

"How did you find me?"

"Figured there were limited places you would go. I searched the stony beach first. This was my second guess. If you weren't here, I was gonna check your house in Corallina." He tapped his nose. "I can't do the scent thing like you can."

"How long do we have to stay here?" Nyel asked, already missing his bed. His room.

My home.

"I told Marina we'd still be there to help with the Bayallon. Thought she could use a couple of days to process."

"That's fair."

The unspoken question fermented on his tongue, turning more acidic by the second. When he could no longer stand its bitter lemon-rind taste, Nyel whispered as if the words themselves might sting.

"Will she tell anyone?"

"I— I don't think so."

"That's not reassuring, Atreus."

"What do you want me to say?" he snapped, "It's not like I've done this before. And I hate to break it to you, but you scared her half to death."

Nyel shrunk back. "I know. I'm so sorry."

"No." Atreus groaned. "I'm sorry. I shouldn't have snapped. It's not your fault. It was an accident."

But that didn't stop Nyel's gut from twisting with guilt. This *was* his fault.

"I have no clue what she'll do," Atreus said honestly. "And that scares the shit out of me."

He poked at the fire, his posture relaxed despite everything.

"You're actually taking this better than I expected," Nyel said as his eyes followed the embers. It was midday, and there was no need for the fire. But it was something to do. And they desperately needed a distraction.

He thought Atreus would turn into a ballistic mess the moment their secret was out.

Maybe this is the calm before the storm.

The taller man shrugged, sitting beside Nyel and resting his elbow on a bent knee.

"Maybe it hasn't sunk in yet. But I don't regret anything."

"You could have stayed hidden. You didn't have to tell Marina about yourself. When I got splashed, it looked like..." Nyel shifted uncomfortably. "Well, for a second, it looked like you were going to take my side."

"I was."

"Why? Not that it mattered; you outed yourself right after, anyway. But why? You told me when I first came to the island that—"

"You were on your own?" Atreus finished, poking the fire with a stick, sending up another flurry of sparks.

"Yeah. Before, well, everything, I thought you'd—" Nyel chewed the inside of his cheek, unsure of how to continue. Sharks, he was bad at this. Why was talking to Atreus about this so freakin' hard?

Atreus paused his poking, letting the edge of the stick burn. The orange glow reflected in his abalone eyes.

"We weren't friends before."

The warmth now filling Nyel's chest had nothing to do with the fire. "Thank you," he said, but it felt inadequate for what Atreus just gave him.

Nyel hugged his knees, letting himself get lost in the dancing flames and thinking about the days ahead. He'd been looking forward to the end-of-season festival since the first one. But would it feel the same now? Would Marina keep their secret?

Nyel was so consumed by his tempestuous thoughts that he didn't notice the day slipping away. He hadn't had a bite to eat but couldn't bring himself to feel hungry. It was late now, and Atreus hadn't spoken a word for hours.

If Nyel were on his comfy mattress at the *pescheria*, he'd be asleep already, probably with a full belly. But too many scenarios raced through his mind to allow for that. Atreus leaned on one arm, similarly lost in thought.

What's going through his head? Is he angry? Regretful? Does he want me to leave?

But asking any of those questions would only make things worse. So he settled on simply watching the man beside him.

Nyel's gaze trailed over the sun-bleached strands hidden in Atreus's curls, tracing down his neck to his prominent Adam's apple. His freckles were more pronounced along his neck and shoulders. While his face bore only a light dusting across the nose, a trail of them traced down his neck like footprints in the sand, skittering across his bare shoulders as if marked by the sea's gentle spray. Nyel's eyes followed the trail lower, lingering on the curve of Atreus's muscled arm before finally resting on the hand splayed against the wooden floor. It was big and calloused from hours working the docks. A few scars dotted his knuckles.

Nyel knew those hands were warm. That they closed around his perfectly. He scooted his hand closer until their pinkies barely touched. Instantly, Atreus flinched, pulling away from the contact.

"S-sorry," Nyel said, embarrassment flooding his cheeks.

"No, it's okay. Surprised me, is all. I'm not used to... " Atreus looked down, and Nyel was surprised to find him flushed.

"Not used to what?"

"I'm— I'm not a *touchy* person."

Nyel thought back to his childhood, filled to bursting with a smothering mother, a doting father, and recently, an aunt who embraced him on every occasion. He'd grown up in a home with kisses, swishing tails, and playful flicks on his fins.

Atreus spent the majority of his life alone. And when he wasn't alone, he was with humans, whom he carefully kept at a distance.

"Sorry." Nyel apologized again.

"I don't hate it," Atreus quickly amended, "It's just—"

"New?"

Atreus nodded. "Yeah. Different."

Atreus placed his hand back on the floor, slowly sliding it across the smooth surface until, once again, their pinkies brushed together.

He held it there, sucking in a breath while Nyel stopped breathing entirely. Tentatively, Nyel lifted his pinky finger, placing it over Atreus's.

"Is this okay?" Nyel whispered like he might frighten the moment away.

Atreus nodded, then lifted his hand and rested it over Nyel's. It closed around him perfectly, as he knew it would.

And it's warm.

"I'm sorry about hugging you earlier. I didn't realize."

"I saw you coming and braced for it. Otherwise, I might have knocked you into the wall," Atreus said, keeping his gaze on their overlapping hands.

But the curtains were drawn, and it was pitch black. A memory resurfaced from their early morning adventure—how Atreus had complained about the flashlight, which he didn't need.

"How do you see so well in the dark?"

"*Rusalki* blood," a voice said directly behind them.

In an instant, they sprung apart, and Atreus had a sharpened stick in his hands before Nyel even realized what was happening.

Nephi laughed from the corner of the room. "Easy boys, it's just me."

"That doesn't make me feel any better," Atreus growled.

Nephi gave a sly grin. "Good."

"Nephi, what are you doing here?" Nyel asked, trying to calm his exploding nerves. "How did you get up here?"

Nephi pointed behind him. "The stairs."

"It squeaks like crazy; we didn't hear a thing." Atreus bit out, still clutching the homemade spear.

"And how is that my fault?" Nephi replied, "I'm stealthier than I look."

Nyel rested a hand on Atreus's arm.

"Easy, Nephi isn't here to cause trouble. Right?" Nyel said with a pointed look.

"Wouldn't dream of it," he replied, which somehow made Nyel even more skeptical.

Atreus lowered the spear but didn't drop it.

"What did you say about being *Ru*— what was that word?" Nyel sat, hoping the other two would do the same. They did, though Atreus's narrowed gaze didn't leave Nephi for even a blink.

Nephi made himself comfortable, stretching and crossing his legs like he owned the place. He sat farthest from the fire, and Nyel thought he saw Nephi snarl in its direction.

"He is half *Rusalki*. They have excellent eyesight in the dark."

"Oh wow, you never told me that," Nyel said, going for a light tone.

"I didn't know," Atreus growled through clenched teeth.

"Another species of Mer that live in the north," Nephi filled in. "Big, barbed with a knack for fighting."

Nyel was amazed. Nephi never spoke about his travels, and now here he was, offering relevant information.

"What else?"

"Well," Nephi said, considering Atreus, "Your sense of smell isn't as good as mine and Nyel's. That's a *Sireni* gift."

"Oh, we knew that one," Nyel said. "I've wondered why Atreus couldn't follow a scent trail."

"Yours is better than mine since you're a pure *sireno*. I'm a mutt with only half the parts. Plus, I fucked one of my nostrils, so I'm running on fifty percent as it is." Nephi said, pointing to his disfigured right nostril.

"What can the *Ra-Maa* do?" Nyel asked before he could stop himself. Nephi stiffened right away, his grin dissolving.

"S-sorry," Nyel said, ducking his head.

"My mother, a *Ra-Maa* woman, gave me my red fins. And that's all the information you're getting." He jerked his chin in Atreus's direction. "And I have no idea what his other half is. Not a Mer I've ever seen."

Nyel didn't miss the way Atreus's shoulders sagged slightly.

"You got any food here?" Nephi barked, "I didn't have a chance to steal anything after I watched your little fiasco at the well."

"You saw that?" Nyel exclaimed. "And you didn't do anything?"

Nephi shrugged him off. "What was I supposed to do? I told you this would happen. Lo and behold, it did. You're lucky only the little woman was with you; if that giant man you live with had been there, you'd have gotten a harpoon through the ribs."

Nyel's insides clenched at the thought of Giovanni turning his hulking form against him—harpoon raised, hate burning in his eyes. He shoved the thought away.

"And if someone had jumped out and come after him, would you have stayed in your hiding place?" Atreus asked accusingly.

Nephi pointed at him with a wink. "Exactly. Sorry, little brother. You and I may be on speaking terms now, but I'm nowhere ready to take a knife for you. Survival of the fittest."

"I care about you too," Nyel said, rolling his eyes.

"I'm just being real."

"Well, at least we can count on you for that since, clearly, we can't count on anything else." Atreus bit back.

"Correct again, Bluey."

"Stop calling me that. I'm not even completely blue."

"Blue-Purply doesn't roll off the tongue," Nephi said, picking at a stray nail. "So what's the status on food?"

Atreus sighed, but Nyel was glad to see him relax somewhat.

"Nothing you'd like. I have some cans of sardines, and that's it."

"I'll eat that." Nephi said, "I'm only half *Sireni*, remember? I rather enjoy the flesh of the once-living."

"Don't say it like that," Nyel cringed.

Atreus stood and dug around in his corner of possessions before tossing a couple of cans at Nephi. "There."

"You should host more often. You have such a knack for it," Nephi deadpanned, making quick work of the lid. Nyel cringed at the sickly smell of flesh and salt.

As the trio sat around the dying embers, Nyel realized something. "I think this is the first time the three of us have spent time together."

They were quiet again.

"It's uncomfortable," Atreus said.

"Let's never do it again," Nephi offered.

"Agreed," Atreus replied quickly, and that was that.

Nephi groaned as he stood, stretching. "I'll take the first watch; you two sleep."

"Watch?" Nyel asked, eyebrows knit in confusion.

"What? Do you really think there aren't hunting parties looking for you right this second? Even on this deceptively peaceful island, we have to be vigilant."

"Nobody is hunting us. Marina won't tell anyone," Atreus said, but he didn't sound certain.

Nephi laughed mirthlessly. "And you actually have faith in that human?"

"I —I do."

"Then you're a fool. They're lying, two-faced creatures with a love for killing anything that's different."

"Sounds like someone else I know," Atreus said, eyes heavy on Nephi.

The two males stared each other down, the tension crackling worse than the fire. Nyel was half-standing, ready to break up a fight, before Nephi laughed.

"This world makes monsters of us all. Still, I won't be the monster that gets its throat sliced while it sleeps. I'm keeping watch." This time, Nyel definitely didn't imagine the snarl as Nephi glared at the dying embers. "Douse that. We don't need it, and it's giving us away."

"Like hell. I'm not putting Nyel in the dark where he can't see. And I'm not sleeping with you around," Atreus hissed. Nyel tensed, waiting for Nephi's anger to flare, but a sly grin once again slid across his brother's scarred face.

"You're finally learning. Fine, then you and I can stare into each other's eyes all night long."

Atreus huffed. "As if."

"Right. You'd rather do that with my brother."

"What is that supposed to mean?" Nyel interjected and hated the way his face went warm.

He didn't mean anything by that. Did he?

"It means what it means. Go to sleep. Apparently, you'll have two guards on duty."

"If you two aren't sleeping, neither am I," Nyel said stubbornly, even though his eyelids felt as heavy as anchors.

"It's an all-night party," Nephi said with a clap, settling by a window and gazing at Baia Vita in the distance.

Atreus made himself busy gathering the firewood around the room, and Nyel sat by the fire feeling useless.

Yeah... this is awkward.

CHAPTER 21

MARINA

SHE WAS IN SHOCK. Even as the sun rose and her father called from below, Marina couldn't make herself move from her bed. Only when the bedroom door creaked open did she finally break free from her statue-like stillness.

"*Piccola*, what is wrong? Where are the boys?" *Papá* asked, worry crinkling his mustache.

Tears welled in her eyes. "They left. Had a family emergency and..."

Her mind finished the thought: *And they are monsters. All this time. They've been lying to us. To me.*

A heavy 'whoosh' sounded beside her as her father sat his bulk on the mattress.

"Did you have a fight, *mia cara*?"

She nodded. "Yeah. Something like that. I thought I knew them better. I thought they trusted me, but..."

Tears fell from her cheeks and onto her clasped hands. She could still feel the scales on her fingertips. How real they were. *Nonno's* stories, right there in her bedroom.

Papá sighed heavily. "These things happen. Let me ask you, are you angry with them?"

"Yes!" she said so fast her hair flew.

And she was. She was so freakin' mad at them. At Nyel, but especially Atreus. She'd known him almost all her life. They'd grown up together in this town, running around every summer. He'd heard her cry through the bedroom walls when she started her first period. And she'd heard him yell in pain as *Papá* dislodged yet another fish-hook from his thumb. She knew his favorite food was red tuna and that he hated wearing shoes. Marina knew him better than anyone.

Or at least... she thought she did. Being distrusted by someone she considered family stung worse than when she had stepped on a sea urchin.

"Can you forgive them?" her father asked.

Marina clenched her fists. She was so angry. And hurt. And shocked.

But... yes. She could.

"Yeah."

"Then that is all that matters." He patted her back affectionately. "When they return, do not prolong it. Speak to them. It will work out."

Marina sighed.

If only you knew Papà.

"Thank you. I should go to town; there are a few things to do before tomorrow."

Her father gave her a prickly kiss on the cheek before leaving her alone.

Of course, she'd forgive Atreus. He was pretty much family. Well — a lot more distant family.

Not even the same species.

The thought sent chills down her spine. Yet the way he'd pleaded with her—the fear in his eyes. It was still him. No matter how weird the whole 'change into a legendary creature with water' thing was. He was still Atty.

But she wasn't about to let him off the hook that easy. He'd still not trusted her with his secret, and that friggin' hurt. Sure, she understood why he did it. There was no shortage of horrible stories about sea monsters in a place like Baia Vita. There was no guarantee how the rest of the island would react to the news. Still...

He should have trusted me.

Marina was in no rush to talk to either of them. Atreus could stay wherever he was hiding until the festival. She'd let him stew with his nerves.

Serves him right. That way, he can think about what he's done.

Not to mention, she had no idea where he was. She wiped the burn out of her eyes before dressing and going to town. The Bayallon still needed her, and Marina Marcello was no quitter. Even if there were *Uomo del mare* running around.

MARINA WALKED FROM CITY HALL, careful to avoid the last uneven step. She didn't really need to meet with the mayor; there was almost nothing left to do to prepare for the race. But talking with the mayor about the course, the number of kids signed up, and whether the hospital would send a nurse in case of an emergency gave her something to do—even for a few minutes.

Marina meandered up the hill, following the trail of flags. The same red flags they'd been tying when everything changed.

Nope! Don't think about that.

She ducked into a side alley, away from the race course. She admired the lights strung across the balconies, replacing the usual clotheslines. Everyone was getting ready for tomorrow.

Maybe I should get back and help Papà fry the fish and — !!!!!

Marina's thoughts were wiped clean as ice-cold water drenched her from head to toe. Several hard bits smacked against her skull, nearly knocking her to the ground. Cubes of ice clattered on the street. Her nose wrinkled as a strong, fishy smell overwhelmed her.

"Oops! Didn't see you there." Leaning over the balcony, Anna and two other girls giggled maliciously from above. "Hey, schoolgirl, what does this say?"

Anna held the bucket so Marina could see the words "Ice" printed clearly on the side. Probably one of the ones her father used to deliver fish.

"I was feeling too hot. Thanks for the refreshing splash!" Marina called, shaking her sopping hair for show.

"Oh, that's right, you're numb to the smell," Anna taunted. "Is this the same water you use to shower?"

They giggled again, and Anna shouted above the others, her voice filled with venom. "You stay outta my way at the festival tomorrow. You hear? I'm getting that dance with him."

Marina rolled her eyes as she walked away, trying to ignore their jabbing words. There was no doubt in her mind who Anna was talking about. The mystery man she'd been with last time. The one who basically told Anna to get lost and chose to stay with Marina.

A whole lotta good that's done me, Marina thought, squeezing more water from her hair.

Marina hadn't seen Mr. Tall-Dark-and-Handsome since catching him putting the moves on another girl. The entire summer went by without another sighting of him, and honestly, Marina had just begun to forget about it. That was until Anna supplied her with a splashing reminder.

"Yeah, you can have him," Marina snapped. She wanted no part of this. "Like I have time to deal with a man."

"But my dear, you haven't had the pleasure of dealing with me."

Marina yelped as the silky voice purred behind her. He was alone, which was odd since Vincenzo hardly went anywhere without his entourage.

This day can't get any worse, can it?

"I'd rather chew glass," Marina said, trying to move past him. He side-stepped, blocking her.

"I can't have that. What a waste that would be, ruining such a mouth."

"Fuck you."

"And there she goes again, spewing filth. No refinement. No training. A gem, yet unpolished."

Alvise looked at her with the kind of disappointment that comes from finding a job half-finished. Like it was Marina's responsibility to 'meet expectations,' and she'd fallen short. As if she owed him a damn thing.

"How you frustrate me," he whispered, though he wore a delighted smile.

"Then I'm doing my job."

"I could make you sparkle brighter than the stars," he said as though she hadn't spoken. "What will it take, my dear? How is that elderly family of yours? Fishing hasn't been good this season. Will there be enough for them to eat this winter?"

Marina clenched her jaw until it hurt. "Get out of my way, Alvise."

"I could make you want for nothing."

"I want you to swallow a fish hook."

"Or," he leaned closer. "I can take it all. Then you'll be forced to beg for everything."

Marina wouldn't back down. Not from him. Not today. She faced him, eyes narrowed. Their faces were much too close. He was doused in rich cologne, and she with fish-gut water.

"Go. To. Hell."

"Only. With. You." His voice glided like a figure skater across the ice. "It's only a matter of time, my little vixen. You will come to me, one way or another."

"I thought I wasn't pretty enough for your collection?" she hissed, barely resisting the urge to spit on his face.

"Not yet. But there is so much to be done with you."

Before she could blink, before she could scream, his hand clamped onto the back of her head, yanking her hair violently. Her chest slammed flush with his as he wrenched her head back, exposing her throat. When she tried to push away, his grip tightened, drawing a whimper from her lips. Alvise hummed, pleased, as though savoring the thought of tasting her skin.

Marina's pulse raced, her limbs weak and unsteady. Her scalp burned from the violent grip, and she could barely draw a breath. The sound of his satisfied hum sent a chill down her spine, anger mixing with helplessness. Her skin prickled with dread as her body betrayed her. Freezing in the face of danger.

"As a maid on my estate, I can shape you into something you can scarcely imagine. Fix all these rough edges. All the impurities. These gorgeous tresses," he lifted a section of hair to his nose, breathing deeply. "They are too precious to waste." He wrinkled his nose. "But let's start with the smell."

Marina shoved him, stumbling as he released her. "D-don't touch me." She faltered, hating how pathetic and scared she sounded.

"What is going on here?" A voice called from behind her.

Alvise straightened, placing both hands in his pockets. "Nothing at all."

"That's not what it sounded like."

Marina turned to the newcomer, and there he was—the beautiful stranger. The man she'd almost successfully forgotten about.

Because, of course, he was here.

His clothes were casual, and his hair was pulled back in a ponytail. But the look of anger on his face was new. And it was far more frightening than she thought possible.

"Let's leave the lady alone; what do you say, Alvise?" he said with a not-so-subtle threat in his tone.

Alvise remained unmoved. "You have no claim to her. As far as I see it, we were having a friendly chat."

"Not all things are objects to be claimed," the stranger snapped. "Especially people."

"Once again, that is where you're wrong."

Marina felt that these two had been down this road before. This conversation felt old, like a battle that had been fought many times.

"It's time for you to go, Alvise."

"It's *Signore* Vincenzo to you." Then, his eyes found Marina. "You have a guard dog. I have to admit, I'm rather disappointed. Can the fox not fight for herself?"

Marina bristled. "I don't! He isn't!"

She was so done with this conversation. Her head hurt where the ice had hit her.

"Alvise, stay the hell away from me and my family," she yelled, hating how her voice wavered. "I'll die before I ever work for you. If you come near me again, you'll regret it."

But the threat sounded hollow even to her own ears. And it must have been just as pathetic to Alvise as his smile stretched ear to ear, revealing perfect teeth.

"I look forward to it. Don't make promises you can't keep, my dear." Alvise's eyes turned to the stranger, running up and down his physique, appraising him as he did with all things. "How far you've fallen." Then he turned on his heel and was gone.

Marina shook as if she were standing naked in a winter storm. Today was too much. She had to get home.

"Are you okay?" the stranger asked.

And like a delayed firework, Marina exploded.

"You!" she shouted. "You had no right to interfere!"

His eyes went wide in alarm. "I'm sorry, I thought he—"

"Thought he what? What was he going to do? It doesn't matter because I can handle myself. I don't need Prince Charming to come running to my rescue. I've dealt with Alvise before, and I'll keep doing it so long as I call this island home!"

When did the tears start falling? Why was she yelling? But now that she'd started, she couldn't stop.

"I'm not one of your playthings. Alright? I'm not an obedient dog you can call when it's convenient, or you're bored. I'm not your personal ray of sunshine, okay? I can't be summer and sunflowers every god-damn second of every day! You can't string me along, promise to care, then disappear the moment I stop smiling like your perfect little doll. I deserve better than that!"

Her voice echoed in the alley. At what point did she stop talking about him? When had the tears and the betrayal morphed her words, directing them toward...Marina didn't want to think about her mother. Not now. Not when she was trying to be angry at this stranger.

She was certain the entire block was listening at this point, but she didn't care. The man rested his hands in his pockets and at least had the decency to look ashamed. If he noticed that her words weren't entirely directed at him, he didn't say anything.

"You're right. I'm sorry."

Marina balked. "That's it?"

He nodded. "That's it. I'm sorry."

"Well, I'm— I'm not done being angry," she admitted, her body trembling with it. The day's emotions spilled over, tipping her already brimming cup after years of keeping it from overflowing one drop at a time.

"Don't stop on my account. Get it out."

"You—" she struggled to come up with something. "You have no right walking around like this. Like you own the place."

"That would be correct. I don't own the space we are currently standing in."

She bristled. "What is that supposed to mean?"

"It means you are right."

"Yes, I am," she snapped.

"Feel better?"

"Not really." But somehow, his words had doused some of the fire in her body.

"Can I ask you something?" he said softly.

"Sure."

"Why are you wet?"

Marina burst into laughter. She must have looked like a lunatic, but at that moment, she couldn't have cared less.

"Because one of your other conquests knows how to hold a grudge. She didn't like that you danced with me during the last festival."

"Oh—I'm sorry. I didn't mean to cause you any trouble—"

"And now that we're on the topic," Marina interrupted. "If you see me tomorrow night at the festival, stay the hell away from me. I've got enough to deal with without adding your jealous groupies to the list."

His jaw clenched, and Marina was ready for him to argue. But he surprised her yet again. "I hear you. And I'll respect your wishes."

"Good. Hopefully, we never run into each other again," she said, spinning and marching away, her fishy hair whipping her face.

"I hope you're wrong, Marina."

She hesitated and almost turned around.

Almost.

As she kicked off her boots by the *pescheria* doors, she couldn't help but think, *he remembered my name.*

But she was done settling for scraps of affection.

I deserve more than the crumbs.

CHAPTER 22

ATREUS

Atreus only let himself sleep when Nephi was gone. The other halfling left before sunrise, finally giving Atreus space to breathe. Nephi was a wildcard in Atreus's routine world. But he supposed there was nothing routine about his world now. His predictable, safe life was gone.

The moment Atreus realized he couldn't let Nyel go changed everything. His old fears paled in comparison to the reality of living without Nyel—the only being who truly knew what he was and chose to stay. And no matter how much he tried to deny it, every choice he made was rooted in that quiet, undeniable truth.

He watched the rise and fall of Nyel's back as the *sireno* slept on the other side of the mattress. Nyel curled like a pup when he slept, taking up as little room as possible. If not for the occasional humming in his throat, Atreus might have forgotten he was there.

He's sleeping so close to me.

Atreus sighed and buried his face into the springy mattress, eyes growing heavier to the familiar smell of smoke. How had this *sireno* infiltrated his defenses so easily? How had Nyel crept past all his walls, broken all his rules—and settled in his heart so deeply that Atreus was ready to risk everything for him?

"The person you were six months ago wouldn't have done it."

Atreus hadn't heard the slimy whisper in weeks. But once again, when his defenses were low, it resurged, clawing its way into his thoughts, demanding his attention.

"You're an idiot. You're throwing it all away. Where will you go when you can't go back? Do you think Nyel will welcome you into his life? With his family? What would his mother say?"

Atreus ignored the toxic mutterings but let his mind settle on the first part. It was true; six months ago, he'd never have made this choice.

It was odd. How could things change so fast?

How could a single person turn the ocean upside down?

RAZOR-SHARP THORNS CUT into his calves. Fleshy white vines dragged him through the soil, towards the pit that waited like an open mouth. Atreus screamed, his nails digging into the ground for purchase. Dirt coated his tongue as he struggled.

Rising all around him were the luminescent white flowers, their cold glow piercing his eyes. Their diamond-shaped petals seemed unnaturally angled, as though they were turned toward him. Watching. They witnessed his demise with an unfeeling gaze, their light offering no warmth, no refuge.

They could have helped. They *should* have helped. But they didn't. The petals only shimmered, indifferent, as the vines tightened their grip and dragged him closer to the waiting abyss.

"You didn't save her!" Atreus shouted at them like a curse.

But the delicate blooms didn't respond. Didn't move. They swayed with the lazy movement of the tide. Unfeeling.

The vines dug through his scales, penetrating muscle and scraping bone.

"You're mine."

"Let me go!"

"You're nothing without me.
Nobody wants you.
Nobody ever will.
I am all you have, all you'll ever have.

Stop fighting. Give in."

"You aren't real!" Atreus cried to the voice that echoed from the pit. The same voice that tormented him in his waking hours. The voice that took root in his mind when his father left. The voice that blinked with the unfeeling glow of nameless flowers.

"I am as real as you are."

"Let me go!" Atreus's fingernails tore as he clawed at the dirt.

"We are one and the same."

"Atreus!"

Someone called to him, but the voice was muffled as though reverberating underwater.

"Wake up!

Atreus gasped and shot upright, nearly colliding with Nyel, who was bent over him, his face pale.

"Where is it?" Atreus shouted, heart in his throat and body ready to face the threat. He grabbed at his ankles.

"There is nothing here. You were having a nightmare," Nyel said soothingly.

"No, it's..." Atreus's eyes darted around wildly, his heart pounding. It was here. It was right here. It.... Was...

As he blinked, his heart rate slowed. Clarity returned, along with a throbbing headache. He rubbed his temples.

"You were thrashing in your sleep."

Atreus swallowed hard. The nightmares were getting worse—perhaps the fear of losing everything he cared about was finally sinking in. He wasn't ready to let it go. Wasn't ready to let Baia Vita fade to memory.

A tentative hand gripped his fingertips.

"You okay?" Nyel asked, and all at once, Atreus was.

This *sireno's* touch was enough to steady the storm within him, grounding him in a way nothing else could. It was enough. Nyel was enough. Once again, Atreus remembered that risking it all had been his choice. A quiet reassurance settled inside him, knowing that if given the chance, he'd do it all again.

Even though it makes no goddamn sense.

Risking his life for one person? It was stupid. Yet he couldn't make himself believe that. Not anymore. Something had shifted deep inside him. It was as if a part of him had awakened, unearthing feelings he didn't fully understand—or perhaps didn't want to. All he knew was that he wasn't the same, and the uncertainty of it both gnawed at him as much as it strangely settled him.

"I know Marina said to meet her at the festival, but can we check and see if she is okay now?" Nyel asked tentatively, and Atreus was relieved to hear him say it.

He couldn't spend another minute in this lighthouse, not knowing if he had a home to return to.

"Yeah. Let's go," Atreus said. They had no possessions to gather, and after making sure the fire was completely smothered, they descended the winding stairs. Normally, Atreus relied on his masterful staging to ward off any curious humans, but given the circumstances, he took extra precautions. Only after he was sure the door's jam would hold did he turn his back on the home he'd known for over a decade.

"Let's do this," he said on an exhale. Nyel nodded, looking just as uncertain as Atreus felt.

Removing his shirt, running onto the sand, and diving into the water was a relief he couldn't quite explain. As he dipped his head beneath an oncoming wave, Atreus sank into the salt water, his fins flaring, relieved from the confines of human skin.

"No matter how much time I spend on land, this always feels right," Nyel said beside him, black-tipped fins flared and jade scales sparkling.

"Yeah. Can take the Mer from the sea but can't take the sea from the Mer."

"Can take— what?" Nyel asked as they swam to Baia Vita, tails swishing in synchronized strokes.

"Never mind. Human expression."

"Do you think she will see us differently?"

"I don't see how she couldn't. We aren't human."

The reality of that grew all the clearer as they approached the bay, dodging fishing boats and nets. There were hardly any fish to catch, and as they passed a net, Atreus tried to herd a few straggling mackerel into its clutches. It was better than nothing. The fact of the matter was that the fish were taken long before reaching the safety of the bay.

Under the water, even this far away, Atreus listened to the steady thrum of massive engines. He couldn't fathom how something so large and made of metal could float, but it did. And it consumed everything in its path.

It was an insatiable maw.

The unforgiving reality was this —the smaller fishing boats of Baia Vita couldn't compete with the power of those ships.

They dried in a hidden alcove between dark rocks, where Atreus slipped on his shirt before stepping onto the open sand. The square was lively with movement, families preparing booths, and city volunteers stringing lights for the night's dancing. Tonight would kick start the celebrations, with the Bayallon taking place the following morning. The streets were abuzz with energy, and upbeat chatter filled the air. There were no screams, no fear, no worries that monsters walked among them.

She didn't say anything.

Even so, he put himself between Nyel and anyone who walked too close. The last time he'd been this wary walking through his home, he was a starving kid. He hoped he'd never have to relive those days as they opened the *pescheria* doors.

Giovanni was hard at work, preparing food at the counter.

"There you are, *ragazzo*! I hope your family is well," he asked sympathetically.

At Nyel's confused expression, Atreus cut in. "They're great. Sorry for leaving the day before everything."

"It's no problem. Family comes first, yes?"

Atreus agreed, and he and Nyel shuffled up the stairs.

Marina sat at the kitchen table, stringing together paper flowers in a long rope for the kids to break through at the finish line. She stopped as they approached. Once again, Atreus put himself before Nyel. The *sireno* was the one she witnessed fully transformed. He might be the one she was wary of now. Atreus needed to reassure Marina, to make her feel safe, and remind her they were still the same—that he would never hurt her. But as her hazel eyes pierced through him, all he could muster was a weak, "Hey."

"Hey," she mimicked, then waved to Nyel. "Hey, Nyel. I'm glad you came."

Nyel waved back but stayed a few paces away.

Marina groaned, dragging her fingers through messy hair, shaking it into an even messier nest of curls.

"Aaah, just come sit down! Jeez, I'm not going to batter and fry you like the fish downstairs."

Atreus laughed even as she cringed.

"Oh good, you thought that was funny. I worried maybe it was too soon."

"I'm not a fish, but the joke landed anyway," he said, taking a chair and ushering Nyel to do the same.

"I'm sorry I made you guys wait so long. To be fair, I had no idea where you went. And I was—*am*, so flippin' mad at you."

Atreus blinked. "Mad? Not— not scared?"

"Well, I was scared at first, but when you explained things, I stopped being scared. I was—*am*, mad. And hurt." She stopped her sewing, staring at the needle in her hand. "You could have trusted me, Atty."

Guilt settled in his stomach, but so did something else. It was warm, and he never wanted to let it go. He cared for this red-headed girl so much.

"I'm sorry. I am. I hope you understand why I did it."

"Yeah. I do. Doesn't make it suck any less."

"I should have trusted you."

"Yeah. You should have. But I'll get over it." Marina's gaze locked on Nyel, who hadn't said a word thus far. "I'm sorry, Nyel."

Nyel blanched, obviously as surprised as Atreus was.

"Sorry for what? We're the ones that lied to you."

She waved him off. "I get it; this is a fishing town, after all. But I had no right to treat you like a monster. That was mean."

"Apology accepted," Nyel said, and Atreus smiled at the way he held back relieved tears.

"What would you like to be called? Just between us, of course. I promise not to say a word to anyone, even *Papà*."

Atreus let out a long breath. "Thank god. I wasn't sure if you—"

"—If I what? Would tell? Seriously? Atty, do you even know me? Jeez. Give me some credit." She threw a paper flower at him.

"Sorry," he said for the millionth time that day, catching the delicate petals. "Uh. We call ourselves Mer. Just Mer is fine."

"Got it. Mer it is. But more importantly,"—she smiled at them both, and the warmth was enough to drive away all the residual fear in Atreus's chest—"it's Atty and Nyel. That's all that matters."

The tension in the air cleared like a gust of wind.

"Thank you," Atreus said.

"Alrighty, no more pouty faces. Stand up so I can hug you both."

They reluctantly stood, allowing Marina's short stature to pull them into an embrace, one arm slung around each of their necks. She held them for a few extra seconds, composing herself. When she released them, there were no tears, but she blinked rapidly.

"There. Now that's out of the way, Nyel, can you help me with these? And Atty, I'm pretty sure *Papà* has his hands full downstairs with the fry."

"You got it."

"And try not to fry yourself while you're down there."

Atreus rolled his eyes as he listened to Nyel and Marina laugh.

The moment Giovanni caught sight of him, his posture relaxed. "Oh, good. It appears you have made amends," he said. "Marina came home so upset last night."

"Um... yeah, we talked it out. It's going to be okay."

"I knew it would, but men get sentimental around my age. I worry for my children."

"Nothing gets past you," Atreus said with a shrug, ever impressed with Giovanni's silent perception.

Children?

"I might be old, but I'm sharper than this knife," he said, handing it to Atreus with a flourish.

Atreus scaled the fish with the curved blade. Giovanni had said children, though surely he meant Marina? Only Marina. Yet the way he said it gave Atreus hope he hadn't dared allow himself.

Stop it. I'm treading dangerous waters as it is.

He'd barely managed to keep this fragile relationship with the humans through what should have been a devastating accident. He had no right to hope for anything more.

"You don't deserve it."

Atreus didn't argue. He knew it was true.

They worked in comfortable silence, Giovanni humming along with whatever opera played on the ancient record player. Occasionally, it skipped and stuttered before resuming its serenade. Atreus didn't care for opera but couldn't deny there was an odd comfort in its monotonous chanting—or at least, that's what it sounded like to him.

The bell rang, and Atreus called out, not turning from his task, "Sorry, we are closed for today. Preparing for tonight."

When no receding footsteps sounded, he turned and was confronted with the most hated face in Baia Vita. Sensing the tension, Giovanni appeared from behind the shelves and stepped forward.

"We are closed today, *Signore* Vincenzo. Our food stall will be open tonight at the festival."

Alvise Vincenzo ignored him, eyes glancing around the old room, taking in all the worn and cracked surfaces. Atreus had to resist the hiss in his chest as Alvise wrinkled his nose at a particularly stained section of the floor.

"Trust me, I take no pleasure in being in this—shop," he finished, as though barely holding back a more offensive word.

"What can we do for you?" Giovanni inquired, ever polite.

"I'm here to deliver these."

Alvise thrust a rolled-up stack of papers at him, making another disgusted expression at the way Giovanni wiped his hands on his apron first.

Atreus glared at the intruder. This was the man hurting his home. Though he and Alvise had no personal history, the Vincenzo empire was buying all the shops, replacing them with soulless chain stores. They drove down prices to the point that local store owners couldn't compete. And worse yet, they owned the fishing organization ruling this part of the Pacific.

They own the ships that are slowly letting us starve.

All this raced through Atreus's mind as Giovanni read the paper. His expression remained steady as he scanned each line, but Atreus caught the subtle twitch of his mustache.

"I understand," Giovanni said, tucking the paper in the back of his pants. "I'll have the payments ready for you at the end of the week."

"Excellent," Alvise smiled. "I trust you know what actions I will take if you fail to meet those payments. I count every cent."

Giovanni nodded. "Your notice made that quite clear."

"What payments?" Atreus asked, frustrated he couldn't read the document himself. "What are you talking about? You own this store."

"But he no longer owns the land it sits on. That title belongs to me," Alvise said with so much mirth, Atreus barely resisted the urge to jump over the counter and hit him.

"How much are the payments?"

"We will make it work," Giovanni said, though there was no conviction in his words.

"I trust you will. I don't want to make another trip to this part of town. The smell alone is enough to make me gag," Alvise finished.

"If you don't like it, you can get the hell out," Atreus growled before he could stop himself.

Alvise stopped mid-turn, eyes lighting up at the resistance. "Is that what you think?"

"You don't want to know what I think," Atreus hissed through gritted teeth.

"Oh, but I do."

A heavy hand rested on his shoulder. "Atreus," Giovanni cautioned.

"Let the mongrel speak; I'm curious what a worthless stray has to say."

"What the hell did you just call me?" Atreus's voice dropped, low and sharp with warning.

"I called you exactly what you are: a stray with no home, no name, no pedigree." Alvise's smirk was venomous. "I know everything about everyone on this island, and you? You're a nobody."

Before the words had even fully landed, Atreus moved. He vaulted over the counter in one fluid motion, his face dangerously close to Alvise's before he even registered what he'd done. His breath was hot, chest heaving as fury coursed through his veins like the venom of a lionfish.

Alvise didn't flinch. Not an inch. He stood his ground, his expression one of cold, calculated disdain.

"Try it, filth," Alvise whispered, his lips curling into a cruel smile. His voice was a taunt, a dare edged with anticipation, like he was aching for Atreus to take the bait. "Give me a reason."

The room was suffocating, the air thick with the threat of violence. Atreus's fists clenched at his sides.

"You don't know who you're messing with," Atreus growled, his words more animal than man.

"And you don't know what I am capable of," Alvise shot back, his eyes glinting like the hooked tip of a lance.

"Atreus!" Giovanni yelled. He'd never raised his voice like that, and it deflated Atreus instantly.

Shit.

"A well-trained stray, so it seems." Alvise tipped his chin up to Atreus's ear, his breath oddly cold. "I own this island, mongrel. And one day, I'll rid it of filth like you."

With shaking restraint, Atreus watched the heir to the Vincenzo empire saunter out of the *pescheria* without a backward glance.

"Atreus," Giovanni said for the third time, but there was softness now.

"I know. I messed up." Atreus shook his head, his fists clenched. He wanted to hit something.

"You assume too much, Atreus. I was going to say how proud I am of you."

Atreus whipped around. "What?"

"It takes a strong man to resist his anger. At your age, I would have flattened him to the floor. You did well."

The juxtaposition of anger and the new swell of emotion left Atreus light-headed.

He's proud of me?

"I'm going to take a walk if that's okay. I'll be back to help."

"That's a good idea. Go wade in the sea. It always brings peace to my soul." His mustache twisted in a rare smile.

Minutes later, Atreus kicked off his shoes and dove into the surf. *Marvassa* embraced him like a mother might a babe, and he changed. He needed to move, to swim, to ease the anger in his chest.

A single phrase played on repeat in his head as he swam until his gills ached with strain.

"A stray with no home, no name, no pedigree—you are a nobody."

NYEL

NYEL'S BODY FELT like it was made of overcooked spaghetti as he sagged with relief. Relief that Marina didn't hate him. That his life on the island wasn't over. And more importantly—Atreus wouldn't be forced to leave.

I didn't ruin his life.

Nyel worked alongside Marina for most of the morning and afternoon. They folded paper flowers and strung them into a makeshift finish line for the kids the following day. He wasn't as crafty as Marina, and his hands were nowhere as steady as Atreus's, but he managed.

When Marina began to hum an incredibly out-of-tune melody, Nyel asked for the name of the song just to get her talking.

"Oh, just a lullaby Mamma used to sing to me."

Nyel paused at this. "That's the first time I've ever heard you talk about her," he probed, hoping he wasn't entering sensitive territory, but the look on Marina's face only confirmed his suspicions.

"Yeah. She was... Mamma had..." Marina chewed on the sentence for a moment, her hands pausing in their task. "Mamma had a big heart."

Nyel continued folding the flowers, listening carefully.

"Her heart was so big she tried to fit the entire world inside. And I think, to some extent, she succeeded. Her paintings changed the world. They touched so many people. She was truly an incredible artist."

There was definitely a 'but,' and Nyel waited for it, afraid that if he interrupted, Marina would stop. And when it came, her voice trembled.

"But with the whole world in her heart, sometimes I think she forgot about little old me."

"And... your dad?"

"Didn't know I existed until I was nine years old," Marina stated matter-of-factly. "Mamma was pregnant when she left Baia Vita. Off to the big city to chase her dreams, and *Papá* couldn't follow her. And I'm glad he didn't. The city would have crushed him."

"So your mom never told him?"

Marina shook her head. "*Papá* didn't know about me until she sent him a letter. She willed everything to me and made me promise to go to school. She died after that." Nyel reached across the table and squeezed Marina's hand. She sniffed loudly, blinking hard. "Jeez, I'm done with crying! *Caspita,* it feels like that's all I've been doing the past two days. My emotions are all over the place."

"That's partially my fault. I'm sorry."

"Don't be. You're here now. That's what matters. Now shut up and fold faster."

Nyel smiled and set to work. This time, he didn't interrupt her tone-deaf humming.

A few hours later, the wafting smell of fried foods met them through the open window. Nyel's stomach growled.

"You can go if you want. I'll finish up; there isn't much left," Marina said, threading another needle.

"Are you sure?" But he was already standing. He'd been looking forward to another festival all season.

"Yeah, go. I'll be at the stand with *Papà* later tonight."

He said goodbye and hurried downstairs, eager to catch up with Atreus so they could enjoy the festivities together. But when he descended the stairs, the *pescheria* was empty. Assuming Atreus had already gone outside, Nyel left the building and waved to Horace, who sat in his rocking chair with Niccolo purring on his lap, soaking in the ambiance.

And what an ambiance it was.

The square was even more decorated than last time. The city volunteers sensed the community's dismay over the harsh season and put in extra effort for tonight.

Strings of lights hung between the buildings, off balconies, and around signposts. Everything pulsed with energy. Potted marigolds lined the dancing square, their yellow blooms catching the light and sparkling as if dusted with glitter.

Every stall was lit up with its own arrangements of shapes and colors. That was where he found Atreus, stringing blue bulbs above the *pescheria's* stall of fried fish and squid on a stick.

Nyel snuck up behind him, a devious smile creeping up his cheeks. When Atreus's arms were raised to string more lights, Nyel pounced, pinching the sides of his waist. Atreus yelled, jumping and dropping the lights.

Nyel erupted in a fit of laughter, falling to his knees at Atreus's incredulous expression.

"It wasn't that funny."

"You sounded like Niccolo in the bath!" Nyel hollered.

"I'm warning you, Ny," Atreus said, shaking his head, "I don't get angry. I get even."

"I'd like to see you try." Nyel bumped his hip into Atreus's and helped him fasten the string of lights. "Are you done? Can we go?" he begged, practically vibrating with excitement.

"You didn't have to wait for me. You could have gone."

"Yeah, but it's more fun with you," Nyel said, then paused at the way Atreus averted his gaze. "What?"

"Nothing. Let's go, wanna play *Bocce* again? I never got my rematch."

"Oh, it's on." Nyel bristled at the challenge.

They played three games of *Bocce.* Nyel won the first one and Atreus the next two.

"Okay, okay, you win. There, you got me back," Nyel said in defeat, gathering the balls and placing them in the basket for the next player.

"That wasn't payback for earlier. Don't worry, that's still coming."

"I'm shaking in my boots," Nyel said with an eye roll.

Atreus bent low, and Nyel felt the warmth of his breath ghosting against his ear.

"You should be."

Nyel fought to keep his body still, resisting the urge to visibly shiver.

"L—let's go see what's going on over there," Nyel said, face growing hot as he touched the shell of his ear.

Music echoed from the square, and the crowd jumped into action as though they'd been waiting for the melody all night.

"Come on! Just like we practiced," Nyel shouted over the volume, grabbing Atreus by the wrist and dragging him to the circle of flowers and glittering lights. He did his best to shake off the heavy thumping in his chest.

The music was jovial, the local troupe pulling out all the stops. An instrument Nyel had never seen before—its center expanding and contracting like the bellows used to stoke a fire—took the lead, its lively, wheezing notes sending the dancing crowd into a frenzy.

They shuffled into the throng and faced one another. Atreus didn't resist; rather, he clasped their hands together and slid the other below Nyel's rib cage, right on the curve of his waist. Nyel sucked in a sharp breath.

"You ready?" Atreus asked.

Nyel only managed a nod as the heat of Atreus's touch melted into his skin.

When the next chorus of bouncing notes took off, so did they. Their practice paid off as they seamlessly blended with the bustle of dancers. They spun, swung, and jumped with the music, and Nyel's body came alive. His heart raced, the smell of sugar and sweat filled the air. The melody of the music threatened to abduct him to new heights.

The final trill of the violin vibrated through the air, signaling the end of the number. Nyel gave one last spin and, with legs wobbly from exertion, half-fell into Atreus's chest. He laughed, lungs heaving for breath as he looked into his dance partner's eyes.

"We killed it out there," he panted, relieved to feel Atreus also short of breath. His ribs expanded beneath Nyel's touch, heart hammering.

"You were great," Atreus complimented, his abalone eyes glittering more than usual.

The string of lights around them dimmed, the music took on a delicate slowness, and the mood shifted. The panting crowd slowed into an *adagio*. The gentle melody floated through the air, mixing with the whispering summer breeze.

Nyel expected Atreus to lead him away but was surprised with an extended hand instead.

"Can I have another?"

Nyel didn't have to think before accepting his hand, letting himself be pulled close until all that separated them was a breath. They swayed in a tender rhythm, hands entwined. Nyel was acutely aware of the heat radiating from Atreus's palm as he guided him by the waist. Nyel fought the urge to let his fingers slide from Atreus's shoulder to the bare skin of his neck. He'd once heard Marina call Atreus's freckles 'angel kisses.' Nyel preferred to think of them as tiny constellations, like a map of stars scattered across his skin. He wondered where they led.

When Nyel lifted his gaze, he found Atreus already looking at him. Thunder thudded against his ribs.

Steady, my heart.

Nyel drew in a deep breath, letting the wild scent of storm fill his lungs. A blend of the untamed sky and something uniquely...him.

Another thud in his chest.

Steady.

ATREUS

WHEN THE MUSIC was fast and loud, Atreus extended his arms wide, maneuvering Nyel in a series of turns and spins. Anything to keep from touching him more than necessary. But now, with the music doing something stupid to his head, Atreus couldn't resist pulling Nyel close. The hand on the *sireno's* waist squeezed fractionally tighter despite his resistance, and when Atreus heard Nyel's little intake of breath, his own breathing stopped entirely.

What am I doing?

He tried uselessly to shoo away the fluttering butterfly wings in his head. His body didn't feel like his own; it was leading him somewhere unknown, and it was all he could do to keep from running away. These feelings were unfamiliar. And if they weren't stampeding through his body, Atreus would have denied they existed at all.

It only grew worse when Nyel's head lifted, and the golden flecks in his honey-brown eyes shone like stars on the surface of a still sea. Something in Atreus stirred then; some creature that he didn't know lived beneath his skin. But it was there now, and it was wide awake.

"Th-this is nice," Nyel stuttered, his voice barely audible over the faint hum of music and laughter from the festival around them. His face was flushed, the glow of the hanging lanterns kissing his skin.

Atreus nodded, not trusting himself to speak. He focused on anything else—the rustling leaves overhead, the distant murmur of the waves lapping against the shore, even the warmth of Nyel's hand in his. But no matter where he tried to anchor his thoughts, his attention kept drifting back to the man in front of him. How close he was. How Atreus wanted him closer. Wanted to keep him there.

"I-I mean," Nyel glanced away, looking at their joined hands as if noticing them for the first time. "It's... really nice," he finished softly, his voice carrying an edge of vulnerability that made something in Atreus tighten.

Atreus's breath hitched. He wasn't sure if it was the music fading, the laughter in the distance, or Nyel's shy smile that made his chest feel like it was made of glass. But it was all too transparent. Too brittle.

Mercifully, the music stopped, the last note hovering in the air with painful softness. And just like that, the spell was broken, and Atreus realized how close they were. He jumped back too fast, and his heart sank at the hurt look on Nyel's face.

"W-wanna to get some food?" he offered just to escape the dancing.

"Sure, food sounds good."

They'd hardly made it ten steps when a friendly fist punched his arm.

"Hey, *Gatto*," Leo said, his voice charming as ever.

Atreus turned, expecting to see Leo's famous, swooning smile. Instead, he recoiled.

Leo was haggard beyond recognition. The bags under his eyes were heavy, and his skin had none of its sun-kissed glow. His cheeks were more hollow than Atreus had ever seen, and there was a tightness to his smile.

"Hey, Leo," Atreus said, unable to hide his concern. "How are you?" he asked, knowing he wouldn't get an honest answer.

"Same old, same old," Leo replied brightly. "You two looked good there," he said, nodding to the dancers.

"Yeah, we practiced," Atreus said, though what he really wanted to do was ask Leo what was going on. He'd been so wrapped up in work that they rarely saw each other anymore, exchanging only brief words as Atreus restocked his boat with chum before Leo was off again. How had Atreus not noticed his decline? Was the new boat not catching enough to make ends meet?

"Hey man, what's going on—" But he was cut off as Leo spoke over him.

"I have to say, though, you were getting some looks on that last one."

"Looks?" Nyel asked.

"More than a few."

"Why?"

"That last number is a pretty famous song around here. Very, uh, for couples."

At the word 'couple,' Atreus's attention snapped away from Leo's concerning appearance to what he was saying.

"Is that a problem?" Atreus asked, more curious than accusing.

Leo shrugged, clearly uncomfortable. "Maybe not in big cities on the mainland, but around here, it won't go over well."

Atreus still didn't understand what Leo was saying, though surprisingly, Nyel had.

"I get it. My mother would have called it 'Unbonded' behavior," he said with an eye roll.

There is that word again. What the hell is this Bond?

But before Atreus had a chance to ask, a smaller voice whined from beside Leo.

"Can we go see Marina now?"

Atreus hadn't even noticed the tuft of blond curls. One of Leo's younger brothers pushed at his side impatiently.

"She's right over there, Edgar; go ask."

"But—" Edgar hesitated, an embarrassed flush creeping to his cheeks.

"If you want to race with the big kids, you have to be a big kid and ask by yourself," Leo encouraged.

"Marina is really nice; you don't have to worry," Nyel reassured.

"I know that," Edgar said, but only looked more horrified.

"Here," Atreus said, reaching into his pocket and pulling out a strawberry fruit tart. He remembered the seller since Marina liked the last one so much and decided to buy her another. "Give her this. Tell her it's from—"

"Atty!" Nyel interrupted. "Tell her it's from Atty."

"You got this, big man. Deep breaths. Go get 'em," Leo said, giving Edgar a small shove. With a determined nod, Edgar walked to the *pescheria's* stall.

Atreus glared at Nyel. "You suck so much."

Nyel laughed, knowing how much the nickname irritated Atreus.

"Why does he need to talk to her anyway?" Atreus asked while simultaneously flicking Nyel in the ear.

"He wants to race with the big kids. He's only a few months away from turning twelve," Leo said, and even in his ragged state, Atreus didn't miss the fondness in his voice.

"He probably won't win. Since he'll be the youngest," Atreus pointed out.

"Edgar knows that. He just wants to race on the bigger course. He's been practicing all summer. And he's been putting off asking for over a week now. I think he has a little crush on the red-headed-wonder. He's at that age where girls are interesting but all the more terrifying."

"That's adorable," Nyel said, rubbing his sore ear.

A panicked voice called out, echoing from the direction of the beach.

"Atreus!" A weathered man streaked with oil and what looked like fresh burns on his hands jogged beside him. "Forgive me, Atreus, but I don't know what to do. My boat, *Fortuna*, I don't know what happened. I've tried everything."

The man looked ready to collapse from stress.

"It's okay. Let's not panic. Let me see what I can do," Atreus said, forcing confidence into his voice. He turned to them. "I'll meet you guys later, alright?"

And without hesitation, he raced to the docks, prepared to save this man's livelihood.

LEOFEL

LEO TRIED. He really did try not to let the sour taste in his mouth ruin his mood. Yet watching the inches between Atreus and Nyel slip away as the music slowed and the lights dimmed left him feeling sick.

He ran his fingers through his curls, trying to get them to stay in place like Atreus's. But as always, the stubborn strands behind his ears refused to submit and stuck out awkwardly.

"Leo, can we go?" Edgar whined.

"Just a minute," he said, patting his brother on the head without tearing his attention away from the pair.

Two men can't be doing things like that. Not in public, anyway. Who the hell do they think they are?

Bitterness coated Leo's tongue at their thoughtlessness. How many times had he suppressed himself, hidden who he was? How many times had he longed to express how he felt about other men? Yet the socially imposed rules he lived by had always held him back.

But tonight was different. Tonight, he was taking a break from the shit-show that was his life. He didn't have time to care what Baia Vita thought of him—because right now, he was already less than the dirt under their boots.

Alvise had made sure of that.

So why not indulge his bleeding heart? What more did he have to lose? His dignity. His pride. His sense of security was all gone. Stolen and placed firmly in Alvise's pocket. Was it so wrong of him to want a sliver of happiness to soothe the hurt?

When Atreus and Nyel finally finished, it was harder than usual for him to put on his charming act. He managed to keep the bite out of his voice only by biting his tongue. A seasoned fisherman Leo recognized limped to them with blisters on his palms, begging for assistance. Given the amount of oil on the man's shirt, Leo could guess that Atreus would be occupied for some time.

It was now or never.

"Hey, Nyel, can I borrow you for a bit?"

"Sure, what's up?"

"Somewhere private?" he coaxed, his heart rate increasing with each breath.

"Is it okay to leave your brother?" Nyel asked.

"He's fine; he'll find a friend in a minute."

Convinced, Nyel followed Leo to a private part of the square. The festivities were still in full view, though the music was diluted to a pleasant hum.

"Hey, Leofel, is everything okay?" Nyel asked, worry creasing his brow, clearly taking in Leo's haggard appearance.

"It's fine. Don't worry about it."

"It's just that... Leo, you don't look so good, and I'm worried there is—,"

"We're not talking about that," Leo snapped, cutting him off, then hating himself when Nyel flinched. "I mean, that's not what I want to talk to you about."

"Okay."

"What I want to say is, well, I've wanted to say it since we became friends, and I know now isn't the best time. I've got a lot going on, and you have a lot, and the season is almost over and..."

And I am blowing this!

Leo couldn't get himself to shut up, dancing around the words he wanted to say but never actually reaching them.

I really like you. I think you're kind and gentle and gorgeous.

The words echoed in his head, and as Leo stared into Nyel's concerned eyes, all at once...he knew he'd never say them.

Not now.

Not with a cord wrapped around his neck. If Leo dragged Nyel into this, pulling him closer to the master who held his chain, this beautiful boy might end up tangled in the links. The revelation hit him so powerfully that he hated himself for not realizing it sooner. Leo forced back the prickle in his eyes before plastering on a smile.

I'm an idiot to think this could ever happen.

"Sorry, I was rambling. I wanted to say that I'd like all of us to have a day together before the end of the season. On the beach." He chewed his lip and added, "You know, me, you, *Gatto*, and Marina if she wants."

Nyel's eyes narrowed, likely suspecting Leo wasn't telling the whole truth. "I'd love that, Leofel," he finally said, with a kindness that nearly broke Leo in two.

I want to kiss him. I want to know how it feels.

Leo knew Nyel's lips would be as soft and gentle as the words he spoke. He knew one kiss could soothe the ache inside him, take the biting edge off his pain, and make him feel—something. Something beyond the constant fear and dread and anger that plagued his every waking thought. The need for relief pressed on him so hard it nearly brought him to his knees. And he knew this beautiful person standing before him could give him that.

Just one kiss.

But Leo forced his spine to remain rigid, shoving down the overwhelming pull to close the distance between them. He cleared his throat roughly.

"It's a plan then. Better get back to Edgar."

And like a kicked dog, Leo hurriedly walked away from Nyel. The moment he turned the corner, he broke into a sprint. He ran from the festival. Ran from the light and the music. The smells and feelings of safety. All a farce. All lies.

Not for me.

He ran to the last place where his world was still his own.

He ran to the beach.

Leo needed to fall apart.

And he didn't want anyone to watch.

CHAPTER 23

NEPHI

Nephi munched on a fried squid on a stick as he slipped around the edges of the festival. It wasn't bad, though he hated how much oil humans used. He chewed it anyway. Food was food. Nobody blinked at the hooded figure that stalked the square like a wolf. It was too easy to steal tasty treats, enough that he wasn't even hungry. He just did it for the sake of doing it.

A stray dog sniffed for crumbs behind a stall.

"Here you go," Nephi crouched down, offering the remainder of his squid. The canine approached him with apprehension in its eyes. Nephi smiled.

"You're the only smart one here. You know there is something dangerous lurking around. Don't you?"

Hunger propelled the mutt close enough to snag the treat before running away.

Nephi wasn't even surprised anymore at the blatant trust the humans had for one another. Not a suspicious bone in their bodies. With the exception of the rich mainlanders who lived on the Estates in the valley, this human settlement was a 'never lock the front doors' kind of place. Even now, with families on the brink of losing everything, thievery was nonexistent.

Easy pickings.

So easy, in fact, it bordered on pathetic. His Pod could ascend from the beaches right now, enjoy the festivities, then slit everyone's throats as they slept. At least the villages they raided in the north were on guard—alert to the potential dangers that loomed in the sea. Nephi had to rely on the powers of a strong drink and Ludo's charm to inhibit their caution enough to take advantage. But that wouldn't be necessary here.

It wouldn't be necessary at all. His Pod, his *real* family, likely assumed he was dead. Succumbed to his wounds and his broken heart.

Nephi watched a group of human children, their sparklers making light strings as they ran. He wondered if it would even be worth it. What was to be gained from destroying a place like this?

"Less humans polluting the sea is always a victory."

He could practically hear his Pod leader, Tariq. And Nephi knew if he were still active, he'd agree. He'd listen and end those children without blinking an eye.

Because they're human. The same humans that took Ludo from me.

One of the children tripped, and as she turned her head, the light of her sparkler illuminated Nephi for a brief moment. He watched with glee as her face went from surprise to terror when she saw the unholy scars and white milky eye.

"Better run. Or I might catch you."

She didn't scream as her stubby legs carried her away from him as fast as she could go. Nephi chuckled to himself; with any luck, she'd have nightmares for weeks. Her sparkler sizzled on the ground, and Nephi snuffed it with his bare foot. But terrorizing the little human didn't bring him as much joy as he'd hoped.

"Damn it all," he cursed, turning from the square, intent on curling up in his rooftop shelter. Maybe his feline friend would offer him some company.

Voices on the edge of the square made him pause. He peeked around the corner to find his brother talking to none other than the source of his obsessions. Leofel looked terrible, and even from a distance, Nephi noticed how he favored his left foot. He was thinner, too, and Nephi didn't like the look on him. He wanted his human to be strong, healthy, and full of vigor.

That way, it will be all the more satisfying to make him crumble.

But asserting his dominance over the broken man hunched in the alley held zero appeal. Nephi wished he'd kept his fried squid and offered it to Leofel, who needed a few extra meals.

Nephi blinked, recoiling at his own train of thought.

What the fuck is wrong with me? Now I want to feed him?

This human was too dangerous. First, Nephi saved his life; now, he wanted to bring him back to health. He had to end this soon.

"I don't want to talk about that," Leo snapped at Nyel, loud enough for Nephi to hear.

"Okay," Nyel replied cautiously.

"What I want to say is, well, I've wanted to say it since we became friends and..."

Leo rambled. He stumbled, and a thin pink sheen came over his hollow cheeks.

Oh? Now, this is interesting. So, my brother has more than one admirer.

A twisting sensation curled in his intestines. He didn't like it.

He recognized the moment that Leo lost his momentum and began backpedaling hard.

"Sorry, I was rambling. I wanted to say that I'd like all of us to have a day together before the end of the season. On the beach."

Nephi smirked.

Coward.

If Leo wanted Nyel, why didn't he take him? Fear of rejection?

Nephi snorted, turning away from the pair.

Pathetic.

Yet, as he contemplated the interaction, Nephi was humbled by his own hypocrisy. If not laying claim to something you wanted was pathetic, then he'd been a coward for weeks. Watching Leo from afar, never daring to make a move. He growled, his frustration boiling.

Nephi wandered, too worked up to return for the night. His bare feet led him around alleys, courtyards with gurgling fountains, and finally, to the rocky edge of the town. He climbed down the familiar black stone until he found himself on the small hidden beach where his troubles began.

And as fate would have it, his biggest trouble was already there to meet him.

"The hell are you doing here?" he barked at Leo, not bothering to rein in his anger. He wanted to rage on this man. To break him. To punish him for being a sore in his side for weeks.

Leo flinched, wiping his face. "Do I need a permit?" he sassed, but his voice was too shaky for any real conviction.

"Maybe I came here for some privacy," Nephi spat.

"Maybe I did too," Leo glared through red-rimmed eyes.

Nephi huffed and took a seat beside Leo on the beach. He watched the waves lap on the darkening sand. Once, twice, three times, the ocean sucked in a breath and let it out again. But neither the serene sound nor the soft waters were enough to quell the anger in his chest.

"You look like shit," he bit out.

And Leo... laughed. Nephi was so taken aback by his sudden mirth that he crooked an eyebrow at him.

Maybe he's finally lost it.

When Leo finally calmed enough to speak, Nephi noticed some of the color return to his lips.

"That's exactly what you said to me last time. Is that how you greet people?"

"I wasn't greeting you," Nephi snapped. "I was stating a fact. You're even uglier than last time."

Leo chuckled again. "Takes one to know one."

At last, some of the biting rage in Nephi's chest... eased. He couldn't tamper down the smirk tugging on the side of his mouth.

"Clearly, whatever hell you're going through isn't enough to stop that tongue of yours."

This time, Leo's smile was sad. "Not yet, at least."

And Nephi hated those fucking words. He didn't want Leo to lose his sharp tongue. His unapologetic tactlessness. He didn't want their chance meetings on the beach to end.

"What are you doing here?" Leo asked, exhaling. "Shouldn't you be up there enjoying the party like all the other people our age?"

"First of all, I'm not your age, and I don't care for crowds," Nephi replied honestly.

"How old are you?"

Nephi drew his eyebrows together. Telling Leo his years wouldn't come back to bite him. Right? What did telling him hurt? Still, as

Nephi opened his mouth to give a piece of himself to this human, his words were laced with caution.

"I've seen twenty-six springs."

"Who the hell says it like that? Just say you're twenty-six years old."

"I do."

"Well, it's weird, and you're older than I expected. I'm twenty." He sighed. It was the kind of sigh that was more than tired. It was the first trace of defeat. Of giving up. "I feel a lot older, though."

"You have a lot on your plate."

"And how would you know that?"

"I have my sources," Nephi replied shortly.

Sure, Nyel had disclosed a few things about Leo, but most of Nephi's information came from his own eyes. It was the only information he trusted anyway.

He'd been watching this town long enough to understand its very essence. The way it breathed and moved. And thus, the way its people breathed and moved. Leo was a supporter of a large family. The weight of which was slowly killing him. The only missing piece in the puzzle was where Leo went on his secret rendezvous into the valley. The perimeter of the estate was heavily guarded, and Nephi couldn't glimpse more than the front door. Given the estate's wealth, it likely belonged to the benefactor of Leo's new boat.

Leo scoffed. "Good to know my friends are spewing my shit all over the island." He pressed the heels of his hands into his eyes. "But it's not like everyone doesn't already talk shit anyway."

"Nyel and Atreus have better things to do than to gossip. I watch. I listen."

"So you're ugly and a creep. Not a lot going for you, stranger."

"Nephi."

"What?"

Nephi took in a gulp of air, suddenly feeling hot. Exposed. He shrugged off his jacket, letting the night's chill ease his skin. "That's my name."

"I—" Leo fell silent, and Nephi shifted uncomfortably in the sand.

"What?" he snapped, narrowing his eyes. His damaged eye was virtually useless in the dark.

"It's... you've never sat on my right."

"What the fuck are you talking about?"

Leo pointed to his face. "I've only seen the other side. And you always keep your damn hood up. I didn't realize the other side wasn't..."

"Burned? Fucked to hell? Well, sorry to disappoint. I'm not completely fucked up. The blast missed the other side. Next time, I'll do a spin and make sure it gets all of me."

Nephi's heart tripped against his ribs as the vulnerable words fell out. Something about Leo made him lower his walls without even noticing. He was cautious for one minute, and the next, he opened himself in a way that would only lead to pain. Nephi clenched his jaw, hating how out of control he was.

It's not him. He's not my Ludo.

"I'm not disappointed," Leo said in a whisper.

He'd moved closer. Close enough for Nephi to see the dark circles under Leo's eyes. The dullness of his golden hair. Close enough to smell the citrus scent on Leo's skin. But his expression...Nephi couldn't make out.

"You were in a blast?" Leo asked in a whisper, and it tickled Nephi's skin.

"I—it..."

Nephi couldn't.

Not about that. Not *ever* about that.

Understanding yellow eyes met his, and Leo cocked his head to the side.

"Your eyes. I've never seen them up close."

Nephi's stomach twisted the same way it had in the alley when he'd seen Leo stumble through a confession. A confession to his younger brother. He knew why Leo was so enraptured. Because Nephi's good eye, brown with flecks of gold, was the same as his brothers. He turned away.

"They're nothing special."

Soft fingertips took his chin, turning his face back to Leo. The touch was as gentle as pattering raindrops.

"No. They're..." Leo searched for the word.

"Familiar?" Nephi supplied, anger flaring.

Leo squinted and cocked his head again, never taking his hand from Nephi's chin.

"Maybe. But it's the way you—" He moved closer, and Nephi held his breath, trapping the scent of bergamot in his lungs. "It's the way you look at things. Like you're studying them. It's... intense."

Fingertips brushed along Nephi's chin, gliding over his jawline before lifting to his cheek. They lingered on the unmarred side, gently caressing the skin. Unable to resist, Nephi leaned into the touch ever so slightly.

My Ludo.

When a second hand rose to stroke his mutilated skin, reality crashed into him like a cresting wave. Nephi jerked away, his breathing and heart rate returning.

"Don't."

Leo retracted his hands, the trance broken. "Sorry."

"You should go home, Leo. You look like you need rest."

Leo huffed awkwardly. "And we're back to how shitty I look."

"I preferred it when you looked healthy," Nephi stumbled.

He felt those yellow eyes watching him for a moment longer before Leo rose.

"Yeah, I should be home. I'll talk to you later. And"—he took a deep breath—"thanks for this."

"Don't thank me; I still think you look like a soggy pile of manure."

Leo laughed and, with a salute, marched away.

Nephi watched him disappear around the stone, wishing they could have talked a little longer.

Get ahold of yourself.

Even though he hated to admit it, Nephi no longer felt the wrathful flame that so often took control—the rage buried so deep inside him that he'd never be rid of it. Only one person in his life could quell those flames, and he was gone. Only one person....

Nephi stared at the spot where Leo had sat only a minute ago. A distinct imprint of his hand pressed into the sand. Nephi reached for it, tracing the outline of Leo's fingertips with the same gentleness Leo used to touch his face.

He wasn't disgusted by me.

Nephi hated the relief. The relief that Ludo wasn't disgusted by his burns. It settled like a fleeting balm over raw nerves, only to ignite into frustration a moment later.

"It's not him!" he shouted to the empty beach.

This was a human. A creature of earth and rock, poisoning the sea and taking without remorse. They had to be eradicated. All of them. These humans needed to remember who the sea belonged to. Nephi raised a fist, intent on smashing the outline of Leo's fingers. But as his hand descended, a memory flashed.

Delicate fair skin.

Tight platinum curls and silver eyes.

Ludo was never scared of him. Never feared him the way Nephi tried to make everyone fear him. Ludo saw through his facade.

"I see what you are not willing to see within yourself," Ludo said, the

ghost of his memory so sharp he could have been right there on the beach.

But that was a memory. And they had been on a different beach. A long time ago.

"You see what you want to see," Nephi had replied.

"I don't think so," Ludomir said, his blond eyelashes fluttering. *"You protect me every time we venture on shore."*

"Monsters make good bodyguards."

"So you keep insisting."

Then Ludo's voice changed. It became a tapestry of sound, echoing as if many voices spoke at once, yet remaining one. It wove into the hairline cracks of the mind, planting hooks before pulling the strings taught—a puppeteer taking control over those who listened, turning them into his marionettes.

A true siren of the sea.

It vibrated in Nephi's ear canal, echoing long after the words were spoken. It was the voice that lured humans to a watery grave. The voice that broke through willpower and bent the mind to Ludo's every whim—an unchallenged weapon.

"Monsters do not resist my call. They come, they consume, and they go. Come now, Nephi. I know what you desire. Now take it."

Ludo leaned in as he spoke, his presence as compelling as his words. His body, every movement and gesture, was as much a tool as his voice—a silent, magnetic call that demanded attention. This was Ludo's greatest weapon. He was a seductionist of the highest order, a master of weaving desire and vulnerability into an inescapable net. With nothing more than a look or the hum of a melody, he could unravel secrets and coax truths to the surface, no matter how deeply they lay buried.

But this wasn't for himself. It was for the Pod. Everything he did, every calculated act of allure, was for their survival, their goals. It wasn't what Ludo wanted. And Nephi knew that. He saw it in the flicker of hesitation behind Ludo's polished performance, in the subtle cracks that only someone who truly knew him would notice.

Nephi's neck stiffened, his head throbbing with the ache of staying away. He wouldn't succumb to Ludo's song.

"I told you not to use that on me."

Ludo's voice regained its normalcy. *"Yet you see my point? Most other Mer would have pounced on me. Used me to fulfill their heart's desire. Why do you hold back?"*

"Because that's not you."

The edge of Ludo's eye crinkled in that all-knowing look he always carried. *"I've met many monsters. And monsters don't take my desires into account."*

Yet Nephi had. He'd watched Ludo for years. He could tell when Ludo genuinely wanted something versus when he was playing the role of seductionist. But Nephi would never take from this male, as others had. If Nephi were going to have him, it would only be because Ludo truly wanted it.

Wanted *him*.

That day never came. Ludo had seen too many violent nights. Felt too many brutal hands to ever want the touch of another. Not in that way. Nephi understood that and still remained by his side. A lover in a way that transcended the need for physical expression. Ludo was the sun. He was daylight and warmth. He was every missing piece in Nephi's fractured soul. He was the day, and Nephi the night. With Ludo by his side, he wasn't just the dark—he was whole.

Now, Nephi was fragmented. Warped and damn right unrecognizable. Even Ludo had never seen him with the scars. Never seen his deformities rise to the surface.

Leo had.

And he wasn't scared of me.

But that wasn't enough to make up for the sins of mankind, and Nephi knew it. This human was dangerous. Maybe Leo was dangerous because he lacked fear. Because he didn't shrink away from the danger Nephi posed.

I'll show him what kind of monster I am.

He crushed the sand beneath his palm, erasing all signs that Leo was ever there. Nephi was a diabolical fiend, born of the ocean and ready to kill anything that walked upon the land. Humans and Mer were enemies, plain and simple. And Nephi never let his enemies live once they were at his mercy.

He stood resolute in his conviction.

Before the season was over, before he returned to the open sea and reunited with his Pod, Leo would die. Nephi would end this unsanctioned obsession and accept what he was at his core.

I'm sorry, my Ludo, but you were wrong.

He was a monster.

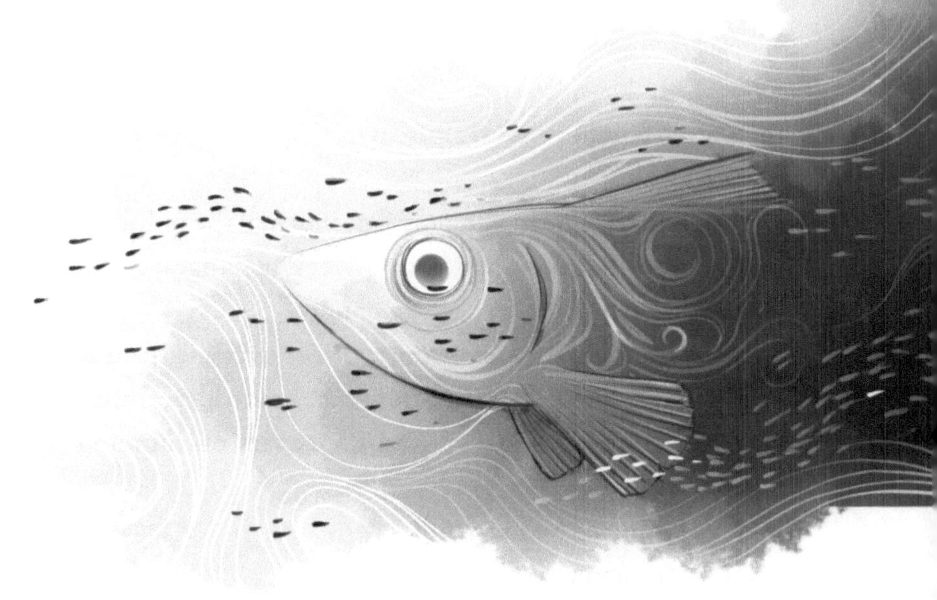

CHAPTER 24

ATREUS

Atreus did his best to stifle a yawn.

"Me too," Nyel agreed, his eyes likewise struggling to stay open.

Atreus hardly slept—and not for the reasons he wished. Instead of enjoying the night away like everyone else on the island, Atreus spent his night helping the poor fisherman whose boat engine had caught fire. He'd managed to get it running again for now, though the vessel wouldn't be truly seaworthy without expensive replacement parts.

It felt like his head had only just touched the pillow when Marina barged into his room like a shipwreck in progress—loud, chaotic, and with zero regard for his exhaustion.

Atreus groaned, pulling the blanket over his head as if it could shield him from her. Marina, however, made it clear that sleeping in wasn't an option as she yanked the covers off him and broke into song.

The Bayallon's a comin',
The Bayallon's a comin',
Oh, won't you help me, please?
Ooooooh yeah—

"Get out!" Atreus yelled, his pillow hitting the door as she ducked behind it.

He listened to her yowling fade down the hall, likely to give Nyel the same rude awakening. But it did the trick; he was up.

It was the morning of the Bayallon, and there was work to be done. Well. In Marina's mind, there was work to be done. In reality, all that was left to do was for the volunteers to take their posts and for Marina to shout the rules to the crowd one more time. Yet that didn't stop her from waking Atreus and Nyel at the first sign of light. They dragged their feet through the courses for the hundredth time, reassuring Marina that everything was perfect. Of course, she triple-checked everything anyway. By the time the town had gathered and the races were underway, Atreus could hardly keep his eyes open.

"*Ai posti, pronti, VIA!*" Marina shouted through a megaphone, and three dozen young racers took off down the lane. It was a short sprint, but watching their uncoordinated waddles was adorable. Adorable enough to tug at the edges of Atreus's mouth despite his tiredness.

"Humans learn to walk so young," Nyel observed through another eye-watering yawn.

"Marina told me they can walk as young as eight months."

"You're kidding."

As they talked, a few of the kids tripped, bouncing on the ground before carrying on.

"I never said they learned to walk well," Atreus amended.

They watched the little ones run, swim (which was more like a chest-deep walk through a makeshift pool), and clamber into a wagon. He had to admit the wagon pull was a huge hit. The parents were fiercely competitive, and watching the kids cling for dear life as they raced to the finish line was the funniest thing he'd seen in ages. The winner broke through the string of paper flowers, and the crowd cheered. Marina hugged the winners and gave them their basket of goodies before restarting the sequence for the middle group of kids.

These kids would swim a short loop in the bay, marked with a floating buoy. A few adults were already on the other end in rowboats as lifeguards.

"Too bad we can't be lifeguards. We'd be better at it," Nyel mused, making Atreus laugh.

"Yeah, that would go over well. It'd be kinda weird if a floundering kid suddenly started to levitate through the water."

Nyel laughed. "No, but seriously. We could help. And in more than just lifeguarding at the Bayallon."

"There you go with your dangerous ideas again," Atreus said dismissively. They'd had this conversation so many times he didn't have the energy to be anxious over it anymore.

"You know I'm right," Nyel singsonged but let the matter rest.

When the lead racers rounded the 'mermaid' fountain, they peddled their bikes like mad to the finish. A young girl with raven-black hair won, much to the delight of her equally dark-haired family.

"Do you ever notice that some humans look different?" Nyel mused.

"They all look different."

"No, some look *really* different. Like that family," he said, nodding to the black-haired group. On closer inspection, their skin was a different shade, and their eyes had a delicate curve at the ends.

"Sure, I guess." Atreus finally said.

"Is it like the different species of Mer?"

"Maybe. But it doesn't seem to bother them as much." He pointed to the only curly-haired figure on the stage. The man was brown-haired and shorter than the others, and clearly the girl's father by the way he spun her around with pride.

"Mixing must not be a problem," Atreus concluded.

"Yeah," Nyel said, his voice dipping at the end. "I wish we were more like that." He stared at the family for a moment before shaking himself. "But change can only happen if we make it happen! Right?" Nyel asked with exaggerated conviction.

"Sure," Atreus replied with a bemused grin.

Nyel punched his arm.

"Hey, what the—!?"

"C'mon, more enthusiasm!"

"I don't know what you want from me!" Atreus laughed. "And you hit like a guppy."

Nyel gasped in mock offense. "Oh, *that's* how you want to play it? You don't know who you're messing with."

"Try it." Atreus smirked, raising his arms in challenge.

The *sireno* lunged, aiming to grab Atreus by the neck and pin him. "Gotcha! Who's the guppy now—hey!"

With a swift spin, Atreus flipped their momentum and locked Nyel into a headlock.

"Okay, okay! I give! *I give!*" Nyel squirmed, trying to wriggle free.

"Say you're a guppy," Atreus teased.

Nyel struggled harder, but keeping him in place was laughably easy.

"Ugh, fine! I'm a guppy."

"Now say I'm a—"

"BOYS!"

Both of them flinched. Atreus released Nyel instantly, hands snapping over his ears.

"Quit messing around!" Marina's voice thundered through the loudspeaker.

"We can hear you fine!" Atreus yelled, rubbing his ears.

"Get to your stations!"

"Aye, aye, captain!" Nyel saluted.

As they trekked up the hill, a man shouted to Atreus. It was the same man whose engine burned out the night before.

"*Signore*, please, from my family as thanks." He offered Atreus a parcel of sweet rolls. "My wife made, very delicious. *Grazie Signore, grazie.*"

Before Atreus could insist it wasn't a big deal, the man was gone. Nyel watched him with smug, raised brows.

"What?"

"And you say the people of this town don't adore you."

Atreus shook his head but couldn't hide his grin. "Whatever. Here, I don't like sweets."

By the time they made it to the top of the hill, Nyel had finished them all. He ate the entire damn bag.

"I've never seen anyone put away sweets like you do," Atreus said, retrieving the bucket from the well.

Nyel licked his fingers clean. "They were delicious. I bet they had sugar in them."

Atreus laughed. "You know what, I bet they did."

They diligently filled the paper cups, lining them up on the table. The final race for the older kids was brutal, and heat exhaustion posed a real risk. The racers would be parched by the time they made it up the hill.

"How do we know when it's started?" Nyel asked.

A distant *'VIA!'* echoed from below them in town as Marina signaled for the kids to start.

"Like that," Atreus said, sitting in the grass. "And now we wait."

The day was perfect, if not a bit hot.

"Marina's done a really good job with this," Nyel said, leaning on his hands in the cool grass.

"Don't let her hear you say that. It'll go right to her head."

"Oh, come on, everyone deserves a little praise."

"She might sing in celebration."

"On the other hand, maybe her confidence is already pretty high."

Both of them laughed. Atreus couldn't get enough of the trilly way Nyel's voice rose in pitch.

"You sound like a bird when you laugh," Atreus said without thinking. Heat rose to his face as the internal thought fell from his mouth.

Nyel cocked a brow at him. "Oh? Like the gulls by the docks?"

"No." Atreus snorted. "I mean like the tree birds. The small ones with the— you know what, never mind."

"No, no, I want to hear it! Which bird?"

"Nope. You lost your chance."

As Nyel made a puppy-dog face, someone crested the hill, jogging towards them.

"Hey, Nyel, *Gatto!* Mind if I join?"

Atreus waved to greet Leo, who appeared to be in better spirits this morning.

"Hey Leofel! Sure, come have a seat," Nyel said, patting the grass on his other side.

Leo sat with a huff. "They've just started the swimming portion. Those kids will be zombies by the time this is over."

"Maybe they'll give their parents some peace," Atreus speculated.

Leo waved his hand. "No way. Give them a couple of hours, and they'll be causing mayhem all over again."

"Did Marina let your brother join the older group?" Nyel asked.

"Yep! He isn't doing half bad, either. Last I checked, he was somewhere in the middle of the pack. But Edgar isn't the strongest swimmer, so it won't surprise me if he's bringing up the rear by the time they get up here."

"It's still admirable of him to try."

"Yep, I'm proud of him. Has more guts than I did at his age."

"I'm sure that's not true," Nyel said.

"It isn't," Atreus confirmed, "I've known him almost a decade. And back then, *he* was the teen causing trouble in town."

Leo raised both hands in surrender. "Guilty. But you weren't innocent either, *Gatto*."

"Only because I was constantly keeping you out of trouble. Someone had to make sure you didn't do anything *too* stupid."

"Wouldn't follow me onto the boats, though."

At this, Atreus shook his head. "Got me there."

"Once a *Gatto*, always a *Gatto*," Leo said, reaching to smack Atreus's shoulder.

Atreus was relieved to see Leo acting like his old self again, but the signs of strain were still obvious. He wasn't okay, and Atreus didn't know how to fix it. But if Leo was content to pretend nothing was wrong, if that's what he needed, Atreus supposed he could pretend too.

"What about you, Nyel? Raise hell where you're from?"

Nyel shrugged. "Not really. My parents kept me pretty busy growing up, and I wasn't big on friends."

"Aw, well, screw them. You've got friends now," he said, tugging

Nyel into a one-armed hug. Atreus stiffened as Nyel's entire left side was pulled flush with Leo's chest. Nyel was shorter, his hair probably tickling Leo's chin. And there was no reason for Leo to grip him so tight—

"Right, *Gatto*?"

"Huh?"

"Weren't you listening? I said Nyel has friends now, right?"

"Oh yeah. Totally. We're friends." But the word tasted funny as it left his mouth.

"See? You've got nothing to worry about," Leo said, finally releasing Nyel.

The sound of crunching gravel and squeaking hinges approached from below.

"Here they come," Leo said, rising to his feet.

Atreus stood as well, and in unison, both extended a hand to Nyel.

Without conscious thought, Atreus narrowed his eyes at Leo, catching the latter off guard. He was immensely satisfied to see Leo's hand hesitate for a fraction of a second, and it looked as though he'd pull away.

But Nyel, oblivious to the silent standoff, reached for both their hands and let them pull him upright. Dusting off his pants, he nodded. "Alright, let's go."

Atreus avoided eye contact after that, but the tension between him and Leo remained—unresolved and catching them both by surprise.

What was that just now? Why am I so uptight?

Atreus had no answer. All he knew was that, at this moment, Leo's presence was annoying the living daylights out of him.

The leaders of the race shot past, not slowing for a second, skipping the water cups they offered. But the next group, with red faces and gasping mouths, stopped their bikes for a drink. Leo helped them refill the cups after the next batch, and pretty soon, only the stragglers at the end remained.

"They've probably already finished at the bottom," Nyel said, craning his neck to see past the curve of buildings blocking their view.

"Marina will wait for everyone before announcing the winner," Atreus said, using his hand to block the sun, searching for the last few racers. A moment later, a single curly blond head slowly made its way up the hill.

"Way to go, Edgar!" Leo shouted, cupping his hands over his mouth. "Whooo! You got this!"

Leo encouraged his brother and jogged alongside the bike, lifting a cup of water to the boy's lips without slowing his pace. When Edgar started the downhill trek, Leo hollered after him.

"See you at the bottom, big man!"

"He did so great," Nyel praised.

"He's come a long way. Proud of that kid," Leo said, fondness making his eyes sparkle. "This wasn't an easy summer for him."

"Let's congratulate him at the bottom." Atreus cleaned up the paper cups and tied them in a bag he'd retrieve later.

As they rounded the corner, they mused about the race and what next year might look like. From this angle, Atreus could see the entire path down to the bay. The hill was steep and cleared of debris for the cyclists.

"There he is!" Nyel shouted as a distant figure barreled down the slope, approaching the final corner.

"Way to go, Edgar—" Leo's cheer died in the air as they watched everything go wrong. The front tire of Edgar's bike shook violently, the wheel coming loose from its spokes. The handlebars jerked from his grasp, and the bike careened into the railing overlooking the sea. For a second, that was it: a ruined bike, some bumps and bruises.

It was as if the world had slowed to a grinding halt. The back of the bike kicked up like a horse, the bars jammed into the railing, and the momentum sent the bike flying.

And Edgar's body flew with it.

He barely had enough time to let out a feeble yelp before disappearing over the edge, falling... falling... falling...

"EDGAR!!!" Leo yelled, diving to the rail, Nyel and Atreus hot on his heels. They searched the cliff yet saw nothing but sharp black rocks jutting from the surface like the cracked teeth of the ocean's maw. Water smashed against stone as the tide surged, bringing wild, white-capped waves that crashed against the cliff face.

Leo's foot was on the railing in less than a second before Nyel wrapped both arms around his waist, hauling him back.

"Leofel, no! The rocks! You can't!"

But Leo wasn't listening as he struggled against Nyel's hold.

"Edgar!" he shouted again, his voice cracking.

The seconds dragged like decades. Leo wouldn't survive the fall. Likely, Edgar hadn't either. And then, with cruel simplicity, only three things existed. Atreus, the sea, and a choice.

He looked to Nyel, who'd half-wrestled Leo to the ground.

Their eyes connected, holding onto one another, sharing a silent conversation that surpassed the need for words. Nyel's gold-speckled eyes widened as Atreus moved.

"Atre—!"

But Atreus didn't hear the rest as wind rushed at him from all sides.

And he fell.

NYEL

"Leofel, stop!" Nyel shouted as Leo half-dragged him to the rails. "The beach! We have to go to the beach."

Leo jerked from his grasp and flew down the lane without a word. Nyel followed but couldn't keep up with Leofel's long sprints. The square flew past in a blur, and in seconds, Nyel's feet met the sand. He wasn't alone. Dozens of the townsfolk witnessed the crash from the base of the hill, and already men ran to the docks, intent on firing up their boats for a rescue mission. But there was no point. The rocks were too cluttered, the waves too unpredictable. The boats couldn't do more than hover around the edges as helpless spectators.

Nyel nearly followed Leo into the surf, his feet halting inches from the water's edge.

"Edgar!" Leo shouted, already waist-deep.

Several men who'd already waded into the water grabbed his shoulders, stopping his progress.

"The waves will tear you to shreds, *ragazzo*! You cannot."

"Let me go!" Leo shouted, hysteria catching in his throat.

Nyel gripped his hair, pulling it with both hands, standing helplessly on the beach.

"Nyel!" Giovanni rushed to him. "Was it Atreus? Did I see Atreus jump into the waves?" he panted.

Nyel couldn't recall the tears pooling in his eyes as he nodded. "Yes, he jumped, I couldn't stop him."

"Dio lo protegga," Giovanni whispered beneath his tousled mustache.

In a flash of red hair, Marina had her arms wrapped around his neck, and Nyel returned her embrace without question.

"Nyel, I'm so sorry, I—"

She pulled back enough for him to see the devastated look on her face. Out of all the people shouting around them, only they understood what truly happened. What Atreus just sacrificed. Only they understood that they might never see Atreus on this island again.

"I couldn't stop him," Nyel broke.

Marina pulled him to her again, whispering so only he could hear. "Can Mer survive a fall like that? Will he be okay?"

Atreus had a much better chance than a human. Better than Edgar. Though the sharp rocks would cut through scale just as easily as skin with enough force.

"I don't know," Nyel said, shaking as he hugged Marina, seeking her comfort.

"Merda," Marina hissed, pulling him even tighter.

The seconds crawled with agonizing slowness, each a ponderous weight dragging through the suffocating summer heat.

Leo had finally stopped trying to muscle past the other men and now knelt in the surf, arms hanging limp at his sides in defeat. He stared in the direction of the rocks with a hazed expression. Nyel wanted to comfort him, to place a hand on his shoulder and remind him he wasn't alone. But Nyel couldn't walk into the surf. With the eyes of the entire village watching the scene unfold, he was trapped.

Should I go after him? Should I sneak away?

Nyel could easily slip away in the chaos. Then what would he do? Even as a Mer, he'd grown up with cautionary tales and threats to stay away from the rocky shores. Even as a Mer, they posed a danger to him.

And what if I find them? What if...

Nyel hugged his middle, nauseated. If he found them... if he found Atreus's lifeless body...

He was going to be sick.

"Over there!"

A voice shouted, and soon, a dozen hands pointed toward the sandbank. A figure rose from the surface, waves breaking over his back and knocking him forward. He emerged from the direction of the sun, its blinding rays forcing Nyel to blink rapidly as the onlookers shielded their eyes. But even through the glare, Nyel knew who it was.

His relief was short-lived. In a few breaths, Atreus would be near enough for everyone to see.

"Oh, *Grazie Dio!*" Leofel's mother, Emelia, broke through the crowd, weeping as she waded through the water at a run. Nyel expected Thomasso to be at her heels, but he was nowhere in sight. "Thank god, thank god I prayed I—"

She halted as Atreus came into view.

Nyel was frozen. The sand beneath his feet may as well have been wet cement. He couldn't move.

He couldn't breathe.

Atreus sloshed through the water, navy, and violet scales glittering in the sunlight. The light hit him so perfectly that his magenta fins cast specks of color on the white beach. A small, still boy lay in his arms, looking more like a doll. Edgar's arm dangled, and his head flopped against Atreus's chest, blond hair obscuring his face.

Nobody moved.

The island held its breath.

Leo was the first person to come alive, dashing to him.

"He's alive! He needs a doctor!" Atreus shouted, his voice shaken and chest heaving as he limped through the water.

Leo halted at the sound of his friend's voice coming from the mouth of a foreign creature. He froze in confusion, but it was enough time for Atreus to transfer Edgar into Leo's arms and step back quickly. The Mer backpedaled until he was waist-deep in the surf, arms raised in surrender.

Emelia darted to Leo, pushing Edgar's curls from his face. "Oh, *mio bambino*," she cried. Then went still as she took in her son's rescuer.

All eyes were glued on Atreus. Everyone asking themselves the same question.

Friend or foe?

Atreus stood there, bleeding into the setting sun. Vulnerable. Alone. A creature carved from the sorrow of the sea.

Nyel's heart ached so much that tears pooled in his eyes, scalding his cheeks as they fell. He couldn't stand it. Couldn't stand to watch Atreus bear the crushing weight of their scrutiny. Not alone. Not anymore.

He shoved his way free of the crowd, stumbling in the sand before diving headfirst into an oncoming wave. Marvassa embraced him, and it felt like coming home. His skin rippled, his hair vanished, and a tail manifested behind him.

Nyel was Mer, and he was done hiding it. He burst from the waves, fins flared, and tail raised.

"You shouldn't have Ny," Atreus whispered to him as he approached.

"I told you before," Nyel said, reaching a webbed hand and intertwining their fingers. "You aren't alone anymore."

ATREUS

He came so close.

So close to not doing it.

Almost let his fear stop him from jumping.

From saving Edgar's life.

All that fear melted away as he lost himself in gold-flecked eyes.

Instinct and adrenaline took over his body as he crashed into unforgiving waters. Each wave struck him as if the ocean was determined to beat him into submission. It hurled him toward the jagged rocks, slamming him against their unyielding mass, sending pain radiating through his ribs and arm. The impact left him gasping, the saltwater stinging every scrape and cut. Somehow, despite the searing pain, Atreus managed to navigate the brutal tide as it tossed him like a rag doll.

By some miracle, Edgar managed to land in the only spot clear of rocks. The water cushioned his fall, and the helpless boy clung to the cliffside just long enough to take one more breath before succumbing to the waves. Atreus found him sinking in the surf, a trail of bubbles leaving his mouth.

Grabbing the boy and rocketing them to the surface took every ounce of strength he had. The sharp ache in his ribs and the numbness creeping into his arm made each stroke agony. Fighting through the maze of rocks with Edgar's deadweight sapped what little remained of his energy. Pure adrenaline allowed him to march through the shallow water, carrying Edgar in his arms. His legs shook beneath him, protesting the weight. If not for the threat of attack from the people he loved, Atreus would have collapsed in the sand.

"He's alive! He needs a doctor," Atreus hastily said, stopping Leo's charge. He was sure Leo would have attacked him if he hadn't spoken. Not that a single human posed any threat, weaponless as he was. Once Edgar was safely in his brother's arms and under his mother's care, all fell silent. Atreus could have sworn that even the ocean waves quieted, waiting for the verdict. Waiting for the people of Baia Vita to pass judgment.

Waiting... for his life to fall apart.

Dark wavy hair cut through the crowd with a cry, crossing the beach and disappearing beneath the waves. Atreus barely had time to process the leap before Nyel surfaced beside him, jade scales catching the light in a way that made his breath hitch.

Their eyes met, and the world narrowed to just the two of them. For a fleeting moment, a golden thread shimmered in the air around Nyel. Tears welled in Atreus's eyes at the sight, the feeling blooming deep in his soul. He wanted Nyel to see it too—to share it with him. But like last time, Atreus was left with the quiet ache of knowing he alone could see its glow.

The delicate thread was nearly invisible in its faintness... but it was there—just like on the night of the fireworks. It felt alive, trying to take hold between them. Terribly fragile, yet insistent, daring to exist in the space they shared. In a place it didn't belong. But without a tether, it hung there, suspended. And Atreus knew it wouldn't last.

Just like last time, it would break... and die.

But for now, it remained, and he would delight in its presence— in Nyel's warmth. The sea surged around them, the high tide roaring as waves struck the shore with force. Yet to Atreus, everything felt hushed, falling into quiet. As mighty waves crested, they bent like bowed heads, as if the ocean itself knelt before the golden light—knelt before *them*.

Whale song echoed far in the distance; whether from the open sea or the depths of his own mind, Atreus didn't know. Didn't care. Because Nyel... was here.

Nyel's jade scales shimmered, shifting to azure before deepening into black—a cascade of colors, shifting and swelling like an oncoming storm. Slowly, Atreus reached out, his fingertips brushing against Nyel's arm, grounding himself in the impossible beauty of it all—the connection, the golden light only he could see, the sense that this was something he would never fully understand.

"You're here," Atreus whispered, his voice unsteady.

"I'm here," Nyel replied.

"You shouldn't have, Ny."

A webbed hand locked with his.

"I told you before. You aren't alone anymore."

Words failed him as he squeezed Nyel's hand. The stunned silence of the crowd pressed in on them like the deepest part of the ocean, the pressure building until Atreus feared he might cave in on himself.

"I—I'm..."

"You can't do this."

The voice spat and hissed, slithering into his mind like a venomous thing. It curled around his doubts, twisting them into truths, feeding on his insecurities like a leech.

*"You're nothing.
You've always been nothing."*

The words dripped with disdain, each syllable sharpened to cut deeper and deeper.

"You think you matter?
That you have any control?"

It laughed, a low, mocking rasp.

"You're a freak. A monster.
They hate you. Hate you.
HATE YOU!"

But then Nyel squeezed him, and the golden light flickered—like the beating heart of a flame—banishing the voice, burning it away like mist under the morning sun.

I'm not alone.

He tried again, this time steady enough to break through the lingering shadows.

"My name is Atreus. I work at the Sleeping Whale *pescheria*. I live in the abandoned lighthouse across the bay. Baia Vita has been my home for most of my life and... I'm a Mer."

His heart wanted to escape his chest and take refuge in the water without him.

"My name is Nyel. I work at the Sleeping Whale *pescheria*. I was born in these waters, and though I've only lived here for a season, Baia Vita feels like home now. I am a *sireno*—a Mer, native to your bay."

The crowd shifted at the sound of their voices. At the *familiar* voices coming out of the mouths of creatures that belonged in fables. When Nyel finished, they stirred. They inched closer, like a hive ready to attack an intruder. Ready to defend its home from something that didn't belong. Atreus took a step backward, ready to run.

"It's them!"

Marina's stout frame burst free of the crowd, splashing into the shallows to stand between them and the onlookers. She held out her arms as though to defend from oncoming projectiles.

"It's still them! The same people you've been working alongside on the docks."

Whispers sounded, but the crowd continued to edge closer. Atreus spotted several of the men reaching for tools at their belts.

Marina's red hair was frazzled into wild knots, which made her appear larger as she shielded them. "Listen to me! I knew about them. I chose to keep their secret because I knew they wouldn't hurt anyone."

"That wasn't your choice to make!" someone called from the crowd.

Others joined in agreement.

"You should have told us!"

"What do they eat!?"

"Are they the ones taking our fish?"

"How can we trust anything with claws like that?"

The voices overlapped with one another, tumbling into an angry crescendo. Marina's arms dropped a few inches, a defeated expression coming over her face. But just as quickly, she raised them again. "I won't let you hurt them!"

"Get out of the way!"

"Stand aside, girl, let us decide."

They were too close now. Atreus worried Marina would soon be yanked from her position. He shifted his feet, ready to push Nyel into the waves.

"SILENCE!!!"

A lion's roar tore through the crowds' squawking, and all fell silent. The assembly parted for the larger-than-life figure as Giovanni made his way forward.

Atreus wanted to throw up. Wanted to melt and become one with the salt and sea.

I've failed him. After all he's done for me... he knows I've been lying to him for years. He hates me. He hates me. He hates me.

The golden light sputtered and dimmed, fading like a dying ember struggling to hold on. Nyel let out an almost imperceptible whimper, and Atreus couldn't tell if he felt the same hollow ache in his chest—or if Atreus was merely projecting his own. But then he realized his hand was clenched around the *sireno's* fingers hard enough to hurt.

He loosened his grip but couldn't stop his entire body from shaking. With fear. With anxiety. With the awful certainty that he was about to be abandoned. For the second time.

Giovanni approached his daughter, but she didn't lower her hands. Marina jutted out her chin in defiance as tears spilled onto her cheeks.

"I won't move, *Papá*." Her words were determined, but the way she said them sounded like a plea.

"I know *bambina mia*." He stroked a wayward strand of hair, and Marina's lip trembled. "But as your father, I ask that you step aside."

Atreus's heart nearly broke in two, watching Marina come undone before a father she loved.

Forced to choose.

"It's okay, Rina," Atreus said loud enough for her to hear.

At the sound of the nickname she'd always wanted, Marina let out a sob. She lowered her arms dutifully and stepped aside.

Atreus stepped fully in front of Nyel as Giovanni approached. The weight of Giovanni's gaze bore down on him. Atreus couldn't bring himself to meet it, couldn't face the disappointment etched in his eyes. Instead, he bowed his head, bracing for whatever punishment Giovanni saw fit to deliver.

He deserved it.

For the lies.

For the deceit.

For almost a decade's worth of memories, laughs, and lessons... all in the company of a creature Giovanni never knew.

He stopped only inches from Atreus, his feet hidden in the surf.

"Lift your head," he commanded, and as though Giovanni had physically forced his muscles to work, Atreus obeyed. The wind blew through his hair. He'd partially dried since surfacing, and *Marvassa* slowly transformed him. What Giovanni saw now was half the human he knew as Atreus— and half a stranger calling itself a Mer.

"Do you understand where you are?" he asked.

"Yes, *Signore*."

"Do you know who I am?"

"Y-yes *Signore*."

"Then who are you?"

Atreus choked, his throat impossibly dry.

"I—I'm...."

He dropped his gaze but instantly lifted it again when Giovanni commanded him.

"Who are you?" Giovanni asked again, his voice terrifyingly calm.

"I'm— me."

Giovanni nodded. "Are you the Atreus I know?"

Was he? Was he truly the person he'd painted himself to be? The person he'd shaped himself to become in order to live among these people? To become one of them? To love them like they were his own flesh and blood?

Is that really me?

"Atreus." Giovanni's voice rumbled so low in his chest it shook the air. "Beneath the skin. Beneath the scales. Are you the Atreus I've grown to know?"

Atreus had hidden himself, lied to bury the truth of what he was. But his love for Baia Vita—for these people, for Giovanni, Horace, Marina, and even the damn cat—none of that was a lie.

It was real. As real as the setting sun. As real as Nyel's steady hand resting against his back. Giving him strength.

The sea may have made me, but this island taught me how to live.

"Yes, *Signore*. Yes, I am."

"And what did I tell you about the formalities?"

Tears welled in Atreus's eyes.

"Yes, Giovanni."

Giovanni nodded approvingly. "As I thought."

The mountain of a man moved to stand beside Atreus, and before he knew what was happening, Giovanni's voice roared, carrying to every ear that listened with unquestionable authority.

"Today, we have discovered the old tales of the *Uomo del Mare* are true. The Men of the Sea live among us! And how fortunate for us that we learn through a man we already know. You've watched Atreus grow alongside your children, watched him work alongside your men. And today, he has saved one of our very own. He is a hero of Baia Vita! And..."

Giovanni reached for the shark tooth necklace, yanking it off his neck and tying it around Atreus's.

"... A man I will proudly call my son."

Atreus must still be in the waters by the cliffs, the waves knocking his head against the rocks. That was the only explanation that made any sense. Yet the solid weight of the leather strap around his neck and the shark tooth resting against his sternum was too heavy to be imagined.

They were real.

This was real.

The villagers, who, moments ago, were poised like a cat ready to pounce, eased at the lion's roar. At his promise that all would be well. Giovanni had made the ultimate gesture of trust, and their fears were quelled.

They exchanged words now with an air of excitement rather than fear, the volume growing.

"Emelia, I suggest you take your boy to Dr. Romano right away," Giovanni said, snapping the golden-haired family back to the present.

"Y-yes, yes, of course," Emelia agreed.

Edgar stirred but remained unable to stand on his own.

Atreus tried to catch Leo's eye, to catch some glimpse that they would be okay. But his old friend refused to meet his gaze as he turned in the direction of the hospital.

Yet the relief, the shock, the absolute mayhem of emotions now seeping out of his pores had at last taken their toll. And if not for Nyel quickly ducking beneath his arm, he would have collapsed to the surf.

"Atreus, you're bleeding!" Nyel cried out as some of Atreus's blood dripped onto his shoulder.

It wasn't a surprise. Atreus was certain adrenaline and fear had worked miracles as the waves tossed him over the rocks. There was no way he'd come out of it with just a few superficial cuts. But none of that mattered.

"A man I will proudly call my son."

If he weren't in shock, he'd have cried like a child.

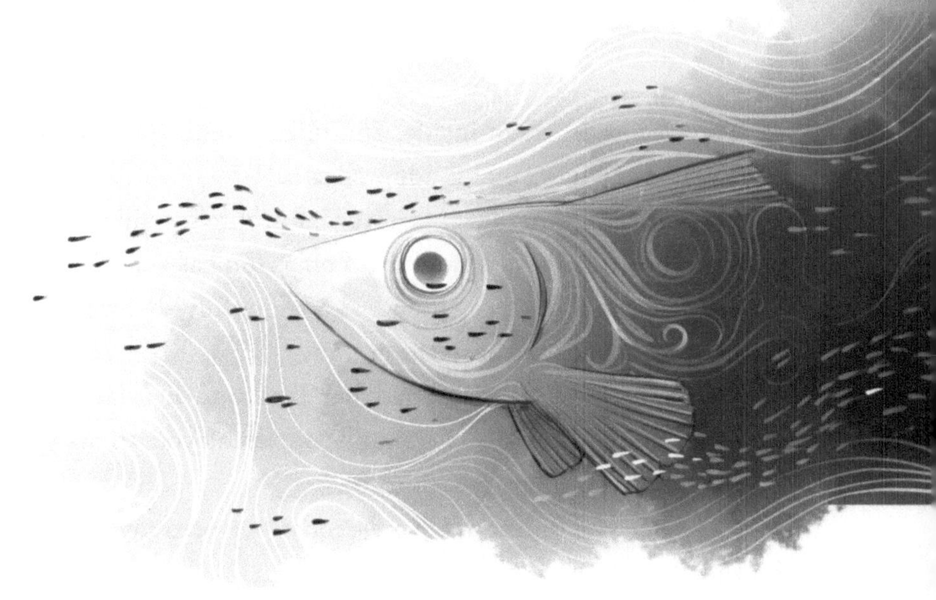

CHAPTER 25

MARINA

ATREUS WAS COVERED in gashes, and by the time they made it to the hospital, he cradled his left arm. Marina had never been inside the new hospital building and indulged herself by admiring the modern decor, sparkling floors, and pristine surfaces as a nurse escorted them into a private room. The cream-colored walls gave the space a warm, inviting feel, while the light blue furniture looked soft enough to sleep in. It was cozy compared to the white sterile buildings on the mainland.

Papà followed them inside, and once Atreus was settled on the bed, he rested a hand on his adopted son.

"Mayor Gianfranchi wants a word. I'm sure he will want to speak with you both as well. I'll hold them off as long as I can."

He squeezed Atreus's shoulder meaningfully before leaving the private room. Marina chased after him.

"*Papà*, wait." Marina buried her face into her father's larger-than-life chest. "*Grazie, Papà*. Thank you, thank you, thank you."

"Why do you thank me, *Cucciola*?"

"Because you didn't make me choose between my father and my brother."

Brother. Atreus was her brother. Some part of her knew that was the spot he occupied in her heart. Now, she could say it out loud. And she'd never stop saying it.

"Watch over him. I imagine he is shaken."

"I will." She kissed her father on his bristly cheek and returned to Atreus's hospital room. He looked tired, but there was a lightness to him she'd never seen.

Like some terrible weight was gone.

A chain finally broken.

"Where does it hurt?" Nyel asked, occupying the chair on the side of the white bed.

"Um... everywhere?"

"You're going to have to narrow it down for us," a woman said, entering the room. "My name is Irena. I am the senior nurse in this hospital."

She observed them each with a warm yet stern gaze. Her no-nonsense blonde bun was streaked with silver, but her hard eyes were betrayed by the tell-tale smile lines around her mouth.

"Which of you is the Mer?"

Marina beamed at the boys. "They are, of course."

Irena inclined her head to Atreus and Nyel. "Welcome. We will do everything we can to help you."

"Th-thanks," Atreus stuttered and winced as he shifted on the mattress.

"The arm first, then." She turned to Marina, "I'm sorry, but only family in the room while we work on him."

"I'm his sister," Marina said, lifting her chin proudly. She took Atreus's good hand as though this settled the matter.

Irena's eyes fell on Nyel.

"I'm the other Mer?" Nyel said as a question.

Irena sighed. "Fine. I'll be right back."

Marina waited for the door to shut before beaming at her brother. "You actually called me Rina."

Atreus grinned, though it looked more like a grimace. "I did."

"Oh, Atty!" she said, throwing her arms around him.

"Ow —OW! Wounded over here!"

When Irena returned, she was followed by a young man with mousy hair and big ears.

"This is a member of our staff in training; he will be helping us today."

"Hi, I'm Stefano," he said, raising a timid hand. Marina thought he looked too young to practice medicine, but what did she know?

They set to work undressing Atreus. Marina and Nyel stepped out while they fitted him with a gown and stitched up his more revealing lacerations. When they were allowed back inside, Marina was surprised that it was Stefano doing most of the work while Irena supervised. It seemed that once tasks needed doing, he left his timidness at the door. With gauze and a needle in his hands, he moved with confident precision. At some point, Irena was called to another room, leaving them alone with the young nurse in training.

"You sure we shouldn't wait for her to come back?" Marina questioned as Stefano readied another syringe with a numbing agent.

"No need."

Atreus hardly winced as Stefano numbed his forearm, and once the feeling was well and truly gone, he set to stitch the gash.

"Are your parents doctors or something?" Marina asked. "You look pretty young to do this."

She thought he'd ignored her entirely while silently stitching the wound, his unblinking focus slightly unnerving. After five minutes, however, he cleaned the area with alcohol and lifted his attention to Marina.

"I'm fifteen. And no. My parents aren't doctors."

Like a spell had broken, once his work was finished, the timid boy at the door was back, making him look young and unsure once again. He fidgeted with a button on his uniform.

"I—I know Dr. Romano personally, and he offered me the training position. And I've been Irena's shadow ever since."

"And you still have much to learn," Irena said, returning to the room.

"Ye-yes, ma'am!" Stefano said, rising so fast his rolly chair hit the opposite wall.

At the end of it all, Atreus needed over thirty stitches across his body and was sent for an X-ray of his arm—a luxury most hospitals couldn't afford.

The massive X-ray machine was housed in a separate, pristine room. It was the kind of equipment so expensive and advanced that many mainland hospitals didn't even have it yet. Marina's eyebrows shot up at the crystal clear black-and-white image of Atreus's bones.

"I'll be back with the results," Irena said, taking the X-rays and snapping her fingers for Stefano to follow.

"It—it was nice to meet you," he said but paused at the door, his eyes darting nervously between Nyel and Atreus.

"They don't bite," Marina said, rolling her eyes. "Even when you do this." She reached over and pinched Nyel hard on the cheek.

"Ow!"

"See?"

"And this one"—she jerked a thumb at Atreus—"took years to figure out how to clean a squid without getting inked. I can't tell you how many times I found him covered in sticky black goop in nothing but his *mutande*."

"You promised never to bring that up," Atreus barked.

Stefano nodded awkwardly and hurried after Irena like a nervous squirrel.

"I can't believe you told him that," Atreus grumbled, but Marina suspected he was more embarrassed that Nyel had heard.

"Oh, calm down, tiger shark, it's what siblings are for."

"You're really playing into this whole sibling thing, aren't you?"

"Abso-freakin'-lutely," Marina said with a pop of her lips. "And I know you're hurt and all, and I should be worried, but this is the best day of my life."

"Alright, Rina," Atreus said, rolling his eyes.

Marina squealed in delight. "Call me your sister."

"You're my sister," he placated.

She squealed again, clapping her hands and wiggling excitedly in her chair. Nyel had to restrain her from jumping on him again.

After several long minutes, Atreus shifted uncomfortably on the bed, the pain starting to take its toll. Marina frowned at the door.

"What is taking the doctor so long?"

"Maybe he is with Edgar?" Nyel suggested.

"He can take his time," Atreus said through gritted teeth, "The kid is more important."

"And I'm happy to report the kid will be just fine," said a voice from the doorway.

Marina's head snapped up. Her mouth fell open as she shot to her feet so quickly that the chair toppled over with a clang.

"You!" she blurted, startling everyone in the room.

The doctor stepped inside, arms spread, white coat billowing open to reveal navy scrubs. "Me."

He strode to the hospital bed, his eyes scanning the fresh stitches crisscrossing Atreus's body.

Marina couldn't believe it. It was him. The stranger. The one she'd danced with at the opening festival. The one she swore she'd never see again—though if she was honest with herself, she wasn't sure she entirely meant it.

Heat flushed her cheeks as the memory resurfaced. She'd been curt, maybe even rude. But in her defense, she'd had a lot on her mind that day. Still, *him?* Of all people?

"You—I can't—you never told me."

"Speechless, I know. I have that effect on people," he said, eyes never leaving his patient as he prompted Atreus to lift an arm so he could inspect the bruising along his ribs.

Marina's face turned a deeper shade of red. A sound escaped her —something between a growl and a strangled screech.

"You're unbelievable!"

"Why, thank you."

"That wasn't—I didn't mean—" she sputtered, her words dissolving as he smirked at her with amused patience.

"Good to see you too," he said with a wink, his shoulder-length hair catching the light like a polished halo as he straightened. Reaching for a yellow folder, he let it fall open and scanned the page. Without looking up, he added, "I like the earrings, by the way."

Marina's hands flew to her ears, pulling out the delicate blue earrings she'd worn for the Bayallon. She hadn't even thought twice about them.

"I wasn't—they're not—it doesn't mean—"

"My dear," he interrupted smoothly, snapping the folder shut, "as much as I'd love to continue this thrilling exchange, I have a patient to address."

"Am I missing something here?" Atreus asked, his eyes darting between the two of them. "Do you two know each other?"

"We've had the pleasure of an acquaintance," the doctor replied, his tone effortlessly charming. "I am Doctor Romano, though you are welcome to call me Mattias. I don't bother with formalities in my hospital."

"So it's you!" Marina blurted, her voice sharper now as realization dawned. Pieces of the puzzle slid into place—this was the infamous doctor all the women in town gossiped about. The smug, cryptic stranger she'd met at the festival. How had she not guessed?

He raised his arms again, flashing that infuriatingly white smile beneath his neatly trimmed beard.

"As we've established," he said smoothly, "it is me."

Marina bristled. "No, I mean you're *the* one! The doctor—the one everyone won't shut up about."

Doctor Romano placed a hand over his chest, bowing slightly in mock humility. "I'm honored."

"I never said I was one of them," Marina shot back, crossing her arms. "As if."

"Oh, your words cut so deeply, Marina," he said, her name rolling off his tongue with practiced ease.

She narrowed her eyes. "Remembered my name this time, did you? Or did you have to look it up before walking in here?"

"I wouldn't be much of a doctor if I didn't know the names of the family of my hospital's very first Mer patient."

"Well, don't let me stop you, *Doctor* Romano," she said, her tone dripping with sarcasm.

"Please," he said, his Cheshire smile widening, "call me Mattias."

"No," Marina snapped, crossing her arms tighter.

His smirk only grew, and she had to fight the urge to smack his stupid, handsome face. She didn't miss the way his gaze lingered on her a moment too long before he turned his attention to Atreus.

"As I said, I am the attending physician, and I want to formally welcome you, Atreus. Even though we are not of the same species, I will do everything in my power to ensure your health and recovery."

"Thanks," Atreus said dryly.

Marina grinned. She wasn't the only one Mattias had rubbed wrong.

"You have a hairline fracture in your forearm. I recommend that at least six hours of your day be spent in the sea to accelerate the healing. This will also close the wounds and dissolve all the stitches we put in. You should be back to normal in about two weeks. I'll have my staff fit you with a water-safe sling in the meantime."

Marina blanched. "How'd you know all that?"

Dr. Romano smirked. "Are you impressed?"

"As if! You wouldn't impress me even if you had a massive—"

"I'd like to hear the answer to that question too," Nyel interjected.

Dr. Romano inclined his head to him. "Welcome, *sireno*; I am also glad to see you here. And I have a vast knowledge about many things."

"That answers nothing," Atreus snapped.

"And yet it answers everything. Do not worry about the charge for this visit, as this hospital's first Mer patient, consider it a courtesy."

He turned to leave, but not before winking at Marina. She pressed her lips together in a harsh line, knowing her face would quickly match her hair.

"What the hell just happened?" Atreus exclaimed the moment the door closed.

Marina couldn't tear her gaze away from where Mattias's— no, Doctor Romano's white coat disappeared. Atreus snapped his fingers in front of her.

"Hey, eyes over here! Don't you be gettin' ideas."

She shook herself. "What?"

"Don't *what* me. As your older brother, I forbid it."

"Forbid what?"

He whipped his finger from the door to her. "Whatever the hell that was."

"There wasn't anything there."

"There kinda was," Nyel mumbled.

"You're not helping," she hissed at him.

"He's got to be like forty years old, absolutely not," Atreus declared.

"That's a bit exaggerated, don't you think?" Marina defended. Why the hell was she defending that jerk? "I seriously doubt he's even close to that. What would you guess, Nyel?"

Nyel shrugged. "I can never tell with humans that have hair on their faces. It's really confusing."

"I'm guessing thirty, thirty-two max," Marina said.

"It doesn't matter because I forbid it as your brother."

"You've been my brother for like an hour," Marina said, but couldn't hold back the smile tugging at her mouth.

"And therefore, it is my right to monitor your love life."

"That's not how that works."

Just as their sibling squabble was about to ignite, the door creaked open, and Irena hushed them with a look. She gave Atreus a mild painkiller and was fastening his sling when another group appeared in the room.

Mayor Gianfranchi entered, followed by Sheriff Fanti and her deputies. The mayor looked ready to faint. Marina couldn't help but feel a twinge of guilt. After all, nearly losing a child during the town's beloved event—and then the whole revelation about water people— must've thrown him for a loop.

"*Uomo del Mare*, how are you feeling?" he asked Atreus, his sweaty brow glistening. He clearly would rather be anywhere else in the world.

"I'll be okay," Atreus said as Irena fastened the sling around his arm. "And please call me Atreus."

"Mayor, please, only family in the room," Irena said with a huff.

"Forgive me, but we have urgent matters to discuss."

"So, is that city hall of yours only for show?"

Mayor Gianfranchi cleared his throat, folding under the nurse's intensity. "I'll see you there then." He exited with his officers trailing behind.

"Honestly, this is a hospital, not a circus," Irena huffed, finishing Atreus's bandages.

"Is he done? Or does Doctor Romano need to check him again?" Marina asked, trying to keep her voice casual.

"No, he is free to go. Why? Would you like me to call the doctor back?"

"That won't be necessary," Atreus cut in. "I'm fine."

Marina chewed the inside of her cheek, irritated with herself and her brother. As they left the hospital, she caught Nyel's knowing smirk.

"And what are you so smiley about?"

"Nothing," he said innocently. "C'mon, the Mayor's waiting for us."

A few paces later, when Atreus was well out of earshot, Nyel leaned in and whispered, "Atreus will need to have his arm checked again. As his sister, it's only right that you tag along."

Marina grinned and playfully bumped her hip into Nyel's, both of them trying to hide their laughter as Atreus shot them a suspicious glare.

NYEL

NYEL FELT THE DIZZYING relief of stepping down from a ledge. His legs trembled, still unsteady from narrowly escaping a fatal fall.

Somehow, they weren't chased from Baia Vita. Instead, they were sitting in the mayor's office. They weren't running for the sea as the people they'd grown to love hurled harpoons at their hearts.

They were alive.

They were okay.

The same couldn't be said for the mayor, who looked like a lobster fresh from the boil. He patted his balding head with a cloth as a layer of moisture accumulated in stress-filled drops.

"Well, as I'm sure you know, this is not what I expected from the Bayallon, and frankly, I have questions."

"We are here to answer them," Nyel supplied, his confidence growing with each second.

Marina and Giovanni sat behind them, while Nyel and Atreus sat directly in front of the mayor's desk. Sheriff Fanti leaned against the wall behind him, her arms folded. Nyel suspected she was there as a guard. They still had a long way to go before they'd be completely trusted.

"Yes well... to begin, I... uh..." Mayor Gianfranchi wiped his upper lip now. "You see, we... our concerns..."

Sheriff Fanti rolled her eyes, straightening. "Are you a threat or not?"

The mayor flinched. "I wasn't going to put it like that, but—are you?"

"No." Nyel and Atreus said at the same time.

"Good. Good," he said, but appeared far from convinced.

"And what of the disappearing fish in the bay? Is that the Mer's work?" Sheriff Fanti pressed.

"Of course we aren't accusing—"

"Yes, we are," she deadpanned as the mayor turned to give her an exasperated look that she ignored.

"The Mer that live in the bay are my people," Nyel said earnestly. "They're like me. We call ourselves *Sireni*, and we are plant-eaters. We don't eat meat of any kind."

"And what about you?" she asked, jerking to Atreus.

Atreus cleared his throat uncomfortably, and Nyel had to resist the urge to place a reassuring hand on his leg.

"I am not *Sireni*. I am half *Rusalki* and… I'm not sure what else. I was separated from my people as a child. I am the only one of my kind in these waters."

"And one Mer that eats fish is hardly enough to account for our losses," the mayor said, and Nyel was glad for his defense.

Nyel was beginning to sweat under Sheriff Fanti's scrutiny and, before he could think better of it, blurted, "We can help!"

All eyes turned to him.

"With what?"

"The fish. We can help if we—"

He cut himself off. Atreus had been against his plan from the beginning. And now that he was faced with the mayor of Baia Vita, Nyel began to doubt its viability.

"Tell them about your idea, Ny. It's a good one." Atreus reached with his good arm, squeezing Nyel on the shoulder.

"I thought you—"

"It's a good plan. I just didn't think we'd get this far."

He smiled, and Nyel felt as though a cyclone had stolen his breath. But far from being afraid of the storm, Nyel wanted to settle at its very core.

"You were right about this from the beginning. I should have listened," Atreus said.

Nyel beamed and dove headfirst into his plan.

He explained how the *Sireni* were suffering from the polluted water. Explained that *Sireni* wanted the ships gone as much as the humans did. Nyel went into detail about how they could work together to accomplish this. With the *Sireni* working as shepherds to herd the fish away from the big ships and towards the bay, they could increase the local fishermen's yields. And as the local fishing grew, the outsourced market would die off. Baia Vita would become less and less dependent on outside sources and return to its self-sufficient roots.

"This all sounds great. In theory," the sheriff said after listening intently.

"What are your concerns, Sheriff? I think that Nyel has made an excellent case," the mayor said, making Nyel's chest bloom.

"This all hinges on the idea that the rest of your people will want to help us. From the sounds of it, your kind went into hiding to stay away. Not work alongside us."

"I'll convince them," Nyel said with so much conviction he almost believed it himself. "For the first time in a long time, our goals are aligned. I'll convince them this is the best way. My village, Corallina, is risking starvation or being forced into colder waters. This is a more appealing alternative."

The Sheriff opened her mouth to argue, but Mayor Gianfranchi cut her off.

"Camilla," he reached into a drawer, throwing a thick stack of papers onto the desk. They landed with a 'thump.'

Nyel couldn't make sense of them but recognized the swishing script that the humans used to sign their names at the bottom of each sheet. All of them began with a letter that resembled an upside-down triangle with a missing side.

"Vincenzo has us in the palm of his hand," the mayor said gravely.

At this, the Sheriff's shoulders sagged. "I understand."

"By spring, there will be nothing left of us."

"We have good people here, Mayor. I left mainland life to protect people like them. These Mer..." Her gaze landed on Nyel. "I don't know you."

"Camilla," the mayor implored, "the mainland is already here. Vincenzo has his claws in all of us. By the end of winter, he'll be buried so deep there won't be any hope of eradicating him."

"I want to protect this place," Atreus spoke up for the first time. "I'll fight for it alongside you."

Giovanni cleared his throat from the back of the room, and all eyes turned to him.

"If I may interject, I can attest to my son's dedication to this island. He has done nothing but uphold our values and maintain our traditions since I've known him as a boy."

The emotion pouring from Atreus was palpable as he reached for the shark's tooth at his chest, but shyly dropped his hand when he caught Nyel watching.

"Furthermore," Giovanni continued, "My family has lived on this land for generations. Never before have I witnessed such a swift decline in who we are. Every night, I pray for a miracle to save us." He opened his hand, gesturing to the two Mer. "And if the resurrection of one of our oldest legends isn't a miracle, I do not know what is."

"Alvise is vile," Marina said. "He won't stop until all of us are under his thumb or driven off. It's bad enough that he took the valley from us, but now he's after everything else. The law doesn't apply to him."

At this, Sheriff Fanti's jaw flexed, teeth grinding.

"Camilla, please," the mayor pleaded, "this is our only chance."

Nyel's heart jumped like a frightened rabbit when the sheriff's eyes landed on him.

"Get your people on board."

"I will," Nyel said, equal parts excited and terrified.

"Then let's set up a meeting!" Mayor Gianfranchi declared before the sheriff could poke more holes in his delicate plan. "Would you be able to get a meeting with your leaders?"

"Uh, we don't have a leader, but I'll figure something out."

"Excellent," the mayor said, slapping the desk. He peeked around the boys to where Giovanni sat silently in the back of the room. "*Signore* Marcello, are you in agreement?"

Giovanni nodded sagely. "I am."

"Excellent, excellent," the mayor repeated, a bit more energy in his movements. He mumbled under his breath. "We might just save this island yet."

MARINA OFFERED him an encouraging wave as he marched into the surf. Nyel waved back, trying to exude a confidence he didn't feel. He took a giant gulp of air. This was it.

"Let's go."

But Nyel stopped knee-deep when he noticed Atreus didn't follow.

"I won't help your chances," he said.

"What are you talking about?"

"You're about to ask a lot from your people. And your people are..." He hesitated before settling on, "set in their ways. It'll be hard enough to get them to surface without a halfling by your side."

Nyel bit the inside of his cheek. Atreus was right, of course, but that didn't mean he liked it.

"It'll get better, Atreus. I'll make it better."

Atreus smiled, though it was weak.

"I know you will."

"I'm on your side, Atreus."

He remembered the first time he spoke those words and truly believed them.

On that night, they stood before each other as Mer, beneath a sky awash in fire and light. And by the look on Atreus's face, he was remembering the same thing.

"I know," he said even softer.

"Say it out loud," Nyel demanded.

Atreus smiled warmly. "I know you're on my side, Ny."

"And that I'm the greatest *Bocce* player there ever was—"

"Get the hell outta here." Atreus rolled his eyes, but not before adding, "You can do this."

Nyel nodded and, without another word, dove into an oncoming wave.

Marvassa greeted him, and he flexed his tail muscles before they were truly there. The change came so naturally to him now that he marveled at how he'd gone his entire life without its touch. He wondered why so many of his people feared its tickling transformation. His stomach clenched in anxiety. Nyel was about to ask them to face that fear. That, and so much more.

"You're making a mistake."

Nyel flinched as a voice sounded far too close, swimming parallel to him in the water.

"Spirits, Nephi! Don't do that."

"You're alarmingly easy to sneak up on."

"I have a lot on my mind," Nyel said, plowing ahead.

"You're making a mistake."

"You said that."

"Mer and humans aren't meant to exist together. There will be blood for this."

Nausea crept up Nyel's throat. "How do you know?"

"I've seen what happens when Mer and people come face to face. It isn't pretty."

"We're going to help each other."

"You're going to kill each other," Nephi pressed. "This little truce you and the *Rusal* have garnered is already about as stable as a sandcastle at high tide."

"You don't know that."

"I do."

"No, you don't!" Nyel rounded on his brother, unintimidated by his flared red fins. "But you'd like that, wouldn't you? You want us to hate each other. You want humans and Mer to fight, and for the life of me, I can't figure out why."

"Why!? You wanna know why!?" Nephi bellowed, getting in Nyel's space. "Because the humans took *everything* from me!"

Nephi's voice echoed through the water, and Nyel jolted at his undiluted fury. His brother's milked-over eye appeared whiter than usual. His scars were more prominent as rage contorted his half-destroyed face.

Humans did this to him.

Now Nyel knew for sure, yet a part of him wondered if there was a deeper wound Nephi hid beneath the scars.

"Why are you still here?" Nyel asked once the echoes of rage dissipated. "Because it's not for Dad. Or for me." Nyel tried not to let the hurt show as he said it.

"I don't know," Nephi admitted.

He's lying.

It was clear as day. The answer was in his eyes—the eyes they shared.

"Do what you want, Nyel," Nephi hissed, turning to leave. But Nyel caught the end of his crimson tailfin, holding him.

"Wait," Nyel's throat filled with wool. "Don't disappear again. Please."

He held his brother's stare before Nephi jerked his tail away and left without another word.

RIPPLE GURGLED LOUDLY, the sound like falling stones, as the sandwinder waggled his stubby tail. His antenna reached out to Nyel as he swam close, like an overgrown toddler asking to be carried. Nyel scratched him behind the antenna.

"Hey buddy, how've you been? Been a good boy?"

Ripple gurgled again, rolling to expose his white belly.

"I wish I could take you to Baia Vita; you'd love it," he said, now using both hands to scratch the hippopotamus-sized beast.

"Nyel, is that you?"

The voice Nyel wanted to hear most greeted him as Sonia swam from the sand hut home, a lively Sabella in her arms.

"Hey, Sonia," he said, kissing his aunt on the cheek before waving a finger for his cousin. "And hello to you, princess."

She cooed at him with delight, her finless tail poking from her clothes.

"It's so good to see you."

Sonia was dazzling alongside her babe. There was a spark of life in her eyes that Nyel hadn't seen since his uncle passed.

"You look good, Sonia. But I need to talk to all of you. There's been a change in situation," he said, taking a reassuring breath.

"And will that change prevent you from seeing your own family?" a second voice huffed from the doorway.

"Hello, Mom," Nyel said, obediently going to place a kiss on his mother's cheek.

"This change in situation better not take you farther away; I barely see you enough as it is. Do you even realize how much your mother worries—"

"Mom," Nyel held up a hand, "If all goes to plan, you'll actually see me more."

This caught his mother's attention. "Well, that's more like it. Come in."

"Actually, I need all of you."

"We're all here," she said. "Your father's inside."

"No," Nyel urged. "Everyone. I need to speak to everyone in Corallina."

It took some doing, but with the promise of seeing her son more often, there was little that could stop Bianca Veritani. Soon, the settlement of *Sireni* crowded together in the center of their village. It wasn't everybody, only those with farms close enough to come quickly, but it was enough that word would spread fast.

The center of Corallina was less of a 'village square' and more of an open plot of sand shaped in a perfect circle. Around the edge, various species of coral added vibrant splashes of color to their otherwise kelp-green world.

Nyel couldn't remember the last time he'd seen so many of them gathered like this, nor could he remember seeing them so deflated. Scales that used to shine were now dull with a sickly gray hue. The *Sireni* reflected the health of their crop. And if the kelp grew gray and sick, so did the people. And given how many gaunt faces now stared at him, Nyel knew that this village was running out of time.

Nyel caught sight of Mr. and Mrs. Ernesti in the front of the group. Chel was beside them with a lanky *sireno* Nyel suspected to be Wyll. She waved, and he returned it, earning a glare from the *sireno* beside her. All eyes were on Nyel as he took his place high on a stone overhang.

A million ways to begin his impossible message raced through his mind. What if they wouldn't listen? What if his strange human clothes marked him as an outsider? He should have changed into traditional sea-grass garb. Too late now. There was only one thing to do: say it.

"I have a message from the humans on the island."

The chatter died instantly. Bodies were still, and eyes wide as fins swayed in the tide like the kelp they so desperately needed to save.

"They know we are here. They know what we are, and they have accepted us."

Easy. Easy.

"I can say with utmost certainty that the ships harvesting fish outside the bay are killing our fields."

"Humans also run those ships," a *sirena* in the middle of the crowd called out.

"Yes, but they aren't the same. The ones polluting the water and the ones living on the island are not the same humans. The people of Baia Vita are also suffering because of these ships. They can't catch enough fish to sustain their way of life. They're dying. Just like we are dying."

"So what do you propose?" This voice came from Mr. Ernesti.

"The humans—" Nyel paused. "*I* came up with the idea that would help everybody."

Nyel dove into his plan, adding details for the Mer that he didn't bother in the mayor's office. When he was done, Mr. Ernesti spoke again.

"So you expect us to give away our precious daylight hours? We should be harvesting whatever kelp we have left. And you're suggesting we play sandwinder for the humans? Herding fish like dumb beasts?"

"That's not at all what he said," Sonia snapped, Sabella sleeping in her arms.

"It won't be like that. We only have to get the fish into the bay, not stand guard like shepherds. And once we coax the fish into shallow waters, Ripple can help push them forward from there." Nyel said, expressing his willingness to share Ripple for the cause.

"I don't like it. It sounds like we will feed the humans for nothing in return."

Nyel clenched his fists. He didn't have time to explain the complexity of human economics. They had to trust him.

"I know it sounds like a lot of work for no reward. Give it time; I promise the ships will leave once Baia Vita begins to heal."

"So what are we supposed to do? Take your word for it?" Wyll spoke up, searching for an approving glance from his hope-to-be father-in-law.

"The mayor wants a meeting. They're waiting for you right now."

The crowd shifted at this. A tangible zing of energy. A primal reaction to the news that another being awaited them. Prey responding to the presence of a predator.

"It's perfectly safe!" Nyel hurried, sensing them drawing away. "They want to meet us. I've been living there for weeks."

"We can tell," Wyll commented, eyeing his clothes.

The noise of the crowd grew, pushing Nyel back.

They won't come. I promised I could do it, and they won't come. I've failed...

"I'll meet them."

Everyone stilled as his aunt swam up beside him.

"If Nyel says it's safe, if he says this is our chance to save our crop and stay in the bay, I trust him. Me *and* Sabella will go."

Sonia's declaration had an instant effect on the crowd. Mer children were rare and precious. If she was willing to bring a babe to this meeting, her trust in him was unconditional. Nyel was suddenly very aware of the weight of that trust.

"I'll go."

Chel rose from the crowd, much to the shock of her parents.

"Oh, um, yeah, me too," Wyll added, joining her. Nyel didn't miss the way Chel beamed at Wyll and intertwined their hands together. Murmurs rose.

"The crop is dying."

"If there is a chance to be rid of the boats, what's the harm in trying?"

"I can herd fish."

Voices of affirmation joined the throng.

"My son is the smartest *sireno* in the seven seas; if he says this will save our fields, then that is that," Bianca said, joining her son.

Nyel was warmed, if not a little embarrassed. His father, Donato, joined with his wife. Pretty soon, Nyel had a team of two dozen *Sireni* ready to surface alongside him. Finally, Mr. Ernesti relented.

"It's this, or risk the dangers of colder waters. I'll go."

The party agreed that Mr. Ernesti would speak for the group when they surfaced. Nyel led them away from the village, away from the safety of the bay, and towards the beach—towards Baia Vita.

CHAPTER 26

LEOFEL

T HE SUN WAS low over the water, but nobody was going home for the night. In fact, Sheriff Fanti and her two deputies were having a hell of a time keeping everyone off the beach. Since word of the *Uomo del Mare* spread within the hour, everyone wanted to catch a glimpse of myth come to life. Spectators leaned eagerly over the railings, squabbling for the best view of the beach.

Leo had no interest in being jostled around and looking over heads just for a glimpse. Instead, he found himself isolated atop the large stones at the base of the cliff. Was it smart to climb the sea-

447

slick rock at high tide? Probably not, but now he had an unobtrusive view of the beach where the mayor now paced trenches into the sand.

Only the mayor, Sheriff Fanti, and her deputies, Signore Marcello and Atreus, were allowed on the beach. Ready to receive their oceanic visitors. Leo couldn't decide if he was excited or scared of what might poke its head from the water.

It was only after Dr. Romano reassured him no fewer than ten times that Edgar was in no immediate danger that Leo finally tore himself away from his brother's hospital bed. Edgar had a number of bumps and bruises, the worst of the injuries being a sprained wrist. Nothing fatal. Nothing life-altering.

Not like the life-altering news that Mer existed. And not in the sea, but among them.

Bile rose to his mouth at the vision swimming behind his eyes. He could see Atreus from his perch. Standing beside Giovanni, a black shark tooth necklace gleaming on his chest. He appeared perfectly normal. Belonging in a way that Leo never did. The necklace was proof of that. Atreus had earned his place, and he wasn't even human.

His *best friend* wasn't human. All those times Atreus made excuses not to swim, even earning himself the nickname *Gatto* - meaning cat for his distaste for the water. Leo laughed humorlessly to himself. He'd been so stupid. But how was he supposed to guess that his best friend was a sea creature? That his best friend wasn't like the rest of them.

And yet, there he stands with a necklace around his neck. While I'm sitting here, hiding on a rock.

And Nyel—Leo didn't know what to think. Every time he thought about him, that strange buzzing sensation would start at the base of his spine and float all the way to his head. Even knowing that Nyel wasn't human couldn't chase those errant feelings away.

He could have told me.

Leo let himself feel betrayed for the first time.

He could have trusted me.

But it was clearer now more than ever that Atreus trusted nobody. Leo had confided in Atreus about his dreams. He'd opened up, but his friend had said nothing, brushing it off with a, "Don't think about it. Move on." The response hurt like a fishhook lodged in his heart, each tug sending fresh waves of pain.

An intense clarity struck him like a lightning bolt, illuminating a distant memory. Goosebumps prickled along Leo's skin, and a sour taste crept into his mouth.

Green and scarlet scales. Fangs. Slitted eyes.

Mer.

A Mer had saved him that day.

I fucking knew it.

Leo gripped his curls until they were painful. There was too much swimming in his head. Worry over his family and fear over what Alvise might do to him had pushed all else from his mind. He hadn't thought of his miraculous survival in weeks. And now... it all made sense.

"It all makes *fucking* sense," he spat, throwing a stone into the waves.

When distant gasps filled the air, Leo's head shot up in time to see a figure rise from the water. He recognized Nyel's clothes right away, but not the being wearing them. Of course, it was Nyel. The Mer had the same skip to his step, the same swing in his arms.

Leo's chest clenched painfully.

He couldn't hear what they were saying, but soon Nyel was diving back into the waves. And when he emerged a second time, he wasn't alone. Over two dozen Mer poked their heads from the water, their muddy green fins floating around them like seaweed.

A part of Leo hadn't believed it. Or at least, had convinced himself that Atreus and Nyel were the only ones. But there they were, a whole community of them, right under their noses.

Most of the Mer remained chest-deep in the water, except a large male who joined Nyel on the beach. He shook hands with the mayor, who looked ready to faint.

An acrid smell of smoke and spice filled Leo's nose.

"When my man reported this to me a few hours ago, I nearly had him shot for spinning fables."

Alvise leaned against his rock, his head just below where Leo's foot hung. Instinctively, he pulled his knees up.

"I had to see it for myself." Alvise blew out another heavy puff from the thick cigar. He gestured to the Mer, a few of which were getting brave enough to walk closer to the beach. There were two women (or Leo assumed so because of their dresses) with the same scale and color as Nyel. They were the first to surface. They looked like minnows, ready to bolt at the slightest sign of danger. One of the women held a baby close to her chest. The infant cried softly, the sound so familiar and normal when there was nothing normal about this situation.

"Beautiful. Absolutely beautiful." Alvise said, and Leo hated the gleam in his eye.

He'd seen it before. Directed at him and the other beautiful people Alvise *collected* at his estate. And as each of the Mer surfaced, taking turns to shake hands with humans, the gleam grew into something far more terrifying.

It was devouring.

It was hungry.

It was a terrible greed that would stop at nothing to sate its desires.

Leo shivered, praying those eyes wouldn't turn on him. But they already had, hadn't they? Leo had already become one of Alvise's many *collectibles*.

"I especially like that small minty one," Alvise said, pointing with the ember bud of the cigar.

Leo squeezed his eyes shut. He didn't need to look to know who'd caught Alvise's deadly gaze. The same Mer had caught Leo's attention, too, after all.

"My men reported a blueish one, too. I don't see it."

Leo stayed quiet.

"Where is he?"

Leo's fists clenched at his pants until the fabric burned in his hands. He wanted to jump into the waves and let the rocks beat him to a pulp.

"Answer my question, pet. You know how I loathe waiting."

Adrenaline spiked, and a cold sweat broke over Leo's brow.

"The beach. With the necklace. Standing by *Signore* Marcello," Leo gritted out through teeth clenched so tight they might crack.

"Ah, the fishmonger's stray. Interesting," Alvise said, smiling through another puff. "Such a beauty. And right under my nose. How interesting."

And before any shred of self-preservation could stop him, the words spilled from Leo in a desperate yell.

"You can't have them!" And he supposed he was a masochist because once the words escaped, he couldn't stop the flow. "They will never be yours. You have nothing on them. No power. They don't owe you a *fucking* thing."

The smile on Alvise's face slowly slid into an expression of sinister neutrality.

"Come down here." When Leo didn't move right away, Alvise sighed as though he'd spent all his remaining patience. "Edgar is in the hospital. Sprained wrist. Bump on the head. Scraped bruises."

"Don't—"

"I'm sure the famous Doctor Romano must have missed something, fool that he is," Alvise said, flicking the ashes. "Perhaps a broken ankle. Maybe a missing finger. Maybe two. I'll have one of my men check, just in case."

Leo slid from the rock, feeling his clothes tear as he descended haphazardly. When he stood beside Alvise, the smell of spices and smoke singed his nose. Alvise took a long pull and blew the smoke directly into Leo's eyes. As he blinked, eyes brimming with tears, a searing pain erupted on the side of his neck.

"Scream, and you'll draw attention to us," Alvise warned.

Leo held in the cry as the cigar's white-hot bud pressed into his flesh. It was over before the smoke had time to clear.

"My estate. One hour."

Alvise left him on the beach, his half-used cigar burning in the sand. Leo clutched at the side of his neck, whimpering with pain. He slid against the rock until his knees hit the sand. The burn was only the beginning of what was to come. He'd pay for his outburst. Leo trembled, his body already rejecting the promise of more pain. The suffering. The humiliation.

He looked into the surf, watching the various shades of green heads bobbing up and down with the waves. Leo searched them frantically, hoping to see a flash of scarlet. A blood-red fin. Slitted eyes that saved his life once before. But there was none.

Nobody was coming to save him now.

With one hand still clamped over his swelling neck, Leo rose and walked to the valley.

Alvise's obedient pet.

NEPHI

The *Marca Stella* burned between his fingers, its wisps of smoke stolen by the ocean breeze. Nephi took another drag from the small cigarette, savoring the burn in his lungs.

He'd barely restrained himself while watching his little brother's stunt on the beach. Atreus had let that oversized human get way too close. Things could have gone south fast.

If it had been Nephi—if he had the Spirit's blessed weapons fused to his body like the other halfling—that human would've lost his head in two seconds flat.

His time on this island was up. He'd known it the moment Bluey leapt over the edge to save the little boy.

Idiot.

Yet, hadn't Nephi been the idiot first? Hadn't he done the exact same thing? And for what—more heartache? More pain? Maybe the Spirits thought he hadn't suffered enough, that he needed to endure more before his soul left this mortal plane and departed for *Thalaren*.

If he was meant to suffer, he might as well find answers. Answers to the questions that haunted him since before his fins matured.

I know where she is. I could find her. Even if it's just to hear her denounce me.

But what good would it do to track down his birth mother? Donato had taken him the moment he was born and fled. If the RaMaa had found them, they would have killed Nephi—baby or not —then his mother.

Even now, nearly three decades later, if her Leviarch ever learned she had broken her vow, she would be executed on the spot.

If Nephi went looking for her, he'd be sealing her fate.

Best to leave it alone.

She's better off not knowing what I've become.

Nephi hissed as the cigarette butt burned his fingertips. He'd forgotten he was even holding it. With a curse, he dropped it to the ground and kicked it away.

The situation on the beach was spiraling. Now, *Sireni* were emerging from the water in droves, greeting their human neighbors.

This island is a sinking ship, pretending there's nothing wrong with its rotting hull.

And Nephi wasn't about to stick around and get caught in the fallout. He stalked away from the beach, hood pulled tight around his face. There was no point in delaying any longer. It was time to leave Baia Vita. For good this time.

His argument with Nyel replayed on a loop in his mind.

"Why are you still here?"

For every wrong reason he could think of. And he was done letting old wounds control him. He would put an end to this and disappear.

"I'm sorry, little brother, but you're better off without me. I'll only be a weight on this sinking ship."

Nephi was built for fighting, not for Kumbaya and alliances. He'd rejoin his Pod. He'd fight. And he'd die—as he should have in the blast that took Ludo.

Took him away from me.

There was only one thing left to do.

Nephi made himself comfortable on the secluded beach, trying to ignore what he knew was taking place on the other side of the island. Humans and Mer coming together to vanquish a common enemy. How fucking poetic.

He didn't have to wait long before a pair of feet crossed the sand and took a seat beside him.

"Knew you'd show up eventually," he said without looking the newcomer's way. "What took you so long—"

The scent of iron and salt and something sour met his nose. It was sour, like spoiled milk. It was acidic in all the wrong ways. It was the residual scent of fear.

Leo's face bore the marks of a brutal beating, swollen and bruised, with a cut above his brow that still oozed blood. His yellow irises stared lifelessly ahead. His shoulders slumped forward as if the act of sitting straight was too much. Every inch of him radiated a haunting emptiness, a hollow shell of the person he once was.

"Well, aren't you going to tell me I look like shit?"

Leo's voice was hoarse. Ruined. Like he'd screamed until his vocal cords frayed and bled. Nephi wanted to comply, to fall into their rehearsed back and forth, but couldn't bring himself to do it.

"You look good."

"Liar," Leo said with a joyless laugh. "And you have your damn hood up again."

"Would you rather I take it off?"

"I like to see who I'm talking to."

Nephi unzipped the jacket, tossing it to the side, leaving him bare-chested and exposed.

"You look good," Leo offered.

"Liar," Nephi said with a wicked grin.

The wound on Leo's face was still bleeding. Fresh.

The insane urge to reach out clawed at Nephi so strongly that he dug his nails into his palms to stop himself.

What the hell am I thinking?

He had come here with a purpose. And he'd be damned if he didn't finish what he started.

"I take it you heard the news. We have new neighbors," Leo said, wiping a drop of blood from his brow and streaking it into his damp curls.

"I did."

"Not surprised, are you?"

Nephi's pulse quickened. "No."

"And why is that Nephi?"

A shiver ran down his spine at the sound of his name, goosebumps making the hairs on his arms stand on end. It was time.

Leo moved, closing the distance between them as he slid across the sand. He was making it too easy, like herring swimming willingly into the hammerhead's maw.

"Look at me, Nephi," he breathed, his eyes searching. Lost.

Nephi obeyed.

Leo's yellow irises were dead. Empty—something vital snuffed out. The unmistakable scent of another man clung to the air around him, stirring something dark in Nephi's chest.

"You look at me the same way *he* does," Leo whispered, "with the same gleam in your eyes." He reached out, stroking Nephi's ruined cheek. Nephi didn't move, didn't flinch. He allowed the touch. "But for some reason," Leo continued, his voice unbearably tender, "I'm not afraid of you."

Nephi took Leo's hand, cradling it as he slid it from his cheek to his nose and mouth. He inhaled deeply, his eyes closing as he tried to imagine... but it wasn't there. Ludo's scent was gone forever. Instead, he caught the earthy aroma of human flesh mixed with a citrusy tang unique to Leo.

"Say it again," Nephi mumbled, his eyes squeezed shut.

"I'm not afraid of you," Leo whispered.

Nephi sighed before smacking Leo's hand away in disgust.

"You should be."

He rose and, in two strides, dove into the waves. Nephi burst from the water in a spray of foam, his crimson fins flaring wide like jagged banners of war. Green scales shimmered in the fading light, each one catching the setting sun like cracked emeralds. Claws flexed, and he bared his razor-like teeth with the promise of suffering. He looked like something dragged from the blackest depths—a creature born of nightmares and forged in hate.

Before Leo could react, Nephi struck, faster than any human could track. In a blink, he had Leo pinned to the sand, one taloned hand clasped firmly around his throat. Yet the scent Nephi craved, the one that sent his blood boiling and his vision red, wasn't there.

No fear.

"Why don't you scream?" he hissed, the sound like a blade dragging against stone.

"Because I'm not afraid," Leo said, his voice steady, almost defiant.

Nephi's grip tightened around Leo's neck, limiting his air. "You have been a sore in my side from the moment I pulled you out of the water."

"Why did you do it?" Leo choked. A question as much as a challenge.

Nephi stared down at him, momentarily stunned. The answer clawed its way up his stomach, retching with shame. "Because you remind me of someone."

He hated the way his voice trembled at the mere memory of Ludo. At the way, even now, he saw traces of him in Leo's curly hair and high cheekbones.

End this. End it now.

"Is he dead?" Leo asked. Nephi bared his teeth in answer. Then, so quietly he almost missed it, Leo whispered, "Did you kill him?"

The corners of Nephi's eyes burned as he glared down at his victim. "Yes," he answered, "I killed him."

"Then do it," Leo said, his tone resigned. He didn't struggle, didn't try to push Nephi away. He surrendered. "I know it's what you've wanted. I saw it in your eyes from the moment we met on this beach. Do it."

Desire and necessity collided in a chaotic dance, tearing Nephi apart. The reality of what he needed gnawed at his insides, while the yearning for what he wanted cut and tore like a hook embedded in his heart.

He couldn't breathe.

One swipe of his claws. And it would be over. Leo's pulse throbbed against his grip, steady and strong, pressing into Nephi's palm like a silent demand. Leo wasn't asking to be spared.

Only acknowledged.

That his life, however short, held even the smallest shred of worth.

Nephi was unraveling at the seams, lost in the agonizing conflict of his own making. Delicate fingers slid around his wrist, not pulling but guiding.

"Do it."

Nephi growled, yanking Leo upright, his talons digging into the skin deep enough to draw blood.

"I hate you," he hissed. "I hate you for reminding me of him. I hate you for not *being* him. I—"

Nephi seized Leo's face and crashed their mouths together. It was hard, brutal, all take and no give. Only now did Leo's hands press against his shoulders, but the fight was weak, barely a resistance at all.

Nephi pulled him in by the neck, deepening the kiss. The human gasped into his mouth, and Nephi took it all. Leo's bottom lip slipped between his—soft, full—just as he'd imagined.

Nephi kissed him

And kissed him,

And Spirits he couldn't stop.

He pressed his mouth against Leo's in a frantic, desperate clash of lips and teeth. And in that moment, Nephi didn't know who he wished this human to be.

A fang caught Leo's lip, pricking the tender skin and drawing a whimper that sent white flames racing down Nephi's spine. The taste of blood followed, sweet and intoxicating, making him lose what little control he had left. Leo's hand slid into the fins atop Nephi's head, and he couldn't suppress the deep rumbling that tore from his throat. Then another hand moved upward, brushing against the melted scales and ruined flesh on his chest.

Nephi flinched as flashes of orange seared through his mind. He shoved Leo to the sand hard enough to send the human sprawling. Panting, Nephi wiped his mouth, swallowing the blood on his tongue.

Leo touched his lip, his fingertips coming away red. His voice was unsteady, almost hysterical. "Is that it, then?"

Nephi stumbled into the surf, his breath ragged, his mind spinning. He had to get away.

"Nephi!" Leo shouted after him, standing now, fists clenched and blood trailing down his chin. "Will you come back?"

"No," Nephi rasped.

Without another word, he dove into the water, the taste of Leo's blood and the memory of his mouth etched into him like a scar.

He wouldn't return to Baia Vita. And he would never see the ghost of Ludo ever again.

CHAPTER 27

ATREUS

I**T SHOULDN'T HAVE** been that easy. It shouldn't have felt so seamless. Yet it was as if Baia Vita had been waiting for them—for the Mer—welcoming them like an old friend with open arms.

The island breathed.

It thrummed with life, and Atreus felt its heartbeat through the soles of his bare feet as he walked the cobblestone streets. Differences melted away, dismissed as effortlessly as if they were no more significant than a preference for one color over another.

It was more than he ever imagined.

More than he ever dreamed.

Because Atreus never dared allow himself to have a dream like this.

The fishing season was extended, and in less than a week, their yield tripled. No—quadrupled. Boats overflowed, nearly capsizing from the weight. Giovanni had to hire a few more young men to help unload the docks that were now buzzing with laughter. Atreus even caught a few overwhelmed tears from the sea-hardened men.

Non-local shops were swiftly boycotted, and within two weeks, many were boarded up. The stores were re-sold, lovingly restored to their original state, and placed back into the hands of islanders who cherished them. Mayor Gianfranchi even complained (with an ear-splitting smile) that he'd never been so busy. At this rate, the ships that marred their horizon would be gone. And the bay would become theirs once more.

The *Sireni* of Corallina had outdone themselves. Nyel told Atreus that nearly half their population had dedicated themselves to herding the fish away from the ships and into the bay. With the Mer openly roaming the island, they witnessed the direct impact of their actions as mainland stores shut their doors. Soon, Corallina's crops would be safe from pollution.

And they all celebrated.

The people of Baia Vita were eager to show their gratitude, offering the Mer food wherever they went—bowls of pasta, fresh fruits and vegetables, and countless pastries. Nyel's love of sugar was clearly not unique, as the *Sireni* devoured the sweets with delight, their hunger finally eased.

It was a time for joy. For rejuvenation and renewal. A time to reclaim what was theirs.

So why did Atreus feel so damn miserable?

He hefted an overflowing crate of mackerel until the wood splintered with a sharp crack. Fish spilled onto the cobblestones in a slick cascade, and the gulls were on them in an instant, shrieking and snatching the slimy bodies.

Atreus grinned. Usually, he would have been scolded for losing the fish. But they were so plentiful now that he even caught a few fishermen offering the gulls free meals.

"The sea birds are part of the island's spirit," they said with a sort of reverence that Atreus hadn't seen in years.

Yet, as the boats returned to dock for the day, Atreus found himself wishing he could persuade the sun to stay in the sky just a little longer.

"You're going to miss my excellent espresso," Marina said over the dinner table.

"My mornings are ruined without them," Atreus replied sarcastically.

"You'll live." She flipped her hair with a flourish. "And Nyel will get them all winter!"

"Yep, sure will," Nyel said, then leaned over to whisper, "Along with the singing."

Atreus must have been more downtrodden than he thought, for that only to encourage a mild grin from him. Nyel noticed and bumped their knees under the table.

"Hey, you okay?" he whispered.

"Oh yeah, sorry, long day," he lied, shoving more salmon into his mouth.

Their conversation went unnoticed because of Horace's animated storytelling, which would have been better appreciated in the theater. They'd tried to be gentle when telling Horace the truth, not wanting to excite the old man too much. But when Atreus dipped his hand into the kitchen sink, the old man shot to his feet with a shout.

"I KNEW IT!"

They'd laughed for hours, and Atreus spent the remainder of the night drying his hand with a towel and rewetting it a dozen times.

"Scales blue as the open sea," Horace mumbled, daring to touch Atreus's wrist. "Though not as dark as Kirill's."

After that, the old man aged backward by the day. Each morning, he sat in his chair outside and watched the Mer come and go through town. He'd even gotten into the habit of randomly stopping people and asking if they would dip their hands in the fountain for him. Every time he asked an actual *Sireni*, they smiled and obliged.

His stories (though they'd listened to them a thousand times) were filled in with even wilder details than before, and he told them as though they'd happened yesterday. Nobody stopped him. And nobody told him the stories of his dear friend Kirill were fables.

Because they weren't.

And he'd known all along.

After helping with the dishes, something he'd never been able to do before, Atreus made his way to bed, settling in for what would be another sleepless night. His head barely hit the pillow when a voice called from the open door.

"Can I talk to you for a minute?" Nyel asked, stepping inside.

Atreus took a steadying breath. "Sure, what's up?" He sounded tight, even to his own ears.

Nyel shifted from one foot to another. "You aren't mad, are you?"

"No," he replied quickly—and it was the truth. He wasn't mad at Nyel or his decision to leave. In fact, Atreus was happy for him.

But the pit in his stomach had only sunk lower with each passing day. And tonight was the last night. Tomorrow, the final morning.

He had no idea what to do with the feelings churning in his chest. So, instead, he reassured Nyel with a playful kick to the shin.

"I'm not mad."

"Promise?"

"I promise."

He wanted to say more. And the way Nyel lingered suggested he wanted to as well. Yet they stood awkwardly, the silence stretching between them, neither willing to break it.

"Well, if that's all, I'm gonna head to bed. Early start tomorrow." Nyel dropped his head. "Yeah."

"Yeeeaaaah." Atreus stretched. "Night then."

"Night."

As Nyel turned to leave, Atreus watched him go, his gaze tracing the elegant lines of his slender frame. For a fleeting second, he was half-tempted to invite Nyel to stay—to spend their last night together in his room, just to bask in the *sireno's* presence a little longer. But the words never came.

Hours later, Atreus lay wide awake, staring at the cobwebs on the ceiling. His mind churned with thoughts of what he could have said —what he wanted to say. By morning, it would be his last chance.

> *"See the lengths he goes through to be rid of you?"*

Atreus squeezed his eyes shut, desperate for sleep to silence the voice gnawing at him from the inside out.

> *"Ready to leave it all behind just to escape you. You're nothing but a burden to him."*

"I tried not to be," Atreus whispered.

> *"He got what he wanted; he doesn't need you anymore."*

"That's not true. He'll come back."

"What if he's already planned
a life without you?
What if tomorrow is the
start of his forever… far away from you?"

Atreus curled in on himself, bracing against the voice's words all through the long hours of the night.

"DON'T MISS ME TOO much, Atty!" Marina gave him a disproportionately strong hug for her short frame.

"I'll cry into my pillow every night you're away."

"Awww, big brother, I love you too," she said, patting his cheek with a slap and skipping onto the barge's deck. "See you on board, Nyel."

This was it. They were going. Marina was going to finish her final semester of school. Nyel would learn how to read and write and do *science* and all sorts of things he couldn't do here.

Couldn't do with Atreus.

It was only for one semester, and deep down, Atreus realized that wasn't a lot of time. But he'd seen things change on Baia Vita in a matter of hours. What would all winter do to Nyel?

"Good luck, *ragazzo*," Giovanni said, laying a knee-buckling hand on Nyel's shoulder. "I'll leave you boys to it then."

As Giovanni walked away, Atreus suddenly felt the platform grow colder. It was just the two of them now. His throat tightened, and for a fleeting moment, he was tempted to follow Giovanni without saying another word. To let the goodbye slip past him, unsaid.

"Well, I'm going," Nyel said, clutching his bag in front of him.

"You'll do great." Atreus's words felt hollow even to his own ears. "Don't forget about us while you're in the big city."

"You know I can't do that. Keep yourself busy, Atreus. Don't get in your head," Nyel said, then with a grin, suggested, "teach Niccolo how to fetch or something."

"Ha. As if that cat will ever do anything he doesn't already want to. And for the record, cats don't fetch."

"I saw the neighbor's dog do it," Nyel countered.

"That's a dog. Dogs and cats are different."

"Oh, right. Maybe dogs will like me more?"

"Maybe," Atreus said, wondering if dogs would like Nyel better than cats. Niccolo always hissed when Nyel was around. Maybe it's because they smelled similar to fish—

—and were they really discussing the merits of cats versus dogs right now!? Of all the things to say, *this* was how they were spending their last moments? Atreus's chest seized. Is this really what he wanted Nyel to remember when he left?

He must have taken too long to respond because Nyel shifted awkwardly. "I better go, or the captain will leave without me. I'll see you in a few months."

Nyel turned toward the vessel, and panic surged through Atreus. Before he could think, his hand shot out, grabbing Nyel's wrist.

"I would have let him drown!" he shouted, unable to control the volume as the words tumbled out of him.

"W-what?" Nyel asked, eyebrows pinched.

"Edgar. During the Bayallon. When he went over, when I got to the railing, I.... I hesitated. Then I saw you and—" He squeezed Nyel's wrist tighter. "I just knew."

Nyel stepped closer, the barge forgotten. "Knew what?" he asked, his voice soft, like coaxing a secret to the surface.

"I knew I had to save him, and I knew that everything would be okay. Even after I changed and everyone saw me for what I was...it would be okay. Even if the humans hated me and rejected what I am... I'd be okay." He slid his hand from Nyel's wrist and intertwined their fingers. "Because I'd still have you."

Nyel's thin, delicate fingers laced with his, grounding Atreus in a way words never could.

"I would have let him drown. I wouldn't have been brave enough to jump. Not without you. So... thank you."

The weight of those two simple words paled in comparison to the gratitude swelling in Atreus's heart. He knew Giovanni felt it, too. So did all of Baia Vita. The island was crawling out of its grave, alive with new purpose—all because of this *sireno*.

Nyel's gaze softened, and he squeezed Atreus's hand.

"I wasn't the one that saved Edgar, Atreus. In the end, you were the one who jumped, and it takes an incredibly brave person to do that."

The warmth of those words filled Atreus's chest, only to be cut short by a slap on his shoulder.

"Brave and stupid!" Nyel forced a glare but couldn't hide the smile hidden beneath. "Don't ever scare me like that again."

"No promises," Atreus replied with a chuckle, then hesitated. "But... can you promise me one thing?"

"What?"

"Write to me?" Heat rushed to his cheeks as the words came out. "Giovanni can read to me, and he'll help me write back and stuff. I just... I want to know you're okay."

Nyel's grip on his hand tightened. "I will. Promise."

Atreus nodded jerkily. "Okay then."

"Okay."

The bellow of the ship's horn cut through the moment, announcing its departure.

"I better go," Nyel said. "See you in a few months."

He pulled away, his fingers slipping from Atreus's grasp. Just as they were about to leave his touch, Atreus caught them again, yanking him back.

Don't go. Don't go. Don't go.

Atreus couldn't breathe. Panic flared, paralyzing his lungs and holding his eyes wide open, as if blinking would make Nyel disappear forever.

The *sireno* glanced at his trapped fingertips.

"I'm coming back, Atreus. You know that, right?" Nyel said softly.

Atreus swallowed hard. He didn't know it. He didn't know anything. Everything was changing so damn fast he—

In one fluid motion, Nyel closed the distance between them, stood on tiptoe, and kissed Atreus's cheek. All racing thoughts stopped dead at the press of soft lips on his skin.

"I'm coming back, Atreus. I promise."

This time, as Nyel leaped from the dock onto the moving barge, Atreus let him go. His hand fell to his side as he watched the *sireno* disappear onto the ship.

He waved as the barge grew smaller in the distance.

A farewell. Not a goodbye.

Because their story was only just beginning.

Acknowledgments

To my amazing husband: You have been my rock, my cheerleader, and my late-night partner-in-crime. From the very first spark of this dream to the final touches of this book, you've been right there with me. You saw my potential even when I doubted myself, and you never stopped encouraging me to chase this. Those long nights we spent together preparing this book are some of my favorite memories, and I could not have done this without your unwavering love and support.

To the wonderful members of my *Mocha's & Manuscripts* group: You have been my lifeline. Your encouragement, feedback, and motivation kept me going when the words felt impossible to find. Writing can be lonely, but with you, it never felt that way. Thank you for being part of this journey and for pushing me to be the best writer I can be.

To my dear friend Aly Hollis. Your support, collaboration, and belief in my work have been invaluable. Thank you for walking this path with me and for reminding me why I love this craft so much.

To my dear Italian friend, Haida: Our long conversations about a silly fanfiction breathed new life into me as a writer. You reignited my passion and excitement for it in ways I didn't think were possible.

Your friendship and encouragement have been such a gift, and I'll always be grateful for the role you've played in this journey.

To my family: Thank you for indulging a young girl's wild dreams of being an author. For reading my cringe-worthy early manuscripts with kindness and patience. For letting me discover myself. Your love and support made all the difference.

To my dogs: You may not know it, but your kisses and unconditional love were exactly what I needed on the nights when giving up felt like the easier choice. You're the real heroes of this book! All six of you...

This book exists because of ALL of you. Thank you for believing in me and in this story. I am forever grateful.

With the Tides,
   Tereza Kane

ABOUT THE AUTHOR

Tereza Kane lives in the rattlesnake deserts of Arizona with her husband and six dogs. She teaches piano lessons by day and writes queer love stories by night. If she isn't cuddling with one of her fur babies or watching nature documentaries, she is likely in the container store buying an unreasonable amount of Tupperware, and someone should probably stop her.